I wave. "Hi there."

He steps around the corner, gun coming up. "On the fucking ground," he barks, just as his partner appears. "*Now!*"

"Fuck no. It's been months since they cleaned this floor."

"The hell with this," the other guy says – the guy with the terrible mirror shades. He jerks his gun up, aims at my chest, pulls the trigger. Or tries to. When it doesn't work, his finger flies to the safety. Which I currently have locked. Which makes him stare down at his gun with a stupid look on his face.

"Yeesh." I wince. "Don't worry. Happens to the best of us, champ."

Praise for
Jackson Ford and The Frost Files

Praise for *The Girl Who Could Move Sh*t with Her Mind*

"Furious, frenetic, fun, and 'f★★k you': All equally valid descriptions of this book and its punk rock chef / psychic warrior protagonist. It's like the X-Men, if everybody was sick of each other's sh★t, they had to work manual labor to pay rent, and Professor X was a sociopathic government stooge. A drunken back-alley brawler of a book."

—Robert Brockway, author of *The Unnoticeables*

"Like *Alias* meets *X-Men*. I loved it." —Maria Lewis

"Ford's debut holds nothing back, delivering a sense of absurd fun and high-speed thrills that more than lives up to that amazing title." —*B&N Sci-Fi & Fantasy Blog*

"Teagan is a frank and funny narrator for this wild ride, which starts off with our heroine falling from the 82nd floor of a skyscraper and pretty much never slows down....A fast-paced, high-adrenaline tale that manages to get into some dark themes without losing its sense of fun." —*Kirkus*

"Ford's breakneck pace keeps the tension high, and the thrills coming the whole way through." —*BookPage*

"The novel unfolds cinematically with loads of breathtaking action, a perfect candidate for film or television adaptation.... [Readers will] want more." —*Booklist*

"Ford's strengths are evident in the taut action sequences and suspenseful pacing."
—*Publishers Weekly*

"The writing and storytelling is as clear and fun as the title indicates."
—*Locus*

Praise for *Random Sh*t Flying Through the Air*

"A fantastic follow-up....Readers who enjoyed Teagan's first brush with disaster will be thrilled to see her pushed beyond her limits in this winning sequel."
—*Publishers Weekly*

"This second book about psychokinetic superspy Teagan is even more suspenseful than *The Girl Who Could Move Sh*t with Her Mind* (2019). The stakes couldn't be higher....The suspense, the danger, and the rocket-fueled pace are all turned up to 11 in this more-than-satisfying sequel."
—*Kirkus*

"This smart, action-packed novel is tighter than its predecessor, and Ford injects just enough exposition that new readers will be able to pick up here. Readers will be back for the next entry."
—*Booklist*

By Jackson Ford

The Girl Who Could Move Sh★t with Her Mind
Random Sh★t Flying Through the Air
Eye of the Sh★t Storm

EYE OF THE SH*T STORM

JACKSON FORD

orbitbooks.net

Copyright © 2021 by Jackson Ford
Excerpt from *The Last Smile in Sunder City* copyright © 2020 by Luke Arnold
Excerpt from *Tracer* copyright © 2015 by Rob Boffard

Cover design by Emily Courdelle and Steve Panton – LBBG
Cover photographs © Shutterstock

Orbit
Hachette Book Group
1290 Avenue of the Americas
New York, NY 10104
orbitbooks.net

First Edition: April 2021
Simultaneously published in Great Britain by Orbit

Orbit is an imprint of Hachette Book Group.
The Orbit name and logo are trademarks of Little, Brown Book Group Limited.

The publisher is not responsible for websites (or their content) that are
not owned by the publisher.

The Hachette Speakers Bureau provides a wide range of authors for speaking events. To find out more, go to www.hachettespeakersbureau.com or call (866) 376-6591.

Library of Congress Control Number: 2020949820

ISBNs: 978-0-316-70277-5 (trade paperback), 978-0-316-70272-0 (ebook)

Printed in the United States of America

LSC-C

Printing 1, 2021

Dedicated to Xzibit, Glendale and Howlin' Rays hot chicken

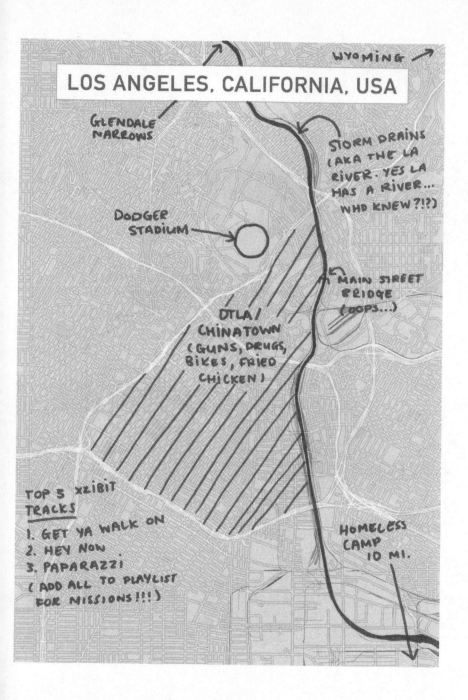

EYE
OF THE
SH*T
STORM

ONE

Teagan

Oh please, like you've never wanted to drive at high speed down a Los Angeles storm drain.

Although I'm guessing your fantasy doesn't involve being chased by a gang of outlaw bikers. Who are shooting automatic weapons at you. And I'm a hundred per cent sure you would prefer not to be in a car holding forty pounds of stolen, high-grade methamphetamine.

It doesn't help that we don't actually have that much room to manoeuvre. The storm drain is three hundred feet wide, but the − let's see − *six* bikes chasing us make it seem a lot smaller. The sides of the drain are steeply sloped − not too steep to drive down, but a bitch to get back up − and there's a channel of water running right down the middle, too deep to cross.

Heat from the late morning sun bakes off the concrete in shimmering waves as Africa goes foot to floor, swerving to avoid a bike that's gotten a little too close. I flinch back, white-knuckling the edges of the van's passenger seat.

"This was a terrible idea!" I shout.

"It was *your* idea!" Annie Cruz roars from the back seat.

"Bullshit! I just wanted to steal their meth. It was you two who thought it would be fun to drop into the storm drain and— *Fuck!*"

A bullet takes out the side mirror, inches from me. Africa reaches across and pulls me down, spitting an angry curse in French.

Another bike comes up alongside us, straddled by a thick-necked goon with bad facial tats. He's carefully aiming a handgun the size of a prime rib roast and clearly hoping to get more than just the wing mirror this time. How the hell does he even stay on the bike with the recoil?

"Buh-bye," I say, reaching out with my mind and jerking the gun out of his hands.

Didn't I mention? I can move things with my mind. It's called psychokinesis – PK for short. The rushing air whips the gun out of sight.

Technically, I'm not supposed to use my ability in public – or in ways that might reveal it to others. My scary government handler doesn't like it. But what is this biker asshole going to do? *No guys, really, she pulled it out of my hands with her mind, I swear! I totally don't have butterfingers ... Why are you laughing? Stop it!*

"Teggan," Africa's Senegalese-inflected roar fills the car. "There's too many. Use your *dëma* powers, huh?"

"I just did! Why do you think we're not getting shot at more?"

"Stop their motorbikes. Break the engines."

"Already tried that!"

When they first started chasing us, I used my PK to crunch the engine internals of one of the bikes, and the result was horrifying. The bike didn't stop neatly, as I'd hoped. Instead, it wobbled and skidded and dumped its driver onto the tarmac at high speed, scraping him to a bloody, comatose pulp. And it's not like these people stopped to put on helmets.

Sure, I'm a psychokinetic government agent, but I do *not* like killing people.

"You have to," Africa snarls. "Otherwise they just chase and chase."

"How about you drive somewhere they *can't* see us, and then we'll—"

"*Watch out!*" Annie screams from the back.

There's a huge, jagged chunk of concrete jutting up from the centre of the channel, resting on a mound of black dirt. Waist-high, more enough to ruin the day for anybody who hits it at speed. The mound of dirt runs down to a long crack, the concrete split and broken, running maybe twenty feet across the storm drain.

Oh yeah. We had an earthquake two months ago. A really big one. Most of the storm drain is fine, but concrete is concrete. Shake it, it cracks.

We only just – *just* – manage to miss the concrete. Africa's driving has gotten better over the past few months, his reaction times and wheel control improving. Behind us, there's a giant, thudding *crunch* as one of the bikes slams into the obstacle.

"Jesus fucking Christ," Annie says. She glances at the meth, which is in an open-top plastic box on the seat next to her. Maybe forty thin Ziploc baggies filled with off-white, greasy-looking powder.

Now it's just four bikes chasing us, and they're a lot further back. I don't think they're going to be able to catch up – and it would take one hell of a lucky shot to hit us. We're accelerating again, approaching the next bridge up – Main Street, I think, a simple four-lane job crossing the storm drain, with thick concrete supports.

"See?" I tell Africa. "We're fine."

He grunts a laugh. "You bloody *toubab*. You nearly get us ki— *Wooooahshit!*"

The biggest SUV I've ever seen is roaring down the sloped side of the storm drain, heading right for us.

It's a black tank, with a bull bar you could use to shift an elephant. Even inside our truck, I can hear the thundering growl of its engine. It bounces as it hits the flat, heading straight for us, thirty feet away and closing fast.

"Teggan?" Africa's voice is high and panicky, and it fucking well should be, because that bull bar is getting very large.

"On it."

I send out my PK in a huge wave, wrapping my mind around the SUV's engine components like you'd close your hand around a glass of water. Then I squeeze, compacting steel and wire and gasoline.

The growling engine cuts off with a giant bang. But the truck doesn't stop. It's simply built up too much speed.

Africa accelerates, turning the wheel to the right, trying to get us some space. Not fast enough. Behind me, Annie sucks in a breath, the kind you make if you're trying to squeeze past someone in a crowded room.

I reach out for the truck's wheels, the body panels, trying to slow it down. But the truck just has too much momentum. Africa twists his body away as that black bull bar fills the window.

There's a giant, world-obliterating *bang*.

The truck crunches into the metal above our vehicle's back left wheel. The spin we go into is so violent that it snaps my head around on my shoulders. Africa is bellowing, fighting with the wheel as the storm drain spins around us, a flash of black as the SUV crosses behind our car – it spun us completely one-eighty – and then it's gone and we're still spinning and Annie is screaming and then another dark shape looms in my window and I have just enough time to realise it's one of the Main Street Bridge supports and—

And then I don't really know what happens.

An eternity of darkness and silence. Punctuated by short bursts of noise and light.

Africa ducking behind the door as a gunshot shatters the driver's window. Broken glass nicking my cheeks.

Annie yelling that we have to get out. From somewhere behind me, there's an odd crackling sound.

More darkness. I'm yanked out of it when Africa starts shaking me. The guy is seven feet tall with hands like dump truck scoops, so it's hard to ignore him when he grabs hold of you. It also alerts me to just how much pain I'm in. My back, my shoulders, my neck . . . oh fuck me, my neck. That is going to *suck* later.

"They are coming," he spits.

"Who's coming?" I say. Or try to. It comes out as "Whsmngz?"

There's something on my face. Something powdery. It's on my skin, my teeth and tongue, up my nose. Jesus, it's in my *eyes*. And it burns: searing, acrid, horrible. I sneeze, and it's like an explosion going off inside my skull.

I sit up, blinking hard against the pain. There's a bag of meth on the dashboard in front of me, split wide open. It must have flown right out of the box and through the gap in the seats when we crashed, smacking into the windshield. Popping like a balloon.

Oh fuck. That's what's on me. Burning my throat and nose and tongue. White powder fills the air around me. The bag that hit the windshield can't be the only one split open, but it looks like it's the only one that happened to explode right in my face. Annie and Africa must gotten some on them too, but I got most of it.

I claw at my skin in horror, hacking, spitting, trying to force the drug out. There's no way you can get high from a face full of the stuff, right? No way. It doesn't work like that . . . you're supposed to snort it or smoke it or . . .

The bikers are riding up, holding very big guns and looking . . . I'm going to go with *annoyed*. It's an image caught perfectly by the bright LA sunlight, their patched leather jackets highlighted just right.

Our ride is totalled. One side bent and smashed from when the SUV hit us, the other mangled from the impact with the bridge support. It's staggering that we're all still alive – if we'd hit at another angle, we might not be.

Which isn't much comfort, because we're on fire.

The hood has popped open, and there are flames visible at the edge. *Big* flames. There's smoke, too, thick and white.

"Don't breathe!" Annie yells. "Just hold it in."

Africa has the presence of mind to bury his mouth and nose in his elbow, but not me. I'm too busy trying to get the awful meth powder out of my face, so I get a big lungful of the smoke. I cough and splutter, twisting my head to one side. My throat closes to a pinhole, cutting off my air. My chest is on fire, my nostrils filling with the sick, acrid tang. The meth powder and the smoke tag team to shred my sinuses to pieces.

We have to get out. We have to get out of here right fucking now. Forget the guys with the guns – we can figure that out afterwards. All I have to do is open the door, get us away from the burning car.

Right then, the bridge above us gives a deep, horrifying groan.

I may have mentioned the big earthquake. You know what big earthquakes do? Besides knocking down buildings and cracking roads and bursting gas mains? They weaken bridge supports. Many of the bridges in LA are off limits to traffic right now, for just that reason.

Apparently, that includes this one.

Africa looks up, then back at me. Above the arm covering his nose and mouth, his eyes are as big as baseballs.

"Teagan," Annie coughs out. "You gotta hold the bridge. You—"

She doesn't get to finish her sentence. At that moment, the support cracks, the concrete splintering in a dozen places.

I throw out my PK, all concerns about revealing my ability forgotten. But I'm not fast enough, not even close.

The bridge collapses, the weakened roadway above our heads breaking up and plummeting towards us, the noise not quite loud enough to drown out our screams.

TWO

Teagan

Maybe I should start at the beginning.

Hi. I'm Teagan Frost. I'm twenty-three years old. I live in Los Angeles, and I like good food, bad movies and terrible rap music. I work for a removals company called China Shop Movers, which is actually a government-run espionage operation. My favourite colour is purple. I drive an '03 black Jeep, which I call the Batmobile.

Believe it or not, I don't usually spend my time getting into vehicular gunfights. Take, for example, the situation I'm in right now. On our little timeline, it's around forty-five minutes before I ingested meth in the middle of a car chase/gun battle/bridge collapse.

We're on the thirtieth floor of a hotel just south of Downtown. The expansive penthouse balcony, a space of marble and granite, is bordered by a chest-high, two-feet-thick wall. Normally hotels don't have balconies, but I guess this place decided it was worth the risk. When the hotel still had paying guests, the fee for one night in the room probably covered the insurance premiums and the services of a good PR firm if someone did decide to do a perfect-ten dive onto San Pedro Street.

It's around ten in the morning, warm for January, with the sun already baking down out of a deep blue sky above the city. Despite the heat, the breeze is warm and gentle this high up, and the view is unreal. Blue skies all the way to the horizon in the north, where dark clouds are starting to build.

The balcony table holds an iced bucket of beers, and classic rock plays from a hidden set of speakers. It's about the nicest situation I've been in for a long time. Well, if you ignore the cracked walls, the messy suite behind us and the many, many men standing around with guns.

I don't remember the name of the hotel, but after the earthquake a few months ago, it's gone derelict. Squatters and looters. Oh, and biker gangs. In particular, the Legends Motorcycle Club, who have taken advantage of LA's upside-down real estate market to get themselves a nice little base of operations.

They insisted on meeting us at a designated location – in this case, the parking lot of a destroyed strip club in Mission Junction – so they could blindfold us and transport us here in one of their SUVs, even though we were able to figure out where we were the second they brought us onto the balcony. Honestly.

The man across the table is called Robert. He has an enormous, sculpted beard that hangs down over his sleeveless, patched vest. Tattooed arms as thick as my thighs – and I am *not* skinny. His body almost overwhelms the cute director's chair he's sitting in, one of about ten dotted across the balcony. Bikers occupy half the chairs, all holding gigantic assault rifles. It's a shame he's called Robert. He's more of a Zeke or Luther or Big Jon. Life sucks sometimes.

Robert isn't actually in charge. He's running the show here, for this deal, but he isn't the President of the Legends. That's someone called Pop, who we haven't met yet.

The only person bigger than Robert is Africa – China Shop's driver and muscle. He's as thin as Robert is thick, the head on his scrawny body so big that it looks like it might roll off. Africa's real name is Idriss Kouamé, although he'll only answer to his nickname.

Normally, Africa's dress sense tends towards the colourful. Purple Lakers jackets, yellow Hammer pants, buttery Timbs. I'm kind of surprised at how subdued he is today: dark suit, slightly baggy on his lanky frame, and a red shirt open at the neck.

He's not actually very good at being muscle. I've watched him try and fight people, and it's like watching a drunk try to dance the macarena. But he does an excellent job of looking scary. He's doing it now as he stands behind Annie's chair, scowling the scowliest scowl that anyone has ever scowled.

Annie Cruz isn't scowling, but she doesn't have to. She doesn't need a facial expression to look scary – it's something she was born with. She's in the director's chair on the other side of the table from Robert, wearing a dark green camo jacket over a black T and jeans. Annie has a buzzcut – she used to have a huge set of dreads, but she shaved them all off recently. Her skin is the colour of brown butter, currently beaded with sweat from the hot sunshine. At least, I hope it's from the sunshine.

If my ability is to move shit with my mind, Annie's ability is moving people. It was her contacts who put us in touch with the Legends. Annie's Army, we call them – a deep network of connects stretching across California. Janitors. Senators. Construction workers. Doctors. Movie stars. Fluffers. Probably half the Lakers. Annie's connects go deep.

Robert keeps glancing at me, and I'm pretty sure I know why. From his perspective, I'm the odd one out. A small-ish woman with short, spiky black hair, dressed in a bright blue Xzibit *Restless* tank top over skinny jeans and Air Jordans. Africa's the muscle, Annie's in charge ... but he can't work out what I'm there for, and it's making him uncomfortable.

Good.

"Y'all want some coffee?" Robert rumbles, addressing Annie. She shakes her head.

"You sure? I make a real good pot of coffee." He gestures to a French press, bumping up against the bag of meth. "Nicaraguan Roast. I let the grounds bloom – that means you pour a little water in, let it sit for a minute before you pour the rest. It really opens up the flavour. You should try some."

There's a gun on the table, different from the ones the bikers have. A really freaking big gun, too, with a bulging scope and a stock you could use to split someone's head open.

The rifle is a modified Heckler and Koch 416, if I remember the mission brief. The Legends are not supposed to have modified Heckler and Koch 416s. Nobody is, except the military. So it's really worrying that this little gang of upstart bikers has a shipment of two hundred they are trying to offload in Los Angeles.

"How much?" Annie says. She sounds distracted, as if only just remembering why we're here. That's not good. She's on point for this mission, and we need her to be on her A-game.

"Ain't you gonna test it?" Robert asks.

"Later." Annie yawns. "We got our own shop."

Robert ignores her, getting to his feet and hauling the rifle towards him. One of his buddies passes him a magazine, which he inserts. "This is the gun that killed Osama."

I can't help myself. "That one in particular? No wonder you're charging so much."

One of the bikers stifles a chuckle. Robert gives him a dirty look. He swings the rifle up, points it into the blue sky and pulls the trigger. Once. Twice. Three times. The shots are loud enough to set my ears ringing.

He turns around, grinning when he sees the looks on our faces. "Come on. Cops won't do nothing. After the Big One, they're running themselves ragged anyway. I could let off a rocket launcher up here, probably." He pauses. "Are you interested in those, by the way? Because we could—"

"No." Annie says. "How much?"

Robert falls silent, as if he can't believe the disrespect we're showing. He puts the rifle back on the table. The irony is, after the quake, government regs on guns are stricter than ever in California. Quite why the government never understands that making something illegal results in a massive black market trade is beyond me.

At last, Robert says, "Three grand per."

Annie doesn't hesitate. "Two."

"Three. Best I can do, even wholesale. You can sell for four, and I got two hundred ready to go as we speak. That's . . . " He frowns, glances at one of the other bikers, a short man with a really bad goatee and a beer belly, holding a rifle almost as big as he is. "Alan, what's the profit on that?"

Alan rolls his eyes upwards, his mouth moving silently. Africa and I exchange a look.

"Two hundred large," Alan says. His voice is nasally, monotone. Like he's an accountant giving a presentation to the board. Hell, for all I know, that's what he was before the quake. With what it did to LA, it wrecked a lot of lives. Maybe Alan's was one of them.

Our mission objectives are simple. We confirm that the Legends are selling guns, and get a favour to take home from this party. We find out as much as we can about their base of operations, which is something I'm super-handy for – and we find out who their supplier is. Then we make an exit, report everything back to our handler, Moira Tanner, who then sends in a team of special forces to do the hard work while we go get a beer somewhere.

Why not just send in the special forces right away, you ask? Because America's finest thick-necked goons don't just go in guns blazing every time they get a whiff of something hinky. They want intel. Sometimes that means long stake-outs and planting bugs and ridiculous disguises, but it's much easier to use your very own psychokinetic, who can case the entire building just by walking through it.

See, moving shit with my mind is only the start of my ability. To move things, I have to sense them, using my mind to track their position in space. That means I can easily build up a picture of my surroundings, even if I can't see them.

I can feel the coins and phones in the pockets of every biker here, the shape of the rings on their fingers and the metal studs on their jackets. My ability also lets me know that there are bikers here we haven't seen yet, other figures who will suddenly appear to tilt the odds if things do go south. I can feel the phone being held by the dude in the hotel room's bathroom, feel it vibrate as he taps at the screen. Another two dudes in the suite's bedroom. One of them is messing around with a pistol in a way that is probably going to get his dick shot off.

I call it echolocation, because I'm super-original and clever.

"Six hundred thousand." Robert rolls the words out. He spreads his hands like he's done a magic trick.

Annie drops her head, as if thinking about it. I sneak a glance at her, and what I see worries me even more. Her eyes are closed, her mouth set in a thin line. Like she's having to gather herself.

I have a sudden urge to check in with Reggie – our boss, back at the office. She's a former Army helicopter pilot who now runs China Shop, and is one hell of a hacker. There's not a whole lot for her to do on this particular job, but she was still heavily involved in the planning, and she's watching us right now. Each of us wear tiny, adhesive pinhole cameras on our shirts, undetectable by any sweeping devices. Sometimes, working for the government means cool toys.

Normally we have comms earpieces, too, but we left those at home. Hard to pretend to be gun-buying criminals when you have one of those in your ears. Anyway, the cameras have a very tiny mic, so Reggie can hear us even if she can't talk to us.

Annie raises her chin. "OK," she says. "Six hundred. But I *am* gonna run some tests, make sure these aren't just stock." She reaches for the gun. "Got a little setup out in Oxnard. Everything gravy, then we come back and settle up."

Robert has the grin of a Hollywood actor: big and white and completely fake. "Hold your horses there. That little sampler doesn't go anywhere without Pop's say so." Is it my imagination, or is there the very slightest waver of his smile as he says the name?

"So get Pop up here," I say.

"Naw, Pop's got more important shit to do. I will call though." He pulls out his own phone ... and stops when another biker pushes open the sliding door to the patio. He's missing an arm, and the other is a forest of tattoos. He's clutching a cellphone, and as he crosses the balcony to Robert, he gives me a completely blank look.

Uh-oh.

The guy bends down and whispers in Robert's ear, like something out of a bad James Bond movie. Robert's expression doesn't change. A weird thought: he enjoys this. Enjoys the

whole rooftop-balcony-meeting, Nicaraguan coffee, sophisti-
cated criminal schtick. It's the kind of thing he'd never have
gotten to do when he was just a shitty street-level biker. For
him, the earthquake represented a growth opportunity.

A sudden quiet settles over the balcony. Even the wind
has stopped.

"OK." Robert claps the edge of the table, gets to his feet.
"Looks like we're all good to go here."

"Thought you needed to call Pop," Annie says.

"Naw, not a problem. Pop says I can do whatever I need
to." He rolls his eyes slightly at me, as if trying to say, *Can you
believe how difficult your partner is being*?

It is very tempting to beat him to death with his own phone.
But I'm a hero and a classy human, so I restrain myself.

"So we can go ahead and test this?" Annie lifts the gun as
she gets to her feet.

"Sure, sure. Answer me one question, though."

"Uh-huh?"

His smile never wavers. "What's China Shop?"

Double uh-oh.

Annie, to her credit, gets it together – just as well, because
I can't keep the alarm off my face. "Moving company. It's the
legit part of our operation."

Robert leans back against the thick balcony railing. "So . . .
you don't do any work for the government?"

Triple uh-oh, quadruple goddamn-it and *all* of the yikes.

We don't get a chance to deny any of it. Three of the bikers
grab hold of Africa. They kick his legs out from underneath
him, grabbing him in a chokehold as he goes over backwards.
Three more hit Annie, wrestling her to the table. Two of them,
Alan and the one-armed guy, grab hold of me, squeezing my
biceps tight. Goddammit, who the *hell* tipped these assholes off?

"Get the fuck off me," Annie snarls.

I need to do something, but I'll have to play this very carefully. I'm not supposed to reveal my ability, even in cases where the people watching are unlikely to alert the media.

What happens next happens really freaking fast.

Robert pulls the modified H&K off the table, whips it up to point at Africa. He aims carefully, centre-mass, not wanting to hit his buddies. Then without another word, he pulls the trigger.

Or tries to. I don't let him. Trigger stays locked. He snarls, chucks the gun to the ground, snatches a rifle from one of his buddies. I lock that one down too, all the while thinking, *Come on, come on, find a way out of this.*

Robert gives up and drops the weapon, jerks his chin at the men holding us. My heart skitter-beats as they heft Africa like a sack of grain. He roars, tries to buck them off. But like I said, he's lanky and skinny and utterly useless in a fight.

And before Annie and I can say anything, before I can switch my PK to the men holding Africa, they lift him onto the balcony wall, and topple him over the edge.

There is a long, horrible second where he's looking right at me. His eyes are wide, terrified. Disbelieving.

His feet flick upwards, as if saluting the deep blue morning sky. Then Africa is gone.

THREE

Teagan

You're probably wondering why I let that happen.

After all, what's to stop me grabbing every object on the balcony, from guns to ashtrays to those cute directors chairs, and using them to beat ten shades of shit out of our biker pals?

That was my first thought too. The problem is that it reveals my ability in a major way. Reggie is always . . . well, *everybody* is always telling me to think before I act. And in this case, I actually do. There's a better, smarter solution here.

Of course, it has a few problems of its own. I need to keep everyone's eyes on me. I can't tell Annie, or Africa. And it may or may not result in us all falling to our deaths.

I go fucking nuts, twisting and yelling. Alan has to plant his feet, jerk back as I try to smash his nose in with the back of my head. One of the other goons grabs my legs, ignoring my furious, angry howls. "You cocksuckers, what the fuck? *What the fuck*? I'll fucking kill you, I'll tear your dicks off and play a drum solo with them, you – *let go!*"

Thinking: *That's it, keep your eyes on me, don't you dare look over that balcony . . .*

With a mutual grunt, Alan and his accomplice lift my

screaming self onto the two-feet-thick railing. Behind me, Annie's breathing is hot, harsh, panicked. "Teagan," she says, and the note of desperation in her voice is terrifying. God, I wish I could tell her what I have planned, even though I'd probably leave out the part where it might kill us all.

I lock eyes with Alan. No matter what happens, I *have* to keep their attention "I'm going to punch a hole in your skull, you bean-counting motherf—"

His expression doesn't change as he and his buddy roll me right off the edge of the balcony railing.

I get a split-second glimpse of Annie, staring at me in horror. Then gravity takes me, clamping onto my stomach. I go head-over-heels backwards, the bright sunlight blinding me. The terror tries to wipe my mind clean, force me to give into it . . .

Just as I land face-first on the floating couch.

It's four stories below the penthouse, hovering in mid-air. It's a two-seater, with thick, squashy foam cushions, and I hit it like a sack of concrete. It punches the air out of my lungs, almost knocks me senseless. I nearly roll right off. But there is a tiny part of my brain that would prefer not die in a stupid way, and it makes me throw out an arm and grab hold. I come to a stop with one leg dangling off the edge, one black Air Jordan waving crazily in the open air.

No time, no time. I shoot the couch back towards the building while I hang on for dear life. A snap of wind sends snarls my hair around my face, and then I'm over the balcony of the twenty-sixth floor suite. That's my cue. I tip the couch sideways, go as loose as possible—

—and roll right onto Africa.

He's lying on the balcony, hyperventilating. Confirmed: his bony-ass frame does *not* make for a soft landing. I yelp as we crash together, rebounding off him and nearly braining myself on the leg of the outside table.

"Teggan, what—?"

My voice is a high-pitched, breathless hiss. "Not now!"

I zip the couch back out into open air, thinking: *Please please please let it be fast enough.*

I don't have a mental lock on Annie. I can move inorganic objects just fine – metal, plastic, whatever – but doing it with organic objects is ridiculously hard. It takes time, and even sensing their position in space takes a *lot* of concentration. Which means that the couch isn't lined up right when Annie comes dropping past the twenty-sixth floor.

She bounces sideways. She must have hit it just right – or wrong. Her legs and arms flail, her scream piercing the air. There's a horrible, nauseating half-second where I'm sure that I'm not going to make it, that I can't move the couch fast enough . . .

Then I do. I zip the couch underneath her, catching Annie on the downward arc of her bounce. Before anything else horrible can happen, I pull her and the couch towards us, not even letting it clear the railing before I dump her onto the balcony.

She rolls, bounces again, throws out her arms like a bouncer doing crowd control. Her face comes to a stop a foot from mine. Her mouth is slightly open, all the colour chased from her caramel skin, forehead shiny with sweat and eyes drifting in and out of focus. Africa grips my shoulder, squeezing so tight that my bones creak.

He opens his mouth to say something, then jerks back when I try to put my hand across it. I snap my head towards Annie, put a finger to my lips. Not that there's any point. She is utterly, completely incapable of speech.

I lower the couch to the balcony, right next to the sliding

doors. There's no sound. Just the whipping rush of the wind beyond the balcony railings.

Then, very distant, from above us: "You see them?"

Another voice. Inaudible.

"Maybe the wind caught 'em." That sounded like Alan the Accountant.

I let out a long, slow, shaky breath. Holy shit. That actually worked.

Of course it fucking worked. It was, if I say so myself, genius. Twisted, insane genius.

Used to be that I could only feel out objects up to about fifty feet away. Over the past couple years, I've gotten a lot stronger. My PK range is up to two hundred feet – and it doesn't matter what's in the way. Plus, I can move fast if I have to. So when I saw Africa about to get the heave-ho, I ran a quick check to find an empty suite below us. Then I zipped open the balcony door, grabbed hold of the couch – which had a nice, handy metal frame – and made Africa a landing pad.

Of course, I didn't just leave it to chance. I find that when you tell people you're going to tear their dicks off and play a drum solo with them, they tend to pay attention – if only because they find it amusing. They didn't notice the thump from below. They didn't care about the person they'd already thrown off a balcony, and especially not when the railing is two feet thick. That type of railing is pretty tough to lean out over – try it, if you don't believe me, next time you meet your gun dealer at a high-end hotel.

I have to force myself to talk. "And *that* is the real meaning of couch-surfing."

Africa is grinning now. He's got it. Shaking his head, staring at me like I'm the craziest thing he's ever seen. "You *dëma*," he says, keeping his voice low.

I'm unsteady on my feet, but somehow I stumble through to

the suite. I was expecting it to be a wreck – this place is home to squatters, after all – but it's surprisingly clean. The bed is made, and there's even a bunch of flowers on the nightstand. Dead flowers, but still.

"We must tell Mrs Tanner," Africa says, as I gently shut the door. "She must know how you handled this, *yaaw*? You did good. She will be impressed."

That gets him a strange look from me. Since when is Africa so keen to keep Tanner informed?

Annie is just inside the door, staring at nothing. I take a step towards her. "You OK?"

She snaps her head up, like a wolf scenting blood. Then she takes two strides, and grabs me by the front of my tank top, lifting me off the ground and slamming me against the wall so hard I nearly bite my tongue.

"What the *fuck* is wrong with you?" she snarls, her mouth inches from my face. Her breath, hot and harsh, smells very faintly of whiskey. She's not drunk, I know that, but she's definitely had some.

"Annie!" Africa tries to insert himself between us, doesn't get anywhere. I just gape. I don't know what else to do. My feet kick at open air.

"We could have been fucking killed," Annie says. She shoves me harder into the wall, then abruptly lets me go. I thump down onto the carpet, nearly losing my balance.

Annie doesn't back off, not even when Africa tries to pull her away. She jams a finger in my face, eyes blazing. "Next time you wanna get us thrown off a fucking balcony, leave me at home. Jesus Christ."

She shoves Africa off, walks into the middle of the suite, her back to us. I'm too stunned to be angry.

To be fair, this isn't the first time Annie and I have taken a

22   JACKSON FORD

high-dive together. Last year, we did a job in a skyscraper in downtown LA – a job that ended up with us trapped on the top floor, with no way out. I may or may not have grabbed Annie and punched us through a window, eighty-something floors up.

Annie is terrified of heights, absolutely one of her worst fears. I'm *still* apologising for that little stunt.

"What is the matter with you?" Africa stops, lowers his voice. "Annie, that is not helpful, huh? Teggan was not the one who threw us."

Damn right. Last time I checked, I actually saved us. Is she mad because I ... what, because I let it happen? What other choice did I have? Reveal my ability? Hope it all worked out?

I thought I made the right decision. It was scary, and dangerous ... but it got us out of a bad situation unhurt, didn't it?

"Annie—" I say.

She snaps up a hand, still not looking at me. "Don't."

"I just ... If I could have told you, I totally would have ... "

"I said: *don't*."

I just saved your life back there. I open my mouth to say it, but Africa clears his throat. Gives me a very firm shake of the head.

My voice is low. "I was only gonna—"

"Mm-mm."

"But—"

"No. Leave it, *yaaw*?"

He's right. If I'm honest, I sort of do know why Annie is being a prick. And it makes me want to throttle her and hug her, both at once.

China Shop used to have a logistics guy. Paul Marino. Ex-Navy quartermaster, a detail-minded pain in the ass ... and Annie's lover. Paul died a few months ago, buried alive by a psychotic little boy named Matthew Schenke, who had the ability to control the earth. It was him who caused the big quake here in LA.

Annie is angry. Grieving. Nothing wrong with that – it's healthy – but the problem is, she's taken a lot of that anger out on me. For months now, she's been cold towards me, snapping at me, sometimes even leaving a room when I walk in. At first, I thought I was imagining it. But it kept happening, and then I mentioned it to Reggie, who said she'd noticed it too.

I didn't kill Paul, but it's as if Annie thinks I had a part in it – that because Matthew came from the same research my parents used to make me, I was partly to blame.

Which hurt, let me tell you.

I eventually got up the courage to ask Annie to ease off on me, without actually mentioning Paul or the boy who killed him. She nodded, said she was sorry, said she was going through some shit. I nodded too and smiled and said it was OK. Then a few days later, things went right back to the way they were.

Annie shakes her head. "Elevator. Let's go." She strides past me, stopping in the suite's entrance hall, by the door. Waits.

When neither Africa nor I move, she gives me a pointed look.

"Oh." I snap my fingers. "Sorry. Yes."

I send my PK out past the door. There's nothing and nobody in the hall, and after a nod from me, Annie steps out. Half the lights aren't working, and the other half flicker on and off, like the world's most depressing rave. Annie lopes to the elevator, jabbing the call button.

"Who the fuck told them about China Shop?" I say to Africa.

A troubled look crosses his face. "I do not know."

"Somebody's trying to get up in our shit."

"We will talk to Reggie later. She might be able to do a trace."

On what? Robert's phone? Maybe – Reggie *is* that good. It would be a real pleasure to find whoever just ruined our op, and exactly how they know about China Shop. Then throw *them* off a building.

That's a problem for later. After we get out of here.

The elevator dings. Annie steps to one side, out of view of the doors. Smart – no point exposing ourselves if the bikers happen to be on their way down to ground level to confirm the kill. That would be an embarrassing way to get caught. Africa and I slip into a door alcove, hiding ourselves from view, and I close my eyes, concentrating on the rising car.

"Clear," I murmur.

The elevator ride is exactly as awkward as you think it is. Let's leave it at that.

The doors open onto a service corridor in the basement – one suffering from the same lighting problems as the floor we were on. Bare concrete, mysterious stains on the walls, janitor's bucket lying on its side. I don't know if the janitor knocked it over today – maybe he stepped out for a smoke, decided he'd pick it up when he got back – or if it fell over in the quake, and just sat there.

The basement might be a dump, but it's a signposted dump – there's a metal plate bolted to the wall, block lettering pointing us to JANITORIAL, LAUNDRY, KITCHEN, UTILITY ROOM. "Employee parking lot should be close," Annie mutters.

"We gonna drive?" Africa moves alongside her. "We left the van back at—"

"I know. We can jack something if we have to."

The tight corridor muffles our footsteps. The adrenaline rush from our little couch stunt is running out, leaving me cold and shivery. Hungry. That's how my PK works – using it requires fuel. Good thing for me that the fuel is usually food and sleep, both things I'm quite fond of.

Shit, maybe there's a kitchen down here. I could snag something. Then again, the hotel's abandoned, so it's not like they're offering room service.

I'm pretty sure Annie and Africa want us to get the hell out right now, but it doesn't look like we're being followed. If the bikers are anywhere, they're one floor above us, confused about why there are no splatted bodies on the sidewalk. Would it really be so bad if I just grabbed a snack?

I send my PK out in a wide arc, searching through the walls, checking for the familiar shape of ovens and utensils and fridges.

And that's when I pick up something . . . kind of odd.

I push between Annie and Africa, sending out my PK in invisible waves of energy. "And now?" Africa says.

"The parking lot's this way," Annie snaps, pointing to a faded sign on the wall.

"Yeah, just a second." I look left and right, make sure that I'm feeling what I think I'm feeling. That the hunger and adrenaline aren't giving me false positives.

My PK leads me back the way we came, down another passage, this one crowded with old, slightly rusty silver food carts. I weave between them, ignoring Africa's hissed questions and Annie's exasperated sighs.

I feel the bikers before I see them. Or rather, I feel their guns. Two big semi-automatic rifles, although not of the modified-psychotic-oversized Army-gun type.

I take a quick peek around the corner. The two men holding them are standing in front of a big double door, which I'm pretty sure is the back entrance to the kitchen. I only get the briefest glimpse of the two, but there's at least one beard, one pair of dumb mirror shades, and a whole lot of very bad tattoos. We must have arrived right at a lull in their conversation. No sooner do I pull back behind the corner, then one of them starts talking about his girlfriend. It's in the bored tone of someone who would very much like to get home to her. *That's OK, homie. Let me send you on your way.*

I slip their gun safeties on, doing it slowly so they don't hear it. Africa and Annie have sidled in behind me.

"OK," I whisper. "Go get 'em."

"What do you mean, *Go get 'em*?"

"Take 'em out. I've taken care of their guns."

"Teagan, what the fuck? What are we doing here?"

"We need to go, now." Africa glances over his shoulder. "We have to—"

"*Hey!*"

That last one comes from the bearded dude. He heard us talking, and has now stuck his head around the corner.

I wave. "Hi there."

He steps around the corner, gun coming up. "On the fucking ground," he barks, just as his partner appears. "*Now!*"

"Fuck no. It's been months since they cleaned this floor."

"The hell with this," the other guy says – the guy with the terrible mirror shades. He jerks his gun up, aims at my chest, pulls the trigger. Or tries to. When it doesn't work, his finger flies to the safety. Which I currently have locked. Which makes him stare down at his gun with a stupid look on his face.

"Yeesh." I wince. "Don't worry. Happens to the best of us, champ."

Bearded guy roars, charges Africa – who decks him right in the mouth, knocks him out cold. Hey, just because the guy isn't good in a fight does *not* mean you want one of his punches connecting.

Beardy crumples like a two dollar card table. His buddy is a little smarter – he ignores his gun, goes for the walkie clipped to his belt. Which goes nowhere, obviously, because I'm holding it in place.

I'll say this for Annie: whatever she's going through, she can move hella fast when it counts. She steps in, twisting from the hip and punching the guy in the solar plexus – once, twice, three times. He falls, gasping like a goldfish, fingers scrabbling at the wet concrete.

"'Scuse us." I step over him, nudging through the door to the kitchen.

"OK, now, Teggan." Africa is breathing hard. "Why you make us come – oh."

I smile, pleased my PK didn't lead me astray. "Yeah."

The doors open up into a big food prep area: long tables, low fluorescent lighting, big plastic bins. There's a faint odour of old food – spinach, oysters, something tangy like sriracha – but it's drowned out by a sharp, urine-like stench. And it's not hard to see why. They don't prep food here any more.

I count at least forty Ziploc bags of meth, stacked neatly on one of the tables. At the far end of the room, a blinking figure in a hazmat suit is poking his head out the door of the main kitchen, wondering who we are and what the hell is going. Behind him are the things that led me here: the beakers and rubber tubing and big ventilation units.

Apparently, it's not just guns the Legends are selling.

I spread my arms, sketch a bow to Annie and Africa. "I'd like to thank the Academy."

FOUR

Teagan

The lab itself is in the main kitchen, through another set of double doors at the other end of the prep area: a mess of equipment and chemicals scattered across disused stove tops.

A meth lab in the kitchen of a busy hotel would never work in regular circumstances, but these are not regular times. Nobody's checking in upstairs any more, or ordering room service – and if there's a nasty smell coming from the vents at street level, who's going to complain? There's so much toxic shit in the air from the quake, it makes the usual LA smog seem like Chanel No. 5.

I didn't sense any of this when we arrived at the hotel. Wasn't really paying attention to my PK.

Someone – one of the meth cooks maybe – has hung a fluffy toy of the RV from *Breaking Bad* on one of the pot hooks. An attempt to make the workplace a little brighter, which is one of the most nauseating things I've ever seen. It makes me irrationally angry. How *dare* these shitbags turn a kitchen – a proud place, a place for art and honest work and good food – into a drug lab? And then make a joke out of it?

I vent some of the rage by snapping all the Bunsen burners,

choking off the plastic tubing with my PK, then fucking up the valves on the chemical tanks. *Kitchen's closed, motherfuckers.*

There are two meth cooks, and no other guards. Not exactly surprising – when your lab is in a hotel already bristling with your people, putting more than a couple to guard the lab seems like overkill. The main doors in the big kitchen are barred and padlocked, so there's only one entrance – the door we came through.

I keep my PK on the alert for any guns approaching the lab, but there's nobody around. It's a little worrying at first, but then again, why would anybody come check on the lab? If you throw three people off a balcony, and their bodies vanish between you and the ground, you don't go hunting in the basement.

My gaze lingers on one of the stoves. It's a Jade Titan, a commercial model with super-powerful gas burners. Man, what must it be like to be in charge of that thing, standing over it with all six burners on full? Steaks sizzling, pasta in the back, sauce reducing. Pastry chef would be melting chocolate in another pot over the boiling water, of course, and there's no way I'd be able to resist—

I sigh, tapping my fingers on the counter.

I have *got* to stop doing this to myself.

I never wanted to be a government agent. Still don't. The only reason I'm doing this job and working for Tanner is because if I don't, she'll hand me over to a bunch of scientists who are itching to cut me open and see what I'm made of. What I really want to do, more than anything in the world, is be a chef. To cook, in a professional kitchen, just like this one. I used to have these big plans about using my off hours from my secret agent job to go to cooking school, eventually figuring a way out of this mess and pursuing what I really wanted.

Problem is, it's not just the threat of dissection that keeps me working for Uncle Sam. There are other people out there like me – other people with abilities. All of them have been bad news. Tanner convinced me that I'm one of the best people to try and stop them. But she also said that I had to commit to it – I couldn't train to be a chef on the side, not when it would distract me from the mission. And as much as I hated to admit it, she was right.

I'm still going to be a chef one day – I don't know how, especially since there are very few cooking schools left in Los Angeles after the quake. But for now, I've had to put all of it on the backburner.

Backburner. Poor word choice, in this case.

Before long, the guards and the two meth cooks are bound and gagged, thanks to a roll of duct tape Africa pulled from his jacket. Of course he has duct tape. If I suddenly needed, I don't know, a printout of the Declaration of Independence, I'm pretty sure I'd find one in Africa's inside pocket, along with coins in ten currencies and a signed copy of Prince's last album.

He stands over the bags of meth, hands on his hips, nodding slowly to himself. Africa doesn't like drugs, and he *especially* doesn't like meth, on account of his girlfriend Jeannette having been addicted to it once upon a time. I met her once, when she was living on the streets, and she was nothing more than a skeleton.

"This is good," he says. "Mrs Tanner will be pleased." He picks up one of the bags, tucks it into his jacket. "We take, we test."

"We'd better call the cops anyway," Annie says, eyeing the captives. I've already gone through their pockets, wanting to make sure none of them made a covert call before we shut them down. Their phones, walkies, wallets and keys sit in a neat pile behind them on the countertop. "Once the Legends find out we were here, they'll shut this place down in a second, set up shop elsewhere."

One of the meth cooks – a guy who looks like Ben Stiller – *mmphs* behind the tape, as if to agree.

The scowl is back on Africa's face. "*Dina le nokh*," he spits at Ben Stiller. Then, to us: "OK. Come. We can call police when we are in the car."

He and Annie move to go, but I linger, resting my hand on the counter. "Hey . . . guys?"

They turn to look at me.

"What if we just took it?" I ask.

Annie screws up her face. "Like . . . to sell?"

"What – no! Why would you even say that? No! God!" I point to the meth. "We'll destroy it."

Ben Stiller growls into his gag again.

"Zip it, Pinkman," I tell him.

"No," Africa says, although he looks unsure. "Too much trouble. It's not part of the mission."

"But listen, hear me out. Right now the LAPD . . . they're kind of stretched thin, right? After the quake? Not to mention the jails and the courts."

"They'll still come investigate a fucking *meth lab*," Annie says. She looks very tired then, stretched too thin herself.

"Yeah, but, like, probably not right away."

"And what about evidence? How's the DA gonna build a case if there's no meth?"

"Look, no matter what we do, this meth is gone. They can't hide the lab, but they *will* hide the meth if they think trouble's coming. At least this way, it's toast."

It's possible we could destroy the drugs here – flush them down the toilet, or dump them into a sink and run the faucet.

But forty bags is a lot. The Legends might not know where we are right now, but I'm not sure we have time to hunt down a bathroom and flush the stuff. And as for dousing it with water in a sink . . . I have no idea if that would work. I know nothing about meth chemistry. They might be able to dry it out, or something . . .

"We can find somewhere to torch it," I continue. "Someone who knows how to do it safely. Africa – dude, you get it, right?"

And he does. He's slowly nodding to himself, lips pursed. I knew he would. Wiping a whole whackload of meth off the map, taking it and burning it – or whatever, I don't actually know the best way to destroy it – is right up his alley.

"Mmm," he says. When Annie snaps a look at him, he says, "You know, it is actually not a bad idea."

"Are you serious?"

"We take the drugs." I walk around the table, tapping my palm a finger. "We get out, and then we call the cops. Maybe they come, maybe they don't, but either way we do some damage. Boom. Done. Chalk one up for the good guys. And let's face it – we're still no closer to finding out where those guns came from. Why not walk away with a win?"

Africa claps me on the shoulder, the sound loud in the low-ceilinged space. "You think smart, huh? Big brain inside that small body."

I slap his hand away, but without much anger. I'll let the condescending comment go, this once. The job's been hairy, but it's turning out OK. Better than OK, in fact. My bad mood from what these jackasses did to this fine kitchen has dissipated, now that I know payback is coming.

Annie pinches the bridge of her nose, looking too exhausted to argue. "And how were you planning to get the shit outta here? You can't just walk down the street with a box of meth. Even in this city."

In answer, I walk over to the pile of the guards' belongings on the counter, scooping up the two sets of keys I find there. "Nobody walks in LA."

Africa grunts a laugh. Annie just sighs. "Fine. Let's go already."

"Yes!" I punch the air. "You will not regret this." I turn to grab the drugs – and my day gets even better. On a shelf nearby, there are three bags of potato chips. I actually *squee* as I dance over to them, jamming them into my pockets. They're my favourite kind, too, the kind that have an ingredients list that takes up the whole back of the packet and which taste like a xenomorph barfing on your tongue. They're the best.

Before long, the meth – all forty-or-so pounds of it – is in a big, plastic storage box. We can't find a lid anywhere, but it doesn't matter. Africa hefts it – yes, I could lift it with my PK, but the last thing I want is to run into somebody while walking next to a floating box. Instead, I do the real hard work of stuffing my face with radioactive chips. I figure I found the place *and* saved our lives with the couch stunt, so I've earned a snack. We leave the same way we came in, and I make sure to crunch the lock on the doors with my PK, jamming them shut. A few good kicks will probably knock them open, but why make things easy?

The employee parking lot is almost empty, a dank and muggy space littered with trash. But there are a couple of vehicles in the spots. A beat-up Prius with a big scratch down one side, and a Mercedes Sprinter. I admit, I was a little worried that the guards parked their cars in another lot somewhere, but one of the sets of keys has a big Mercedes logo, and the van opens right up.

Africa holds out the box to me, then gets behind the wheel. I climb in next to Africa, Annie scooching in on the second row of seats, bringing the meth with her. There are no shouts of alarm, no running feet.

There's a metal gate at the top of the ramp, next to a card reader, but that's no more barrier to me than anything else I've used my PK on today. As we drive up the ramp into the blazing, muggy afternoon, I wind down the window, casually lean my arm out. The chips filled a hole all right, but I'm going to need something more substantial. Fried chicken, maybe . . . yes, *definitely* fried chicken. With slaw.

And you know what? I freaking earned it. *We* freaking earned it. I'm still seriously pissed at whoever decided to mess with us by telling the bikers who we really were . . . but we turned a bad situation into a good one. We didn't die, and we severely disrupted the Legends' shit. And the best part? We're getting away. They don't even know we're down here.

The ramp comes out onto the sidewalk, on the east side of the hotel. As we crest the top, I glance to my right, and find myself looking straight at Robert the biker.

He, Alan and half a dozen of their leather-clad friends are walking in our direction. They come to a dead halt. Eyes widening, mouths parting in stunned surprise.

Which quickly turns to blazing, barely controlled fury.

"Um," I say. "Shit."

"Africa, *fucking drive!*" Annie yells, as Robert pulls a gun from out the crack of his ass. He fires, the bullet going wide. Alan and one of his buddies bolt for a black SUV parked on the side of the road, but Africa is already reacting, spinning the wheel and jamming the gas, the Sprinter's tires squealing as we hit the tarmac.

You can probably figure out the rest.

FIVE

Teagan

And now I'm trapped under a collapsed bridge, in a burning van, having just taken a faceful of meth, while a biker gang shoots at me and my friends with automatic weapons.

We've all been there.

The slabs of concrete crushing the van are huge, truck-sized, multiple tons each, way too heavy for me to manipulate with my PK. The only thing I can do is reinforce the roof of the van, *making* it stay in place as the huge weight from the collapsed bridge tries to crush it. And it's not going to last for ever – it's taking every bit of energy I have to hold it up, and it's already starting to buckle.

It's almost completely dark, with only the van's puny interior light on. We're all on the floor, down where the air is cleaner. Africa and I are down in the footwells, our sleeves over our mouths, Annie out of sight in the back. My throat and sinuses feel like they've been scoured with lye. I can't stop coughing, and I'm lightheaded. It's making it very, very difficult to keep the focus on the roof. And the big, blaring thought running through my terrified brain is: *meth you just did meth oh shit oh shit.*

"Teag—" Annie's voice dissolves in a hail of coughing.

"Yeah, I know!"

"Wait, I will get us out." Africa lifts a giant leg, starts kicking at the door. I help, putting some of my PK into the metal. But that takes my focus off the roof, which gives a threatening groan.

"Hang on." Annie's hand appears over the edge of the passenger seat, flailing, as if she's trying to answer a question in class. "I think I can—"

A rumble from above drowns out her voice – more of the bridge collapsing, the slabs settling, putting even more weight onto the car. From somewhere in the real world, there are distant shouts. The Legends, still out there.

And in the background: the crackling hiss of flames. It would be really nice if the rubble we're trapped under could have smothered them, but apparently there's still air down here.

Both of you focus on that door. I'll hold up the roof. That's what I want to say. Those are the words in my head. In reality, I get out the word "*Both*—" before my lungs seize up and my throat seizes up and I dissolve in a hacking burst of coughs. The smoke is everywhere now.

I've been buried alive before. Literally buried alive. Matthew Schenke, the four-year-old with the power to cause earthquakes, dropped me into the ground. Somehow, I got out of that mess, my PK going into overdrive and moving organic matter for the first time. I've had some bad nightmares since that day, nightmares where I can't move the soil around me no matter how hard I try and I'm stuck down there for ever. I'm feeling the same panic now – the same scrabbling, wide-eyed terror. Only this time, my PK isn't going to do the job. There's just too much concrete, too much weight, too much to focus on. *We're going to die in here, we're go*—

Oh.

Ooooh shi

i

i

i

i

iiiiit.

There's a trick you see on videos where they start with a shot of someone's face, then zoom out to show that face surrounded by other faces, then *keep* zooming out further and further until it turns out all those faces make up a colour-coded map of the United States.

That just happened to me.

And my psychokinesis.

I feel ... *everything*.

The storm drain surface. The vehicles. The burning wires in the chassis of our van. The broken bridge slabs. The metal railings. The dust particles in the air. The bikers' guns. The hip flask one of them has in his pocket. Their vehicles.

Holy fuck. It's more than that.

I can feel the *bikers*.

Normally, my PK only works on inorganic objects – metal, plastic, glass. It's a limitation I've had my entire life. When Matthew Schenke buried me, my PK kicked into overdrive, and I managed for the first time to manipulate an organic substance – the soil I was buried in. It was the loosest grip possible, and it took every ounce of effort I had. I haven't been able to replicate it since.

Not any more. The meth has taken a look at my PK limits, cocked an eye and blown them away.

The bikers. A bird, whirling above the storm drain. Three rats, skittering up the sloped side. The cars parked in a lot nearby. The bystanders pressed up against the chain-link fence at the edge of the storm drain, watching the chaos below with open mouths. The water – holy fuck, I think I can feel the water in the drain's concrete channel, silky and quick and dark.

I can move all of these things. I know I can. I have never been this clear, this focused. My heart is going insane in my chest, my skin bathed in sweat, my face and throat on fire . . . but I am as calm and clean as if I just stepped out of a hot spring.

Africa and Annie are yelling. They sound very far away. Tiny photos in the mosaic, part of a larger whole.

"It's OK," I hear myself say – and this time, my lungs and throat comply. "I got this."

The people at the top of the storm drain – the onlookers. They have phones. *They'll see me. Video me. I can't use my PK here, not in public, I—*

Sure I can.

I can't believe I never thought of it before. It's so *simple.*

I reach out. Grab every single phone I can find. Thirty or so – some in pockets, some already held in clammy fingers, filming the action. My range must be half a mile now, way further than I've ever gone. I gently grip every phone with my mind, feeling their smooth surfaces, the texture of their power buttons, the fingerprint oil on their touchscreens . . .

And then I *squeeze.*

Dive deep into each and every phone and crush the chips.

The phones die instantly, bricked. The outsides unchanged, the internals a mess of broken silicon. There are a few security cameras on the buildings surrounding the storm drain, and I take care of those too. A thought tugs at me: our little pinhole cameras, the ones broadcasting back to Reggie. I break them, too, although it comes with a little guilty twinge. *Sorry, Reggie. Can't be too careful.*

People will see what's about to happen. They'll swear it's true. And maybe that might have consequences for me, somewhere down the line. But there'll be no photos or videos, none, no evidence at all.

Africa claws at me, and I reach out and take his hand, letting him know it's going to be OK.

Then I go to work.

I tear away the bridge slabs. Just lift them right off. Every single one, like they're made of foam. Daylight floods the van's interior as I move the pieces of the broken bridge to one side, out of the way. I don't throw them, or put them in a place where someone might think, *how the hell did they land up over there*? I just give us a bit of space to breathe.

The slabs give out a crunching *bang* as they impact the surface of the storm drain. The bikers have stopped in their tracks, except for one or two who take a step back.

With a small smile, I rip the doors off our van.

All of them.

I blink – a movement that feels like it takes aeons. When I open my eyes, after a million years, Annie and Africa have exited the van, staggering away from it on the opposite side to the bikers.

I take my time. Clamber out of the van, not worried about being shot – I've shut down the bikers' guns, almost as an afterthought. I stretch extravagantly, and the crick in my back feels delightful. I'm bursting with energy, raw and pure. It's like I've had the best sleep ever, deep, dark, dreamless, and now I'm awake and I'm under blue sky and there's nothing I can't do. God, why did I think meth was bad? It's fucking *awesome*.

A thought intrudes. Jeannette – Africa's girlfriend. An image of her when we first crossed paths. A skeletal crust of a person, hunched, body stripped clean. Screeching and snarling like an animal.

But the distance between her and what I'm feeling now is immense. It's easy to push the thought away.

I stare at the stunned, trembling biker gang, some of whom are desperately trying to shoot me. I'm barely aware. My mind is a thousand miles away.

My parents made me. And not just in the Biblical sense. They were gifted geneticists, light years ahead of anybody else, and they wanted to create a soldier who could end wars before they started. Turns out, not even they could put multiple abilities in one person, so they split them between me, and my big brother and sister. Adam didn't need to sleep. Chloe could see in infrared, picking up heat signatures.

What would their abilities have been like on meth? I don't know about Adam, but Chloe ... her vision would be an explosion of colour. A billion shades of heat and light, dazzling, hypnotic.

Chloe and Adam are gone. Adam went insane, his mind shredded from never having slept. My parents had to lock him away, and his twin Chloe – poor, deluded Chloe – let him out. He killed them all, almost killed me too.

I miss them so much. All of them. *Especially* Chloe.

The thought of her brings hot, bittersweet tears to my eyes. I would have loved to share this with her. I can picture us on the ranch in Wyoming, both of us high off our fucking tits, riding horses through the forest and laughing, her seeing every colour of the universe while I move objects half a mile away. She should be here. With me. We should be doing this together.

There's a box at the back of my mind where I put all the bad shit. Don't get it twisted: it's not like I have a box of bubbling, evil darkness threatening to take over. That's just not me. A lot of horrible things have happened in my life, but I've dealt with them. I spent a long time dealing with them, thank you very much, and although I can't get rid of them, I have found a place to put them.

When I picture it, I actually see a dusty, slightly tattered box on a high shelf in the closet. The kind you don't really think about until you need to get something from it.

What can I say? Therapy works. Even when you're imprisoned in a government facility.

I don't like to pull the box down too often – it's not a fun experience. But now, it's as if the contents have no power over me. Like I can hold them in my hands, turning them this way and that.

My real name isn't Teagan Frost. Back when I was still hanging with Chloe and Adam, I was plain old Emily Jameson. Em. It's been a long time since I even thought of myself as Em, and the memory is so bittersweet that it almost makes me cry.

Almost.

One of the bikers throws his gun, hurls it away like it's poisonous. I smile slowly at him. He makes the sign of the cross, does it again.

I'm still levitating some of the bridge slabs. I let them drop, and the bikers break. Two of them sprint right at me, eyes wide and fearful, wielding their guns like clubs.

I tilt my head, and the bikers go flying. Thrown right into the air, my PK manipulating their bodies like it was nothing. Moving organic matter used to be almost impossible, but not any more. They yell and flail their limbs, crashing into the narrow channel of water running down the centre of the storm drain.

Another biker, coming at me from the side, trying to flank me. He's got a big-ass combat knife, seven inches of serrated steel. I stop both the knife and his arm so suddenly that his ulna breaks, and his scream of pain is sweet.

There's music. No: humming. *I'm* humming, and it takes me a very long second to recognise the tune: the opening bars of "The Next Episode", by Dre and Snoop.

More phones are in the area, the people on the surrounding streets coming to investigate the ruckus. I brick them all, reaching out and crushing them with a single thought. It's scary how good it feels to be this powerful, scary because I keep thinking of Jeannette. I ignore the thoughts, grabbing hold of two of the black SUVs, sending them flying like a grenade went off underneath them, *boom*, just end over end, metal and glass crunching.

Holy shit. I'm actually horny.

Sex is usually off the table for me. I lose control of my PK when I come, throwing everything around me into the air. As you can imagine, that severely limits *who* I can sleep with. Why yes: it sucks exactly as much as you think it does. I've mostly dealt with it by not thinking about it, *not* making sexual pleasure into something I chase, and I've been pretty successful thus far.

I'm not a virgin. I popped my cherry with a bartender here in LA, getting him drunk and taking him into the woods to fuck, where my PK wouldn't have any inorganic objects to grab onto. It sucked. I hated it. I stopped trying.

Now? Jesus Christ with a butt-plug, I am ready to fuck anything that moves. It's like all the sex I could have been having these past few years has built and built and built, and now it's all clamouring for release.

Every one of our pursuers is on the run, booking it up the

sides of the channel. I raise my arms, eyes closed, grinning at the sky, and trip the bikers up. What the South Africans call an ankle tap. I don't really want to keep them here. I just want to remind them who they're fucking with. It distracts me from the hot, flushed feeling of need.

All at once, my legs turn to jelly. I don't feel woozy or anything – I've never felt so clear. But the lower half of my body isn't paying attention. I sit down clumsily, amid the fire and rubble and smoke, the blue sky above me, and the storm building to the north, at my back.

The van we were driving is still burning behind us, nothing more than a gutted shell now. At least we took care of the meth. I lie down, head resting on the concrete. After what I just did, I should feel drained, wiped out. But I'm still so freakin' *wired*. If my legs were actually listening to me, I'd start running. Probably in the direction of the nearest human being, so we could find a hotel room somewhere and fuck each other's brains out. I giggle, my fingers twitching.

A shadow falls over me – no, two shadows. Annie and Africa. Oh good – they made it.

"Shit." Annie's voice is pinpoint-sharp, like it's coming from inside my head. "That was . . . "

"Yaaw, Teggan, what did you do?" Africa doesn't sound pissed. He sounds amazed. His eyes are wide, his shoulders and knees twitching. Annie too.

Looks like I'm not the only one who got a dose of the powdery meth. Although I think I got it a lot worse than they did.

I'm starting to get a headache. Building insistently at the back of my skull. Africa is still talking, the words coming in a rushing torrent. "When I see you lift the bridge, I try circle around to cut off the biking gang, you know, maybe make sure they do not spring a surprise, but then you throw them, *yaaaaaa*, like nothing, I never see you do that before. Hey, lotta people saw you, what you did, there gonna be all sorts of videos and Snapchat things out there, *yaaw*?"

Suddenly, he gets a look on his face. A horrified, disgusted look, as if he's only now realising that we're all high. And he's probably thinking of Jeannette too. She's clean now, but she's relapsed before, something Africa refuses to talk about. Africa has had to chase her more than once, find her in the mess of Skid Row, go back to the world of homelessness and addiction that he thought he'd escaped.

"Relax," I tell him. "I took care of the phones."

I push myself to a sitting position, *refusing* to give into the thoughts – after all, it's not like I did meth on purpose. All the same, there are . . . a *lot* of people out there now, on either side of the storm drain, pushed up against the chain link fence and gawking at me. Twenty, thirty, maybe more. And I just gave them the full Teagan experience, something I am explicitly not supposed to do. Ever. There won't be video, no proof, but . . .

I may be in trouble.

Good thing the worried part of brain isn't driving the bus. I tilt my head back, warbling at the sky in a fake-deep voice. "*Smoke meth every day.*"

"What you mean, *smoke meth every day*?" Africa goggles at me, horror spreading across his face. "That is a very bad idea."

"No, dumb-dumb, it's like the last line of the Dre song. "The Next Episode"? Nate Dogg telling you to smoke weed every day?"

Another giggle worms its way out of me. I should stop that.

"You know what would make this better?" I tell them. "Fried chicken. Annie? How 'bout it?"

And Annie does the oddest thing.

She drops to one knee and grabs hold of my shoulders. Like

she's about to start shaking me, yelling at me for revealing my ability. Except: she doesn't. There's no anger on her face. There's just . . .

I don't know what it is. There's longing there. And fear. And worry. Exasperation. Desperation. Anger. All of it, buried in the lines around her eyes and the set of her mouth, the flare of her nostrils. It pushes through the high she must be feeling, something raw and red. I stare at her, unable to look away. Not knowing what to do.

Before I can figure it out, the look is gone. Annie pulls me to my feet, as if she was planning to do that all along.

"Ya," Africa says, dazed. "Food is good."

"*Yay!*" I throw my arms high, the weird moment with Annie forgotten. "*Fried chicken for everyone!*"

SIX

Reggie

Regina McCormick ends the call with Africa – she can barely understand what he's saying at the best of times, even when he isn't speaking at ten thousand miles an hour – and takes a long, shaky breath. Her diaphragm is even worse than usual today, and the sound that rolls out of her is weak and wheezy.

"What the hell?" she murmurs.

She doesn't even know why she's surprised any more. The insanity of what she saw on China Shop's video feed before the pinhole cams cut out? The ... whatever the hell it was that Teagan just did, at the Main Street Bridge? Or – lest we forget – the fact that *someone* knew about their mission, and tipped off the Legends?

Africa told her that Teagan thinks she took care of any cameras, but if she missed even one, revealed her ability to others, then they're in trouble. Reggie quickly scans social media. There are a few people claiming they saw something ... but no video, or photos. None at all.

Of course, if there were, Reggie would already have gotten a call from Moira Tanner. Not a pleasant one either. She glances at her cell, sitting in its slot on the right of her wheelchair. Reggie frowns, picking up the phone – it's difficult, with the lack of mobility in her fingers, but the phone's case has a specially designed ring on the back, slotting over her middle finger.

No missed calls. That's good. As long as Moira isn't calling, everything will be all right.

All the same . . . *Damn it, Teagan.* The girl could do a thousand jobs perfectly, using that insane ability of hers without a hitch, clean getaway. But when a job did go bad, it happened fast, it happened messy and Teagan somehow always ended up making it worse. There were definitely witnesses, even if they didn't know what they were seeing, or get anything on tape. And what about the bikers? What will they do?

China Shop is going to need one hell of a debrief. They'll get their story straight, figure out how to present this as a win to Moira. Reggie winces. Maybe she should call Africa back, get some real answers – or take him up on his offer to join them for a meal, something which exhausts her even thinking about. Then again, what good will it do? It's all over, and anything Africa or Annie tell her – and it would have to be those two, because you can't get a serious answer out of Teagan even on a good day – would only prompt more questions. Best she do it later, when she's had a chance to do some actual research on her end.

Maybe she *should* go, meet up with the crew, *demand* some answers. No – it's far more important to find out who it was that told the Legends about them, mid-mission. Or what if—

Hell. Maybe she should take a breath – *ha* – and get some tea. That's what she should damn well do.

Reggie taps the joystick on her chair with the back of her right hand, reversing out of her Rig – the huge, six-screen setup she runs China Shop from. As always, she feels a tiny pang as she rolls away. Being locked into her Rig makes her feel like a pilot again.

As she manoeuvres her chair, the bag hanging on the back catches against the edge of the desk. It's a bag Reggie loves, that she's had on the back of her chair for ever – or since she visited Taos, anyway – made of multicoloured cloth in Native American patterns. It holds her tools and an extra scarf and a water bottle, and despite her limited mobility, she can reach round and pull it towards her. But she keeps catching it on the furniture in this new office, and she's started to wonder if she should move it, or get a different one.

The earthquake destroyed China Shop's old offices in Venice Beach. Their new setup is in an apartment block on West 228th Street in Torrance. A two-bed, two-bathroom new build that survived the big quake. Reggie works out of one bedroom, lives out of another – both are off a narrow, undecorated hall, which is itself off a larger living area. Moira paid the contractor a substantial fee to widen the doors for Reggie's chair, raise the countertops, even build a special roll-in shower. Give the woman this: she's a ruthless operator, but she has always looked after Reggie's physical needs. After all, they go back a long way.

Of course, the gigantic payout from the Army after her accident certainly helped. It's paid for Reggie's physical rehab, her medicine and equipment. It's paid for her carers over the years. It will probably continue to do so for the rest of her life. Reggie doesn't know if the payout happened because of Moira's involvement, and she never asked. Something tells her the woman would never admit to it.

The bright lights in the hall don't Reggie's mood. She can't help glancing down at the hand on the joystick, at the small liver spots forming on the back, particularly the one behind the middle knuckle that looks like the state of Maine. She'd googled it of course – the liver spots, not the state of Maine – because how could you not? *Solar lentigines* (as Google called them) *are very common in adults older than fifty.*

Reggie – a healthy forty-eight, thank you very much – had huffed when she read that and, aware that she was alone in her office, raised her right middle finger at the screen. As far as she could lift it from her useless hand, anyway.

She'd dropped it immediately, muttering "Drama queen," under her breath, smiling at the words. When she wasn't working with China Shop, Reggie spent some of her off hours working with an amateur theatre troupe in Anaheim – a disability-friendly crew that put on productions of Shakespeare, Tennessee Williams, even a few original scripts. The playhouse is no more, of course. Damn quake. Reggie pushes the memory out of her mind. She's got quite enough pain to deal with right now.

The living room is open-plan, with a small kitchenette, patches of sunlight from the windows gleaming off the chrome fixtures. Reggie heads in there now, eyes on the automatic tea-maker on a low shelf. Teagan bought it for her birthday, which touched Reggie no end, and it's a marvel. She hardly needs to do more than lift a big-handled cup – her stack always has straws in it, something else Teagan makes a point to take care of – and stick it in the machine.

Reggie sips her chamomile, trying to quiet her mind. Ignore the fluttering in her diaphragm and the burning pain in her thighs. Above all, ignore the clusterbomb of the living room.

It's where China Shop does the planning for their jobs, on a large whiteboard marked with savage scrawls. Stacks of paper, on both the low table and the floor. Empty mugs and takeout coffee cups, Post-it notes. Boxes of clothing, for when the team need to disguise themselves as city workers or security guards or cops. A flash of annoyance – those should be in the van, Africa should have taken care of that. Then again, did Reggie even mention it to him? Or is it another item on her to-do list that she hasn't gotten to?

Of course it is.

Reggie never used to be in charge of clothing and paperwork and supplies. That was Paul's job, when he was still alive. Paul Marino could be frustrating to work with, petty and pompous. But he was a superb logistics man, a former Navy quartermaster who lived and breathed details. He made China Shop work, doing all the things nobody else wanted to do.

Reggie misses him – and not just because of his professional skills. He was an ass sometimes, but he was a good man – and deeply good to Annie, with whom he'd formed a pretty unbelievable bond. Reggie sips her tea, hoping Annie's doing better today. Hoping the job has distracted her from her grief.

The China Shop budget is generous. Their tools, vehicle, systems infrastructure, offices, all top-notch. Moira has always seen to it that Reggie is comfortable, and has everything she needs. Except for one, very deliberate thing.

She's held off getting them a new logistics man, saying that she hadn't found anyone she trusted to do the job, that a couple of qualified candidates fell through. On the face of it, the fact that she hadn't replaced Paul is ridiculous. But that's too simple. No, there was no logistics man because Moira is trying to send a message to Reggie: *If you want to run China Shop so badly, then it's all on you.*

After the earthquake, Reggie had to stand up to Moira to keep her job. Which was right, dammit, because she *was* good at it. But it had been a close-run thing, and Moira clearly hadn't been happy about it.

Reggie is a world-class hacker, and there's not a system in the world that can keep her out. But when it comes to running a covert group of operatives, dealing with all the details, she doesn't have it. No point bullshitting. Teagan and Annie and Africa help out, do their best, and they've certainly raised the lack of a new logistics guy before – well, Teagan and Africa anyway. Annie tends to leave the room whenever the subject comes up. But they're not all that good at it either.

Since Paul died, their planning, logistics and supplies have been a disaster. And invoices! Reggie grimaces at the thought.

Reggie's mother used to boast about her daughter. *My Regina's good at everything. Whatever she puts her mind to.* Her mom was wrong about that – well, mostly wrong. Being good at things didn't mean squat if you couldn't do those things any more. No, her true skill, her real talent, was reinvention.

Being a high school track star was fine and well, but it didn't mean squat when her times weren't going to get her a scholarship, much less to the Olympics. She didn't have the money for college; hardly anybody in Shreveport did. So Reggie joined the Army, and a secondment to the CIA as an analyst turned into a permanent post. After a year or two on the Baltics desk, they put her in the field, working out of Bosnia.

At the time, she'd been deeply worried that she'd never make it, and was pleasantly surprised at how well she adapted to the brutal strain of deep cover. When Bosnia went south, after what happened in Nemila, she'd put that gift for reinvention to good use. She'd gone back to the Army, retrained as a pilot. She was good enough at it that they let her fly Apache helicopters – one of the first black women to ever do so.

Of course, the true test of her gift came at the end of a Taliban RPG in Helmand. But she rose to it, remaking herself yet again: not just carving out a life for herself with no legs and

barely any arm movement, but teaching herself how to code –
and code damn well, thank you very much. Well enough to
do it professionally for the US government, the only constant
throughout her working life. Uncle Sam would always find a
place for those who were willing to remake themselves.

A rueful smile sneaks across Reggie's face. Moira wants to
test her? See what Regina Gillian McCormick is made out of?
Fine. Regina Gillian McCormick made it out of Shreveport,
Louisiana. She wasn't defeated by what happened in Nemila,
she wasn't defeated by a Taliban RPG and a busted C6 verte-
bra, and she is damn sure not going to let a pile of paperwork
claim that particular honour.

Her phone rings. *Well, there you go.* Did she really think
Moira wouldn't find out about the way the job ended? Reggie
sighs, putting the cup on the counter and fishing the phone out
of its holder, already planning how she's going to frame this.

Only, it's not Moira. It's a number Reggie doesn't recognise.

She frowns, then her face clears – probably someone
wanting some boxes shifted. China Shop still has a cover as
a removals company, and after the quake, their services have
been in demand.

"Answer call," she says. There's a beep as it connects.
"China Shop Movers?"

The voice on the other end is confident, female. "May I
speak to Regina McCormick?"

"This is she."

"Oh hi, great, Regina. My name is Darcy Lorenzo. I'm
calling from DCA Talent?"

" . . . I'm sorry, where?"

"DCA Talent. We manage actors in the industry. I wanted
to talk to you about—"

"You manage actors."

"Uh-huh. So listen, I saw you play Titania at the Roadhouse. I wasn't actually supposed to be there that night – I work with actors all day, so I try to give myself a break." Darcy Lorenzo laughs, a tinkling sound that puts an absurd image in Reggie's mind of a champagne flute smashing to bits on a hard floor. Why on earth is this woman calling her? "But a friend of mine dragged me along. I have to say, you blew me away."

"Um. Thank you?" It was months ago that Reggie played Titania, the fairy queen in *A Midsummer Night's Dream*.

"I've kind of kept you in the back of my mind," Lorenzo says. "Just when we're going through casting notes, you know. I wasn't sure I'd find a role that's right for you, you know, since . . . " For the first time, the woman sounds unsure.

"Since I'm in a chair," Reggie says, a note of steel entering her voice.

"Right, yes, exactly." Lorenzo actually sounds relieved. "As I said, I kept you in mind and . . . well, I think I've come across a role you'd be perfect for. I tracked down the folks who own the theatre you performed at, and got your number. Do you have an agent right now?"

"An agent?"

"It's totally fine if not. Actually, better than fine, because it gets me in on the Regina McCormick ground floor." Another tinkly laugh.

Reggie clears her throat. "I'm not—"

Available. She was going to say, *I'm not available.*

And she isn't! There's way too much to do. She has to deal with the aftermath of what Teagan did, for one thing, and . . . God, so much else.

Lorenzo continues as if she hadn't spoken. "Now as far as I know, this casting call is agency-only, but of course I'd be happy to submit it on your behalf. No commitment – we'd talk about that if they gave you a callback – but I speak for everyone here when I say we'd be delighted to represent you. Are you able to film an audition? On your phone is fine."

"I . . . yes, I . . . "

"Outstanding. If you give me your email, I'll send over the scene – I can't say too much about what the project is right now, NDAs and all that, so don't worry about putting it in context. Just hit us with your best shot."

In a daze, Reggie gives the woman her personal email address. After they hang up, she spends a long time staring at her phone.

Reggie might not be from LA, but she's an actress, and she has some idea of how these things work. And what just happened . . . shouldn't happen. Agencies don't even cold-approach actors with two good feet under them. Actors with disabilities? Reggie's an optimist, but she's never shied away from reality. She certainly isn't going to start now. Hollywood can be brutal, and no casting director is going to go through the hassle of casting a quad or a para when they can just pick someone bankable and have them occupy a wheelchair on set. They did that with Denzel, didn't they? Had him play a full quad on that old 90s movie, the serial killer thing with Angelina. *The Bone Collector.*

Except: just because it doesn't usually happen, doesn't mean it won't *ever* happen.

This is insane. Reggie's dreamed of going pro, sure, pleasant daydreams spurred on by the almost liquid thrill she got as she rolled out onto the playhouse stage in Anaheim. But actually doing it? Come on.

Before she can process this thought, her phone – still in her hand – rings again. And this time, there's no debate who it is. Reggie knows, even before she looks at the phone screen.

"Answer call," she says, trying to ignore the pitter-pat of her heart. "Moira. It's all under control. I haven't found any evidence of what Teagan—"

Tanner cuts her off. Her breathy New England voice sounds unusually harassed. "Where is the team now?"

"They're getting some food. What's going on?"

"We have a situation."

SEVEN

Teagan

When you're in LA, and you've just wrapped up a hard day busting meth labs and beating up biker gangs, where do you go for a good meal?

Howlin' Ray's.

Howlin'. Motherfuckin'. Ray's.

The greatest hot chicken in history. Fine, that may or may not be true, but who cares? As I take a bite of the sandwich, the glorious, crispy breast, firm bun and tangy slaw compact together into a magnificent, salty, crunchy, garlicky delicious mouthful. At that moment, I am a hundred per cent sure that there has never been a better bird.

And that's *before* the burn hits you. This is Nashville hot chicken, and I like mine so spicy it burns the top three layers off my tongue.

The quake torpedoed a lot of LA's finest restaurants. Which was a bummer, obviously. But LA's food scene is known for its food trucks and hole-in-the-wall operations, and it didn't take much for those spots to start up again. Ray's was one of the first to come back. It's in a little spot in a Chinatown food

court, and even post-quake, the line is always nuts. I nearly
went insane waiting for our turn.

I'm still high on the meth, although I'm no longer in super-
mega-ultra-apocalypse PK mode. There's an uncomfortable
hollow feeling in the pit of my stomach, one that's been
building for the past half hour though – a feeling I'm trying
real hard to ignore. And I can't stop clenching my muscles.
My shoulders and lats and quads are tight and hard, almost
vibrating.

The food court is rammed, despite it being only noon. A
seething mess of noisy people, making the already-sweltering
space even hotter. It's elbow-room only at the tables, whole
families jammed up against construction workers and business
people in suits, the floor a mess of discarded serviettes and
food splatters. Places like Ray's have become focal points for
entire sections of the city – buzzing hangouts where you're
almost certain to see somebody you know, no matter the
time of day.

Once we retrieved our van – which, thank fuck, wasn't
too far from the Main Street Bridge – it took us for ever
to find a place to park here. Guess not even an apocalyptic
earthquake can solve LA's parking problem. All the same, the
sheer number of people out getting food gives me hope. LA's
hurting, but it isn't dead yet.

There's not one but *two* chicken sandwiches for me, a quar-
tet of jumbo tenders for Africa, with shake fries and collard
greens. Annie has a slim plate of wings. She's barely looked
at me since we left the Main Street Bridge. Africa's attention,
though, has been entirely on me. My little meth episode horrified him, even if it was accidental. He kept asking me if I'm
OK, offering me water over and over again until I wanted
to hit him.

The dose of meth he and Annie got wasn't anywhere nearly as big as mine. They're already coming down, and although neither of them look especially comfortable, and probably won't be for a while, they're going to make it out OK.

Not sure I can say the same for me. I am still flying.

I smash through the first sandwich in four giant bites, every cell in my body awake and screaming for sustenance. When it's done, my tray is a mess of dribbled sauce and pickles, but I don't care. I smack my lips, reach for the second sandwich. Annie has hardly touched her wings. She's just sitting, shoulders tense, not looking at anything.

I tease out a hunk of pickle jammed between my teeth. "Your food OK?"

She doesn't respond.

"Annie? Earth to Annie? If it's bad, we can send it back. Or is it not hot enough? They'd probably give you some sauce in a cup if you want."

I trail off when Africa gives me a minute shake of the head. He's chewing at a tender, arms tucked in so he doesn't jab the woman sitting next to him.

He's right. I should leave it alone. Annie's got a lot of shit to deal with, and if she wants to sit and stew, that's fine.

Except: the part of my brain that understands this isn't in control. I'm still vaguely pissed at Annie for getting angry with me, for no goddamn reason. This feeling sits alongside the joy I'm getting from my sandwich, and they are *not* easy roommates. It's bringing out a weird passive-agressive vibe in me that I'm not sure I like.

"Here," I say, offering her my second sandwich. "You should try this. It's *really* fucking good."

"I'm fine," she mutters, not looking at me, her voice almost swallowed by the noise of the crowd.

"I don't know what they do to it. I think it's the marinade, but it might also be the oil? I get the feeling they fry the stuff in chilli oil. I saw a trick like that once on—"

"I'm *fine*."

It's a snarl, backed up by a flash of anger on her face, a look so harsh and sudden that I actually lean back a little.

I take a bite of my second sandwich, to stop myself saying anything else. It doesn't taste nearly as good as the first one. The headache at the base of my skull is more insistent now, as is the yawning emptiness in the pit of my stomach. My fucking shoulders are starting to ache – I can't relax them, no matter how much I roll my neck. I'm clenching my teeth, too, and my legs are starting to tremble. I don't feel good any more. And I have a horrible feeling it's about to get a lot worse.

Africa has noticed. "You are lucky. It was powder, not rocks. That means the chemicals were weak. You must keep drinking water, OK? Because you are going to crash, and much worse than Annie and I are now. And after we are done here—"

"Dude, I'm fine."

"Maybe now. Maybe for a few more hours. But then . . . " He shakes his head, no doubt thinking of his girlfriend. "You think you know, but you don't. You will want more, and Teggan, you *cannot* let yourself take any."

His voice is making my headache worse. "I won't. Can we drop this? Please?"

He looks like he wants to keep going. Instead, he goes back to his food, shaking his head. Like he doesn't understand.

We sit in silence for a few minutes. I will myself to eat that second sandwich . . . and can't do it.

Africa finishes another tender. "OK, so. Now that the job is finished, we must talk about what to do next. Mrs Tanner will want a full report. Especially about the thing with the bridge. We must make sure to tell her that the Legends, they won't be a problem any more, huh?"

I finally swallow. "Got that right." I prod the air with a hunk of sandwich. "Cook meth in my city, get a bridge shoved up your ass."

"Eh, take this serious." He puts down his next tender, locks eyes with me. "We cannot just say, *hey, we took care of the problem.* There are still the guns. And it is important for us to be honest – and she has to know what happened when your power go crazy from the meth, huh?" He holds up a hand. "I know you say there are no videos and what what, but you cannot be sure. And I know lots of people see it anyway. Even in here, people are talking about it."

"Who cares?" I grin, an expression that feels like I have to wedge it onto my face with a crowbar. The headache is starting to get gnarly now, a furnace at the back of my head. "Let them talk. You hear some of the stories coming out of LA these days? You know there are a bunch of people who swear blind they saw an actual devil – like a horned devil – crawling out a quake crack in Pomona? You think anybody's gonna believe—?"

"Not sure that's the same thing as you throwing a bunch of shit around the LA River," Annie mutters.

I blink at her. "The what?"

"The LA River, man."

"What river? That was a storm drain."

"Eh, come now," Africa says. "No distraction. We must talk about—"

"You cannot be this dense," says Annie.

"Rude. I'm not dense, I'm just confused. That was a river?"

Annie glances at Africa. "Back me up here."

"Yes yes, the LA River, I know. Now, when we talk to Mrs Tanner—"

I blink. "What fucking river are you guys talking about?"

"Jesus Christ." Annie pulls out her phone, dials up Google Maps. She un-pinches her fingers to zoom out on a map of LA, tapping on a winding path that bisects the city, north to south. "Here. Runs from the Santa Susana Mountains all the way to Long Beach."

"That's a *river*?" I say.

"Yes!"

"But it was . . . that's a storm drain!"

"Culvert, technically, but whatever. Army Corps of Engineers buried the river in concrete in the late thirties, after this massive flood. Now all that's left is that channel of water running down the middle – easier to control, I guess. And to be fair, they didn't concrete the whole thing. There are spots up in Glendale, where it's still an actual river, with banks and plants and shit."

I don't ask how Annie knows all this stuff. She's big into the history of LA, always has been. And while I'm not happy that she's giving me shit – again – at least she's participating. She's not shutting us out. And the conversation distracts me from my head and my stomach and my iron-hard, vibrating muscles.

"It's basically falling apart, anyway," Annie is saying. "Concrete's all fucked up, mostly because the Engineer Corps can't build for shit. They're the ones who did the levees in New Orleans – remember Katrina?"

"But how can they even do that?" Africa says, pointing at Annie's phone. "It must be a big river, *yaaw*."

"*Of course* it was big. Took 'em twenty years. But they got it done. Just up and wiped a whole river out of existence under a shit-ton of concrete. Anyway, Teagan, you can't seriously tell me you don't know about it."

"I—"

"You're telling me ..." Annie closes her eyes, takes a deep breath. "You're telling me you've been in LA for over two years, doing a job where we drive back and forth across the river—?"

"Storm drain," I mutter. Fuck, are my *eyes* vibrating? It feels like it. I'm twitchy and hot, nervous, irritable.

"*River*, three or four times a week ... and you just never register that it's there? What about LA River Drive? What you think they named that after?"

"... River Phoenix?"

She sighs, dropping her head and rubbing her eyes with the heels of her hands. "Fuck me, you just live in your own world, don't you?"

Africa clears his throat pointedly. "When we meet with Reggie, we must explain everything so she can make a full report to Mrs. Tanner."

"Yeah, OK." I should eat the last bite of my sandwich, still oozing delicious sauce. But I'm not hungry any more. Not even a little bit. "Why you got such a hard-on for Tanner anyway?"

"What do you mean?"

"You've been doing this for months now. *Mrs Tanner says*, and *what would Mrs Tanner think*, and *we must tell Mrs Tanner*. What gives, dude?"

The words coming out of my mouth are nasty, childish even. I don't like them even as I say them, and I'm starting to feel pretty nasty and childish myself. Is it the meth talking? Or me?

Then again, Tanner isn't exactly my favourite person right now. We know she's been investigating where the earthquake kid, Matthew Schenke, came from – a place in New Mexico that he called the School. And yet, I have no idea what Tanner has found, if she's found anything. She's shared diddly-squat.

She's no slouch, which means she must have something ...
but her keeping us in the dark, pissing around with losers like
the Legends when there's a bigger threat out there, is starting
to grate. Africa being intent on pleasing her makes it worse.

I expect him to get angry, like Annie, but he just sits quietly
for a moment, nodding to himself, as if genuinely considering it.

"It is difficult, what she does," he says eventually. I swear
his voice has gotten deeper, his Senegalese accent more pro-
nounced. "She is trying to do good things in a world that is
not good. It is not right that we lie to her. That is not fair."

"Might be easier if she was less of an asshole," I mutter. God,
why do I sound so fucking *petty*?

"She is not an asshole."

"She totally is."

Abruptly, Annie gets up, pushing her tray back.

"You're done already?" I say.

"Mm." She winces as she tries to lever her leg out from
under the table without kicking the person next to her. "I'll
catch y'all later."

"Where are you going?"

She looks right at me then. And I swear, there's the ghost
of that look she gave me after the bridge collapse. The one I
couldn't figure out.

"Home," she says. "Reggie wants me, tell her I'll be in
tomorrow."

Africa leans across – he's got the reach for it – and squeezes
her shoulder. I want to do something similar, make up for
being such an ass before. She doesn't deserve that. But I'm on
the other side of the table, and it's way too awkward. My teeth
itch. Can you even have itchy teeth?

All at once, an image flickers into my mind: an old anti-drug
poster, or internet ad, or something. An addict, mouth slightly

open to reveal brown, rotting stumps. *Meth mouth*. It takes everything I have not to retch. No way I'm letting that happen.

"You not need a lift?" Africa says to Annie. "We have the van back now."

"Nah, I'm good. One of my boys can come pick me up. Or I'll Uber or something."

I wince. Ridesharing has come back to LA, which is good, but we aren't talking dozens of cars on the road. She could be waiting a while.

The whole city is like that at the moment. Superficially OK, but very far from back to normal. Right after the quake, there was a lot of international assistance to help us get back on our feet. The Japanese, especially, helped out with rebuilding some of the freeways – they know a thing or two about how to survive earthquakes. But then some politicians in Congress made a stink about it, and there were federal funding investigations, and lawsuits, and leaked memos, and before long Los Angeles was stuck swimming in place. Whatever rebuilding money there was got rerouted through a dozen different agencies and local government groups, all of which seem to hate each other, and none of which seem to know what to do with the cash. It makes my brain hurt just thinking about it.

Annie nods to us, turning to go, sidestepping around a smiling, overweight man juggling a baby and a tray of food. As she does, I get a look past her to the other side of the food court.

Nic Delacourt is here.

He's sitting with a group of buddies at one of the green plastic tables, all of them sharing a huge bucket of chicken. They're all wearing old, mud-spattered clothes and yellow high-vis vests.

Which is strange as hell, because Nic is a lawyer, working for the District Attorney's office. Last time I checked, judges

didn't permit high-vis vests in courtrooms. He'd been vol-
unteering with quake relief, I know that much ... but it's
the middle of the day, on a weekday. Wouldn't he be at the
courthouse in Inglewood?

Nic has his back to me, but I'd recognise him anywhere.
He's big, with broad shoulders and a bald head shining under
the court's bright lights. He's doing a very Nic thing – gesturing wildly as he eats, making a point with a chicken drumstick,
waving it in the air. He must be in the middle of a story, or
a joke; everyone else at the table is listening to him intently,
good-natured smiles on their faces. They look tired, weary
even ... but happy.

And I can picture the expression on Nic's face without even
thinking about it.

I shut my eyes, take a deep breath. Of all the things I do
not need to think about now, my sort-of-ex-crush is at the
top of the list.

Africa frowns, follows my gaze. "Hey – it's your boyfriend, huh?"

"Uh, no."

"No, it is. It's Nic, ya?"

"I mean, he's not my boyfriend—"

"*Hey!* Nic! We over here!"

I have never wanted to stick a fork in someone's eye so badly.
Just fucking jam it in there.

"Dude, it's fine," I hiss through my clenched, grinding
teeth. Nic still hasn't responded, so maybe I can shut this down
before it starts.

But no, Nic's heard his name, he's looking up, and now
Africa is waving.

I have to resist the urge to leap across the table and break his
arm. Not that I'd be able to. Trying to stop him saying hello

to someone we know in a public place would be like trying to restrain a hundred-pound German shepherd from eating a fresh rib-eye.

And now Nic is getting up, a strange expression on his face – the weird look you get when you don't quite recognise the person shouting your name, and are frantically trying to remember if you've met them before.

"I'm Africa." My dipshit colleague's voice is a sonic boom over the food court.

"No!" I twist my body around, wishing I had invisibility powers instead of psychokinesis. "No. Shut the fuck up. Africa!"

"I work with Teggan! For the China Shop!"

Nic is halfway over to us when he spots me. It's at the exact distance where it's too awkward for him to turn around and pretend he didn't.

His expression goes from puzzlement, to annoyance, and then to a kind of controlled blankness. He pauses for a second, then slowly makes his way over.

Nic and I were friends for a long time, joined at the hip by a mutual love of food. He knows about my ability – I may or may not have dragged him headfirst into one of our escapades last year. In the past, I've wanted to date him. He's wanted to date me. The problem is, those two things have never happened at the same time.

During the whole quake thing, he wanted me to do more, help people using my ability. When I tried to explain why I *couldn't* reveal my ability, he said some . . . ugly things. Accused me of being selfish, said he was embarrassed for me.

Yes, I know I just threw my ability out in public today. It probably wasn't the smartest decision, but I was high on meth at the time so shut up.

Nic apologised later. Of course he did. He's not a bad guy.

He wanted to reconnect, sent text after text after text. Problem is, I didn't know what to say, and it became one of those problems that you just ignore and hope it goes away. I missed him, but I was also mad at him, and in the wake of Paul's death, I didn't want to start untangling whatever situation Nic and I had. So I ghosted him. I didn't plan on it. It's just that one day, I realised I hadn't replied to his last text for a while, and I couldn't think of anything good to say, so I just . . . left it. Not proud of it, but there you go.

We haven't spoken in months.

How does Africa know him anyway? I'm sure I've mentioned the big guy to Nic once or twice, but they've never been introduced. *Yeah, we're gonna have to talk about that.*

You want to know the most fucked-up thing? Nic is one of the only people in the world I *can* date. He knows about my ability, after all – and more importantly, he knows about what happens to it during sex. Back in the day, I managed to convince Tanner that I had the right to be with someone. Not even I can blame her for how fucked-up things got after.

So what have I been doing this whole time, where I don't want to date and I can't have sex? Let's just say I've gotten very good at not thinking about shit. Which has been especially hard lately, let me tell you, even before the meth made me ultra-horny – a feeling which has utterly and completely vanished, by the way, swallowed by the hollowness in the pit of my stomach.

Nic isn't the only person I've thought about romantically – there's a guy called Jonas Schmidt, a German tech bro who happens to be that much-sought-after combo of insanely rich, ridiculously hot and genuine. He helped us out during the quake, and we definitely had something. Or at least, I think we did.

Jonas doesn't know about my ability. I haven't seen him

since the quake, and that's not going to change. All the same, over the past few months, he's been in my thoughts more than Nic has.

"My brother!" Africa pumps Nic's hand hard, even though Nic clearly still doesn't know who he is. "Good to see you, huh?"

"Yeah, you too." Nic cuts a glance at me, and my cheeks go red.

"Hey, Nic," I say, putting as much confidence into my voice as I can. Trying to pretend I'm not still high on fucking meth. Hoping he doesn't notice. God, what if he does? Then again, fuck him.

"Hey," he says. The word is a balloon: bright and shiny on the outside, nothing but hollow space inside.

We fall silent. Africa, finally, picks up on the vibe. His eyes dart between us. "I was . . . Teggan and me, we were just eating some chicken from Ray's. You had it too, *yaaw*?"

"Uh, yeah. It's good."

More silence.

"How have you been?" I try.

"Oh, you know. We been working out in SB still; it's pretty crazy out there."

"Oh yes, I have many friends in San Bernadino," Africa says, clearly delighted to find a conversational ice floe to crawl onto in this freezing sea of awkwardness. "Very bad stuff. The buildings, they not up to code. Not like in Downtown. One of my oldest friends, Trevor, he tell me there still no power out there sometimes."

"It's pretty crazy," Nic says again, hands in his back pockets.

"You're still at the DA's office?" I ask, eyeing the high-vis vest.

"Gave it up. I'm doing quake relief full time now."

"For real?"

He shrugs, like he's had this conversation before. "Aw, you know. They're kind of running on a reduced staff at the moment anyway. They don't really need me."

Please. I might not have spoken to Nic much over the past couple of months, but I know him. He gets off on helping people. All the same, to quit his position . . . leave a promising legal career behind . . .

Africa nudges him, a move which actually staggers Nic. "I forget you are a lawyer! Hey, let me ask you: let us say I want to buy a property here in Los Angeles, but because of the quake the owner has just left it. If I cannot find them, must I legally pay them if I go and take the land?"

We both stare at him.

"Um," Nic says. "I don't really . . ."

"Myself and Jeannette – she is my girlfriend – we are looking to buy property. We think maybe we open a business here, on the side, you know, and we find this one place that maybe—"

My phone rings.

I am not a big talking-on-the-phone person, but I don't think I've ever been so happy to get a call. I don't even care if it's someone pretending to be the IRS, demanding I pay my taxes using Best Buy gift cards.

Fortunately, that isn't the case. "It's Reggie," I tell Africa. Then, to Nic: "Sorry, man, I gotta take this."

"OK, yeah, sure. Good to see you."

"You too, man."

We're talking over each other now, both of us super-enthusiastic. "Take care."

"Yeah absolutely, for sure."

He leaves quickly, zigzagging back to his table. Africa gives me a confused look.

I move my thumb to answer the call, then stop. "When did you guys even meet? I never introduced you."

"We didn't. I find him on the Facebook."

"Excuse me?"

"Ya, you mention your boyfriend, so I'm curious, you know?"

"OK, one, that is creepy as shit, and two—"

"Teggan." He nods at the phone.

"We are not done talking about this, just so you know." I hit the answer button. "'Sup?"

It takes me a good few seconds to understand what Reggie is saying. She's talking *really* fast, and that cool Louisiana accent of hers is turning every second word to chowder.

"Slow down," I tell her, trying to make sense of it all, my drug-addled brain not helping. "Wait – Reggie, no, slow down, I can't hear ... Hold up, what do you mean *electrified*?"

EIGHT

Reggie

The satellite photo on Reggie's screen looks mundane, but it makes the hairs on the back of her neck prickle.

It shows a self-storage unit in Glendale – the kind of facility that has sprouted everywhere in the US, appearing near highway off-ramps and industrial areas. Big Green Storage, the company is called. The kind of outfit that offers a concrete-and-steel box with a roller door for the low, low price of $21.95 a month (*First month free!!!*). The building that houses these particular concrete and steel boxes is three stories high, linked by elevators and fire stairs. It is identical to hundreds of other storage units across the US.

Except for one tiny detail.

The Glendale franchise of Big Green Storage was run, as most of these places were, by one permanent employee. Reggie looked him up: Art Levinson, a forty-something man with a driver's licence photo which made him look as if he'd just heard that a distant, half-remembered cousin had just died. Just another poor bastard working for a little over minimum wage in the great state of California.

At around eleven that morning, Art had been in what passed

for the building's office, making himself a cup of coffee, when his hand had started to vibrate. "Buzz," he told the 911 operator on the call Reggie pulled. "Like I was holding my phone, and it started ringing, only my phone was all the way over on the desk. That kind of buzzing vibration mode, you know?"

Reggie has to play the audio back a few times before she understands the story, because by the time Art had managed to place the call, he was hysterical.

The buzzing sensation had stopped as soon as Art had taken his hand off the coffee machine. When he touched it again, the buzz was stronger. He'd thought it was another earthquake at first, or even just a regular tremor. But nothing in the office was moving, as it would during a quake.

It was then that Art realised that his shoes were buzzing, too. He'd gripped the edge of the table the coffee machine stood on, and snatched his hand away with a yelp. "Red-hot," he kept repeating on the call. "Like my skin was on fire. The whole damn thing was a red-hot joy buzzer."

By then, Art's feet had started to feel the same way, stinging and burning inside his shoes. He'd leapt for his desk, all but throwing himself onto it, his coffee mug shattering across the floor.

There was no relief on top of the desk. It hurt him just as bad.

"It was an electric shock," he told the operator. His voice on the tape is garbled. "I've had them before, touched a live wire once or twice, I do DIY amps and stuff at home, and I know what it feels like. But I knew that couldn't be true, because the desk was made of wood. *You can't run a current through wood.*"

This last was said with a kind of hysterical, desperate confusion.

Art had boogied off the desk and boogied right the hell out of the office. By then, every single surface he touched – be it wood, metal, plastic, concrete, his shoes, his clothes – felt like grabbing hold of a live wire. There was a stench by that point: seared plastic, ozone. Art flew out there, howling, barrelling out of the office door into the parking lot. Five feet out, he tripped, sprawling on the concrete surface – then leapt back up with a distraught cry when it shocked him too.

Ten feet or so out from the building, the sensation began to drop away. Art had somehow made it across the street to a warehouse, borrowed a cellphone to call 911.

The cops came, along with an ambulance. Art couldn't tell them if there was anyone else in the building – tenants could come and go as they pleased without signing in, and the truck-sized security gates were on the other side of the building.

Art was physically fine, albeit shaken. But none of the first responders could get within ten feet of the building. It wasn't a hard boundary, but as they approached, the concrete began to shock them.

The storage unit, and the parking lot around it, had become electrified.

Reggie makes herself focus. The *how* can come later – it's the *what* that concerns her now. She works fast, pulling up info on the building. Owners, blueprints, current tenants. Satellite imagery. The police presence will make things tricky, especially if they call in another agency like the FBI. Moira can probably take care of that, holding the folks at the Bureau off until China Shop gets in place, but that doesn't mean they have all night. They need to work fast.

The cameras are all down, of course – torched by the electricity coursing through the building – but she digs in deep, going through the owners' server. It's not difficult. Self-storage companies aren't exactly the Pentagon when it comes to systems security.

Reggie quickly grabs the past twenty-four hours, finds the time the cameras went down – 9.58 a.m., a little over two hours ago. Reggie skips back an hour, runs it at high speed. Nobody around. Nothing out of the ordinary, in either the reception or the dimly lit corridors.

Reggie growls. Seems like the *what* will have to wait until China Shop get there.

Maybe this isn't as mysterious as it seems. She knows a little about electricity, has a basic knowledge of computer systems and copper wiring. Could it just be a disconnected power cable? One of the big utility cables buried underground, perhaps . . .

But even cursory research shows that the biggest power cable in the world couldn't cause what is happening at the storage unit. Electricity, when you get down to it, is nothing more than the movement of electrons between atoms. In some materials, like metal and water, those electrons move easily. In others – wood, rubber, concrete – it's near-impossible to separate them, which is why electrical wires have rubber sheaths.

Metal and water conduct electricity, concrete and wood and rubber resist it, and not even the most powerful electrical current in the world could overcome that resistance.

Except whatever is causing this *has* overcome the resistance. It's made electrons move where they shouldn't. It's turned resistors into conductors.

Christ – what about the *air*? They haven't even thought about that yet. Whatever is doing this is able to electrify concrete and wood – who's to say that electricity won't affect the air as well? The oxygen and hydrogen molecules in the building?

What the hell are they dealing with here?

Reggie pulls up the satellite image of the building again,

biting her bottom lip. Where is the energy actually coming from? What's the source? And shouldn't that amount of electricity set things on fire? Nobody's called the fire brigade, and from what Reggie can tell, the building isn't ablaze. A thought pops into her head, and she digs into the LA Fire Department servers. There: some alarms in the building *have* been tripped, which means there are at least one or two small fires inside. Whatever caused this—

Reggie lets out a frustrated huff. *Whatever is causing this? Stop being a fool.* There's a *person* behind this – a person with abilities, like Teagan. Is it someone Teagan's age, like Jake – the other psychokinetic they'd tangled with last year? Or was it another Matthew Schenke, a child with insane powers?

It's easy to imagine whole streets electrified, families cooked in their apartments, city blocks turned lethal. Grass and wood and water and tarmac loaded with enough voltage to kill. A smoking, ruined city, with nothing and nobody alive. She has to remind herself that she can't accept the electricity theory at face value. Art might be wrong, the cops might be wrong, and if . . .

The screens swim in front of her. She closes her eyes, leans back, makes herself take a few deep, shaking breaths. Her diaphragm protests, tightening up. Her internal thermostat, never reliable at the best of times, is going haywire. Sweat slicks her forehead and neck, although the office is cool.

She knows what it is, of course. It's the feeling she gets when she's trapped. When she can't see a way out.

It's the feeling of Nemila.

When the CIA put her in the field, they sent her to Bosnia. Her cover was as a peacekeeper with NATO. Her real mission was different. She was to destabilise the Serbs from the inside, disrupt their operations, using her official cover as a shield.

It was how she met Moira Tanner. Reggie fell into being a spook; Moira became one because there was never anything else she wanted to do.

They worked surprisingly well together. The polished daughter of a New England brahmin, and the scrappy recruit from the worst town in Louisiana. It was when they ran solo that there was trouble. Reggie was good at a lot of things, but never quite got the hang of deep cover operations. Her biggest success – acquiring a list of people the Serbs wanted to take out in Sarajevo – turned to ash. The Serbs found out. Took her to a farmhouse outside Nemila. And they . . .

Well. Moira got there before it got really bad. Which doesn't stop Reggie remembering the house, the room they put her in: empty of furniture (save for the chair they tied her to) with a child's crayon drawing of flowers still on the wall. She remembers the jumper cables, the batteries. The fists and feet.

And she remembers the sweet, cloying taste. The taste of fear. Of being trapped, with absolutely nowhere to go.

She's felt it plenty of times since then. After her accident in Afghanistan, when she woke up in the hospital. The long nights that followed. The therapy sessions. Somehow, she found a way through all of those – found a way out the trap. But now . . .

It's not just the appearance of another person with abilities that scares her. She's dealt with plenty of those – hell, one of them bought her a tea-maker for her birthday. So why does she feel like she's standing in the presence of something much bigger than she is? Why does she feel like she is under-equipped to deal with it, like she has been drained of her energy and her decision-making ability by the sheer, solid reality of running China Shop?

Darcy Lorenzo's voice, running through her head: *I've come across a role you'd be perfect in.*

She grunts. What is she doing? Whatever fantasy role might be on offer somewhere, whatever life might or might not be waiting for her after she sends in her audition, it doesn't matter. She has a job to do. Regina McCormick has never stepped back from a job in her life, and she is sure as hell not going to start now.

All the same, the thoughts won't go away. They play at the back of her mind, bright and quick, like fireflies.

Her phone buzzes, startling her. "Answer call," she says. "Speaker."

"I've talked to my contact at the FBI," Moira says. She's walking – actually it sounds like she's jogging, her voice harsh and hot. "He's going to get his LA field team to hold off until we've had a look, and he'll let us use their cover."

"Roger that. There are windbreakers and ID in the van – I'll tell Annie to get ready."

"Not her." Tanner breaks off to spit an order, hissing at someone else to hurry. "I want Mr Kouamé on point for this operation."

Africa.

The command catches Reggie off guard. "May I ask why?"

"I also want to be patched directly into the team feed," Tanner says, ignoring the question. "Do it now."

Reggie complies, manipulating the oversized trackball, pulling up the team's comm channel. The system the team uses is a step up from the military's old Warfighter Information Network Tactical programme, and it's a marvel. From her Rig, Reggie has access to as much data as she can handle, as well as crystal-clear audio and video. The team still has their earpieces, and there are spare pinhole cameras in the van . . .

Moira is perfectly within her rights to oversee things . . . but she has never requested access to the system during an op before. Not once. It makes Reggie deeply uneasy.

When the *Join* request from Washington doesn't come through. Reggie waits a beat, then says, "Moira, I'm not getting anything this end. Did you—?"

She's cut off when Tanner barks, "What do you mean, there's no connection? Fix it!"

It takes Reggie a second to realise that Moira isn't speaking to her. "Still nothing here," she says. "Waiting on your handshake."

There's a scuffling sound, as if Moira is passing the phone from hand to hand. "It's a problem on our side," she snaps. "They're having trouble getting a good connection. Jesus Christ."

Reggie raises an eyebrow. Moira Tanner swearing? Dear God, it must be the end times. It certainly will be for whoever runs Moira's communications in Washington, if they can't get the connection working.

Wait a minute . . .

First, someone disrupts the China Shop job with the Legends, blowing their cover. Now, there's a communications issue with Washington. It can't be a coincidence.

She quickly briefs Moira, being as succinct as she can. When she's done, Moira is silent. "Run diagnostics," she says after a few seconds. "See if there's been a network intrusion – we can coordinate on our side. Signature- and anomaly-based detection."

"Do you want the team to stand by on site?"

"No. Keep them in play – we need to know what we're dealing with. But they are to approach and observe *only*, they are *not* to engage. You are to stay in contact with Mr Kouamé, and I want updates on this line the second you hear anything."

"I could find a way to patch you in somehow, a phone connection or—"

"I don't want some broken-telephone link where I'm hearing everything second-hand. I want full audio and video. Just call me with any developments."

"Moira . . . is this someone from the same place as Matthew Schenke? The same School?"

Perhaps now Moira will share what she knows. She's been investigating the source of these extranormal individuals, but so far, she's kept China Shop in the dark. Two months since they found out about the supposed School in New Mexico, and nothing. Whatever Moira Tanner has, she's keeping it very close to her chest.

When Tanner speaks, her voice is sub-arctic. "We don't know. But we will know if your team performs."

"What if it is? What's the plan?"

"It will be communicated to you in due course. Stay with your team, run those diagnostics. Tanner out."

NINE

Teagan

By 2 p.m., we're in Glendale, in the Valley, and my stomach wants to crawl out of my mouth.

I mean that literally. Not the food inside the stomach – the stomach itself. It's like the muscles in the lining have become sentient and want to make a bid for freedom. Right up out of my mouth, over my tongue and teeth, and head for the horizon. I sit in the back of the China Shop van, breathing very carefully, and not opening my mouth even a little bit.

I can't stop thinking about what I've done to myself. What if this is permanent? What if I never stop feeling like this?

Annie's still with us. Africa and I managed to get her before she left – she was standing on the curb outside Ray's, waiting for her ride. I desperately need to ask her if she thinks I'll be OK. But every time the words get to the tip of my tongue, even worse paranoia drags them back. I can't let Annie think I'm a meth addict. She'll ... she'll ...

I don't know what she'll do. And Africa. He must hate me. God, they're going to kick me out of China Shop, make me go back to Waco, let me get cut open. Neither Annie nor Africa have looked at me since we left Ray's. Fuck them. They don't know what it's like. Well, no, they do, because they got a little of the stuff, but nothing like I did. I got an entire faceful. They're fine. They're peachy. They can't feel the horror that is my stomach, or the searing, blinding pain at the back of my skull. Like ants, digging tiny mandibles into my flesh. *Fuck them fuck them fuck them.*

I've never felt like this before. It's the polar opposite of what the meth felt like before. Instead of the open, clear freedom, all I get are invisible prison bars, my cell shrinking by the minute, crushing my chest. *If I can just find more meth . . . even a little bit . . . I wouldn't feel so—*

No. No way. *Stop it.*

I take everything back. I hate meth. I don't care how powerful it makes me, I'm never touching it again.

Africa's driving, Annie riding shotgun. She didn't look happy to see us. Then I told her what Reggie said, and she looked both furious, and very, very scared.

I don't blame her.

We pull off San Fernando into an industrial area, the road lined with warehouses and vacant lots. It's not hard to find our destination. It's the one further down the block surrounded by flashing red and blue lights.

Africa comes to a stop on the opposite side of the street. "That is it?"

"Nah, it's the other warehouse with a zillion cops around it," Annie murmurs. There's no venom in her words. It's like she says them on autopilot.

I want to remind her that it isn't actually a warehouse, but I don't trust myself to open my mouth. I'm still trying to get a handle on this – it'd be tough to process, even when I'm *not* on a horrifying meth comedown. You can't electrify concrete. Or wood. I don't even know how you do that without the entire building exploding.

Except: something – or some*one* – has.

It shouldn't be hard to believe. I can move shit with my mind, and last year I met a boy who could cause earthquakes. But there is something about this situation, something about the *way* it tells the laws of physics to go fuck themselves, that scares me. Bad.

"Yo, Teagan." Annie doesn't look away from the building. "Get the shit."

"*Hmmm . . . grerp.*"

"Come on, let's go. The jackets and IDs."

"*Hrrrrrroookay.*"

The whole world does a loop-de-loop as I get to my feet, the tools lining the walls of the van doubling and tripling in front of me. I nearly thump back down, and it's a goddamn miracle I manage to stay standing. I'm sweating buckets, but I can't stop shivering.

I regret everything.

FBI. Jackets. ID. Yes. But where do I even look? Since Paul died, the back of the China Shop van has been a disorganised mess. Bins overflowing with clothes, tools lying everywhere, duffel bags, a can of paint – from the surveillance job we did in San Jacinto, maybe? And a whole bulging folder of fake IDs.

I start with that. Or try to. The letters are moving a *lot*. There are multiple IDs with my own photo on them, and I swear the little smile I have on them mocks me.

"Teagan, what's the hold-up?" Annie doesn't wait for my response, clambering into the back and taking the ID folder, flipping through it. "Just get the jackets. They're in that bin right there."

The jackets should be easier. They're not. When Paul was around, they'd be neatly folded and itemised. Now? They're a mess, sleeves everywhere, some folded, others balled up.

Sorting through them right now is like trying to solve a Rubik's Cube after a whole bottle of tequila. In the end, Annie has to help.

She hates me. I let Paul die. She's going to let me suffer, she's going to make me do the job, even though she knows I'm sick. Oh God. I can't do this. There's nothing for it. I have to get more meth. Maybe there's some in the front passenger seat, where I first got a dose . . . no, that was in a different van, not this one, shit. Shit.

That image again: brown teeth in a pinched, ugly face. *Meth mouth.* I squeeze my eyes shut, tears leaking from them. My throat feels like a straw that's been left outside in the hot sun, shrivelled and kinked.

Then we're outside. I'm wearing my jacket. There's an ID around my neck. I have no memory of putting either of them on. The clouds on the northern horizon have gotten darker, despite the sun still burning high in the sky.

"Reggie, come in," Annie is saying. "You got anything for us?"

I don't even realise Annie put a comms unit in my ear until Reggie's voice comes over the group channel. "Nothing. Security cams are fried across the storage unit, and I'm not getting anything useful from the surrounding buildings. Nothing on traffic, no online chatter, nothing on the secure channels. Whatever this is, nobody's seen it before."

"What about the dude who called it in? The caretaker or whatever?"

"They took him to the hospital. We can follow up later, but I want you to check out the scene first."

"You cannot put electricity in concrete," Africa says. His jacket is both enormous and somehow *still* too small for him.

Over, I think. *You should say "Over" at the end of each*

transmission. Paul insisted on it. None of us ever listened to him, not even Annie.

"Reggie," Annie says quietly. "Are we *absolutely* sure this is a . . . " She flicks a glance at me. "You know. A Teagan situation. Someone like her."

I don't have the energy to tell her that calling it a *Teagan situation* is kind of rude. I don't think actually I'm able to speak.

"Because maybe there's just a . . . " Annie scratches her head. "Shit, I don't know a fault or something. A loose wire that's—"

"Ain't no loose wire causing this. But right now, there's no way to be sure – not without any footage or eyewitnesses to confirm. You folks are on observation duty. Local law enforcement's not equipped to deal with this – they don't even know people like Teagan exist."

Which may change, after my little stunt in the storm drain, but whatever.

"But if it is a person, then why?" Africa tugs at his jacket cuff. "Why electrify an entire building? For what?"

"Honey, I have no idea," Reggie replies.

"Is it a hostage thing?" Annie asks.

"No. There've been no demands, no anything. Just an electrified building. Now listen – Moira's asked to be connected directly."

Ah. The only thing that could make this day worse. Having Moira Tanner see what we see, and listen to our every word. Another burst of hot, staticky paranoia: if Tanner finds out that I'm high, what will she do?

Reggie isn't finished though. "But it looks like there are some problems with the connection in Washington. She'll join us when she's able."

"Problems?" Annie bites her lip. "Reggie, you don't think—?"

"I'm running diagnostics now. Chances are, it's just a glitch, but we have to assume the worst."

"What do you want us to do?"

"Proceed with the mission. And one more thing: Africa's on point for this job. Moira's request."

There's a second of stunned silence. Then Annie says, "I'm sorry, what the *fuck*?"

"Eh." Africa glares at her, looking both offended and pleased at once.

I don't hear Reggie's response. The comedown is doing horrible things to my sense of time, because suddenly we're across the street and heading for the police line. Blue and red, the lights piercing my brain.

Annie approaches one of the uniformed cops, a middle-aged, heavyset dude with a bad goatee. He shouts at her to keep back, then blinks when she holds up the FBI identification. What are we going to do if the real feds show up? Then again, maybe Reggie and Tanner will keep this off their radar . . .

Another skip forward. Africa is bending down, hissing at me to get it together. Which is a bit like telling a broken egg to fix itself. Annie is in conversation with a detective, a woman with cornrows and a gold badge hanging down over her black polo.

"And you haven't been inside?" Annie is saying. She sounds pissed.

"Can't even get close." Like Annie, the detective has a slight Latinx accent.

"What about drones? I know LAPD got a few — shit, even something from your evidence lockup—"

"You think we ain't tried that?" The detective runs a hand down her face, looking tired and confused. "Most of the building is normal inside. Couple small fires, but that's it. But when we got to the second floor, the drone . . . went down."

The detective looks over at me, her gaze lingering. Probably thinking that I look mighty out of it for an FBI agent. Also that I don't actually look like an FBI agent in the slightest, despite the windbreaker.

"Detective, we don't have time for this," Annie says. "What do you mean *it went down?*"

"It's not really clear on the tape. There's this shadow, from something just out of camera view. Then bam. No control, no video, nothing. Listen, if the FBI are assuming command then—"

Aaaaand fast-forward.

No cops any more. I think we're on the other side of the building, in an empty parking lot. I'm sitting down with my back against something – a car? I don't know – and Annie and Africa are having one mother of an argument.

"—way she can do that." Annie jerks a finger at me. "She can barely stand up. Look at her fucking pupils, man!"

"We cannot go in there ourselves," Africa says, scowling. "We cannot even get near it. I am in command of this mission, and—"

"I don't give a shit, bro. She's done. You think she's gonna be able to just stand outside and echolocate what's in there?"

"We know she has good range. We have seen it, yes?"

"Listen, jackass, I've been doing this longer than you. I don't care if you're Tanner's new flavour of the month – you don't understand how Teagan's shit works. Yeah, she's got range – *if* she's in good shape, or if her body goes into fight-or-flight."

Or if I'm high. I feel like I should mention that, but I can't get the words out.

"So we get her into that," Africa says. "Fight-or-flight."

"Oh, and how you gonna do that? You gonna hit her? Shoot at her? If you even try anything . . . " Annie takes a breath, visibly calms herself. "It doesn't even matter. We could have her fly a camera in there and it'd just be the same as the drone. Zap."

"But we have to confirm. I have orders from Mrs Tanner."

Not *we* have orders. *I* have orders.

Why the fuck did Tanner put Africa in charge? It's not that he can't do it – he's more than proven himself since he joined the team, despite his category-five-hurricane personality. But leadership material? Running missions? While someone as seasoned as Annie is walking around?

"Orders to *observe*," Annie is saying. "Right now, I don't observe shit."

"And I am saying that is not good enough!"

Africa crouches down in front of me, snapping his fingers in front of my face, each one like a thunderclap. "Teggan, are you good? We need you to scan the inside."

"Did you not hear a fucking word I just said? She's *done*. We're not making her do that. You of all people should know what a meth comedown looks like."

Africa rounds on her. This time, he speaks slowly. Quietly.

"Do not ever speak of that to me again," he says. "You know nothing."

"I've been on these streets longer than you, jackass, you think I don't—?"

Another time skip.

Usually, I can speak for myself, but my mouth is way too dry. It's the Mojave Desert in there.

"Then we must come up with something." Africa touches his earpiece, as if checking whether or not she's connected. "Mrs Tanner will be expecting answers."

Annie's nostrils flare. "I know you got a hard-on for impressing her, but this is not the fucking time."

"Yo." My voice is barely there, but it suddenly seems very important to make myself heard. "I think I'm gonna throw up."

Annie doesn't hear me. "We fall back. We come up with a new plan. Because if you think I'm letting her—"

"Yeah, definitely gonna throw up. 'Scuse me."

I lean over and retch both chicken sandwiches onto the blacktop.

I'd love to say the puking stops there, but it does not. My head is a balloon in a hurricane, and my stomach is a howling maw of death. I retch stomach acid, saliva dripping from my gasping mouth, my whole world shrunk down to a tiny point where it's just me and the pain.

Just a tiny little bit of meth. That's all I need. It's not even about the pain I'm feeling now—

Liar.

—it's about how good I was. I was perfect and clean and free, the absolute best version of myself. What's so bad about wanting to be that way again?

Hands on my back. No idea whether it's Annie, or Africa. They're both talking, their voices blurred and indistinct. I'm going to die. That's what going to happen. The finality of it almost crushes me.

I don't die. I may not be human – not technically, anyway – but my body acts like it. And when humans puke, they usually feel better. The fog in my mind clears, just a little.

A person is causing this electrical shit – there's no doubt in my mind. Someone with abilities like mine. Matthew Schenke was the last one I ran into, and he was a psychopath, using his ability to destroy as much as he could.

Right now, inside that building, is someone who came from the same place Matthew Schenke did — I'm sure of it, more sure than I've ever been of anything.

Which means that if we don't find a way to stop this, a lot of people could get hurt.

There's also the fact that I *cannot* let Tanner get to whoever is doing this before I do. She'll spirit them away, maybe even to the same facility she held me in before deploying me in Los Angeles, and she'll tell us nothing. I'll never find out about how these people are using my parents' research.

Worse: what if she just decides, *fuck it*? Decides not to risk a second Matthew Schenke situation, and just nukes the building with a Hellfire missile? If you don't think she'd deploy a weapon of war on US soil, you don't know Moira Tanner.

I straighten up, still on my knees. Annie's sort of right — echolocating through an entire building is probably more than I can handle right now, demands more concentration than I can spare. But vomiting my guts out has cleared my head, just a little, and I still have some PK left. I can feel it, feel the objects around me, fuzzy but distinct.

I think about Tanner. About Waco. About Hellfire missiles. About Matthew Schenke and Paul Marino. About what's at stake if I don't knuckle up.

"Hey, guys," I say carefully. "I've got a wild idea ... "

TEN

Teagan

Nobody liked my wild idea.

Annie got so angry I thought she was about to punch me. Africa called me crazy, a *dëma*, a mad woman. "I forbid it," he kept saying. Reggie was about as enthusiastic, telling me to back off, observation *only*.

I told them that unless we actually got inside, we were observing dick. We were standing there staring stupidly at a building, waiting for something to happen.

These facts are all true. But they're feeling very academic now that I'm actually in here.

How am I inside? Without being electrocuted? Glad you asked.

Back when Paul was still around, he and I had to get onto the roof of a hangar at Van Nuys Airport this one time. We stood on a thick sheet of metal – the kind they use for roofing – which I then floated upwards with my PK, like a magic carpet ride.

It's a good trick. And if you want to navigate an electrified building, where the walls and floor and ceiling will kill you, a PK-powered hoverboard is the way to go.

Whoever is doing this hasn't electrified the air itself, or the drone the cops sent in wouldn't have gotten through the front door. I'm guessing it's possible – if we're talking electrons here, there's really no difference between air molecules and the molecules in the walls or ceiling – but it hasn't happened. We don't know why. The only thing I can think of is that if it is a person doing this, they might not want to electrify things they have to breathe.

I'm not actually on a metal sheet right now. There wasn't one handy. I'm on a car door, one that I ripped off a little Prius we found in the back lot. It made my idea seem even more dodgy than it was already, and did not, shall we say, inspire confidence in Annie and Africa.

They agreed – under protest – to keep the cops at bay, making sure they didn't get near the rear of the building. They're FBI, after all. While they were doing that. I got in through one of the storage unit's back roller doors, opening it with my PK. And yes, before you ask, it's a lot harder right now. I am not exactly operating at peak capacity. Which Annie and Africa reminded me of, multiple times. Annie kept telling me that my pupils were so big, she couldn't see my irises any more.

But I did it. I'm inside. Heading down one of the corridors, hunkered down on the car door, two feet off the floor. Trying very, very hard not to touch anything. You know that game, The Floor is Lava? This is the grown-up version. And in keeping with all things adult, the consequences of fucking up here are *so* much worse.

Well, maybe. The receptionist didn't die – he just said touching anything hurt a lot. But he managed to escape, and there's no telling what would happen if I touched a surface and had nowhere to run. Still, right now, nobody's dead. Hopefully we can keep it that way.

"Teggan." Africa's voice is hella staticky in my ear – the electricity must be causing some interference. "What do you see?"

"Nothing so far," I murmur. Shit, even the act of talking makes it harder to stay balanced.

It doesn't help that it's like a horror movie in here. The lights are burned out, as you'd expect. I'm wearing chunky night vision goggles – Annie retrieved them from the van. They give everything a sickly green tint, which does not make the dank, concrete corridors any more appealing. Normally, I'd fall over myself for the chance to use night vision goggles. But right now, I'd kill for actual light.

Crappy linoleum floor panels. Concrete walls, with big metal roller doors every few feet, huge padlocks on each one. A low ceiling, also concrete, with lines of dead fluorescent lights. That's it. This place is a maze – there's not even an exit sign anywhere, which I'm sure has to violate a few laws. Would an exit sign keep working through all this? They use radio-active gas for their light, don't they? How would electricity . . .

The burst of adrenaline and clear-headedness I got from puking has almost gone. I'm paranoid again, twitchy, my stomach and my head aching. I can't keep a thought in my head. I'm desperate for more meth one second, then recoiling in horror from the idea a moment later. The air stinks of smoke – not an intense smell, but definitely there. Most probably from the fires Reggie mentioned. I'm still struggling to understand how the entire building isn't on fire, but then again, what do I know about electricity?

And the storage unit feels . . . *wrong*. There's a taste to the air, metallic and oily. The air feels thick, too – the kind of thick you get when you're walking through a pea-soup fog. It may not be carrying electricity itself, but it is *not* happy about being here. There's a very low sound in the background that reminds me of a generator, or an AC vent. A low hum. I can't shake the feeling that the deeper I go, the more electricity there is coursing through the walls and floor.

I'm breathing way too hard, and it has nothing to do with the meth comedown. Whoever's doing this is powerful. *Really* freaking powerful.

Why is it that every time I encounter someone else with abilities, I feel like I'm playing catch-up? Just once, I'd like to be the person with the biggest dick.

Underneath me, the door wobbles. Normally, levitating myself like this would be easy. Not today, though. Today, it's taking a lot out of me.

Holy shit – movement. At the far end of the corridor. A dark shape, flickering in the corner of my eye. I whip my head round, but the shape isn't there any more. It's gone. Except it's not – it's right behind me, about to fall on me, and I can feel it, I—

I snap my head back. There's nothing there. Of course there's nothing there. I'm seeing things now. Because if there really *was* something there, the night vision goggles would paint it green . . . right?

Fan-fucking-tastic. Bad enough that the comedown makes me feel like ass, it has to make me hallucinate too?

Something nearby explodes. *Pow.* Like a balloon popping. There's no flash of light, but it still makes me jump. The shift in my centre of gravity rocks the door underneath me. I start to drift, heading right for one of the roller doors.

"Oh," I say. "Oh shit. Ooooh shit. Shit shit sh—"

With an effort of will, I pull my platform from the roller door, drifting to a wobbly stop in the middle of the passage. Another second, and I'd have been bacon.

I slap myself. Then I do it again, despite the fact that it hurts a lot more than it should. "Get it together, bitch, come on."

Which is when I see the body.

The passage dog-legs off to my right, more roller doors and concrete and padlocks. Lying in the middle of the passage is the smoking body of a man. His right arm is splayed out in front of him, like he died trying to crawl to safety.

My gorge rises, subsides, then rises again. I crouch down on my floating door, hugging my knees to my chest. There are little pinpricks of light going off behind my closed eyelids, and my skin feels like an evil witch is raking her pointed nails across it, very slowly. The headache has subsided, a little, but it's still there, a burning knot at the base of my skull.

Somehow, I manage to keep my stomach under control – throwing up on an electrified floor would cook the puke. I think if I have to smell that right now, I'll just implode.

"There's a body here," I say, keying my earpiece.

No answer. The static doesn't even change.

I've got to check it out, even though I really don't want to. Odds are it's not the source of whatever is causing this . . . but I can't just breeze past it.

I float over, trying to look everywhere at once, listening for the slightest noise. It would be just perfect if someone with electricity powers got the drop on me right now. That would really cap off this whole day.

The man is lying face down. He's wearing a cheap green windbreaker over torn blue jeans. Bright red New Balance kicks. His hair is dark, cut short, and there's a wedding ring on his left hand, which rests to one side of his body. His jacket is smoking, very gently.

There's no one around. Not a sound.

I let out a breath. Whoever the source of the electricity is, it's not this guy. He's just some poor schlub who was in the wrong place at the wrong time. *Sorry, buddy.*

Guess I was right. The electricity *is* more powerful the deeper you go. Good news for the receptionist. Very bad news for yours truly.

Anger wakes me up, a nice sharp bolt of it, like an icicle sprouting in my chest. It clears my head a little more. God, I am going to kick the ass of whoever is doing this.

But where the hell do I find them?

I slowly spin my platform, my muddled brain puzzling it out. The power source — I'm just going to call them that from now on — is still here. Still in the building. They have to be. So if I was them, where would I hide?

Nobody's going to sit back and just be like, *Wow, guess the electrified storage unit of death is off limits for ever, oh well, have a good day everybody!* They'd investigate. If I'm the power source, I'd know that, so I'd put myself at the furthest possible point from any entrance. I'd go to the top floor, as close to the middle of the building as I could get.

Yes, I admit, the logic is a little fuzzy. But I'm just saying. If could generate a million volts with my fingertips, that's where I would go.

The elevator is obviously a non-starter, even if it was still working, which I doubt. It takes me a while to find the stairs — I hit a couple of dead ends first, and more than once I'm turned back by an actual fire. One of the lockers is ablaze, bright and hot enough that I have to pull up my goggles. It doesn't look like the fire has spread yet — say what you like about concrete and metal, they don't burn easily.

The stairs, when I eventually do get there, are a surprising pain in the ass to navigate. They're tight, which makes not touching the walls and ceiling a challenge. Still nothing but static on my earpiece, and the hot, harsh sound of my breath in the dark. More than once, I catch movement at the corners of my vision — flickering dark shapes, like before. I'm almost certain that I'm seeing things, but I might not be. As you can imagine, that only adds to the paranoia.

I hit the top floor. There's another explosive pop – distant this time, something else in the building giving up the ghost. It doesn't make me jump, fortunately, but it sharpens the edge on my nerves. My stomach is hitching again. If I—

There's a noise. One I definitely haven't heard before.

At first, I think it's metal creaking – you know that high-pitched sound it sometimes makes if it's under pressure? Only, it's not that. It's . . .

Sobbing?

Sobbing.

Someone down here is crying. It sounds like a woman, high-pitched. Soft and distant . . . but there, all right.

Got you.

Only: I might be wrong. It could be someone else, another employee who somehow found a way to stay safe from the electricity. I can't assume anything.

Slowly, oh so slowly, I float towards the source of the sound. Several times, I have to stop and listen hard – the tight corridors twist and multiply the sobbing, disguising its direction.

But my ears are good, despite the loud rap music I pour into them on an almost daily basis. I keep moving, doubling back when I have to, getting closer and closer. I don't know which direction I'm heading in, but I have a feeling I'm getting close to the edge of the storage unit.

More light, flaring in my goggles. I pull them up, blinking away sweat, expecting to see something else on fire. What I see, instead, is actual light. Like, electric light. Coming from around the corner of the corridor.

I hover in place, suddenly more scared than I've been in a long time. The sobbing is very loud, and it's definitely coming from right around the corner.

Now that I'm here, I realise I don't actually have a plan.

Because of course I fucking don't. Although in my defence, I've been a little preoccupied with not dying, not freaking out and not throwing up.

The person behind the corner may or may not be causing this. They may be a frightened civilian who has somehow kept themselves safe. Either way, this is one situation where the element of surprise may *not* be in my favour. When you have someone who can wield this much power, the last thing you want to do is startle them. It would be like a party where the birthday girl kills everyone after they turn on the lights and yell "Surprise!"

I'm pretty sure I couldn't stop a bolt of electricity, not even if I smoked all the meth on Planet Earth. Which leaves me with . . . what, exactly?

Easy. I identify myself. I let them know I'm here.

If I surprise them, I'll get electrocuted. If I tell them I'm here and they're bad news, like Matthew Schenke, I may still get electrocuted . . . but there's a chance I won't.

There's another option of course. *Leave. Get the hell out of here. Tell Tanner where this person is, and let her handle it. She can send in a special forces team. Nuke the site from orbit. Anything.*

Instead, I clear my throat, and say, "Hello?"

The sobbing stops immediately. Somehow, the silence is even worse.

I lick my dry, cracked lips. "I'm . . . Listen, I'm going to come round the corner, OK? Please don't zap me. I just wanna talk."

Nothing.

I wait for a real superhero to burst in and save the day.

Still nothing.

So I grip the edges of the hovering car door, and float around the corner.

ELEVEN

Teagan

It's not a secret lair. It's not even a room. It's just another corridor. Same roller doors. Same grimy floor.

Except in the middle of that floor, sitting with his arms
around his knees, is a boy.

Blinking up at me in astonishment.

He's four or five, with black hair that hangs down his forehead in a spiky fringe. Vietnamese heritage, with dark skin
and a round face. The skin around his eyes is puffy, the cheeks
shiny with tears.

A single fluorescent light buzzes on the ceiling, flickering
and grimy, but alive. I have no idea how it's still working when
the entire building is a live wire.

The boy wears an oversized black T-shirt, pipe-cleaner arms
poking out the sleeves. He's wearing tiny sneakers which used
to be white, and neat blue jeans with a big rip just below the
right knee.

For a few seconds, we just look at each other. Me, floating
on my car door two feet off the electrified floor. Him, sitting
on that exact same floor.

"Are you with my dad?" the kid says.

To say I'm not expecting the question is the understatement of the century. But on its heels comes a wave of relief – he's not going to zap me, or at least he's not going to zap me right away.

"Um," I say. "Um. I ... yeah. Ah. No. No, I'm not. I'm ... sorry."

He looks down at the floor. He doesn't start sobbing again, but his shoulders are trembling.

"I'm Teagan," I say.

"My name is Leo," he mumbles.

"Hi, Le—"

"My name is Leo Nguyen and I am four and my dad's name is Clarence and his number is 505-222-8870 and we live in Albkeekee."

My brain scrambles, until I realise he's trying to say *Albuquerque*.

"Wow," I say. "OK. Let's just—"

"Why are you flying?"

I open my mouth to tell him about my ability, but the words won't come. In an ideal world, I'd be in a dark room on a soft bed, with lots of water, maybe watching a nature documentary narrated by Morgan Freeman. Instead, I'm here. And if I don't get it together, this is going to go very badly.

Fortunately, he doesn't seem to mind that I don't answer. "I'm hiding from the, from the Zigzag Man," he says.

"Who ... ?" I clear my throat. "Who is that?"

Leo doesn't answer. He buries his head in the space made by his arms, which are still wrapped around his knees.

What kind of dad just leaves his kid alone like this? Then again, if you're trying to keep pursuers away from your child, leading them on a diversion makes sense.

Problem is, that answer only leads to more questions. What

the hell were they doing here? Why come all the way to LA from New Mexico?

I lick my lips, suddenly aware of how thirsty I am. Like down-an-entire-six-pack thirsty. The corridor swims in front of me, the anxiety and paranoia and insistent pain fighting for control. *Keep it together.*

What I wouldn't give for some direction from Reggie right now. To hear Annie's voice, Africa's. No chance. There's not even any static on the earpiece any more. I'm not actually sure it's still working.

"Hey Leo?" I say, trying to sound casual. "Can I . . . ? Would you mind if I sat down next to you?"

He doesn't respond.

"I'm kind of tired." I try on a smile, which feels like an XXL sweater on an S body. "Would that be cool? Because the floor next to you is OK, right?"

"I only made the zaps start, like, over there." He points back in the direction I came in.

It takes me a second to understand what he's saying – and when I do, my stomach drops.

It's not just that he has power. He has control over it. He can electrify solid surfaces, but not the air. He can create a . . . I guess you'd call it a safety zone around himself.

It makes a weird kind of sense sense. I have a range for my PK, and it's easy enough for me to lift something far away while leaving closer objects untouched, even though I can wrap my PK energy around both. Maybe his control over electrons works the same way. He tells the ones at a distance to start moving, while keeping the ones close to him static.

And that, right there, is the scariest thing of all. He has more control over his power at age four than I did at age twenty. And his *range* . . . He's affecting hundreds of feet in one go. The electric charge might get weaker at the edges of that range, but still. Damn.

Who the hell *is* this kid?

"So it's good for me to step off?" I ask. "OK. Cool. I'm gonna just ..."

Step off my nice, safe platform onto a floor that may or may or not kill me, based on a little kid saying it's OK.

Slowly, I move the car door towards the ground, aiming for a spot as close as I can to the boy. He doesn't react, doesn't even look up.

"Leo? Hey, Leo?" I point. "That spot there isn't electrified, right? Next to you?"

He says nothing.

"I really don't want to step off if—"

He shrugs without looking up. "It's fine."

I'm about to push him – you know, get confirmation that I'm not about to die – but something tells me not to. This boy might not be as murderous as Matthew Schenke, but he's very much on edge.

Three inches above the ground. Two.

I close my eyes, and take the step.

I'm so primed for the shock that there's a nanosecond where I actually feel it, my muscles going rigid, my heart seizing in my chest. When nothing happens, when my foot comes to a stop on the floor without a bazillion volts exploding through me, I'm hit with a case of the shakes so bad that I almost fall over.

I step off the car door fully, then lower it to the ground next to me. Then I sit down next to Leo. Very, very carefully.

He's acting like I'm not even there, looking away from me, his shoulders still trembling. He's scrawnier up close. Even his spiky fringe looks too big for him.

"So," I say – and realise I'm about to clap him on the

shoulder. I jerk my hand back, which fortunately is not something he notices. I shouldn't be scared of him; he hasn't tried to hurt me directly. Not yet anyway. He's letting me sit next to him. But it's like sitting next to a Bullmastiff pup – one of those breeds that gets to the size of a house by six months. It's too young to know that it shouldn't bite you.

"Hey," I say gently. "Why was the ... Zigzag Man, right? Why was he chasing you?"

"He makes you see things."

Well, that's not creepy at all.

"You were with your dad?" I ask, changing tack. He nods. "Can you tell me why he brought you here?"

He shrugs. A little boy shrug, left shoulder up, then right, then both down. "We were s'posed to go Compton." Again, with the same over-emphasis, like the word is hard to remember.

"What's in Compton?" It's in South-Central LA, maybe an hour's drive in traffic. Mostly black and Latinx – but didn't I read that there's a tiny Asian community there now too? Not much, maybe a thousand people, but still ...

"My uncle," Leo says. "He lives at, at 860 East Glencoe." Running the words together, as if it's something he was made to memorise, but doesn't fully understand.

OK. I get it. His dad brings him to LA for ... reasons. This Zigzag Guy chases them. They end up here, Leo's dad leaves him – to lead their pursuer away, maybe? – and Leo electrifies the whole building. Good way to stay safe, I guess.

There are a *lot* of gaps in that story, but it's a start.

"Did you come from the School?" I say. Almost whispering it.
"The what?"

"The ... the School? Out in Albuquerque. There would have been more people like you there."

He stares at me, four-year-old eyes blinking in confusion.

I try another tack. "Did you . . . " I pause. "Did you know a boy named Matthew? Matthew Schenke."

A shake of the head. "Mm-mm."

"He could move dirt around. With his mind."

The second I mention the word *dirt*, a look of horror crosses Leo's face. "Lucas. I hate him!"

Me too, kid. I shiver at the thought, the sensation of being buried in hot, concrete soil bubbling to the top of my mind. Lucas. Guess Matthew wasn't his real name.

My gut clenches. It's a different sensation from before — there's no nausea this time, no hollow feeling. It's like someone reaches down my throat, grabs hold of my guts and *squeezes*. I close my eyes, trying to breathe.

I have to keep it together if I'm going to get this kid out of here. I'll get him to turn off his ability, and we can just walk out. No harm, no foul.

What the fuck do I do now?

Let's say I do convince him to walk out with me — which is about as likely as 2Pac and Biggie suddenly bursting in to save the day. I hand him over to the team, and I know exactly what happens then. He vanishes. Tanner whisks him away to a secure facility — maybe even the one I was kept in, after Wyoming went to shit. After my brother killed my whole family, burned everything down, and the government found me.

Thinking of the facility is the exact worst thing I could possibly do right now. The anxiety and paranoia bubbling around my brain amplifies the memories, twisting and distorting them.

Waco.

A cluster of shitty, prefab buildings in the middle of a Texan nowhere. Shitty and prefab on the outside, anyway. Inside, they housed one of the most secure holding facilities on the planet. A facility built just for me. Teenage me, ripped away from everything she knew and loved, locked in a cell with no windows.

I can smell it all over again: the disinfectant, the shitty meatloaf and overcooked chicken legs they brought me for my meals, the sweet, cloying scent of the gas they used to knock me out when I went nuts. The psychiatrists, never the same person, none of them looking at me as anything but a freak. The tests. The constant, grinding, unending tests. The hours alone, knowing I'd never leave, so deep in the hole that I went beyond crying. The memories are so potent I nearly choke. On a good day, they stay firmly locked away in the back of mind. Not today. Today, the demons are in charge.

I was in the facility for four years before Tanner presented me with her deal: work for her, outside the walls.

Leo won't just be there for four years. They'll keep him there for much, much longer. His entire childhood. He'll never see another boy or girl his age, never speak to anybody who doesn't want something from him.

Jesus Christ.

Could I get him into the cops? Get him into ... fuck, I don't know, child witness protection? But that doesn't stop Tanner — it just makes it harder for her.

And what about the Zigzag Man? *He makes you see things —* that's what Leo said. Does that mean he has abilities? How safe would Leo be?

My mind runs away with itself, unable to stop. Maybe the Zigzag Man wants to hurt Leo and his dad — that's one thing. But what if it's more than that? Leo came from the same place Matthew did. Who's to say that they don't want to use his ability? He's already able to electrify a massive building without breaking a sweat. What would happen if they plugged him into the power grid? Or a water source – the LA Aqueduct, for instance, the big channel out of the Owens River to the north, the one that supplies the whole city?

I'll tell you what happens. A lot of people die. Instantly. Hundreds, maybe thousands.

Why the hell would anybody do that? What's the endgame here?

I have no idea how to answer that.

China Shop. I get Annie and Africa to help me—

I grimace. They won't help me – not on this. It sticks in my gut to say it, but we are not going to be on the same wavelength at the moment. We haven't been for a while. *Maybe* Annie might have been on my side with this, but for whatever damn reason, she despises me right now. And Africa? He'll point-blank refuse to keep Tanner out of the loop, especially since he thinks I'm not in my right mind. Reggie might help . . . but it's a big might.

I've already been here way too long. The whole team will be going nuts, trying to contact me. And by now, Tanner's probably considering contingencies. She might not send a missile into the building with me inside it – in her own twisted way, she values my life, and she doesn't actually want to hurt me. But if she thinks I'm dead, she won't hesitate.

Worse: even if she thinks I'm alive, someone above her might make the call. Tanner might be pretty high up in the intelligence community, but she's not number one. She reports to people, too. People who don't know me, or care if I make it through this.

"Hey," I say. Keeping him talking won't solve the problem, but it might buy me some time to come up with a plan that doesn't completely suck. "Can you tell me about the School? Anything you remember." Well, OK, he never actually said

he knew what the School was ... but if he knew Matthew –
Lucas – then they were probably there at the same time. Right?

"I want my dad."

"I know. We'll go find him in a minute. But if you
could just—"

He looks at me then, and it's like he's seeing me for the
first time.

"I want my dad," he says again. "I gotta stay here until he
comes back."

Which is crazy all on its own, because how is dear old dad
going to get back inside if Leo's electrified the place? It's little
kid logic at work. Jesus, this whole situation is *nuts*.

"OK, that's fine, that's totally fine, we can just wait here. I
just want to find out about the School you were at. Who was
the boss there? Was there like a teacher, or—?"

But he's hunkered down into himself, head almost tucked
into his armpit. "I can't talk to people without, without my
dad," he says again. And this time, there's an edge to his voice.

Right then, it's like the air gets thicker. Like the feeling
you get right before a thunderstorm, when the whole world
goes still.

The Bullmastiff pup, showing his teeth. And why wouldn't
he? This kid might not be a tiny psychopath, but who knows
what he's been through before today?

Which, of course, doesn't stop a cold, greasy sweat from
breaking out on my forehead.

I don't always think things through. But I've been trying
really hard lately – trying to make the *right* decision, not just
the first one that pops into my head. So: what's the right thing
to do here?

Keep this kid safe. Keep him out of harm's way. No matter
how you look at it, that's the responsible choice.

The problem is, he's not safe here, and he's not safe with China Shop. So: what's left?

Which is when I say something that I know I'm going to regret, even before the words leave my mouth.

"Leo, listen to me," I say quietly. "Your dad can't get back in here."

"Why not? I can stop the 'lectricity if—"

"But how will you know he's out there?"

"I got a phone."

"But . . . but, Leo, there's no signal here. Not while your electricity's on."

He blinks at me, as if he doesn't understand what I'm saying.

I'm guessing he knows he has the ability to kill people – he can control his electricity, after all. But he's scared, and he's not thinking. He didn't think about how his dad would get back inside. He didn't think about the cops arriving. And he didn't think about the other people in the building, or the ones who came to check it out.

He looks down at the ground.

"I think I did a bad thing," he mumbles.

"Oh, hey," I say, reaching out to touch him, stopping myself just in time.

The only thought I can hold my head is: *get him the fuck out of here. Get him somewhere safe.*

"Leo . . . if you come with me, I *promise* I'll get you to your dad."

It's a long time before he answers. When he does, there's a different look in his eyes. A hard look. A look you shouldn't see on someone his age.

"If you're helping the Zigzag Man," he says, "I'll zap you."

" . . . I know."

"Or if you make me do anything I don't wanna."

"Got it."

Slowly, I reach out for his hand, stopping just short. He hesitates for a few seconds, then takes it. His skin is warm, and very dry.

Despite my heart pounding hard in my chest, I manage a smile – and it feels like a genuine one this time. I give his hand a squeeze, then get to my feet, gently pulling him with me.

OK. Step one complete. Earn the trust of the little boy who could kill me instantly whenever he chooses. Time for step two.

"Hey, Leo," I say. "Do you like hide and seek?"

"Huh?"

"Never mind." I give his hand a squeeze. "Come on."

TWELVE

Teagan

The scariest part of exiting the Big Green Storage building isn't the cops. It isn't the fact that I'm going AWOL on my team.

It's Leo.

I'm not talking about his ability – he's actually stopped discharging electricity into the building now, or at least, we're inside his safety radius. It's how he slips in quietly behind me as we head for the exit, moving quickly and quietly, his sneakers barely audible on the scuffed floor. He doesn't make a peep. Kids aren't usually this obedient, or this careful.

What kind of life has he been living, that he knows how to move this quietly?

We're just coming up the stairs to ground level, our way lit by the flashlight on my phone. The nausea and headache subsided a little when I was speaking to Leo, but now they're back with a vengeance. I make myself focus on putting one foot in front of the other, then doing it again, and again.

If I remember right, the south-west wall of the building is closest to the edge of the lot – no more than a few feet of open concrete, which is probably where they stash the dumpsters. Then, a tall chain link fence. From the brief look I got before I came in here, the land beyond the fence is undeveloped. Wide open. There won't be much cover – and it's broad daylight out there, which means I'm going to have to time this very carefully.

Shit. There's a thought. I'm currently carrying two things that will allow Reggie to track me – my comms earpiece, and my phone. Both government issue, with built-in scramblers. Encryption. Whatever the fuck it's called. Reggie controls them, which means she could *definitely* track me if she wanted, even if they were turned off. I winkle out the earpiece, using my PK to crunch its internals to pieces, doing it before I can second-guess myself.

I glance down at my phone – shit, it's only 3 p.m.? I feel like I've been here for hours. I shake it off, wrap my PK around the internals, getting ready to do to them what I did to my earpiece. I pause for a second, trying to figure out if there's *any* way to avoid doing this.

And that's enough to make me think of Waco again. Of the cells and the tests, the knowledge that I might never get out of there. That my family was dead, and no one was coming to rescue me.

I won't subject Leo to that. Not gonna happen.

This feels wrong. I've never turned my back on the team – not once, not ever. No matter how much we argue, or whatever crazy shit we get into, we've always been together. Doing this feels horrible. Sickening. It's impossible not to hear Reggie's calm voice, breaking down a problem, analysing it as she sips chamomile. Annie's smile, back when it actually existed. Africa's laugh, his giant hands pulling me into a bear hug. Am I really doing this?

"Sorry, Reggie," I mutter. The phone goes dead as I snap a couple of key chips inside.

Which is when I realise I just killed our only source of light.

Oh, this is going well.

"Is it broke?" Leo says.

"Something like that. Sorry, dude. You're not scared of the dark are you?"

"No," he says, in a small voice. Then: "I've got one."

"Got one what?"

There's the click of an unlocking phone, and more torchlight blinds us. At that moment, there's a footstep from behind my back.

I whirl, sucking in a startled, horrified breath. In that instant, I know what I'm going to see. It's an image so clear in my mind, that I don't doubt it, not for a second. I'm going to find Jeannette there. Africa's girlfriend. Here, somehow, leering at me through a mouthful of rotting, brown teeth, reaching for me—

There's nothing. No Jeannette. No anybody. An empty corridor, with nothing but flickering shadows.

"Are you OK?" Leo asks.

I can't unclench my fists. "Fine," I say, barely aware I spoke. The meth comedown . . . it's making me see things that aren't there, I know it is. So why can't I shake the idea that there really was someone there? That even now, they're waiting to strike?

"It's my dad's phone," Leo says, dropping the light. "He gave it to me to play *Dr Panda Town*."

"Is that right?" I say, still distracted, running my finger over the sticker on the phone case, a unicorn smoking a massive joint. A long time ago, my phone got stolen, right in the middle of me being framed for murder – yes, this is the kind of life I lead. Africa found it, and he knew it was mine because of the sticker.

God, I miss the old Africa. Before he was part of China Shop. Before he became obsessed with the job.

I pocket the phone. It's dead, beyond even the best tracking Reggie can deploy, but I have no intention of leaving it for anyone to find. I pocket the comms earpiece too.

Most of the police presence is on the opposite side of the building, near the road. That's where all the black-and-whites are. Of course, the cops aren't stupid. They've got people watching the doors, back and front. In theory, nobody gets in or out of this building.

Which is a good strategy, if you assume that whoever you're watching for will actually be using a door.

I echolocate, throwing out a wave of PK. It doesn't take me long to find what I'm looking for.

With Leo in tow – still eerily silent – I walk over to one of the storage lockers close to the stairs. I can tell from my PK that there isn't much inside this one, and I quickly pop the lock with my mind, rolling up the door. The locker is almost empty, with just a couple of dusty boxes stacked against one wall. On one of the boxes, in big black Sharpie letters, is the word: *TOYS*. Which would be fine, if someone hadn't drawn a ;-) next to the word.

Honestly, I'd rather not know.

"In here," I whisper to Leo, ducking underneath the door. I sound pretty calm, given the insanity I'm currently involved in. He says nothing, not even a little *woah* at me using my powers. Then again, the first time he met me, I was on a magic carpet. And he grew up with kids who could move the earth around at will, along with God knows what else.

Once we're inside the dark locker, I close the door behind us. Nothing I can do about the snapped padlock – I'll just have to hope nobody notices. Instead, I concentrate on the exterior wall, feeling my way along it. "Please be cheap," I mutter. "Please, please, please be—"

Yes. Just as I thought. Big Green Storage are cheapskates. Their walls are prefab, with no insulation: just outer cladding, and a layer of concrete maybe half a foot thick.

We think of concrete as uniform. An impenetrable surface. In reality, it's uneven, rough, filled with weak spots and pressure points where the mix wasn't quite right – *especially* in cheap-ass buildings like this one. Finding those weak spots with my PK is easy, even when I'm not operating at what I'd call peak capacity.

I do a quick burst of echolocation, throwing it out as far as I can in the direction of the fence – no people on the other side of the wall, and yes, there are a couple of dumpsters close by.

"Are we gonna hide in here?" Leo stage-whispers.

"No. Hey, watch this."

The concrete groans. Shudders. Starts to crumble inward. The air fills with thick dust – Jesus, I hope this shit isn't toxic. Too late to worry about that now.

In seconds, there's a big hole in the wall, a rough semicircle of about four feet, exposing the cladding behind it. Daylight floods in, sending a lance of pain right through my eyes, so sharp that I have to squeeze them shut.

I pause for a second, waiting for the sound of cops shouting – or Annie and Africa figuring out what I'm doing. Nothing.

I let out a breath, and punch through the exterior cladding. It's synthetic, and it's even less trouble than the concrete, splintering and snapping. Somehow, even that little move is enough to make the comedown worse, amplifying the headache.

"How about that, huh?" I say to Leo, through gritted teeth.

He just blinks back at me. Then he looks at the hole I made. "What if it was stronger?"

"Huh?"

"The wall. Could you still make a hole?"

"Of course." I smile at him – or try to, anyway. "I'm pretty strong."

"OK."

"What?" I say. "I am!"

"Are we gonna be with my dad soon?"

"We . . . Sure, I . . . Yeah, yes, we are, we're gonna find him now, come on."

I duck through the gap, my cheeks feeling weirdly hot. Did this kid just throw shade on my ability? Does he not *know* that I moved an entire broken bridge only a few hours ago? I have a sudden urge to tell him, but clamp down on it. Now is not the time.

We come out between two dumpsters. Another burst of echolocation confirms there aren't any cops near us. I can feel one – or rather, his gun – walking the perimeter over to our left, his back to us. Another two on our right, behind the corner of the building. Watching the doors, just liked I figured.

Annie and Africa don't have firearms of their own. Wherever they are, it isn't this side of the building. Somewhere close, there's the *whup-whup* of a police chopper. I send my PK upwards, hunting for it, but even on a good day, it'd be too far away.

But I was also right about the fence. It's no more than ten feet from the wall.

I reach out and in one movement, rip the links up from where they're buried in the dirt, bending them outwards. Several of them snap with a loud *pang*, but fortunately, the chopper is still close enough to mask the sound.

The skin on my neck prickles. Suddenly, I'm dead sure that either Annie or Africa is going to step into view, demanding to know what in the fuck I'm doing.

And what the fuck am I doing? Exactly? It's all very well to say I'm saving Leo's life, keeping him out of Tanner's clutches, but let's be real. This whole plan is all sizzle, no steak.

Annie and Africa don't appear. Nobody does.

It's not too late. You could just find the crew. Claim you meant to do it all along.

And then I'll never find out about where Leo came from. Or who the hell is using my parents' research to create kids with abilities. And Leo will vanish, swallowed by the same government system that held onto me for so long.

I turn to him. "Ready?"

Before I've even said the words, he bolts. Sprinting towards the gap.

"Oh, fuck." I scuttle after him. "Leo. Leo!"

He ducks his head as he shoots through the fence, heading into the scrubland beyond. I'm a little bigger than him – obviously – and when I try to go through, a broken piece of metal nearly skewers me in the eye. Another catches at my jacket collar, nearly yanking me off my feet. My stomach notices these things, and decides it wants in on the action too, lurching uncomfortably.

The scrubland is a strip, maybe fifty feet wide: dirt and bushes and trash, with a rough, unpaved track cutting down the middle. Up ahead, the ground drops off abruptly. There's a very distant peal of thunder from the north. Even now, when the heat of the day has started to drain off, the clouds are still there, hunkering on the horizon. When that storm finally breaks, it's going to be a monster.

Hopefully we're not around when it does.

Leo is crouched down a few feet away, squatting next to a spiky bush. I stumble over, doing everything I can to stay upright. "Dude, stop. You can't just run off like that."

He ignores me. I drop to my knees next to him, breathing hard.

"Where's my dad?" he says.

"Look—"

"You," says a voice. "Stop right there."

THIRTEEN

Reggie

It's been a long time since Reggie felt angry about her accident.

There have been some tough times, to be sure. Learning how to breathe again was only the start – getting out of her own head was much harder, and Reggie spent plenty of time with an Air Force-appointed psych working things out. But she got hurt serving her country, and in Regina McCormick's book, that meant she didn't get hurt for nothing.

She has never been angrier than she is now. She has never felt more stuck, or helpless, or frustrated. Crammed into this crappy chair in this crappy office in this crappy part of a crappy city, when an entire mission is coming to pieces and she can't do a single thing about it.

Moira still hasn't managed to resolve her connection issues with the team's feeds, and is in an even more foul mood than usual. And that was *before* Reggie told her that Teagan had gone into the storage unit.

"She's not here," Africa growls over the comms. "No contact, nothing." He and Annie are in the front parking lot now, their cameras facing towards a line of frustrated cops. Flickering red-and-blue distort the image. Reggie's hands fly across her trackballs, her eyes darting left and right across the screens as she uses every trick she has to hone in on Teagan's comms unit. No video, no audio. Nothing.

Teagan has dropped off the face of the planet.

At least whoever has intruded on their network hasn't managed to torch all their comms, just a few elements. Reggie has checked and rechecked her system, looking for any evidence of intrusion. But there's nothing. No failed logins, no port scans, no malware or trojans. No one but she and Moira have accessed any of their files. It's the same in Washington, where they've been unable to find evidence of an intrusion.

It's very possible that all of this is just poor timing. A horrible coincidence, their comms going screwy right when the team needs them the most. Except: it's coming right after an anonymous phone call nearly torpedoed a job for them. Reggie hates coincidences.

"Electricity must be interfering," Annie says, exhaustion edging her words.

"Have you checked the perimeter?" Reggie asks.

"Ya," Africa replies. Annie's turned towards him on the pinhole camera feed, and there's no escaping how frustrated he looks. The desperate worry in his eyes. "And we are checking again. She did not come out anywhere. We not see her."

Annie says, "Reggie: the cops are starting to ask questions. I don't know how long we can keep this whole FBI thing going ... "

"Leave that to Moira. She'll handle it. Just find Teagan."

"And we keep telling you," Africa bellows. "She is—"

Abruptly, he goes silent.

Reggie isn't usually one to allow someone to take that kind of tone with her. This time, she barely notices. "Check again. The whole perimeter."

"Reggie," Annie says. "You don't think . . ."

She doesn't finish the thought. She doesn't have to. The horrified, hesitant note in her voice says plenty. As far as they know, touching the building won't kill you, even if it hurts like hell. But they have no idea if it's the same the whole way through. If Teagan got stuck, couldn't get away from the shocks . . .

"I refuse to believe," Reggie says slowly, "that someone as much of a pain in the ass as Teagan Frost is dead."

Annie makes a sound that might, under better circumstances, be a laugh.

"She's there all right," Reggie continues. "She just can't hear us. Keep—"

"Wait," Africa says.

"What?"

"Something . . . it's different now."

The two video feeds turn to look towards the storage unit.

Reggie has to suppress the urge to raise her voice. "Different *how*? Talk to me."

It's Annie who answers. "The hum's stopped. There was this, like . . . buzzing sound coming from the building. Subsonic. I don't know if you could hear it on the comms – like from an electric fence, you know? It's not there any more."

"Ya, I feel it too," Africa says. "You don't think maybe . . . ?"

"Shit, one of the cops has figured it out." Annie's camera swings towards the police line, where a uniformed officer is approaching – the same one who briefed them when they arrived, it looks like. Annie's voice rises to a yell. "Hey! Step away from the scene, right now!" She mutes her connection, presumably so she can shouts at the cops without deafening everyone on the channel.

"Hold on," Africa says. "I have an idea. Boss Paul – did he keep a volt measure machine in the van?"

It takes Reggie a second to work out what he's saying. "A . . . what, like a voltmeter?"

"Ya."

"Should be in the middle tool drawer," Annie says, breaking off from scolding one of the officers. Africa moves towards the van, his camera feed bouncing as he runs.

Reggie tries to raise Teagan again, knowing it won't do any good but doing it anyway. Nothing. The woman has gone completely dark.

Dark. Not dead. Not a chance, not Teagan Frost, not after all she's been through.

If she was dead, Reggie thinks, *there'd be no more China Shop. I wouldn't work for the government any more. I'd be free.*

The thought is so horrifying that Reggie physically recoils, grunting and turning her head away, as if she'd just bitten into something rotten.

"OK, got it." Africa's voice snaps her out of it. He's in the van, the feed showing a messy tool drawer. In his huge hand is the voltmeter, a device used for measuring live electrical connections. Reggie cannot for the life of her fathom why Paul would have had one in the first place, but then again, Paul treated all equipment like condoms. Better to have and not need, than need and not have.

A bittersweet pang at the thought. Paul would have gone bright red if you'd said the word *condom* to him.

"Good thinking," Reggie says. And it is. He can hold the voltmeter out ahead of him, letting the two wires trail along the ground. He'll be able to see straightaway if the current in the concrete starts increasing. "Hurry."

"Nothing," Africa says. He's looking down at the voltmeter's twin wires, now brushing the concrete surface of the parking lot. "Still nothing . . . getting closer to the building now."

"All right, I got the cops to hold off for a minute," Annie cuts in. "But Reggie, sooner or later, this shit is gonna blow up in our—"

The wires touch the concrete lip of the storage unit's loading dock. The audio distorts – Africa letting out a held breath. "Nothing. Voltmeter is quiet."

"Teagan," Annie says. "Teagan, do you copy? Come back." Then, as if she's forgotten she's on an open line: "Come on, *gordita*, say something."

Reggie licks her lips, looking between the windows on her monitors, trying to find anything that might help – building blueprints, the feeds from Annie and Africa. Tanner said she's getting live satellite imagery up, but it's not quite ready yet. *That* has nothing to do with whoever is disrupting their communications; just good old orbital physics, not playing ball. Not even the US government has satellites watching everywhere all the time.

They are not in control of this situation. Not even close. *She*, Reggie, is not in control of this situation.

"OK," Annie says. "I'm going in."

Reggie's eyes go wide. "Like hell you are."

"It's not electrified any more, Reggie."

"And if it suddenly dials up again while you're inside? Did you think of that?"

"*Of course* I'm thinking of that. But what other choice do we have? Teagan's in there—"

"And she's probably still hovering above the floor."

"No, no, no, listen." Africa pauses, as if getting his thoughts in order. "Annie is right. I don't think it's gonna go electric again. I think it's finished."

"How can you be so sure?"

"OK, so maybe whoever has the power is trying to lure

people in. They want us to think it's safe, and then we come in, and *bang*! More people dead. But what I am thinking is, that does not make sense. They only kill a few people that way, and then Mrs Tanner decides to destroy the whole building anyway – even if they don't know who she is, they must know someone will fire a missile or drop a bomb, huh? It is not worth it for them."

"No, that can't be—"

"Reggie," Annie says. "Either we're gonna go inside the unit, or someone else is. Cops, the real FBI, NSA, whoever decides to leapfrog Tanner on the chain of command."

"You're putting yourselves in danger."

Annie makes a sound that might be a laugh. "Won't be the first time that bitch almost cost me my life." She doesn't say if she's referring to Tanner, or Teagan.

"None of us have any infiltration training. They drill special forces for months on that alone—"

"Teagan went in, didn't she?"

"And she has extranormal abilities. You don't."

It's a feeble argument. Truth is, China Shop has been involved in some pretty hairy ops over the years. They may not have traditional training, but they can handle themselves.

"If we wait for the cavalry," Annie says, "whoever's messing with us will be in the wind. We have to go in now."

"We sweep floor by floor," Africa says, speaking as if the matter is settled. "Front to back. Check all the storage doors – Teagan may be inside one."

"Africa," Reggie says. "Stand *down*."

"Sorry, Reggie," Annie replies. "I'm with the big guy. This is happening."

Reggie opens her mouth to protest, but it turns out she has absolutely no idea what to say. Because Annie and Africa are right. If they don't go in, this whole situation is going to end up even more FUBAR than it is already.

Oh, Lord.

Reggie sits in the office in Torrance, watching as Annie and Africa make their way inside. Africa, grunting as he hefts the heavy roller door on the loading dock. Annie, ducking through. Africa has already passed her a pair of chunky night vision goggles, is wearing some himself. They make him look like an alien invader, a beanstalk-thin body with a huge pair of protruding eyes.

Reggie's feeds go to low-light mode, bathing the building's interior in green. She watches, neck muscles taut as steel cables, as Annie and Africa slowly clear the floor. They ignore the units with padlocks on them, but even then, progress takes an age.

There's hardly any sound. Just their breathing, and the occasional "Clear". They might not be special forces, might be exhausted and still coming down off a meth high, but they're not doing a bad job. Despite her nerves, Reggie is proud of her team.

It's a feeling that gets pushed into the background the more they explore the complex. There's at least one body – an employee, it looks like – but nothing else. No Teagan. No individual with electricity powers. Nothing.

"There's nobody here," Africa says eventually. His video feed shows him staring at a brick wall, then turning to look at Annie. Her expression is unreadable.

"That doesn't make sense," Reggie says. "Are you sure—?"

"We've checked the whole place," Annie replies.

"Check again."

"She isn't here. And she's still not answering comms."

"I said, check it – oh, hell."

Her phone is buzzing. Tanner, wanting another update.

"Just keep looking," Reggie says. "She has to be there."

But even as she answers Tanner's call, she knows that's not true. She saw how thorough Annie and Africa were. Unless there are secret doors not shown on the blueprints, her most important team member has vanished into thin air.

"Report," Tanner says.

Reggie opens her mouth to tell Tanner that Teagan is missing – and stops.

"Ms McCormick?" There's a cold edge in Tanner's voice now. "I said, report."

On screen, Africa and Annie are caught in each other's camera feeds. Green ghosts, haunting an empty building.

"Ms McCor— Oh Christ, of all the times for the cell towers to—"

"We're still looking," Reggie says.

The lie slips out before she can stop it. It's as if it was there all along, just waiting for its chance.

"Say again?"

"Teagan is . . . she's still in the building, going floor by floor. Nothing yet."

Tanner lets out a frustrated sigh. "Tell Ms Frost to pick up the pace. I have my director breathing down my neck, and half the FBI demanding my head on a platter."

" . . . Copy that."

Tanner ends the call.

It takes an almost physical effort for Reggie to lock down her thoughts. She's more amazed at herself than angry – she can't recall the last time she lied to Moira Tanner. There was no point, has never *been* any point. Moira might be tough to work with, but she has always wanted China Shop to succeed – Teagan might have trouble seeing that, but Reggie sure doesn't.

So what in the blue hell was that?

Reggie almost laughs. A first-year psychology student could figure this out. Part of her wants Moira to call her out. To fire her. Because then she'd be free from China Shop, free to do whatever the hell she wanted, audition for Darcy Lorenzo, kick off a new career and—

Reggie makes a noise that is part snarl, part groan. Regina McCormick, CIA analyst and operative, does not lie. Warrant Officer Regina McCormick of the 162nd Aviation, 1st Battalion (Assault Helicopter) *does not lie*. She'll be damned if Regina McCormick of China Shop does.

Of course, that ship has sailed. The lie has been told. Still. It wasn't big. Nothing she can't explain away. If they do find Teagan, it will pass by unnoticed.

"Reggie?" Annie says.

"I want you both to split up," Reggie hears herself say. Her heart feels as if it's skipping every third beat, and there's a very strange taste in her mouth. "Search the storage unit again."

"But—"

"*Again*, Annie. Top to bottom. Then I want you to start looking in the surrounding area. Anywhere you think she might have gone."

"Why would she run without telling us?" Africa asks.

"I don't know, honey. But she's gotta be somewhere, so get to searching. Have the LAPD assist if you can, you can cover more ground that way."

"They will not follow us. They are already—"

"I don't *care*, Africa. Find Teagan, you hear me? *Find her.*"

FOURTEEN

Teagan

The cop is middle-aged, with an untidy beard and the weary eyes of a man who never quite got that detective's badge.

I can't use my ability here. That would make a bad situation exponentially worse. I can't run, because this is Los Angeles, and he'll shoot me. And I can't do nothing, because Leo – a boy who can electrify things that you thought could never be electrified – will send a zillion volts through the dirt and cook the cop where he stands.

"What are you doing here?" the cop says.

The question blindsides me. I was expecting something along the lines of *Get on the ground and don't fucking move.*

"Um . . ."

It's not a good answer. The cop takes a step closer. I get in front of Leo instinctively, shielding him. My pulse thunders in my ears.

The cop jerks his chin. "Move along."

"I . . . what?"

"You can't be here. This is a crime scene. If you need a place to stay, there's a big camp down the river a ways. Under the 105."

The cop isn't seeing two people with extranormal abilities, one of whom just electrified an entire building. He's seeing a scared, haggard-looking woman – who looks, funnily enough, like she's coming down off a meth binge – and a small child.

There might be an FBI windbreaker on my back, but it's one that's been torn and shredded by our run through the fence, scuffed with dirt, looking like it came from a gift shop. More importantly, he's seeing us on *this* side of the fence.

He can't have seen us come through, or seen me make the hole. If that were the case, he'd be a lot more aggressive. We've moved far enough away from the fence that he thinks we're just passing through. The poor son of a bitch is on patrol duty, and to him, we're nothing more than a couple of drifters – just two of the thousands moving in and around LA in the aftermath of the quake.

Fuck it. I'll take it.

"What happened in there?" I say. "Seems like a lotta your buddies are out."

"Nothing important, ma'am. Move along now."

I can't resist sketching a salute as I hustle Leo past the cop. He eyeballs us before turning back to the fence.

"This way," I mutter to Leo, trying to keep my voice steady. Mercifully, the kid's in duckling mode again, sticking close behind me.

We head directly away from the storage unit, moving towards the drop-off I spotted earlier. The land rises a little as we get close, the soil rougher, with more rocks pushing up through it. I'm expecting the same on the other side of the drop, but instead, it's concrete. A long slope of it, running down to a wide channel.

The LA River.

See, Annie? I know what it is now.

Unlike the section we tangled with the Legends on, this part of the river isn't concreted over. The sloping sides are, sure, but the flat part is a wide expanse of packed dirt and scrubby vegetation. A few bamboo groves sprout here and there, spreading jagged shadows. The actual channel of water is right at the bottom of the slope, on our side. No telling how deep it is, but it's not flowing all that fast. There's no one around.

Why did they concrete one part of the river, and not up here? Annie would know. If—

I close my eyes. Annie can't help me now.

We need to get as far away as we can. It's going to be a lot trickier here than it is on the river. There might be more places to hide up top, but there will also be more people. On the river, we should be in the clear.

"We're gonna head down there," I tell Leo, pointing. I'm worried he's going to protest, but he just nods.

Now that we're out in the sun, the meth comedown has ebbed a little. I'm still headachey and nauseous, but at least I'm not seeing things. I don't imagine anyone creeping up behind me.

The slope is too steep for us to walk, so we scoot down on our backsides. Weirdly, it's kind of fun, and I smile at Leo, hoping he feels the same way. But he's turned away from me, looking north, towards the building clouds.

The water runs in a shallow channel, around ten feet wide. I'm worried that it's going to be too deep to cross, but close-up, it looks like it barely comes up to my ankles. The other side is flat, hard-packed dirt, like the scrubland above, maybe two hundred feet to the opposite concrete slope.

We reach the bottom, still scooching on our backsides. I'm just wondering how to cross the water when I slip, dropping towards the channel. I throw a hand out to stabilise myself, which works for about half a second. Then I skid, arms flailing, right into the water. It's only ankle-deep here, but it's enough to completely soak my legs and my butt.

I sit in the shallow flow, breathing very hard through my nose, trying to think of nothing at all.

Leo manages to avoid ass-planting like me, but he can't stop his feet hitting the water. His jeans are soaked all the way to the rip in his knee.

I don't have the faintest idea where we're actually going to go. Even trying to picture Glendale on my mental map of LA is like trying to see through thick mist. But if we can get further down the river, and up the far slope, there might be somewhere we can go. A café, maybe, or – what the hell – a homeless shelter. Get something to eat and drink. Figure out our next move.

"OK," I tell Leo, forcing a smile onto my face. "It's not deep. Come on."

He shakes his head. Wraps his arms around his knees.

"Come on," I say, the smile faltering. What is with this kid? He's already wet, isn't he?

"It's cold," he says.

"Yeah, well—"

"Where's my dad?"

"He's ... I promised you I'd get you back with him, and that's exactly what I'm gonna do, OK?"

"You said he was outside."

"No, I didn't." Am I seriously having this debate while sitting in a pool of water? I get unsteadily to my feet, the current eddying around my ankles. "I said I'd get you to him."

"No, but, you said, he couldn't get back in." He hugs his knees tighter.

"I did, but—"

"*No.*" Long and drawn out. He shakes his head vigorously, then points. "If he's up there, then, we need to go up there too. I dunno why we're down here."

Oh. I get what's happening here.

"Leo." I wade across to him. "We *can't* go back up there. We don't even know if your dad is—"

"Why?"

"Why what?"

"Why can't we go there?"

"Because . . . " I falter. "Because the cops will arrest us."

He won't look at me.

"Your dad couldn't get back in to find you, and I know I said I'd get you back to him, but we *have* to go."

In response, he hunkers down into himself.

"You're not the Zigzag Man," he says. I'm pretty sure he meant to say *with* the Zigzag Man, but that's not what came out. "But I don't like you. You're a liar."

It is very, very hard not to start screaming.

An adult would understand this. An adult would get that trying to find someone here is a bad idea. An adult would agree that we need to get somewhere safe. Leo is not an adult. Obviously. And in his mind, his dad is waiting for him somewhere around here.

I don't want to lie to him. That'll just backfire later. And lest we forget, Leo can instantly kill anything he doesn't like.

Getting angry or frustrated here will solve nothing. So despite my exhaustion, despite the horrible, leaden feeling in my body, despite the unbearable urge to crawl into a cave and sleep for a thousand years, I stop. Force myself to think.

I take a deep breath, and plop down next to him, relieved to be off my feet. Even if the concrete is freezing under my wet backside.

"Leo," I say quietly. "I didn't lie."

"My dad says that if you lie to someone, it means you don't love them."

"That's ... true, I guess. But, Leo, I swear, I wasn't lying. I just ... forgot to explain myself."

He blinks up at me, not understanding.

"Your dad *might* be up there. If he is, they won't let him in the building."

"But he's gonna come find me!"

"Yes, he will. But he might not be able to. You understand what I'm saying? I know you only zapped the building because you were scared, but ... "

Another deep breath, trying not to picture the body I came across. "But it made other people scared too. That's why I came, because my friends and I were scared and wanted to find out what was happening."

He says nothing.

"If your dad is up there, they won't let him in. And if we go up there now, they'll take you away from him."

"They will?"

"Yeah. So we need to get somewhere safe. OK?"

He chews his lip. "My dad always says you need a plan."

"He's smart." I don't know what else to say.

"Super-smart. Like that time we went to the BioPark but it was closed, so we went for ice cream instead."

"The ... BioPark?"

His eyes light up, maybe for the first time. "It's like a zoo? They have a giraffe and a Kododo dragon and a turtle with red feet." His gaze drops, as if he remembers where we are.

I'm about to speak when he says "We gotta go to ... to 860 East Glencoe. The place in Compton." He stumbles a little over the words. "We gotta go there."

He picks at the concrete surface, prying up a loose chunk. It makes me think of what Annie said, about how the Army Corps of Engineers built it – just like they built the levees that collapsed during Hurricane Katrina.

"Maybe my dad went there," Leo is saying.

Maybe he did.

And maybe, if I get Leo there, his dad will be so grateful that he'll tell me what the hell the School is, and who's running it.

Getting there is going to take some doing. We're in the Glendale Narrows right now, and Compton is almost twenty miles directly south of us. I need a ride . . . but that comes with its own problems. It's not just the fact that the roads are a mess right now. It's Reggie. She'll be checking out every damn security camera in a fifty-block radius . . . and I only have to get unlucky once.

We could walk it – just go right down the river, straight shot, all the way past Downtown Los Angeles – DTLA, as we call it – then through Commerce, Bell Gardens, Downey. Hop out when we get to Compton. That keeps us off the roads, and away from any cameras – or at least, away from most of them. But it has its own problems. If we're going to walk, we need food, and water.

I can't just go into a random restaurant. For one, it's not exactly what you'd call safe – by now, Reggie and the crew must know I've gone AWOL, which means they'll be in full search mode. For two, I have almost no money. Oh, I have a couple of cards in my pocket, but using them would be like putting up a neon sign. And the five bucks in cash and change I have won't get us far. The quake, sadly, didn't make things in LA much cheaper.

And it's only the start – even if Leo and his dad are reunited in Compton, even if Mr Nguyen gives me the low down, we still need to find something more permanent. Something that keeps Leo safe from Tanner ... and from the Zigzag Man. Whoever the hell he is.

I need some help.

Annie and Africa are out, obviously. Same for Reggie. And whoever helps me will have to be someone who won't call the cops when I show up with a strange little boy. Somehow, I don't think claiming Leo is a mysterious family member who just showed up one day is going to cut it.

It has to be someone who knows what I can do. Who knows about the world of shit I immerse myself in on a regular basis. The last thing I need is to have to explain why I can move shit with my mind and why Leo can zap anything he touches.

Which, really, leaves exactly one person.

I close my eyes, making myself run through other names in my head. Literally *anybody* else. I cycle through a bunch of foodies I hang out with, a woman I got friendly with at a yoga class last year, even Manuel, who runs the mini-market at the corner of my block – or used to, before it was wrecked by the quake. No go. None of them know about my ability.

You can't call him. For one thing, you broke your phone. You don't know his number by heart, and—

Aaaaand Google backs up all my contacts online. I can use Leo's phone and just call it right up.

God. Fucking. *Argh.*

"Hey," I say to Leo. "Would you mind if I used your phone real quick?"

FIFTEEN

Teagan

"Hello?" Nic Delacourt says.

Actually it's more of a grunt than a word. Like he's just woken up from a really deep sleep. He must have crashed out after he got home from Howlin' Ray's – makes sense, if he's been moving rubble and working with his hands on the early shift.

I take a deep breath. "Um. Hey."

Silence.

I'm about to speak again when he says, "Who is this?"

"It's . . . it's me."

"Who the fuck is me?"

Is he still half asleep? I know I'm on a different number, but he has to recognise my voice, right?

"It's Teagan," I say. Leo gives me a weird look. Behind us, a police siren goes off, piercing the night air as a cruiser speeds away.

"How're you doing?" I say, when he doesn't respond.

"Tired. Look . . . sorry, it's been a really long day. I kind of got home and just passed out. Can we do this tomorrow?"

"Can we do . . . what tomorrow?"

"Tomorrow's too late," Leo whispers.

"Yeah, I know, Leo, stop it." I wave him away.

"Who's that?" Nic asks.

"Doesn't matter. Nic, I'm in trouble. I need help."

I'm not sure what I was expecting. A sudden alertness. A clipped "Where are you?" I was not expecting more silence.

"You still there?" I ask. "I've got a real problem, man. I could definitely use—"

"What kind of problem?"

The same dull, resigned tone.

"One I can't really talk about over the phone." I shift on the concrete – God, my ass is *freezing* now.

He laughs. Tries to, anyway. "Sure. Of course. Why'd you even call me, Teags?"

"What do you mean, why did I call you? Did you not hear me when I mentioned my *massive problem*?"

"Oh yeah, I heard. But what I want to know is, why am I the person who has to come rescue you?"

"I don't—"

"You got Annie. The big dude, what's his name . . . Africa. Your girl Reggie. Shit, you could probably get whatever fucking secret agency you work for to bring in the marines, if you need an assist. Why me, man?"

"Because you're my *friend*!"

"Oh, is that what we are? Cool. Thanks for the clarification. Been wondering about that for a while now."

"Nic . . ."

"You know what, actually, Teags, sorry, but I've been working since ass-o-clock this morning, and I gotta do the same thing tomorrow. I need sleep. I'll talk to you when I wake up."

"We gotta cross the river," Leo says. "It's cold here."

Nic barely manages to stifle a yawn. "Yo, who the fuck *is* that with you?"

I bite down very hard on my frustration. "Nic. I know you probably don't like me very much right now. But I *really* need your help. I've got a kid with me. His name's Leo . . ."

"What do you mean a kid?"

"A boy. He's like three—"

"I'm four!"

"Four, sorry. He's four years old, and we can't find his dad."

"Hold on, hold on. You want me to come get you because of some lost kid? Jesus fuck, Teagan, go to the cops or child services or something, man. I don't even work as a lawyer any more. Let me sleep."

"He's like me," I say, through gritted teeth. "He can do what I do. Well, not exactly, he's got a different ability, but . . ."

Another beat of silence. Then: "Well, what about China Shop? Isn't this what y'all are about?"

"I can't go to the team for this one."

"Why not?"

"It'll take way too much time to explain over the phone." I talk quickly, before he can object. "It actually doesn't matter right now. Please, please help us. We just need some food and water, and *maybe* a ride somewhere."

"Last time I helped you, you blew up my apartment."

I grimace. Back when I was framed for murder, the team and I used his home to lay low for a little bit. That didn't work, because a little while after we got there, a special forces team showed up and I accidentally totally destroyed the apartment when we tried to escape. I've never lived that one down, even when we were still on speaking terms.

"And by the way," he says. "Don't give me that *it'll take way too much time to explain over the phone* bullshit, OK? I don't think

EYE OF THE SH*T STORM

that's ever been true for anyone. You want me to come find you, I want to be damn sure I'm not walking into something that might get me killed."

"Nic, we don't—"

"Tell me, Teagan."

So I do. Well, the CliffsNotes version anyway – I leave out the part about being high on meth. The story takes a few minutes – Leo is getting antsy next to me, and my fuzzy brain keeps wanting to jump ahead. But we get there.

It'll have to be enough. I don't know what else I can say to convince him.

"Sheee-it," he says, after yet another silence.

"Uh-huh."

"You can't electrify a building. It doesn't—"

"Yes, it does; Reggie explained it. It's something to do with electrons. I didn't really understand it myself."

He gives a deep sigh, then stretches. I know this because I hear the click in his back, which sounds like a gun going off.

"Where are you guys?"

"Seriously? Oh shit, thank you. Thank you, Nic, you will not reg—"

"Teagan. Tell me where you are."

"Right. Sorry. We're in the LA River right now, up in Glendale. We're near that building I mentioned – Big Green Storage. But listen, do *not* come up this way, it's full of cops, and Annie and Africa are probably still there too."

"Yeah, I figured. What's on the other side of the storm dr— river?"

I look up. There are buildings visible at the top of the slope, but they're as anonymous as they come. "Honestly? Kind of hard to tell."

"Wait, wait ... Glendale means ... OK, that's probably

Griffith Park. You could get to the ... Actually, hold up." Scuffling sounds, the rustle of fabric. "Better idea."

"OK?"

"We could be fucking around for hours trying to find each other with street signs – half them shits got knocked down in the quake anyway. But if you're in the river in Glendale, there's this spot I know south of you guys, in Frogtown. Adam's Gym. They're right by the river, and they've got this big-ass rotating sign on top of the building. You can see it for miles, and I know for a fact it's still there. Get to the gym, meet me out front."

"What if I just, I don't know, drop a pin somewhere? Share it with you?"

"Nah. Cell service is still spotty. It's been fine for me today, but the last thing we want is for me to lose data at the wrong time. Oh, and you probably don't want to be carrying a phone around if you don't want your team to find you."

Give him this: he might not be a lawyer any more, but he's got the mind of one. Reggie might not know about Leo's phone, but who's to say she won't start scanning for signals in the area? Or checking to see if I'm signed into my contacts? Shit, maybe she's even done it already ...

No point worrying about that now. "Adam's Gym. Big-ass sign on the roof. Roger that."

Nic ends the call. Doesn't even say bye.

Well, that was fun.

Not like this next bit is going to be any better. "Up for a walk?" I say to Leo.

"Why were you fighting?" Leo says.

"I—"

"You can't, can't fight with friends."

"He's ... it's ... he is, it's just ... " I trail off. How do describe the concept of *ghosting* to a four-year-old? Leo's smart, but he's not that smart.

I break the moment by getting to my feet. The only place to stand is in the ankle-deep water. Not like my feet aren't soaked anyway. To the north, the brewing thunderstorm gives off another low rumble. The clouds are above our heads now, slowly edging towards covering the sun.

Nic's comment about the phone comes back to me – it's very possible that Reggie could track it, and it would make sense to destroy it in the same way I wrecked mine. But that would leave us without any sort of communication, and the last thing I want is for us to get lost, or miss Nic somewhere. I don't care how visible this sign is – I want options.

I settle for turning the phone off. Reggie might still be able to track it, but she'd have to suspect I was using it first. I think that's a stretch, and I can live with the odds. For now.

"It doesn't sound like it's too far," I say. "Ready?"

"Are we going to the place right now? The one with, where my dad is?"

He must mean Compton. No point lying to him again. I kneel in front of him. "Not right away. It's pretty far, and I don't have a car. The person I just called is gonna help us, but we gotta go meet him. We're gonna find your dad, though, bud. I promise."

Leo takes an age to respond. He literally chews his lip for a minute. But then he looks up at me, his eyes bright.

"OK."

SIXTEEN

Teagan

It's harder going than I thought it would be. And I did *not* think it would be easy.

The water tracks a serpentine course between the sloped, concrete sides. The ankle-deep section we started in quickly gives way to knee-deep, then waist-deep water. I was hoping we could just walk alongside it, along the hard-packed dirt. But the bushes and vegetation are thicker than I thought they'd be, cut through with little offshoots from the main stream. We spend too much time clambering across slippery rocks, pushing through undergrowth and thick, almost impenetrable clumps of bamboo.

There's hardly any wildlife – no birds, and definitely no fish in the green-brown water. It's the lack of birds that bothers me the most. This much vegetation, you'd expect to see *something*.

The sun has edged behind the cloud bank, plunging the world into that weird pre-storm half-light. It's not raining yet – small mercies, I guess – but the air is muggy, almost syrupy. It's doing nothing for my comedown. I've slipped into a kind of queasy, uneven trance, concentrating on putting one foot in front of the other, and doing my best *not* to concentrate on the pounding headache and the hollow, yawning howl in my gut.

The area we're heading to, Frogtown, isn't actually an official place. It's a local nickname for Elysian Valley, a neighbourhood just to the north of Dodger Stadium, bordered in the west by the 5 freeway. I have no idea why it's called Frogtown, and it wasn't exactly an appropriate question to ask Nic. All I know is, it's south of where we are now. We keep pushing south, and everything will be OK.

Every so often, there's a structure at the top of the concrete slope – a flat wall, like a billboard, maybe ten feet tall by twenty wide. The bottom sits flush with the top of the concrete slope. They appear in clusters, three or four at a time, on both sides of the river, and there doesn't appear to be any logic to where they're placed. This being LA, they're riddled with graffiti. Some pretty good pieces, too. I spot some WRDSMTH, some Kim West, even one piece that looks like a Mr Cartoon job.

But what the hell are the walls the graf is painted on? I stare at them for the longest time before it hits me: flood barriers. The City of Los Angeles is putting up some extra insurance in case a real big dump happens.

What I don't get is why the barriers are spaced so strangely. Is it strategic? Like, they've worked out where a potential flood would breach the edges of the river? Are they trying to protect specific buildings? Maybe the quake knocked the others down . . . only, I don't see any debris.

Annie would know. Hell, I can hear her now. *Damn city builds some, stops for a while, builds some more, tears some more down cos they ain't up to code or some shit. Same motherfuckers moving folks out of their neighbourhoods, letting developers come in. It ain't right, man.*

It's hard not to dwell on how angry she's been lately. How most of it seems to have been directed at me. The thoughts taste bitter. I get that she's grieving, I do, but . . .

I really thought she and I were doing better. We've never seen eye to eye, but we were . . . well, not friends, exactly, but friend*ly*. That's gone. Blown away like smoke.

Leo doesn't talk much. Just follows, head down, carefully placing his feet. I'd like to say it's a companionable silence, but it isn't. Unease radiates off him. Like he could change his mind at any second.

And really, if he did, what could I do about it? Maybe I could knock him out or something, drag him with me, only what the hell do I know about knocking people out? I've got as much chance of giving him a brain haemorrhage as I do of sending him to sleep.

And I'm pretty sure if I try, he'll just zap me out of existence.

These are not fun thoughts. I block them out by thinking about cooking. Running through recipes in my head, techniques I've used, techniques I want to try. When I actually have a decent kitchen again. When I go to cooking school—

I yank back from that thought like it burned me – a sensation I'm all too familiar with.

When you're saving the world – or at least, keeping this little part of it safe – it's hard to become a professional chef. I might hate Moira Tanner, but she was right about that. All the same, having to put aside that dream . . . hurt.

It's no fun thinking about any of that. So instead, my mind switches to thinking about Nic.

So much better.

What kind of vengeful, sadistic God arranges things so that the only person I can turn to is one I ghosted? With good reason, by the way. Nic Delacourt said some pretty awful things to me after the quake, and yeah, he apologised after-wards, but that didn't make me any less pissed at him.

To be fair, I never intended to just leave him hanging. I'm not that terrible. I just couldn't figure out what to say to his messages. I tried out a dozen responses in my head, but every time I'd try typing one, I'd end deleting it. After a while, it just got awkward. In the end, I just kind of . . . left it.

Ugh. Maybe I *am* that terrible.

Don't forget what he *said, too. The way he looked at you when he called you selfish, for not revealing your ability. A sorry is not going to erase how that look made you feel.*

We haven't gone very far – maybe just around the first big bend in the river, a little over a mile – before I notice that there's something wrong with Leo. You know, beyond the whole freaked-out-kid-with-lethal-superpowers-thing.

He's limping. Dragging his left foot. And he's doing some-thing weird with his hand, which is twitching in irregular jerks. He wasn't doing that before, I'm sure of it.

I frown. "You OK there, dude?"

"Fine," he says, sullen. Oh yeah, his left foot is messed up – scratch that, his entire left *leg*. It's jerking, too, just like his hand.

"Did you hurt yourself somewhere?" I say. I don't remember seeing him trip or anything, but I'm so zonked that there's a chance I just missed it.

He drags his twitching foot over a bump on the hard-packed surface. "It's just my wiggles."

"I'm sorry, your what now?"

"My wiggles. When I make 'lectricity, my foot starts wig-gling." He blinks down at his jerking wrist. "And my hand."

"Leo, dude, those aren't just *wiggles*."

"They don't hurt," he says. He sounds confused, like he doesn't understand why I'm making a big deal out of this.

"OK . . . does this happen every time?"

"Only when I zap things for a while. Or zap a really big thing." He scratches his nose with his good hand. "I can't really use my 'lectricity while I got wiggles."

Electricity. Isn't that how nerves work? Is his ability affecting his nervous system somehow? Jesus, what is it doing to his *brain*?

If I push my power too hard, my body drains itself of energy. If I push myself *really* hard, my PK goes really fuzzy. It's super-hard to lift anything, or even sense it.

On the surface, Leo's *wiggles* make sense. They're the result of his ability being pushed too hard. So why do I feel cold thinking about them? Why do they send a shiver of worry up my spine?

Maybe it's because they cause a physical reaction – an actual movement I can see. Or maybe it's because he can't use his ability until they go away. It's as if he gets a super-charged version of my PK's feedback, like he's experiencing it all at once.

Who the hell did this to him? And why?

"Do you . . . ?" I shake my head. "Do you need help? Like a piggyback or something?"

"I'm OK," he insists. "Sometimes, when it happened, Dr Ajay would give me an ice cream."

For a second, just a second, he smiles.

Man, listen. Leo Nguyen from Albuquerque has the greatest smile. It fills up his entire face, makes his nose wrinkle. It is *impossible* not to look at it, and not feel a little bit better.

Then it's gone. Just like that. Replaced by the same mis-trustful look – only even more now. Like he's said too much.

"Who's Dr Ajay?" I say, filing the name away for later.

In response, he just shrugs.

I don't know if he doesn't want to tell me, or if he doesn't know how. I don't remember being four years old all that well, but I'm pretty sure I wasn't too communicative, either. Especially about stuff I didn't really understand.

Which doesn't stop it being ridiculously frustrating.

We've been walking for a couple of miles now, and aside from the sloped sides, there's no concrete anywhere. It's a literal river: a snaking channel, bordered by dirt and foliage. And it's a lot deeper now. I can't see the bottom, but it's got that thick, heavy look of deep water.

Must be fun to go kayaking here. Maybe, after this shitstorm is all over, I'll come back and do that. Someone must have set up a business renting canoes to jackasses like me. It might be fun to row row row my ass down the river in the middle of a city, just me and a six-pack and my headphones.

Leo yells. Points, his hand twitching.

We're just coming around a sharp bend in the river, and what Leo is pointing at is a sign. Massive, bright green, neon. It's maybe two hundred yards away, above the west bank, and it brings a huge smile to my face.

Give Nic this: he picked a good target. You'd have to be blind to miss it. You can probably see it from space.

"All right!" I hold up my hand for a high-five from Leo, but he ignores me, limping even faster towards the sign.

"Not cool, man," I mutter. But I follow.

The bamboo groves are more numerous here, and it's getting hard to find a route between them. It looks like we can get up the slope in a little gap just ahead of us. There's a flood barrier at the top, but we can slip around it if—

Wait.

"I'm hungry," Leo says. "Can we get cheeseburgers when we meet your friend? Hey – come on!"

"Just a second." I look back towards the bend, squinting, focusing my PK. It's like trying to start a car on a cold morning, but I get there.

Someone's coming.

So? It's not like the river is your own private walking path. There must be a bunch of other people who use it.

I feel lightheaded all of a sudden. Woozy. Like I've had too much whiskey. It's ... *different* from the meth hangover, somehow. Fluffy, instead of actively awful. I blink hard, try to shake it off.

It might be one of the team – I'm pretty sure either Africa or Annie would have tried the river, sooner or later – or the cops. Maybe even the one that caught us outside the fence. But it's just the one person – I'm pretty sure the cops wouldn't come alone. Whoever it is is moving fast.

That's not what worries me though. I can't sense the person themselves, but I can feel what they're carrying. It's a twitch at the edge of my mind, like you might get if a gust of wind rippled your shirt collar. Whoever they are, they're carrying a hypodermic needle.

A big one.

Before I can act on this, a voice calls out my name. And my mouth falls open.

"Teagan? Are you there?"

It's a male voice. Clear, calm. German accent. A voice I know.

As I watch, staring in stunned silence, the speaker steps around a clutch of bamboo.

He's in his early thirties, with an artfully messy spike of blond hair over a clean-shaven face. A pair of aviator shades sit perched on his forehead. He wears a well-cut dark suit over a white V-neck T-shirt. Despite the dirt, his leather loafers are immaculate, and his ice-blue eyes shine with a hot, bright energy. When he sees me, his face splits in a huge smile. "There you are," he says.

I last saw him in person during the quake. On his private jet at Van Nuys Airport. But I've seen him since, in my most private thoughts. Even though I knew I'd probably never see him again.

And yet, amazingly, impossibly, here he is. In the middle of the LA River. Right in front of me.

Jonas Schmidt.

SEVENTEEN

Reggie

Right when Reggie's day couldn't get any worse, Annie's camera starts to glitch.

She's on the 2, the part of the freeway that crosses the river, looking south, when the feed goes black. "Annie." Reggie says, frowning. "Check your video."

A hiss of static. "Shit, hold up." There's a rustle of fabric. "Looks OK to me. Can you reboot it?"

Reggie does so. Still nothing – the same black screen. There are no error messages, and the connection looks good. The audio's still fine – Reggie can hear Annie's phone in the background, beeping with texts. Annie hasn't been idle, reaching out to several of her contacts, trying to see if there's anybody in the Glendale area who might have seen something. So far, she's come up empty.

For the thousandth time, Reggie scans their systems. Nothing. She has run multiple threat detection packages, looked in every nook and cranny, and she can't find evidence of an intrusion.

Africa's feed is crystal clear. "I have finished checking the park on the west side of the river," he says. "She is not here."

Reggie's eyes flick to the map on one of the other screens. "We're going to need more boots on the ground. Africa: head back to the storage unit. See if you can get the LAPD to help with the search."

"They may not listen," he rumbles. "They are already not trusting us."

"Make it happen," she snaps. "Annie: head south and check the Atwater area"

"Why Atwater?"

"She might have tried to pick up transport – she's more likely to get a cab or an Uber there than in Silver Lake." If the girl is even able to call an Uber. Reggie can't get a bead on her phone. It's that, more than anything else, that concerns her. She should have been able to trace it even with the device turned off. The only way it would go dead on her is if the battery was removed, or the phone destroyed.

"OK," Annie says. "But I'm pretty sure—"

There's a hiss of static, then nothing.

"Annie, come back?" Reggie says. She reboots everything yet again. No connection, to either audio or video.

Annie's comms are dead in the water.

"Shit." It's said quietly, under her breath. If she makes it any louder, she won't be able to control her temper. And if that happens, then tonight will go from bad to catastrophic.

China Shop is an experiment. A team designed to handle black bag jobs that other teams aren't able to handle, and to do it fast and efficiently. They may not be special forces, but there's no one better for pulling off intrusion jobs, break-ins, recon. Teagan's ability, backed up by Annie's contacts and Reggie's computer skills, make them uniquely suited to what they do.

The problem is, they are not ready for the current situation. Reggie doesn't know why Los Angeles seems to be a magnet for individuals with abilities. The other psychokinetic, Jake, was an anomaly – a one-off, she thought. Coincidence. Matthew Schenke was not. He was *sent* here, directed, pointed in the right direction by . . . someone. Whoever runs, or ran, the mysterious School.

And now it's happening again.

After the earthquake, Tanner should have vastly expanded the team. Added actual military personnel: trackers, snipers, demolitions experts. Operators to back China Shop up when things went south. Why the hell hasn't Tanner gone that route?

But of course, Reggie knows why. It's about control with Moira Tanner. It always has been. She doesn't want more people – more people would mean she'd need to give up some autonomy. And just because China Shop is run from an off-books black budget doesn't mean that budget is limitless – or that the people who control the purse strings don't keep a close watch on what gets spent. Just because the budget isn't run by a traditional senate subcommittee doesn't mean it's not tightly controlled.

By keeping it small, Moira Tanner keeps an iron grip on her little project. It's very easy to see her keeping her superiors in the dark about . . . well, everything.

"Annie's down," Reggie tells Africa.

"What do you mean, down?"

"Her comms are offline."

Africa is silent for a long moment. Then he says, "OK. Here is what we do. You must connect me with Mrs Tanner. I will keep her updated while you fix the communication with Annie, huh?"

"Excuse me?"

"If there is a technical problem, fixing it must be what you are doing. You must not have to worry about other things. I will keep Mrs Tanner informed while I keep looking."

China Shop has always been made up of contradictory personalities. Reggie has always prided herself in being the calm voice of reason, the one who kept the team together. She has never lost her temper, never gotten angry, even when stress levels were high. Reggie may be the team's hacker, but her real role is and always has been as peacemaker.

Which is what makes her next words so surprising.

"Let's get one thing straight, honey," she snaps. "This is my operation. All comms go through me, and the Rig." The Army was a long time ago, but she hasn't lost the steel voice of command. "You do not get to give me orders, Africa. Are we clear?"

Another long silence.

"Are we *clear*?"

" . . . Ya."

"Good."

She has never taken that tone with anybody in China Shop. There's never been any need. *What the hell is happening to me?*

"I can't connect you with Annie," she says, forcing herself to focus. "There's a technical problem on the Washington side. But it changes nothing: head back to the storage unit, and find me some more bodies to help with the search."

When Africa speaks again, he sounds resigned. "What did Mrs Tanner say? When she hear about Teagan?"

"She . . ."

And once more, the lie is there.

Reggie knows she's going to run with it even before the words leave her mouth. Even though she only digs herself deeper and deeper by telling it. Even though there's no good reason to do so. She is powerless before the urge, already speaking before she can second-guess herself.

"She wasn't pleased. But she's as concerned as we are, and she's doing what she can to help. Now get going."

Inwardly, she is stunned at how easily the lie slips outs. Once again, it is not a huge lie. It's a small one, really, almost inconsequential. Something that could be attributed later to a miscommunication. And in any case, she's not telling the lie just *because*. She's telling it to keep Africa in play. She's telling it to buy herself time. It's completely understandable, and nothing she can't fix.

"Uh-huh," Africa says, sounding unsure. "OK. Please tell me if she has anything for me, huh?"

"I . . . Yes, I will. Keep looking."

EIGHTEEN

Teagan

My brain short-circuits. Every thought I have stops cold.

Jonas Schmidt isn't here. He can't be. This is the meth, playing games with me, making me see things again.

Except: it's different this time. This isn't a flicker at the edge of my vision, or the feeling of someone coming up behind me. This isn't my paranoid, agitated, anxious brain conjuring something out of thin air.

It's Jonas. He's real.

Standing right in front of me, wearing a wide smile, the skin around his eyes crinkling and his perfect cheekbones standing out. The German billionaire I've had a crush on for the past four months, who I thought I'd only ever see again on his Instagram photos.

"It's good to see you, Teagan," he says.

"Wh . . . ?" It's more a breath than a word.

"It took me quite some time to find you." He scratches the stubble on his jaw. "I admit, I was not expecting to have to go wading through a river."

Leo is trying to talk to me. I don't register his words. I'm barely aware of them.

"Jonas . . ." I lick my lips. "How did you . . . ? What are you doing here?"

"We're all waiting for you." He gestures up river. "Africa, Annie, Regina. All of China Shop. My jet is on the tarmac at Van Nuys. We can get you out of the country." An urgent look comes onto his face. "But only if we hurry."

"What about Leo?" I turn to introduce him, which is when the weirdest thing happens.

I *can't* turn.

Leo is behind me, standing just off to my left . . . but I can't look away from Jonas.

"Oh yes." Jonas takes a step forward. "We know all about young Mr Nguyen. He can come too."

Why can't I look at Leo? Why can't I turn around?

Jonas's smile is even wider now. "It's all right," he says, patting the air. "You're safe."

And I am. I know it in my bones. Jonas is here, which means everything is going to be fine. I can stop running. I can stop fighting the comedown and finally, finally sleep. I can stop . . .

The hypodermic.

It's still there. Behind me, in motion, as if whoever is holding it is still walking. I can just sense it with my PK. There must be someone with Jonas, but why would they . . . ?

Leo isn't talking any more.

He's screaming.

But it's coming from a long way away, and it's someone else's problem. The thought slips away. Everything is slipping away. I'm coasting down, down, down, into a hole that is warm and dark and snuggly, and if I just let go . . .

"Come into my house, Teagan," Jonas says kindly. "You will be safe there. Nothing can hurt you inside the walls."

There's this thing I used to do when I was a kid, and I had

a nightmare. I called it the Emergency Blink. If a bad dream took me, I just had to blink. Even though I couldn't, even though my eyes were already closed, the simple act of trying to blink in the dream would often let me escape it. I haven't used the technique in ... Jesus, almost a decade.

But something is telling me that I need to use it now.

I squeeze my eyes shut. Relax. Squeeze. Relax. I'm still in the dark place, still warm and comfy ... but now I can hear Leo more clearly. Hear what he's screaming.

And what he's screaming is: "*Zigzag Man!*"

"You aren't real," I tell Jonas.

It takes everything I have. I hadn't realised until this moment how badly I wanted him to be real. To be there, in front of me, ready to whisk me away on his private jet and keep me safe.

"You ... " I take a deep breath. "Aren't. *Real.*"

It's like someone snaps their fingers. I jerk, almost toppling over, righting myself just in time. Jonas vanishes. Just ... *poof.* There one moment, gone the next.

And finally, I turn towards Leo.

He's on the ground, pinned there by a black bear.

No – not a bear. My mind isn't working like it should. It's a huge man, head the size of a cannonball, straggly black hair streaked with grey. His gigantic beard is streaked with grey, too, spreading out from under a bandanna like a fungal growth. The bandanna and his clothes are black: leather jacket, cargo pants, heavy black boots caked with river dirt. He's turned slightly away from me, a massive hand holding Leo down.

And in the other hand, the hypodermic.

"*Help me!*" Leo shouts, reaching out for me. "I can't zap him, I got the wiggles, *help*—"

The man puts his elbow on Leo's chest, clamps a hand over

his mouth. He moves the needle towards Leo's neck – or tries to, because at that moment I grab hold of it with my PK. I don't have the focus to tear it away, not yet, but I stop it in its tracks.

"All right," I say, wiping my mouth with a trembling hand. "Put the pigsticker down and back the fuck off, before I—"

"You are in my house."

The man's speaks quickly, the words blurring together. His voice is soft, almost gentle. He doesn't turn around, and I can't tell if he's speaking to me, or Leo, or no one at all.

"My house only speaks the truth. My house has walls that go on for ever."

"Please!" Leo screams.

The needle slips free of my grip, inches towards the boy's neck. "My house has doors that open but never close, and it lies, oh it lies it lies. The little children will not be quiet no they will never ever ever ever be quiet, not until we *make them*, but they will still whisper yes they will—"

"Teagan?" Jonas says.

He's standing on the spot where the Zigzag Man was holding Leo down – both of them have vanished. Jonas tilts his head, smiling kindly.

"You've been through a lot," he says. "You can see people in the house but it grows and grows and you can never reach them. Let me help you."

And once again, I'm falling, falling, sliding back down into the warm dark. The thoughts of Leo and the Zigzag Man are fading away, no matter how hard I try to hold onto them.

Except: it's different this time. There's another voice. One I haven't heard before.

A man's voice.

At first, the words blend into one, smearing themselves

across my mind. It takes me a second to understand them. "Put
it down, right now. You hear me? Get off him . . . Wait, what
are you doing? *What are you doing to me?*"

I raise my head, which takes a year, a decade, a millennium.
I push back the darkness – it's like trying to push aside thick
vines in a jungle.

The Zigzag Man and Leo reappear. And with them:

Nic.

He's wearing jeans and a white Clippers jersey. And he's
down on all fours a few feet away, his body shaking. As I
watch, he collapses, hugging himself, shaking like a leaf.

Jonas puts a hand on my shoulder – he got behind me
somehow. "Come with me," he whispers, and the darkness
closes in.

And then second voice reaches us. Out of sight to my right,
on the other side of a bamboo grove. A woman, yelling, furious, her heavy feet thundering on packed dirt.

At that moment, as the full horror of the situation slams
into me, Jonas pulls me backwards. The ground and the sky
change places, the whole world vanishing behind a curtain of
warm darkness.

This time, I don't welcome it. Because even as I fall, I'm
aware of it: aware that something (*Zigzag Man Zigzag Man*) has
pulled me out of reality.

What happens next happens in snatches. Bright flashes of
light, penetrating the black.

Nic, up one knee, lurching to his feet.

The Zigzag Man is on his feet too, backing away from
something. Arm held up, as if to shield himself. Then, a
moment later: running away. Just booking it back upriver.

I shout Leo's name. Or try to. My mouth is so dry that I
quite literally can't speak.

Footsteps, behind me. Hands under my arms, pulling me up, setting me on my feet. My brain is still trying to get out from under the warm dark, and all the blood leaves my head at once. The hands hold me up, keeping me steady as my body stabilises. I'm shaking, jerking my head left and right, terrified I'll see Jonas Schmidt again.

Behind me, Nic coughs as he gets to his feet. Which brings the oddest thought. If he's still down, then who's holding me?

"Teagan, what the fuck is wrong with you?"

The hands turn me around, and I'm looking up at Annie Cruz.

NINETEEN

Teagan

So you know that call between me and Nic? Where I asked him to come help us? Pretty awkward, right?

Take that awkwardness. Triple it. Quadruple it. Imagine it as nuclear-level awkward emitting from an awkward-class star in the Totes Awks constellation.

That's what the next few minutes are like, after the Zigzag Man escapes.

Annie stands off to one side of the bamboo grove, her back to us, arms folded. She's so angry she can't actually speak to me.

I don't know how she and Nic knew to find us down in the river – we never made it up to the gym, which is where he told us to wait. I don't know what she's doing here, how she knew where we were, where Africa is, whether or not she's still in communication with Reggie, who must be going out of her mind right now.

I have no idea why the Zigzag Man could affect me and Nic, but couldn't affect her. Why he bolted when she showed up. When Nic told her what happened – that he made us see things – she looked at him like he'd gone crazy.

Leo is close by, crouched at the edge of the river, idly scratching at the dirt. One of the first things I did when I could actually move again was to rush over to check on him, but he just told me he was fine. His voice was as flat and featureless as a prairie.

"I'm gonna need you to explain to me what the hell just happened back there," Nic says to me, his arms crossed tightly over his chest.

"What do you want me to tell you?" I don't mean to sound so sharp. I was so convinced that Jonas Schmidt was there. It felt so *real* . . . but in hindsight, it also made no sense at all. In the aftermath of the attack, the exhaustion has returned, the numb limbs and leaden stomach.

"We come find you and him –" Nic nods at Leo " – and there's some . . . some *guy* who makes you see—"

His mouth snaps shut, and he looks away.

"What did you see?" I ask quietly.

"Doesn't matter. Look, who *was* he?"

"I don't know."

"And why didn't his powers work on Annie? Or on . . . Leo, right?"

"I don't know."

"Please. Another person with powers, and you're just—"

"What do you want from me, man? We don't have a WhatsApp group. I have no idea who that was, or how his ability works."

"The Zigzag Man," Leo says. He's still scratching at the dirt.

Nic tilts his head. "The who?" He's actually shivering, his shoulders shaking. Christ, what the hell did he see?

"The Zigzag Man. He was chasing me and my dad."

"Why's he called the Zigzag Man?"

"It's just what he's called."

I have to bite down on the urge to tell Leo that isn't good enough. God, I keep forgetting how young he is.

Annie makes a disgusted sound. "Oh, y'all got cute names now?"

"It's just his name," Leo says to the dirt.

"I don't care what he's called, what you're called, whatever the hell you're trying to do. You're lucky I don't just—"

"*Annie.*" I step between her and Leo. "Fall back. Right now."

She bares her teeth — something I get the feeling she does without meaning to — then turns away.

I don't care how angry she is. Leo is *not* the one who killed Paul. I'm guessing that particular argument wouldn't fly with her right now. All the same, she does not get to be angry at a scared little boy.

Nic starts towards Leo, but I pull him back. "Hold on. Just wait a second." I point at Annie. "How did—?"

"What, Annie? I called her. Before I came to get you."

"You . . . *why?*"

"Oh, yeah, sure, I'm gonna walk into a Teagan situation by my damn self. Why the f—?" He glances at Leo. "Why *wouldn't* I call her? She told me where she was, and I picked her up."

Shit. I told him I couldn't work with the China Shop guys on this, but I never told him not to reach out himself. Truly? I didn't think it was an option. It just never occurred to me that Nic knew any of them.

I change tack. "How did you even have her number anyway?"

"We've spoken a couple of times."

"What do you mean? When?"

"After the whole thing with Jake, where you blew up my apartment? She bought me lunch. Guerrilla Tacos."

Of course. Annie's Army. If you're Annie, and your whole MO is digging up useful contacts, why *wouldn't* you want someone in the District Attorney's office?

"You never said anything," I tell him.

He shrugs. "Honestly? It never came up."

"Seriously? You couldn't have mentioned—?"

"Oh, you do *not* get to talk about not telling people things," Annie says, without turning around.

Ouch. OK, fair. Maybe I should draw a line under this particular conversation. "How did you guys even know where to find us? We weren't at the gym yet."

"Heard him screaming." Nic nods to Leo.

The kid still has the damn wiggles, worse than before. His leg twitches, foot jerking. Nic gazes at him for a moment before turning back to me. "Figured something was going down, so we came to help."

I bow my head, trying to force back the heat blossoming on my cheeks. "Thanks. That was ... yeah."

Annie mutters something evil-sounding, shaking her head.

"Where's Africa?" I say, looking around, half-expecting the big guy to pop up from behind a chunk of bamboo.

"Hunting for *you*," Annie replies.

"You ... you didn't tell him about Nic calling you?"

For the first time, Annie's fury fades. Just a little. She looks over her shoulder at us, an unreadable expression on her face.

"Dude is getting way too close to Tanner," she says. "He's playing his own game."

"He's *always* played his own game."

"Yeah, but this is different. That's why I ditched my comms and my phone – I wanted to figure out what you were doing before we pulled him or Reggie in. And what *are* we doing, Teagan? Please explain this to me, because I'm having a real hard time figuring this out."

I lift an eyebrow at Nic. "Did you not tell her what we talked about? On the call?"

"Oh, he did," Annie says. "I just think it's bull."

"Annie, look—"

"No, you look. What are you trying to do here? *Save* this kid? After everything that's happened? And you do it by ditching us? What if I hadn't been here when this ... this Zigzag guy showed up? You *cannot* put yourself in danger like that. You just plan on wandering around with *him*?" She jabs a finger at Leo, who flinches. "What exactly were you gonna do? After Nic came and got you?"

Even Nic tries to interject now, but Annie brushes him aside. "I knew you were reckless, but I never thought you were stupid. This? This was some major stupid shit."

In the quiet that follows, the only sound is the running water in the channel.

I want to be angry. I don't like being yelled at. But I don't like lying to myself either, and I would be if I pretended there wasn't a tiny core of truth inside Annie's words.

"I just wanted ..." *Keep it together.* "I just wanted some answers. Ever since the whole earthquake thing, we've known this threat is out there – that someone was making kids with abilities. I was tired of not knowing. I figured if I kept Leo safe ... if I could get him to his dad ... " I swallow. "They'll lock him away you know. In Waco, where I was. Or someplace worse. The things they'll do to him ... "

More uncomfortable silence.

"Where were y'all going, anyway?" Annie asks.

I explain about Compton, about where we think Leo's dad

is. Nic and Annie listen, stony-faced. When I finish, neither of them say anything for a long moment.

Annie pinches the bridge of her nose, squeezing her eyes shut. "Compton."

"Yeah. It's where his uncle lives. If his dad is anywhere, it'll be there. And Annie, look . . . I know you're angry, but I could really use your help. We *cannot* let this kid get taken by either Tanner, or whoever the hell this Zigzag Man is."

Above us, a gull calls, whirling in the late afternoon sky against the cloud. Despite the mugginess, a chill sneaks across my exposed skin.

If Annie says no, I don't know what I'm going to do.

I have to believe that she'll understand. Neither of us, after all, work for Tanner by choice. Well, kind of – I definitely don't have a choice, and the only choice Annie has is working for Tanner, or trying to find a job that'll employ ex-cons. That's no choice at all. Maybe, just maybe, she'll understand that it's finally time to stop doing what Tanner wants us to. It's not about us any more. It's about Leo, and making sure he doesn't suffer what I suffered.

Please. You just want to know where he came from. Don't pretend like you want to help him for no reward.

I push the thoughts back, watching Annie.

And eventually, after an age, she nods.

The relief is unbelievable. "Thank you."

She scoffs. "If I don't, you'll just get yourself killed."

"Want me to bring my car around?" Nic says.

"Nah, I don't think so. Teagan – I'm assuming y'all got another phone? One Reggie can't track?"

"Um, yeah. Yes."

"Cool. OK. We'll roll with that. Here's what we're gonna—"

"Hold up." I turn to Nic. If Annie's here, then I don't need to involve him. I owe him big time, but right now, I think the biggest favour I can do for him is to leave him out of it. This whole situation is already FUBAR, and the last thing I want is him hurt. He doesn't deserve that, no matter what ugly things he may have said to me. "Nic, you should head out. Annie and I can—

"Where's the kid?" he says suddenly.

He's looking towards the water. Annie and I follow his gaze, and my blood goes cold.

Leo is gone.

TWENTY

Teagan

Nic takes off running, heading for the water.

I would like it noted for the record that I, too, start running. The problem is, my legs are very short, and my addiction to salted caramel ice cream makes it hard for me to compete in a foot race. I am also ... well, let's go with *not my best self* right now.

What I do have is a pair of lungs, and I make good use of them, screaming Leo's name. He's been taken, I'm sure of it – we should have seen it coming. The fucking Zigzag asshole circled back around, saw us arguing, took the opportunity. How could we be so *stupid*?

Nic reaches the water, skidding to a halt. "*Fuck.*" He spits the word, clearly on the same wavelength as me.

They can't have gone far. This time, I'll be ready. I'll have my PK good to go, a few choice projectiles locked and loaded. Let's see how he uses that cute illusion trick when I ram a concrete slab up his ass at a hundred miles an hour.

At that moment, I spot Leo. He's still limping, but he's moving surprisingly fast, heading alongside the water. I cannot describe the relief – it's like I've been walking in a desert, only for someone to dump a bucket of ice water on my head. *Holy shit. He's OK.*

Nic takes off, racing for Leo. This time, I don't bother sprinting behind them. I don't think I could, anyway. The relief has turned my legs to jelly. Jesus, where the hell is Annie?

Leo must hear Nic behind him, because he turns around mid-stride. "Go away!" he yells, his little boy voice cutting through the night air.

"Just stop for a second," Nic shouts.

"I said go—"

I know what's going to happen before it actually does. And there is no time to shout a warning.

Kids are not very coordinated, and most four-year-olds don't run well. The only reason Leo got so far away is because we were too busy arguing, and despite his twitching leg, he's built up a good head of speed. So when he half-turns, running on one good leg, right on the edge of the deep-running channel . . .

His eyes actually meet mine as he falls. Just for a split-second. The look in them is one of total surprise.

Then, with an enormous splash, he topples into the LA River.

"No, no, no!" Nic sprints faster, reaching the spot where Leo fell.

Leo's head and two waving arms explode above the surface. He shrieks, hands flailing – and immediately goes under again.

"*Leo!*" I shriek. I can use my PK – if there's something to grab, I can lift him right out. But he's panicking, and he might not know to hold on. I'm going to have to dive in after him—

Nic gets there first. He kicks his shoes off in mid-run, doing an exaggerated knees-up manoeuvre. The left one doesn't come off all the way, and he has to hop on one leg for a second or two while he yanks it away. Then he takes a leaping stride, and plunges into the water.

It's flowing fast. I hadn't realised *how* fast. I can't see Leo at all. Nic is already damn near fifty yards away, his muscular arms swinging through the air as he paddles.

I claw at my dirty FBI windbreaker, hurling it to the ground. There's actually nothing nearby for my PK to use, no handy pole or carelessly discarded life raft, so I'm going to have to swim for it.

Annie grabs me by the arm, so suddenly that I nearly topple over backwards. I didn't even realise she was there.

"What the fuck are you doing?" she hisses.

"Going in after him!"

"Your man's got him already."

"What?"

Annie points. "There!"

Nic is swimming across the current now, heading for the shore. He's on his back, using one arm to paddle. His other holds a very small, very still figure.

I shake off from Annie, start running again, ignoring her shouted warnings. She curses, sprints past me, reaching the shore just as Nic does. As I get there, she skids to her knees, reaching in and hauling him and Leo out of the water. They both flop onto the riverbank.

And Leo . . .

He's alive.

Gasping, coughing, sobbing, shivering . . . but alive.

Jesus Christ.

I sit down on the dirt. Hard. Hang my head.

I am the worst kidnapper ever.

Annie mutters something that I swear is *Should have let the kid drown.* I want to tell her to shut the fuck up, but I just don't have the energy right now.

Nic holds on tight to Leo, his big arms wrapped around him. "It's OK," he's saying, over and over, rocking the boy back and forth. He gets to his feet, legs shaking, still holding Leo in his arms.

"No, it's not." Leo's leg and arm are still jerking. "She said we was gonna get my dad but the Zigzag Man came and she . . . "

You want to feel helpless? You want to feel like a terrible human being? Look into the face of a child who realises you weren't able to protect them.

Nic pulls Leo into a huge hug, wrapping his arms around the crying boy.

"Leo, right?" he says, after a few moments.

"Uh-huh."

"Well, that's kind of weird." Nic has an odd smile on his face.

"Weird?" Leo looks suspicious, but he's distracted now, his attention no longer on me.

"Because that's my name too. Well, my middle name. Nicolas Leonardo Delacorte." He smiles. "Like the Ninja Turtle."

"And like the painter."

Nic makes an impressed face. "That's right. Like the painter."

"I was named after him, but I don't really like that stuff."

"Not sure I do either." He gestures to me. "Give me your jacket."

I strip it off, handing it over, and Nic wraps it around Leo's shivering shoulders. Above us, the clouds give out a gentle burp of thunder.

"Hey, listen," Nic says to Leo. He doesn't put a hand on his shoulder or anything, just looks him right in the eyes. "You can't run off like that. What if we hadn't been there?"

"I didn't *wanna* fall in," Leo mumbles.

"Well, you kind of did." Nic smirks. "Now I'm all wet too." He gives an exaggerated shiver.

"I have to find my dad."

"I know. But—"

Leo looks at me. "But the Zigzag Man came, and he made her see stuff and she couldn't do anything. I don't like her."

OK, enough's enough. I open my mouth to defend myself, but Annie stops me with a look.

A half-smile plays around Nic's mouth. "Yeah, well, I don't like her much either."

"Um, hi?" I wave. "Standing right here, dude."

"I'm scared," Leo says.

"I know, my man." Nic tells him. "I know. But right now, we can't link up with your pops if we're having to fight everybody." He leans in. "It's not just the ... what did you call him? The Zigzag Man? With what you can do, there are a lot of other people who want to take you. They aren't like *bad*, really, but they won't want to find your dad. I can tell you that much."

Leo is still shivering, but he's calmed right down. "OK."

Fine, I admit it: Nic is much better with kids than I am.

Annie shakes her head, muttering something. The look on her face is one of utter disgust. I stare at her, my mind in turmoil – surely she didn't *want* Leo to drown? No way she's that cold.

"If we're gonna do this," she says, resigned, "we gotta stay on the river."

I push back the ugly thoughts. "Wouldn't a car be better?"

"Not with Reggie watching the roads. She'll have traffic

cams up. Even if she doesn't think to check for Nic's ride, she might get lucky. I know she's got some crazy facial recognition stuff."

A coldness sneaks into my stomach, squats there. I can't bear talking about Reggie like she's the enemy. It's all kinds of wrong. But if Leo ends up on her radar, then he'll be on Tanner's. That can't happen. I send a silent apology winging its way to her.

"Plus," Annie says, "they *still* haven't shifted most of the debris from when that one skyscraper collapsed in Downtown. It'd take us hours just to get around it."

I roll the idea over in my head. "I don't know. I don't like the idea of staying on the river. Compton is *far*."

"Oh yeah. Like twenty miles. I'm not saying we have to walk it all, though. A car in the storm drain's probably too conspicuous – people notice that kind of stuff, even now, and we couldn't get one in here until we get to the paved part downriver anyway. But a couple of bikes might get us down there."

"I just—"

"Don't get me wrong, I think this whole thing is all kinds of messed up. But if we are really are gonna do this, then yeah, the river's the best chance we got."

I bend over, hands on my knees. Annie's right. And as much as she thinks I'm an idiot, she's probably the best person to have with me right now. I didn't think that way before, but . . .

"Listen, Nic," I say, picking up my thought from before Leo ran. "Thank you so much for coming. It . . . " I clear my throat. "I appreciate it. But you don't have to stick around. We can take him from here."

Nic wavers, chewing his lower lip, then nods.

"I'm gonna put you down for a sec, bud," he says to Leo. But when he tries to do so, Leo won't let him go.

"I don't wanna go if you're, if you're not here," the boy says, his voice muffled by Nic's shirt.

"Come on, my man." Nic says gently. Once again, he tries unsuccessfully to put him down.

Leo holds on even tighter. "*No-o-o-ooo.*"

There's an awkward moment where Nic has actually let go of him, but Leo is still hanging off his neck. Nic gives me a helpless look, and I just shake my head. I don't have the first clue what to do here.

"I don't want you to go." The despair in Leo's voice is unbelievable – the kind of thing you should never hear from a child. "If the Zigzag Man comes back, or if ... if ... " His voice dissolves into sobs. The whole day, everything he's been through, just spilling out of him.

Nic can do nothing but hold him, stroking his hair and telling him it's going to be OK. Even when it isn't.

I don't know what to do here. I can't *make* Nic stay – not after I gave him the OK to head on out. But if Leo won't move without him, then we're screwed. I can't drag the boy to Compton, and I don't know if we have time for me to sit around and argue with him.

Something I may have mentioned already: Nic's a decent dude. Whatever our issues, he's fundamentally a good person. So when he looks at us and says, "Guess I'm sticking around," I'm only a little bit surprised.

"I got some snacks in the car, I think," Nic continues. "Protein bars." He gets to his feet. "We should stick together though. In case the Zigzag guy comes back."

"What's a protein bar?" Leo says.

Nic winks at him. "Like a boring chocolate bar. Come on – let's get outta here."

TWENTY-ONE

Teagan

"I can feel the storm," Leo says.

It's the first words he's spoken since we started walking again. For half an hour now, we've been trudging in silence down the river. Nic and Leo in front – the boy won't move more than a few feet away from Nic. Me in the middle. Annie somewhere in the rear. Now, Leo has stopped walking, squinting up at the low-hanging, heavy clouds. It's around four o'clock.

"Well, that's not creepy at all," I mutter.

"We can see the clouds too, bud," Nic says.

"I mean like . . . " He hunts for the words. "It's like, talking to me."

I stare at him. "The clouds are talking to you."

"Yes." He gives me a solemn nod.

"Can you . . . ?" I hunt for the right words. "Can you control it? Control the lightning from here?"

"Um . . . I dunno. Maybe."

"How about we leave that one alone for now?" Nic claps him on the shoulder, keeps walking.

We weave through more groves of thick bamboo, pick our way between piles of trash and bushes so overgrown and interlocked that they require huge detours. I've completely lost track of where we are — I *think* we're in Elysian Valley, just south of Glendale, but for all I know we could be way past it.

I am somewhere north of tired. Between the meth come-down, the fight with the Legends and some jerk-off planting illusions in my brain, it's taking every ounce of effort I have just to keep walking.

If you'd found a way to become a cook, this would never have hap-pened. You'd be in a kitchen somewhere, probably paying your dues working in prep, debearding mussels or chopping cucumbers or cleaning grease traps or squeezing julienned potatoes to get the liquid out so the chef can make rösti which of course she'd let you taste and—

Right then, my right foot snags something, and I trip.

It happens in slow-motion. I actually see the ground rush-ing up to meet me. I have enough time to think that this is the time I go down for good — if I end up horizontal, I'm not getting up again.

Annie catches me, grabbing my arm in an iron grip. I wobble in place, the world swimming in front of me, a nice little shot of adrenaline zipping around my system.

Holy shit. I think I just fell asleep for a second there.

"Nice catch," I tell Annie.

She lets go, giving me a dark look before striding off.

"What?" I say, to her retreating back.

"Just be more careful."

"Yeah, well, it's been a long day."

I'm alongside her then, and I just catch her rolling her eyes.

Everybody's got their pet peeves. Mine are eye rolls. "Sorry, Annie, am I being a drag? My bad. I'll try not to pass out on you."

"OK," she says. Her even tone — like the kind you'd use on a crazy person — just stokes the fire.

"Hey, what the hell is your problem?" I say.

"I don't have a problem."

"Then why are you angry with me?"

"I'm not angry," she says, stepping very carefully over what looks like the remains of a fire, a charred pile of blackened coals, long since dead. An empty can lies wedged in the middle, like a buried artefact.

"Come on. Don't get me wrong, I owe you for the assist back there, but I didn't *ask* you to come get us."

"True. He did." She gestures at Nic, who is still walking with Leo.

"That's what I'm saying though. I know you think I can't handle myself—"

"You can't."

"Says you."

"You'll just get your ass killed."

That does it. "Annie, I can turn anything into a weapon. If somebody comes at me with a knife or a gun or a ... or a fucking two-by-four, I can shut that shit down. You've *seen* me do it. So stop pretending like I'm this delicate flower."

"Let's get one thing straight here." She says it loud enough that Nic and Leo turn around. "You can do whatever you want. I don't give a fuck. Get yourself hurt, killed, whatever. That's one thing. But here's what you can't seem to get through your thick skull – it *won't* just be you. It'll be me, Africa, Reggie. It'll be him." She points at Nic. "You think you're invincible. But you're not, and neither are the people around you. I don't want to have to be your collateral damage."

"I didn't ask for any of this." I all but hiss the words. "Not a single fucking second of it. That's what *you* can't seem to get through your *thick* skull."

It's like she doesn't hear me. "In one day – one freaking

day – you've got us all involved in a gunfight, kidnapped a little kid, and by the way, don't think I can't see that you're still high off your tits. Look at your pupils, man."

The line sounds weirdly familiar, and all at once, it comes to me. *Bad Boys II*. Martin Lawrence, high on ecstasy, Will Smith giving him shit and saying the exact same line. Martin guffawing, asking how the hell he can look at his own pupils, crossing his eyes. I get a sudden urge to say the same thing to Annie, let her chew on that for a bit.

This is . . . *insane*. Does she think I got high on purpose? That I *wanted* to keep going after our dust-up with the Legends?

"Woah, woah, what?" Nic says.

Annie half-laughs. "She ain't tell you? Homegirl here took a faceful of meth a few hours ago. She's still coming down."

The look on Nic's face isn't disbelief. It's worse. It's more like resignation – like he knew, but didn't have the energy to ask.

I turn my attention back to Annie. "I don't believe you. If it was up to me, I'd be working in a restaurant somewhere. I wouldn't even know you. So—"

"*Hey,*" Nic bellows.

He's got a good bellow. He's spent enough time in court, after all.

I'm expecting him to say something like *We don't have time for this.* He doesn't. Just looks between us, eyes flashing.

Next to him, Leo is staring daggers too. It's almost funny – like he's trying to copy Nic. Hell, maybe he is.

Annie spits something ugly in Spanish. She strides away from me, moving past Nic, putting distance between her and us.

I have a sudden urge to throw something at her. Even just something small. Give her a little reminder that actually, yes, I can handle myself . . .

Which she would probably use as evidence that I think I'm invincible. *Oh yeah, using your voodoo in public again, like nothing can happen.*

The comedown is making itself known again. The same yawning pit in my stomach, the aching pinch at the base of my skull. A couple of fun and exciting new symptoms too: the skin on my arms has started to prickle, and my tongue feels fat and dry, my mouth parched. It's stopped coming in waves now — it's become a constant presence, something I just have to ride out. No wonder people get addicted to meth. If living without it feels like this, then why *not* stay on it all the time? Where would I even get some, anyway? I might have taken down a meth lab this morning, but I don't actually know where to buy it on the street. I'd only need a tiny bit, a few grains maybe, just enough to stop feeling so goddamn awful all the time . . .

I grunt. There is no way — no way, ever — that I'm touching that shit again. I can't. I won't.

At least I'm not hallucinating any more. There are no flickering movements at the edge of my vision, no feeling that someone is walking up behind me. *Except for the vision of Jonas Schmidt you just had. Why settle for meth hallucinations when you can have the real thing, thanks to your friendly neighbourhood Zigzag Man?*

We're right alongside the river now, on a narrow path, maybe six feet, made of hardpacked, uneven dirt. On our left, the rushing water. On our right, more bamboo, thick and dark. There's a smell of rotting garbage somewhere, worming into my nostrils and squatting there.

Leo glances over his shoulder at me. "Ugh," I say, grinning, trying to force the bad vibes away. "Stinks right?"

"She got mad you." He points at Annie, a trudging figure fifty feet ahead of us. "Did you do something bad?"

I sigh. "She thinks I did."

"Are you gonna say sorry?"

"It's . . . Maybe. I dunno."

"She shouldn't be mad if you didn't do anything," Leo says, thoughtful. "Is *she* gonna say sorry?"

It's a few seconds before I answer. The anger and adrenaline has faded a little, enough to give me a bit of distance. And common sense. "She's just . . . she lost someone close to . . . well, she lost one of her friends. She isn't herself, so I don't wanna like, make her say sorry."

"Did he die?"

" . . . He did. Yeah."

"Oh." He thinks for a moment. "She must be sad."

I don't really know what to say to that. Nic has gone quiet, watching the two of us.

"How did he die?" Leo asks.

The question doesn't so much catch me off guard as sneak up behind me and put me in a chokehold. "Um. Well. I. He just—"

We almost walk smack into Annie.

She's come to a dead halt, just around a small bend in the river. Nic and I stop dead – he instinctively pulls Leo back, a hand on his shoulder.

"Annie, wh—?" I start to say.

She cuts me off, snapping up a clenched fist, not looking at me.

There are voices. *Angry* voices.

The narrow path continues alongside the river, the bamboo groves on the right. But there's a gap just ahead, a space between two of the groves. The voices – three men, it sounds like – are coming from inside the groves. One of them is shouting, fearful, panicked, telling someone to leave him alone. The *someone* in question snarls back, the words turned to mush by the thick bamboo and the running water.

Nic and I exchange a glance. *Well, that can't be good.*

Annie looks back at us. She's still pissed, but it's taken a backseat for now. She flicks her raised hand twice, gesturing us to move forward, past the groves. Then she puts a finger to her lips.

I'm not wild about leaving whoever's doing the shouting in a bind. But we don't know what's going on in there, and we are very much on the clock. I give Annie a nod. Nic is clearly on the same page, flashing her a thumbs-up.

"We gotta help," Leo hisses.

"Not this time," Nic whispers back.

"But they're in trouble!"

"No. We don't know who they are. We have to keep going."

He subsides, still casting nervous glances at the source of the sound.

We move in single file now, Annie in front, then Nic and Leo, with me bringing up the rear. Inside the groves, the man who wanted to be left alone is angrier now, swearing at who-ever's trying to mess with him. And there's another sound, too: the low growl of a dog.

As I reach the gap in the bamboo, there's a *thud*, and the man cries out.

"They're hurting him," Leo whispers, moving like he's ready to step off the path towards the groves. Nic darts towards him, dropping into a crouch, urgently whispering at him to leave it.

I really wish he wasn't right. I'm no fan of leaving people in the shit, but there are times to play hero, and now is not one of them. It sticks in my throat, but there it is.

I come up behind Leo, hustling him along. Annie is already urging us to hurry, beckoning us from further down the path.

There's another thud – and a *yelp*, the sound of an animal in pain. A small dog skids into view, tumbling, as if thrown.

"Doggy!" Leo yells.

The voices stop abruptly.

Oh, shit.

TWENTY-TWO

Teagan

Leo doesn't get to run off this time. Nic takes care of that. He jumps in front of the kid, grabbing his shoulders.

Just in time for one of the attackers to step into the path.

He's built like a fire hydrant, short and stocky, and the bright red hoodie he's wearing doesn't help. His body might be muscular, but his face is pudgy, his head topped with a grey, flat-brimmed New Era fitted. He reminds me of a douchebag tech bro – someone marketing smart coffee cups or an app-powered juicer.

If he's surprised to see three people and a little kid walking down the river, he gives no sign. "Nothing going on here," he says loudly, an annoying smirk on his face.

The dog scrambles to its feet next to him. It's a little Jack Russell, I think – one that looks like it's been living in a dumpster. Mangy fur, ribs showing. Not quite feral, but on its way there.

The dog is limping slightly, but it still manages to snarl at the man. He responds by stepping on it – not hard enough to hurt, but enough to pin the dog to the dirt.

"Help!" It's the voice of whoever the douchebag was hassling, and this time, he sounds terrified. "Help me!"

Leo wrenches out of Nic's grip.

"Leo, no!" Nic lunges for him, just missing. Leo does stop, however, coming to a halt a few feet from the man built like a fire hydrant. His tiny shoulders tremble with rage.

Fire Hydrant's smirk grows wider. "Oh, you like dogs, dude? You can have this one if you want." He lifts the foot pinning the Jack Russell. Before the dog can get up, he plants his boot on its side and shoves. It skids towards Leo in a mad scramble, yapping, trying and failing to get its feet underneath it.

As that happens, a second man stumbles out from behind a dense cluster of bamboo stalks. He's wearing a suit, his tie yanked down. He's in his late fifties, with a pinched, lined face – one with a massive shiner below his right eye. He stumbles, catches himself – only to go down when a second man steps into view and gives him a good shove.

This happy asshole is as tall and thin as his buddy is stocky. He wears a ratty white T over jeans, and in his hand, there's the glint of a knife. Not that I need a reflection to see it; my PK picks it up just fine.

The dog is on its feet now, barking hysterically, but too terrified to rush the two men. Leo balls his tiny hands into fists.

"Leo, come on," Nic says.

"Hey, Lars," says the guy in the white T. "What we got going on here?"

Lars – Fire Hydrant – scratches his jaw. "Just some tourists. Move the fuck on, tourists."

"I'll zap you!" Leo yells at him. He lurches forward, dropping to his knees and putting his hands on the ground, his face twisted in concentration. Problem is, he still has the wiggles – his hand is twitching like crazy. So, as you'd expect, absolutely nothing happens.

"Uh, OK," says Lars.

With a strangled howl, Leo leaps up, and bolts towards them. Before we can do anything, he leapfrogs the Jack Russell, and slams into Lars, planting his hands on the man's thigh. He must have the tiniest bit of juice now, because Lars jerks, jittering backwards and clapping his hands to the spot Leo tagged. "Ah! Shit. What the hell?"

The thin man reaches over and give the kid a massive shove. Leo goes sprawling, thudding into the dirt.

Welp. Guess we're involved now.

I step forward, a serene smile on my face. "Hi. I'm Teagan."

Lars grins right back. "Hey, little girl."

"Oh, we're doing the *little girl* thing. Cool. Cool, cool, cool."

"Teagan," Annie growls. She steps in front of me, getting between me and Lars. The dog is going *nuts*.

Suit-and-tie makes a move. He tries to shove Lars' partner, but the guy just bats him away, reaching down for the knife. Which I grab hold of with my PK and jerk it out of his hand.

"The fuck?" he says, as it clatters to the ground

Annie and Nic are both staring at me in horror.

I twitch the knife where it lies on the ground. Little movements, nothing crazy. Just when the dude's fingers touch the knife. He probably thinks something is going on – scratch that, he *definitely* thinks something weird is going on – but to everybody not in the Teagan Circle of Friendship and Awesomeness, it just looks like he has butterfingers.

"Hell is wrong with you?" Lars steps backwards, reaching down for the skittering knife.

"Problem?" I say, as I skitter the knife out of the man's grip once again. He actually hesitates before going for it, like it's a snake that may or may not be poisonous. His eyes are huge, the confusion and horror written on his face.

Leo snaps that amazing smile at me. This time, I snap one right back.

Lars spins, as if looking for an attacker. His piggy little eyes settle on me, and he charges.

I raise an eyebrow. I can't grab his Timbs – they're rubber and suede, organic material, which is a little beyond me right now. What I *can* grab are the metal shoelace eyelets. Grab them, yank them backwards. Which means dear old Lars goes ass over tits. He *whuffs*, the air knocked out of his lungs, rolling over and curling into a foetal position.

All at once, the thin man decides he's had enough. He stops going for the knife, straightens up, bolts towards us. He leapfrogs the trembling Lars, shoving past Nic, heading back down the path the way we came. The dog sends a few yaps at his retreating back, as if telling him that he'd *better* run.

I give Lars a shove with my foot, just like he did the dog. He stumbles, nearly falls over as he staggers between Nic and Annie to the river. Then he turns, steadies himself.

"We just wanted some food!" he yells, his voice an octave higher than before. "We're hungry, man."

There's a strangled howl from behind us. The man in the suit rushes into view, holding the knife. He takes two big strides, like a long jumper. Then, using his whole body, he hurls the knife at Lars.

It misses – of course it misses; do you know how hard it is to throw a knife properly? – and splashes into the river. Lars takes off running, vanishing into the darkness.

For a second, all is still and calm. No sound but the man in the suit's ragged breathing, and the soft rush of the LA River.

"Unbelievable." Annie puts her hands over her face.

Leo slowly gets to his feet. His hand is twitching again. "That was *awesome!*"

"Hold up, sorry, what exactly just happened here?" Nic says.
Leo points at me. "She moved stuff."

The dog decides it wants in on this conversation, and starts
barking, bouncing around our feet.

"Unbelievable," Annie says again. Drawing the word out
as she looks me. "You just can't control yourself, can you?"

"I controlled things just fine, thank you. That's why we're
still breathing."

The man in the suit clears his throat. It's a loud sound,
almost a smoker's cough, and it cuts through the conversation.
Only the dog refuses to stop, yapping and barking.

"I don't suppose," the man says, "that any of you folks would
like a cup of coffee?"

TWENTY-THREE

Teagan

The man's name is Grant. His dog is called Bradley Cooper. While Grant makes us coffee, Bradley Cooper crawls into Leo's lap for a cuddle.

How does Grant make us coffee? Easy. His microwave.

There is an actual, full-size microwave sitting on the ground in the middle of the bamboo grove, wired directly into a power line above us. The connection is such a ghetto mess of cables and resistors and transformers – or whatever the hell they're called – that I can't make head or tail of it. I debate whether or not to ask Leo if it's actually safe, but just because he can control electricity doesn't mean he'll be able to give me an answer. Ask him what a transformer is, and he'll probably start talking about robot cars.

Not that I care. Because I have coffee, bitches. It might be instant coffee from a can, but it is the single greatest cup of coffee I have ever had.

Grant hasn't stopped talking since we saved him. I was worried he was going to demand to know exactly *how* Leo and I did that, but he just breezed right past it. He ushered us into his little spot in the bamboo, jabbering away, like he hasn't spoken to a human being in years.

"You have to be so careful on the river these days," he's saying now, gesticulating with a hand smeared with grime. There's a wedding ring on one finger, but no sign of a partner anywhere. "This isn't the first time Bradley and I have run into trouble. This was a bad one, though, not like the last time I got jumped. That one was drunk, he could barely take two steps without falling over. I pretty much *walked* away from him. This time though? Oh man ... let's just say I'm glad you folks showed up."

I just sip my coffee and let his chatter wash over me. Mostly what I'm doing is marvelling at his setup. It's not just the microwave. Grant's carved himself a little home out of the bamboo, occupying an empty spot between the two groves. It's all but invisible from the sloped side and the land above it, and there's only one entrance from the river side. It's not exactly what you'd call roomy though, especially with Grant's possessions: three duffel bags of clothes, a surprisingly neat sleeping bag and mat, bottles of water. And the microwave, of course.

Nic and I sit on upturned plastic crates, drinking our coffee. Annie leans up against one of the bamboo trunks, staring at nothing. She protested hard when Grant insisted on making us coffee, but he wouldn't take no for an answer. Neither would I to be honest.

"Anyway, you're welcome to stay as long as you like," Grant says. "There's not all that much space, I know, but I'm sure we could work it out if you folks wanted to catch a few Zs."

Right then, there's another rumble of thunder from above. There's a little bit of sunlight still – the sun has dropped lower in the sky, escaping the growing cloud cover as it sinks towards the horizon.

He winces. "OK, all right, it might be a little too wet to

sleep out in the open. Doesn't rain much here – well, I'm sure you folks know that, you're Angelenos, I can tell – but when it does, hoo boy. When that happens, I usually go to the big camp downriver, under the freeway."

It's the one the cop from before was talking about. I've never been there, but I've seen it on the news a few times. One of the big freeway junctions over the storm drain was really unstable after the quake, so the government put a whole bunch of scaffolding and supports in. Then there were lawsuits and committee hearings and God knows what else, because that's how the government do, and the propped-up freeways just sat there.

Combine that with a million people who have lost their houses and their jobs, and you get a gigantic, impromptu homeless camp. Why yes: it *is* an incredibly stupid idea to set up a massive camp in the middle of the storm drain, right in the path of any floods. There have been an endless number of hot takes and long reads online, exploring why these people have actually made camp in such an unstable place. I'll be honest: I'm a little hazy on the reasons. From what I can tell, it's because they have nowhere else to go, although I have no idea how true that really is.

"How long have you been out here?" Nic asks.

The question seems to catch Grant off guard. "Me? Oh, wow. Since the Big One, at least."

"What's the Big One?" Leo asks. He's sitting cross-legged on the ground, rubbing Bradley Cooper's belly.

"He's not from around here," I explain.

"Oh, wow, OK." Grant's smile is awkward – probably because he wants to ask *why* we're hanging around with a kid who isn't from around here. "Sorry, little fella. I meant the quake. Two months ago? Three? I'll be honest, I lost track of time . . ."

In the silence that follows, Annie pushes off the bamboo, gives us a pointed look. "We should get going."

Grant leaps to his feet. "No, no, no, please, you certainly aren't imposing. Are you sure I can't make you any coffee? I might even have a teabag or two if—"

"I'm fine, thank you," says Annie, with exaggerated politeness.

"We'll head out after we're finished drinking ours," I tell her. Actually, I think I'll ask Grant for a second. Maybe a third. Instant or not, this shit is *good*.

Nic's eyes land on the microwave, and he chuckles. "How did you even . . . ?"

"The microwave?" He winks. He actually winks. "Little bit of elbow grease and a prayer. Even insulated the wires properly, in case it gets wet." He points to the darkening clouds.

"For real, though. How?"

"I'm an electrical engineer. Well, I was. I used to work on traction substations – you know, for rail networks." He sighs. "But, after the Big One, a bunch of us got laid off. Trains ain't really running any more. I tried to get work, but you know how it is." He brightens. "Anyway, if you can find your way around a transformer, it's pretty easy to hook up a microwave. Beats eating cold meals all day, I'll tell you that. I actually stole it after my landlord kicked me out." His mouth twists in a strange smile. "I almost didn't, but . . . well, I wasn't thinking straight."

" . . . I'm sorry," Nic says.

"What? No, don't be! God no, no no no. I'm doing just fine."

"You were literally getting robbed when we came by," I say.

His smile falters. "Anyway, it's not so bad," he says, utterly ignoring my point. "I actually had a job interview today." He plucks at his suit lapel.

"Right on," Nic says. "For an engineer position?"

"Yes. Well, kind of. It's more of a contract thing. Company that runs trash compactors needs a few of their units looked at." He barks another laugh, this one sounding just a little more forced than before. "Lots of trash after the Big One, as I'm sure you can imagine!"

My belly rumbles. God, when did I last have any food? Howlin' Ray's, that's when, and I puked that up back at the storage unit.

"Was that your stomach?" Grant says, his mouth twisted in a smile.

" . . . No?"

"Like hell. They heard that from space. God, you must think I'm so rude, not offering you folks anything to eat. I should have mentioned that – I'm almost out myself, actually. I'd just eaten dinner when those two thugs arrived. I don't think they believed me when I told them. Lots of hungry people around these days." He leaps up, roots around in one of the duffels, comes up with a sad-looking bag of ramen noodles. "This is all I've got left, I'm afraid. I'd be happy to cook it up for you, if you want?"

He holds the bag out to me, but I shake my head. I don't care how hungry I am, I am *not* stealing a homeless dude's last meal.

"What are you gonna do when you run out of food?" Leo says, scratching Bradley Cooper's belly.

"Excellent question. Truth be told, young man, I think I need to move on anyway. Like I said, tonight wasn't the first time I've been robbed – or nearly robbed, I suppose."

With one more questioning glance at me – *you sure?* – he stows the ramen in his bag. I close my eyes, telling my growling stomach to quit it. The food problem is one I've been ignoring, but pretty soon, it's going to become too big to do so. It's not just me – it's Leo, too. He must be running on empty – although give him this, he hasn't complained yet. I'm kind of impressed with him, actually.

If all this had happened before the quake, I would have suggested we go find a restaurant or a diner. Hell, a Starbucks. That's not really an option right now. It's not just that we'd risk being spotted on surveillance cameras – it's that we could burn literal hours trying to find a working kitchen. They're mighty thin on the ground these days. Sure, maybe we get lucky – find a convenience store that's still open or something – but even then, we'd spend a while hunting for it.

"I'll head to that camp I mentioned," Grant says, as if he knows what I'm thinking. "Lots of people there now. Safety in numbers and all that."

"What about your stuff?" Leo asks.

Grant says nothing for a few moments, busying himself with the bag. "I used to do a fair bit of hiking – walked Runyon Canyon all the time. I don't mind hefting a bag or two. I'll just take what I need."

"You gonna put a microwave on your back?" Nic asks.

His reply is a weary smile. "I'll leave that for other people to use. I don't think anybody's stupid enough to try unhook it from the power line, after all. Maybe someone else can get a cooked meal or two out of it."

"We could come with you," I say. "We're kind of heading down the river too."

"Oh, you're welcome to join Bradley and me, for sure. But remember, I just ate. It's hours of walking, and I'll be doing it on a full stomach. You sure I can't give you some—?"

"Positive. Thank you though."

He taps his chin. "Come to think of it, you folks might want to check out the FEMA outpost."

"What FEMA outpost?" Nic says.

"What's a FEMA?" Leo asks.

"Federal Emergency Management Agency," Annie says absently. She keeps looking back towards the water, arms folded tight across her chest. "They're the ones who ..."

She stops. Goes dead still.

And I think I know why.

"Yeah, they've still got an operation in LA," Grant is saying. "Soup kitchen, water point, basic clinic. You might have to wait a while – it gets pretty crowded – and they definitely don't let you stay, or else I'd never have been on the river at all. But it's a lot closer than the camp I'm going to, probably no more than a forty-minute walk from here."

"Where?" I ask. I already know what he's going to say.

"Dodger Stadium." He points. "It's up a hill or two, but I'm pretty sure you can get there all right. You can definitely handle yourselves if there's trouble!"

Annie says nothing, staring out at the rushing water, chewing her lip. Nic senses the change, sends a questioning glance my way.

Dodger Stadium. Somewhere I hoped I'd never have to go back to.

The place where Paul died.

TWENTY-FOUR

Reggie

And with one phone call, Reggie's world comes crashing down.

"We think we've got it," Moira says. "We're going to make a fix here, then reboot the entire system from our end to reset the encryption. That should take care of the issue, and should bring the video and audio links back online. I want your team ready to give me a full update."

It takes a lot of effort for Reggie to respond. "Copy."

Moira ends the call without another word.

All at once, Reggie doesn't want to be in the office. Or even in the building. She wants to be far, far away from here, somewhere she can deal with everything that's happened tonight. Where she can actually make a good decision, for once: an *informed* decision. She actually goes as far as to move her hand towards the chair's joystick, meaning to push back from the monitors, turn her country ass around and *go*.

But she has never run away in her life, not ever, and she sure as hell isn't going to start now.

Isn't that why you told the lie in the first place? Running away is what you want.

Reggie shuts down that thought before it can get going.

She's got to deal with this. She can't do anything about Annie – that connection is still down, and won't be back online until Tanner reboots the system. But at the very least, she can get Africa onside.

She calls him on the comms. "Listen very carefully—"

He cuts her off. "I am on the other side of the number 5 freeway. I cannot do this by myself, Reggie – there is too much ground. Where is Annie now? I did not hear her say anything."

"Africa, Moira doesn't know."

"What?"

"About Teagan. I . . . She doesn't know Teagan is missing."

"*What?*"

There is no other choice here. No way out of this particular hole Reggie has dug for herself. This is the problem with lies. You can't just tell them and be done. You have to keep them alive, keep feeding them, so they don't feed on you. And the problem with *that* is the myriad smaller lies that spring up to keep the big one alive.

Reggie is still coming to grips with why she lied in the first place. Still trying to wrap her head around it. There is a chance she can still salvage this, but not if Moira talks to Africa.

"I told her Teagan was still in the building," she says, keeping her tone nice and even. "That we hadn't found anything."

Silence. Then Africa says, "I do not understand."

"She thinks Teagan—"

"You told her a lie?"

"I didn't have a choice. I wanted to give us time to *find* Teagan."

"So she does not know. This is bad, Reggie. This is very bad. We cannot leave her in the dark like this, *yaaw*? Why you tell me now, anyway?"

Reggie hisses a frustrated breath. "They figured out how to fix the system. All video feeds will be back online soon."

Another long silence as he digests this. For Reggie, it's the longest silence of her life. At any moment, there's going to be a connection request from Moira, a bright little notification on her screen.

After a few seconds, Africa simply says, "Mm."

"Africa, listen to me. You *cannot* tell Moira about Teagan. If she thinks the girl's gone AWOL, then all hell will rain down."

"Mmmm-mm-mm." She can picture him now. Head slowly shaking, lips pursed, finger up to his ear – something both she and Annie have told him to stop doing multiple times.

If he rolls on me, it's over.

And she is not ready to leave. She is not ready to make the leap into the dark just yet.

"It is a very bad thing you have done," Africa says slowly.

"I'm aware."

"I do not understand why. We have to tell her the truth—"

"No! No. I'm going to handle this, but I need you to help me. We are going to find Teagan, and Annie, and we're going to figure it all out."

"Do not ask me to do this, Reggie."

She should have seen this coming. Africa idolises Moira Tanner, so asking him to lie to her, especially when he's been lied to himself . . .

Moira's *Join* request blinks up on her screen.

She opens her mouth to plead with Africa, but finds she has no idea what to say. She'd just be repeating herself.

Her mind races. Moira's rebooted the system, which means the issues with Annie's system should be fixed, too. Reggie quickly brings her feed up on screen – she's going to have to do this fast, get Annie on the same page.

Except: Annie's feed is still dark. There's nothing there. No audio, no video.

"Oh, hell," Reggie murmurs. For a long moment, she doesn't move. She has lost control of this situation, dug a hole far too deep to climb out of.

And she has no idea what to do next.

As if in a dream, she accepts the *Join* request. There's nothing else to do.

"Tanner here. Mr Kouamé, report."

No answer.

"Mr Kouamé." Tanner sounds dangerous. "I said, report. Ms McCormick, are we *still* having technical—?"

"We find nothing in the building, Mrs Tanner," Africa says in a flat voice.

For a second, Reggie is sure she's misheard.

"It is not electrified any more," Africa continues. "Teagan and Annie and me, we are now hunting in Glendale."

Reggie's breath releases in a choked gasp. Tanner, fortunately, doesn't appear to have heard it. "What's your strategy?" the woman snaps.

Reggie steps in, amazed at how smooth she sounds. "We're going street by street. Africa's moving south, Teagan north."

"That's far too much ground to cover."

"We know. Right now, I've got Annie helping the LAPD work the scene – we may be able to find forensic evidence that will point us in the right direction." She keeps her voice even, certain that this is the lie that will get her caught – the idea of Annie working with the LAPD is laughable. "If necessary, we can lean on the police to help coordinate the search."

"I expected results by now," Tanner says, but there's no venom in her words – just ragged exhaustion. "If the situation has expanded beyond the original scene, then some real-time drone imagery might be helpful. I'll coordinate it from here, and I'll lean on the police department to provide some helicopter support. Ms Frost, what's your status?"

Africa steps in. "We are having issues with the connection, for both her and Annie."

Tanner's fury threatens to boil over. "I see," she says, icy calm. "Ms McCormick: is this a result of the intrusion?"

"I don't believe so." Reggie's mouth is bone dry. "We think their comms may have been affected by . . . well, by whatever is behind this electricity business."

"Mr Kouamé," Tanner says. "Keep searching. You're in charge on the ground. Let's lock this down."

"Ya, Mrs Tanner."

"Ms McCormick, a word please."

Here it comes. Reggie mutes Africa's connection, tries to keep her voice steady. "Yes?"

Moira sighs.

It's not a sigh of exasperation, or anger. It's the sigh of someone who has gone beyond exhaustion.

"How are you holding up?" Moira asks.

Reggie pauses, not sure how to respond. She can count the number of times Moira Tanner has expressed interest in her well-being without even troubling the double digits.

"As well as could be expected," she says.

"That's good." Another sigh. "I owe you an apology."

" . . . OK?"

"After Mr Marino died, I knew we'd have to replace him." The words come haltingly, as if she's not sure how to arrange them. "And over the past few months, I've had to convince my superiors again and again of China Shop's usefulness. That's Washington for you. Results don't matter, only favours."

"And then there was the search for this ... School. We've been digging and digging, and getting nowhere. So I didn't make replacing Mr Marino as much of a priority as I should have. And now we have another situation, a situation in which his input and logistical expertise – or that of someone like him – would have been invaluable."

Reggie says nothing.

"I know that a lot is being asked of you right now," Moira says. "But, Reggie: whatever I said before, you're doing a fine job. I want you to continue quarterbacking this. We will provide support and information from here as we can."

Moira has called Reggie by her first name before – they were colleagues in Serbia, after all – but not for years. Twenty years now – Christ, has it really been that long? It has, of course it has, because almost nobody knows Moira Tanner better than Reggie, and right now, Moira Tanner is scared.

That, more than anything, drops the bottom out of Reggie's stomach. Moira is scared, she is trusting Reggie to keep this together ... and Reggie has been lying to her.

"Moira," she says. "I can't find any evidence of intrusion on the network. The comms issues—"

"I know. We don't always get to operate in perfect conditions. I wouldn't trust them if they came along. Just do what you can, and so will we. That's all we have."

Somehow, Reggie manages to speak. "Copy that."

"Leave this line open for now. Tanner out."

Reggie's shoulders sag. She stares down at her hands, at the markings on the skin. Her fingers barely shake at all. *I am in over my head*, she thinks. *I am drowning.*

The thought has an elegance to it, a terrifying simplicity.

She picks up her phone, briefly mutes her comms connection, so she can dictate a text message to Africa without Tanner hearing. "Thank you," she says, the words appearing on her phone screen, the message sending automatically as she pauses.

The reply takes longer to arrive than she would have expected. *We must find them now.*

Reggie starts to dictate another message, wanting to let him know how much she appreciates it, but then a second text arrives from him. As she reads it, her mouth falls open.

I think I know where they are going.

TWENTY-FIVE

Teagan

Grant walks with us as far as the 110 freeway bridge, then points us up a steep rise to the west.

"Stadium's maybe twenty minutes up that hill," he says. He's got one of the duffels on his back, his frame bowed from the weight. He's holding two more, one in either hand, and he utterly refused Nic's offer to help carry it. "FEMA's a twenty-four-hour operation, so you don't have to worry about closing time or anything."

"Thanks," I say, wishing I could inject a little more enthusiasm into my voice. It's a lot chillier now, although there's still no rain. Winter in Los Angeles is still pretty warm most of the time, but it can get down to the forties and thirties sometimes.

Bradley Cooper barks, dancing around Leo's feet. The kid crouches to scratch him, and the dog rolls onto his back for a belly rub. Problem is, he rolls right into a muddy puddle that smells like shit. May, in fact, be actual shit.

"Gross," Leo grins.

"Bradley, no!" Grant pulls the dog away, laughing.

"Thanks," Nic says, holding out a hand. "Appreciate the help, bro."

"Think nothing of it." Grant shakes. "I'm the one who owes *you*. I'm just sorry I couldn't feed you."

"The coffee was enough," I tell him. "Hey – you're not worried about those guys coming after you? The ones from before?"

"A little, yeah. But they headed off upriver, so if they turn back I've got a head start, if nothing else."

His gaze lands on Annie. She's staring up at the horizon, jaw set. She hasn't said a word since we left Grant's camp.

"I hope you folks find what you're looking for," Grant says. He looks from Annie to Leo, a slightly worried expression on his face.

"We're gonna find my dad," Leo says.

Grant nods. "Well, I'm sure he's trying to find you, too, young sir. Don't you worry. And you're in good hands with your friends.

He shakes my hand, gives Annie a friendly nod and vanishes into the darkness.

And of course, it's not twenty minutes up the hill. It's a good hour. The ground is a mess, uneven and cracked, with downed trees and piles of trash everywhere. And the hill is a *lot* steeper than it looked from the river. It's dusk now, and the low light makes it tough going. I have to use Leo's cellphone flashlight to show us the way.

Leo's nerve issues have almost completely gone. Chasing off the men trying to mug Grant – and getting to play with Bradley Cooper – seems to have given him a little more energy. He keeps moving too far ahead, scrambling over fallen trees and vanishing into dips in the hillside. Nic has to call him back more than once.

Annie is lagging, falling behind. Nic notices, is on the verge of calling back to her, but stops when I put a hand on his shoulder. "This is where Paul . . ." I say. "Where he . . . you know."

"For real? Here?"

"Well, around here. Up near the stadium."

Mercifully, our path doesn't take us past the place where we first fought Matthew Schenke. An uncomfortable silence still settles over us, though, one that has nothing to do with exhaustion. Leo is the only one who doesn't appear to notice, bounding across the hillside, urging us to hurry. I just focus on putting one foot in front of the other, telling my growling stomach to calm the fuck down.

We cross through a small neighbourhood, bounded on both sides by wilderness. Many of the houses are ruins, and those that are still upright are dark and silent. Beyond the houses, there's a freeway, also empty. You know how strange it is to see a Los Angeles freeway completely empty of traffic? It's like walking on an alien planet.

I get jumpier the closer we get to the stadium. If I was the Zigzag Man, this is where I'd strike. I'm constantly checking in with my PK, checking if there's anybody approaching. Alert for any freaky false positives my mind throws out, thanks to the meth.

Leo is still in view, about thirty feet ahead of us. "Do you think they'll have cheeseburgers?"

"Let's hope so," Nic says.

"Maybe my dad'll be there too. Come on!"

The last time I was at the stadium, it felt like everybody and their dog was trying to get inside. The crush of people outside the entrance tunnels was insane. They've left their mark. Windblown trash covers the surface of the parking lot, potato chip wrappers and coffee cups and plastic water bottles — so many plastic water bottles. There are more military vehicles here than last time, troop carriers and flatbed trucks and Humvees. A few National Guard soldiers standing around, looking bored. They glance at us as we approach, and I'm suddenly sure they're going to order us to stop, that they know who we are and who Leo is.

But their expressions don't change. We're just another group of people looking for food. Fine by me. Right now, anonymity is what I want.

Nic asks one of the troops where we should go. He's a youngish guy wearing wraparound sunglasses, despite the fact that it's, you know, night. "Head through Tunnel K," he says, waving in the general direction of the stadium.

We're halfway across the parking lot before I think to check for Annie. She's stopped dead a little way from the soldier we spoke to. Her hands are jammed deep in her pockets, head down, as if she's thinking hard.

I'm prepared for her to be behind us, but I'm not prepared for her to be *this* far behind. I jog back to her, telling Nic and Leo I'll catch up.

"Annie?"

She gives a quick shake of her head, still not looking at me.

I take a deep breath. "Look, I get it. Paul was—"

"Can't do it."

I thought there'd be a shouting match. Honestly? I could have handled that. It's nothing I haven't gotten from her before. What I didn't expect was the hopelessness in her voice. Like she's had the wind knocked out of her.

"We're not gonna be here long. We're just gonna get food and go. We won't even go near where Paul . . ."

Another shake of the head. She's actually trembling, like the temperature's dropped.

"I don't want to," she says.

I'm about to argue with her, tell her to pull it together. But something about the way she says it — carefully enunciating each syllable, as if each word is a fragile egg that might crack from the slightest pressure — stops me.

Annie shakes her head again. "I thought I could do it, but I can't."

"OK," I hear myself say, even though I don't exactly know what I'm agreeing to. Is she going to stay here? Or—?

"I'll meet you back down at the river," she says. "At the bridge from before. The one you went crazy on."

"Wait, what? The Main Street Bridge? It's here?"

"Nearby, yeah." She clears her throat. She still hasn't looked at me, is still carefully stepping over each word. "Little way south. You can't miss it."

"Sure. Just look for the bridge that's completely destroyed."

Annie doesn't even respond to the joke — which, now that I've heard myself say it, is sort of a relief. She leaves without another word, heading back the way we came.

I rejoin Nic and Leo, tell them where Annie plans to meet us. "Is that a good idea?" Nic asks.

"It's a terrible idea, but *you* go make her come with us."

"Dude." He spreads his hands, gives me a pointed look.

"Fine, sorry, it's been a long day. I'll try to rein myself in."

"Amazing," he says. "You use sarcasm even while you're promising me you won't use sarcasm. It's not helpful, man."

"*Whatever.* Can we get some food? Please?"

God, *this* is why I don't hang out with him any more. Having your deficiencies and fuck-ups pointed out to you again and again gets mighty tiresome after a while.

We make our way across the parking lot in silence. I was expecting more vehicles and people closer to the stadium, but there are actually fewer — as if nobody wants to get too close.

It's only when we finally spot Tunnel K — an easy job, thanks to the giant white K printed on the wall above it — that we actually see a larger group of people. Maybe ten or twenty of them, huddled in a loose line, waiting for the soldiers to wave them in. My stomach growls again, and I have to force myself not to start thinking of my favourite foods. I'm pretty sure the only thing they've got inside are cheese sandwiches and bottled water, but fuck it, I'll take it.

"Are you guys in love?" Leo says.

I nearly trip over my feet. "I'm sorry, what?"

"No," Nic says, not looking me. "We aren't in love."

"Are you sure? Cos—"

"Hold up," Nic says, pointing. "Isn't that . . . ?"

He's talking to me, not Leo. And as I follow his finger, my stomach drops three inches.

We're maybe fifty feet from the line, in an open stretch of parking lot. The person Nic is pointing at is marching out of the shadows of the stadium wall, heading right towards us. Seven feet tall, fists like ham hocks. FBI windbreaker open, snapping in the breeze.

Africa.

TWENTY-SIX

Teagan

Under the circumstances – a government agent kidnapping a child with abilities and going on the run from her secret agent crew – you'd think a little discretion would be called for.

But this is Africa we're talking about.

"You think you can run from *me*?" he bellows.

The walls of the stadium shake. Car alarms go off. All the birds in a ten-mile radius shoot skyward with a panicked squawk. And every single person in the line, every National Guard soldier, *all of them* turn to stare at us.

Africa doesn't notice. "Why you do this? Huh? You run from me, run from Reggie. Mrs Tanner not know where anybody is." He apparently decides that English isn't going to cut it, because his words dissolve into a chaotic mix of French and Wolof.

How the hell is he here? How did he know where to find us?

"Hey." Nic steps into Africa's path, patting the air with raised hands. "How about we go talk somewhere?"

Africa blinks, as if noticing Nic for the first time. "What you doing here? Teggan – why is Nic . . . ?"

He trails off as his eyes focus on Leo. The boy stares back at him in horror.

"Who is he?" Africa jabs a finger at Leo. "Who is this boy?"

"My name is Leo Nguyen and I am four and my dad's name is Clarence and his number is—"

"My man." Nic puts a hand on Africa's shoulder. "Let's just calm down for a second."

"Everything OK here?" It's the National Guard soldier from before, the one with the ridiculous wraparound sunnies. He's got a twang to his accent that I hadn't noticed until now – Oklahoma, maybe, or Nebraska. Somewhere flat and empty. He's got the kind of pale, freckly skin that probably turns lobster red after about five seconds of sunlight.

Africa rounds on him. "No! Nothing is OK! And is even worse now that you are sticking your nose in—"

I squeeze between Africa and the soldier. "We're totally fine here. Sorry about that – just a little friendly argument, that's all."

The soldier looks dubious. "Keep it on the down-low, all right?" He gestures to the line of people, most of whom are goggling at us. "Lotta scared folks here already without you going off half-cocked."

"Don't you tell me half-cock, you bloody *toubab*."

"Africa!" I hiss.

The soldier gives us another long, suspicious look, but moves away. Leo has shuffled behind Nic, gripping his hand tight.

"Explain to me," Africa says. "Now. Why you run? And *who is this boy*?"

And as he says it, Leo's identity falls into place. He actually takes a step back.

I close my eyes. No point denying it. "Yeah."

"Teggan . . ."

"Yeah. He's . . . he has abilities."

He stares at me. "Teggan, my comms system is muted now. I mute it as soon as I see you, because Mrs Tanner is listening. My camera is still working –" he taps his chest, and my heart climbs into my throat "– but I have put it on my shirt, here, behind the jacket. For a little while, they can think it might be a mistake, *yaaw*? Like I do it by accident. But I know I have to give you chance to explain before I tell her and Reggie that I find you. We do not have much time, so please, tell me what is going on."

Africa was homeless when I first met him. I can still see him hanging out in Skid Row: cutting through the crowd in front of the LA Mission, his clothes a mismatched riot of colour, a man with a thousand connections and a million tall stories. Someone who life had kicked in the teeth more than once, and whose personality was a reaction to a world that didn't seem to want him very much.

Moira Tanner brought him into China Shop by threatening him. That's what she does – she gets people to act against their own self-interest. I don't know what the threat was, whether it was arrest, deportation, exposing whatever secrets he has. But I bet not even she predicted just how much he'd throw himself into the role, embrace the weird realities of working for the government. He's fallen in love with this job. The idea of doing what I did – of sabotaging an active mission, jeopardising this incredible opportunity – must be utterly insane to him.

He's led a very weird life. But I think China Shop was the first time he realised that all of his experiences, all his stories – the made-up ones, and the real ones – can't compare to what the world is *really* like. It sobered him up. Made him more serious. And I don't think I fully understood that until now.

"It's . . ." I lick my lips, trying to get my words in some sort of coherent order. "We can't let Tanner have him. You get that, right? He'll land up in Waco, or somewhere worse."

"We can *help* him."

"No, dude, listen. Please. This is a bad idea. Tanner won't help him. She'll use him. You know that."

Behind me, Leo turns to Nic, his voice fearful. "What does that mean?"

"All of us," Africa says slowly. "All of China Shop Movers. You, me, Annie, Reggie and Mrs Tanner as well. Paul, when he was still here. We all work together for the same goal. And I know you sometimes do crazy things, but I always think, she is still part of the team, and she will do what is right." He gestures at Leo. "What is right about stealing a young boy? About going behind our backs? And you—" He points at Nic. "You help her! I know you are aware of her *dëma* powers, you know what we do, so why—?"

"She didn't steal me." Leo finds a tiny grain of courage, stepping out from behind Nic's legs. "Leave us alone or . . . or I'll zap you."

"Nobody's zapping anybody," I say, holding my hands out. I can *feel* the crowd looking at us, as well as the soldier, still watching us from near a parked Humvee.

Africa crouches down, which still makes him about two feet taller than Leo. "Why don't you come with me, huh? I work with the government. We can keep you safe." The kid stares back at him in horror.

"OK," Nic says. "Everybody just take a big, deep breath, all right?"

"Give me the boy," Africa says slowly. "Give him to me now, and I will not tell Mrs Tanner that you took him. I will let her know that we found him together."

I don't want this. I don't want Africa as an enemy – not after everything we've been through, all that shit with the quake, all the times we've helped each other. We've known each other for a long time. We have fought, we have argued.

Fuck it – we've saved the world together. Hearing him talk like this, hearing him *threaten me* . . .

But there's no way I'm turning Leo over. That would be the worst thing I could do. I'd never forgive myself.

"Can't do that," I say. I straighten up to my full height – five three, but you work with what you've got. "Africa, listen to me. We are talking about the life of a child. If you do this, that's over. He won't be dead, but he may as well be."

I don't even care if Leo hears this – I *have* to make Africa understand. "There are things bigger than China Shop, and this is one of them. Please, dude. *Think.*"

Just for a second, Africa hesitates. The tiniest flicker of doubt crosses his face, his eyes narrowing very slightly. He runs his tongue across his upper lip – I don't even think he knows he's doing it. *Yes. Come on. Make the right decision, big guy.*

Which is when Nic decides to save the day.

Maybe he thinks I'm not going to convince Africa, or just decides enough is enough. He steps forward, raises his chin slightly. "OK, I've heard enough. You need to know that I am the legal representative for this woman, Teagan Frost, also known as Emily Jameson. I am also the legal representative for this child, Leo Nguyen. They are my clients."

I gape at him. "Nic, what are you doing?"

He ignores me, puffing his chest out. "My clients are American citizens, and enjoy the rights and privileges afforded by our constitution, and by the rule of law. You wish to detain Mr Nguyen. He is with Ms Frost and myself of his own free will – we are acting *in loco parentis* until his biological father is found, a fact the child will be more than happy to confirm. He *can* be detained by an authorised law enforcement officer with the proper identification, but since you don't have any, I'd ask you to politely fuck off."

A shutter comes down on Africa's face. Closed for business. Expression as hard and unyielding as a steel door.

Doesn't Nic get it? Africa used to be homeless. He spent *years* living in the cracks. His enemies were people who spoke exactly like Nic is speaking now. Lawyers and judges and case officers and cops.

"You talk to me," Africa says slowly. It's the complete opposite of how he was before. There's no yelling now. No gesturing. His voice is quiet, as still as a calm sea, with dark shapes swimming just below the surface. "You talk to *me* about the law."

"I want this to be clear," Nic continues. "You've presented no ID, and no arrest warrant. If you act against my clients, or if you try to detain them in any way, you should know that I will be contacting the Los Angeles Police Department and informing them of a kidnapping."

"Nic," I say. "Shut the fuck up right—"

Africa shoves Nic aside, reaches out, and grabs hold of Leo Nguyen.

It's one of those situations which you know is going to end badly even before you fully understand what's happening – but you can't do a single thing to stop it. You just stand there with a stupid look on your face, unable to move, unable to even speak.

"Leave me *alone!*" Leo yells.

And on the last word, he discharges a huge burst of electricity into Africa.

TWENTY-SEVEN

Teagan

There's a giant *bang*, and Africa goes flying.

He shoots backwards, his feet leaving the ground, his huge arms flailing. There's a split-second where I get a look at his face, and what's there is total, sincere confusion. Like he genuinely cannot *believe* this is happening to him.

He flies ten feet, slamming into the door of the nearby Humvee, right by the soldier with the wraparound shades. The man dives for cover as Africa slides to the ground, the stunned expression still on his face.

Nic grabs for Leo, way too fucking late. I have to use my PK to grab hold of his watch, stop him from touching the kid and getting his own dose of *zap*. Nic's wrist jerks, and he winces in pain, eyes flicking over to me.

"*Leave me alone!*" Leo yells again, little fists balled.

"Drop your weapon!" The soldier with the shades rips his rifle up. His aim lingers on Leo, before swinging over to me, as if he can't comprehend what he just saw. He's young – my age, maybe even less. The rifle barrel trembles as he draws a bead on us. I put my hands automatically, even as I lock the gun down, jamming the safety catch in place.

The crowd at the stadium entrance scatters, tripping over each other to get away. Africa is still sprawled, blinking in stunned disbelief. His clothes are smoking – it's probably only his size that's kept him conscious after a hit like that.

"Christmas elves!" I yell. I read once that if you want to defuse a fight, you should start yelling nonsense – something about how it short-circuits the aggression response in peoples' brains. "Monocles! LeBron James! Panna cotta! Um . . . "

"What are you doing?" Nic shouts. He's frozen in place, one foot slightly lifted, as if getting ready to break into a run. His voice is a lot higher than it normally is.

"Shut up, I'm thinking! Netflix! Netflix and Chill!"

"I said, drop it!" the soldier yells. There's the thunder of boot-clad feet. More guardsmen appear, coming in with rifles up, yelling at the onlookers to get back. They're approaching us in a loose semicircle, yelling at us to get on the ground.

Well. That didn't work.

"Listen to me," Nic shouts, Leo quaking behind his legs. "These are my clients, and—"

"Nic, *enough*." For some reason, my voice stops the guardsmen yelling, just for a second. As if they want a little more time to assess why, exactly, I'm not getting on the ground.

I lift my hands, fingers spread, making eye contact with the young guardsman – or as much as I can with his mirrored sunglasses, anyway. Showing him I'm not a threat. If we play this right, we can just walk out of here. Africa's down for the count, probably trying to figure out what planet he's on. The guardsmen haven't got the means to stop us. We're not getting any food here, that much is certain . . . but we can probably get back to the river.

"Leo," I say, holding out my hand behind me. "Come on. Let's go."

"I—"

"It's OK." I flash him a smile. "Nobody's gonna hurt you."

"Down. On the fucking. *Ground*."

"Yeah, nah," I mutter. "Leo?"

I hear him take a breath behind me, like he's about to start sobbing again. But it's just like before, when we were leaving the storage unit. If he trusts you – or at least, if he thinks you aren't going to hurt him – he'll do as he's told. There are soft footsteps, and then a small hand slips into mine. *Oh, thank fuck*.

"Nic, you too," I say. Then, to the guardsmen: "We're gonna leave now. OK? There's no weapon, no harm, no foul. We're just gonna go."

The guardsman with the mirrored shades glances at the soldier on his right, a woman with a long ponytail. For the first time, they seem unsure. I can use that. All I have to do is start walking.

Africa is on his feet now, unsteady, using the Humvee for support. Gaze burning a hole in the back of Leo's head. I take a step forward – and from behind me, there's a sharp *click*.

One of the guardsmen – a woman barely out of her teens, it looks like – tried to fire, the gun pointed right at my head. In her panic, she pulls the trigger again, then a third time. Her thumb frantically works the safety, the confusion on her face growing.

So much for trigger discipline.

I meet the woman's eyes. "Let's all just—"

With a yell, she drops her rifle, claws at her waist for her sidearm. I've locked it down before she's even drawn it, holding the trigger in place for good measure. "Nobody wants any trouble," I say, raising my voice. "We—"

One of the guardsmen rushes us.

It might be the wraparound shades guy, but I can't be sure.

Whoever it is throws their rifle to one side, sprints straight for Leo, as if intending to scoop him up and get him away from danger.

He doesn't get there. Before I can react, before anybody can do anything, Leo screams—

—and a bomb goes off.

That's what it feels like. A huge, ear-splitting bang, a flash of intense white light.

I stagger, clapping my hands to my ears, blinking against tears that double and triple my vision.

The guardsman who rushed us has been thrown backwards – and unlike Africa, he's not moving. He lies in a tangled heap, one arm thrown over his chest, like he got drunk and passed out.

For a long second, not a single person moves. Nobody says a thing. All except for Leo, who is huddled in a ball on the rough concrete. He's still screaming.

The woman who pulled her trigger takes a step forward, blinking in shock, when it happens again.

In the split-second available to me before the flash and the ferocious *bang* wipes my brain clean, I get a good look at exactly what he's doing.

I thought Leo was just delivering electric charge through the ground. He wasn't. Not even close.

Lightning.

The kid is literally calling down the lightning.

He's ripping the charge from the heavy clouds above, pulling down an enormous bolt of raw electricity. For a moment, the woman he's targeted is a dark, agonised silhouette against a backdrop of burning, horrible white light. Then it's gone, and she's down, and I have no time to process what the fuck I just saw before two more bolts of lightning come cracking down.

Now I *am* blind. Blind and deaf. I drop, not knowing what else to do, terror squeezing my stomach in a clawed fist. I curl into a ball as more lightning comes hammering down. In the gaps between the bolts, there are screams. Horrified, disbelieving. Cut short.

There's nothing I can do. There is no part of my ability that can stop this. Whatever power Leo is tapping into, it's bigger than him, bigger than me.

Move. But I can't. My legs won't listen to me. I curl tighter and try to calm my hammering heart and hope and pray that Nic is OK.

In the storage unit, Leo had this … safety radius, I guess you'd call it. He made sure the electricity he was putting out didn't affect the area around him. I have to hope it's the same thing here – that the lightning won't fry us. But if there really is a safety radius, and the guardsmen are outside it …

Bang.

Bang.

Bang.

And after what seems like years – decades – it finally stops.

An insane ringing fills my ears. But behind the sound, there are others. Crackling fire. A woman sobbing. Running footsteps.

There's no more screaming. I don't think there's anyone left to do it.

Slowly, I sit up. It's like my mind takes a second or two to catch up to my eyes, and I have to blink a few times before the afterimages in my vision fade.

Bodies.

At least five. guardsmen, mainly, lying in sprawled, broken heaps. There are objects dotted between them, and it takes me a second to recognise them – they're clothes, military fatigues, torn and shredded, ripped right off them. Shoes, too, scattered everywhere. Behind us, the crowd at the stadium entrance has scattered. There are small fires everywhere, and a big one on the Humvee, which is fully ablaze. The air stinks of ozone and gasoline. A rifle lies abandoned on the concrete.

Shit – Africa!

I'm so certain I'm going to see him among the bodies that a cry actually forces its way out of my throat. But he's not among them. He's nowhere to be seen.

Leo. He's still crouched down, still shaking. Nic is up on his knees, staring at him.

I get to my knees too. Doing so brings on another dose of double vision, and I have to stop for a second to let it pass.

I've been in danger before. You can't live the life I lead without landing in multiple fucked-up situations. But I think this is the first time there was genuinely nothing I could do.

I couldn't stop it. I couldn't run. I was completely helpless. All I had was blind hope that I wouldn't die – and it was only through blind luck that I didn't.

Leo looks over at me – and his eyes roll back in his skull. His left hand twitches, then his whole arm. He tilts sideways, slumping onto the parking lot surface, his body jackhammering.

This isn't like before, when he almost laughed at his leg and his wrist twitching. This is way, way worse.

"Nic," I say.

He doesn't appear to hear me.

"Nic, help him." I'm not sure I've got the strength right now to carry Leo myself.

Nic looks up at me, then over at Leo. Moving as if in a dream, he makes his way to the boy. It's impossible to miss how he hesitates before scooping him off the ground. Like he's scared to touch him.

But then he has the boy in his arms, straightening up and walking in long, jerky strides away from the stadium. Somehow, I manage to follow.

TWENTY-EIGHT

Teagan

Over the past few years, I've become very familiar with the giant spurt of adrenaline you get after surviving something that should have killed you.

It always arrives around five minutes *after* I nearly die, beginning with a prickle on my arms, a delightful tremor in my fingers. Then a feeling of well-being, flooding through me, quickly growing to a kind of hysterical euphoria. It's like an old friend by now. One I've been hanging out with for so long that I know everything they're going to do before they do it.

It also makes me wildly uncoordinated. As we stumble back down the slope towards the river in the growing dusk, I have to watch my feet, make sure I don't faceplant. My ears are still ringing, and my balance is shot to shit. God knows how Nic is doing – he's carrying a twitching Leo behind me, his feet heavy on the hard earth of the hillside. Behind us, the sirens have started.

We are so fucked.

We went to the stadium to get food and water, to keep us going for the long night ahead. We were supposed to slip in and out, just three more poor souls looking for shelter, souls nobody would miss when they made their exit and resumed their stealthy trek down the LA River. Instead, we not only completely failed to get any food and water, but we also sent up a giant signal flare for anybody looking for us. It's not just Tanner and Reggie. If the Zigzag Man didn't know where we were, he does now.

Fucking Africa.

I hope he's OK.

And I hope catches a horrific case of genital itch because, seriously, *what the hell*?

Lost in my thoughts, I almost run headlong into a tree. I just catch myself, sagging against it, resting my cheek on the rough bark.

Nic doesn't stop to check if I'm all right. Leo has stopped shaking now, but he's unconscious, a dead weight in Nic's arms.

We're not being chased – mostly because there's nobody really left up there to chase us – but it's not a good idea to hang around. With a groan, I push myself off the tree, start moving.

It's a lot faster going down the hill than going up. Also, a lot harder on the quads. It takes me a few minutes to realise we're not heading back down to the river – or if we are, we're not going down the way we came up.

When I mention this to Nic, he doesn't respond. I have to ask again before he looks at me, blinking slowly, like he just woke up.

"There's a quicker way to the Main Street Bridge," he mutters.

"How—?"

"'Cross Broadway, then through the LA State Park."

" . . . 'K."

I kind of grey out for a little while. I just follow Nic, my mind trailing ten feet behind me. We cross an empty four-lane street at the bottom of the slope, then a set of train tracks. There are no trains in sight, the tracks silent and still. I have to work really hard not to trip over them.

How can it be so damn quiet? After the insanity we just went through, the whole city should be on high alert. But there's nothing. Like none of it happened.

We hit the park, which is barely worthy of the name. It's a barren stretch of dirt, pockmarked with distantly-spaced bushes. As we enter, I come to a wobbling halt, hands on my knees, a stitch burning in my side and the muscles in my legs twitching. Like I've got my own case of the wiggles to deal with.

"Teagan, let's go." Nic says.

"Just a second."

"We don't have a second."

"Yeah, don't care." I sit down hard, giggling. Actually giggling. What can I say? Adrenaline makes you do weird shit.

He grunts, looks away.

"By the way, just what the hell was that?" I ask. "Back there?"

"What the hell was what?" He's distracted, glancing in the direction of the tracks, as if he's expecting pursuers to come rumbling across them at any moment. Leo gives a particularly bad twitch, just then, which makes Nic look down at the boy in his arms. For half a second, a flicker of terror dances across his face. Like he's been carrying a bomb.

"*Objection, your honour, my client pleads the fifth,*" I say. "All that."

Here's another side-effect of adrenaline: it makes it impossible to lock down your emotions. They whipsaw wildly, joy turning to fury in a nanosecond. It's why I giggled as I slid down the tree, and it's why I can't control the sudden, irrational anger.

"You can't just take a kid without a warrant," he says.

"What fucking world are you living in?" I was on the verge of convincing Africa. I'd opened up a tiny crack in his armour, and if I'd just had a few more seconds, *everything* that happened back there could have been avoided. Africa is a dipshit, true, and we wouldn't even have gotten into that situation if it wasn't for him ... but he was starting to see reason. He'd realised what was at stake. If Nic had just shut the fuck up, Leo wouldn't have gone apeshit, and those National guardsmen might still be alive. We'd have food, water, maybe a new ally. "You have a law degree. I thought they only gave those out to smart people. So explain to me why you thought talking about the constitution and *in loco fucking parentis* was going to help back there."

"Careful," he says.

"Get this straight. In my world, there are no warrants. No court protections. We are right out on the fucking edge. You wanna go talk to Tanner about the law? She doesn't care, you idiot. You can throw down clever legal arguments, and hide behind as many laws as you want, and it will mean precisely dick. She'll grab that Constitution you're waving in her face, and use it to light her cigarette. And by the way, you wanna talk like that to fucking Africa? *Of all people?*"

He looks at me then. Really looks at me. Like he's seeing me for the first time.

"I am a black man living in America," he says slowly, not taking his eyes off me. "You don't get to talk to me about not being protected by the law. Not ever."

"That's not what I ... "

"I don't give a fuck." His voice is monotone, cold as a switchblade. "I know *exactly* what it's like to live in that world. I went to work for the District Attorney for no money so I could find a way out of it. I don't need some white girl telling me I don't understand what it's like."

Abruptly, he turns, walks off into the darkness.

I want to call after him. Say ... shit, I don't know. That I'm sorry. That I overreacted. That it doesn't matter how right he is, because people still died up there – and wouldn't have if he'd just let me handle it. I'm furious with myself, more embarrassed than I've ever been in my entire life – but I'm also furious with Nic. He has to know that wasn't what I meant, he—

I drop my chin to my chest, groan long and hard.

In the end, I do the only thing I can. I get to my feet, and I keep walking.

Annie said she'd meet us at the Main Street Bridge – the one that is now a huge pile of rubble, thanks to the little car chase we had with the Legends biker gang. It's south of us now, no more than a quarter-mile, just down Wilhardt and left up Main. But we get to the intersection of Wilhardt and Naud, and we can't go any further. There's a gigantic sinkhole at the far end of the intersection, cordoned off by tattered yellow police tape.

Nic rubs his jaw. "OK. We can head up there." He points to the north-east "Up Naud. Drop into the river."

"Won't that add like an hour to the trip?" My voice sounds dead. It's started to rain heavily: big, fat, cold drops spattering my arms and neck and wrists. Leo's little lightning strikes must have opened up the clouds. It's not a downpour, not yet, but the rain is steady and hard.

Nic gives me a pitying look. "It'll add about five minutes. Come on."

Turns out, Nic is right. In minutes, we hit the concrete slope heading down into the storm drain. I keep my eyes on my feet, not wanting to fall over again – which is totally within the realm of possibility. I'm expecting more hard-packed dirt at the bottom of the slope, but the concrete doesn't stop.

I look up, startled. We've reached the covered-over section of the river, where the entire storm drain is concrete, end to end. The river itself is in a channel running down the centre of the drain. The flat, even surface feels odd under my sneakers.

Nic is maybe fifty yards ahead of me, walking without looking back, moving awkwardly across the concrete. He's still holding the unconscious Leo. Jesus, I haven't even had a minute to think about the boy. This isn't just what he calls the wiggles – and what he did with the lightning was clearly very different to how he electrified the storage unit. It drained his tank completely, and God knows what nerve damage it's doing to him now.

Who did this to him? Who gave him this ability? And what the hell are they trying to accomplish?

Nic moves up the slope slightly, manoeuvring around a cracked part of the concrete. As I follow, my anger turns on him. How dare he tell me I'm being racist? How can he possibly think that? He has to know what I meant, and he just took it in the worst way possible. And just to be totally clear, *I* wasn't the one who took the Africa situation from dangerous to completely fucked-up. That was all on him.

Which doesn't change the fact that I still tried to tell a black American about how the law wouldn't protect me. There is no sugar-coating that. I didn't even *consider* how it would come across.

It's not that I don't see race. People who say that deserve to get their teeth knocked out. But I thought it didn't matter. I told myself I lived in a diverse, accepting city – that whatever its problems, it still didn't matter that much what race you were. Hell, I worked – *work* – with people of colour. Annie is Latinx. Reggie and Africa are black. If—

I let out a frustrated sigh. File all that alongside *I can't be racist, some of my best friends are black.*

Nic made the wrong move with Africa. No question. But it was a move he made for the right reasons. He's a successful lawyer – or was – and being black meant he had to work twice as hard for it. He would take justifiable pride in his skills. And here's me, telling him he was wrong for doing it. Telling him he can't possibly understand the situation that Africa and I live with.

All at once, I'm *disgusted* with myself. Nic relied on training, experience, and self-belief to try and fix a bad situation. When it didn't work, I told him it was because that training, experience and self-belief wasn't good enough. I, a white person without even a high school diploma to her name, told the black lawyer that he didn't understand how the law worked.

But people died. If Nic hadn't jumped in, Africa would have let us go. You were almost there.

If, if, if.

There's the distant *blat* of a siren from behind me. I whirl around anyway, as if the cops were sneaking up on us. The empty storm drain doesn't exactly calm me down. The amount of people coming after us is growing. Africa. Reggie. The Zigzag Man. Hell, even the National Guard now – Leo might have done some damage, but I can't believe they'll just let it go. They're coming for us.

I am a bundle of nerves, and at this point I am actually looking forward to meeting up with Annie – if possible, the only person who is angrier at me right now than Nic.

The bridge is just ahead. A hulking shape in the darkness. "Can you see Annie?" I shout to Nic. He doesn't reply.

As we get closer to the ruins of the bridge, the river changes.

By river, I mean the water in the centre channel. It's burst its banks, gushing over the top and spreading across the concrete. We try to avoid it, but we can't stop it lapping over the top of our shoes, soaking our socks.

At first, I think it's just the rain — that what I'm seeing is normal. Annoying, but OK. Then I realise what's happening. It's doing this because of the collapsed bridge, which is acting as a dam, the river water bunching up against the crushed concrete slabs. Worse: debris has started to collect. Trash, old tires, hunks of dead bamboo. A floating, swirling mass of flotsam. It doesn't look like the water is completely dammed yet; some of it is finding a way through, sneaking through the gaps in the wrecked bridge. But add even a little more debris into the mix ... maybe stuff that's floating towards us from upriver, right now ... and if the rain keeps up ...

I shake myself out of it. A flood is the least of my worries. Not when I'm in a concrete channel with sloped sides I can climb quickly.

"Annie?" I shout. "You there?"

Nic speaks over his shoulder, raising his voice so I can hear. "I think I saw someone up there." He adjusts his grip on Leo, lifting his arm to point, indicating a spot at the top of the slope, up at the part where Main Street becomes the Main Street Bridge.

"Is it Annie?"

"Dunno. Let's go."

"How is ... ? Is Leo OK?"

"Still out."

That's the extent of our conversation.

We make our way up the sloped side of the channel, coming out under a miraculously-still-upright power line on Main

Street itself, which is empty of traffic. On the other side of the
street, there's a figure, silhouetted against a distant streetlamp.
Annie. Has to be.

"Over here," I shout, passing Nic and moving to a slow jog.
Man – now we have to explain to her about what went down
at Dodger. That's going to be a fun conversation, although it's
not like she can get any more pissed at me than she is already.

As I cross the street, I stop cold.

It's not Annie. It's not even a woman.

It's Robert.

The frontman for the Legends. The biker gang from
this morning.

Same patched leather vest, same hulking, tattooed arms.
Beneath his bushy beard, there's a very faint smile.

And around him, moving slowly out of the shadows:
more of them.

I don't know how these jack-offs knew where we'd be. I
don't care either. I have had one hell of a night, and I'm not
about to let goth Santa Claus and his elves make it any worse.
And since they know what I can do already, I figure I have
free rein to throw some more concrete slabs at them.

Except—

Where are their guns?

They don't have any rifles with them. No pistols or shot-
guns. Not a single firearm.

The hairs on the back of my neck prickle. I never thought
the *absence* of guns would scare me, but it does. I quickly scan
the environment – nobody around, no phones pointed at us.
A couple of security cameras. I crunch the insides of those,
turn my attention back to the bikers. There's a concrete trash
bin on its side at my two o'clock. That's a good start. I reach
over and grab it, lifting it upwards.

"Uh-uh." Robert lifts a finger. "You might not want to do that."

"You might not want to try and stop me."

"I'm sorry – who the fuck are these people?" says Nic.

Robert ignores him. "Just saying," he tells me. "Your friend probably won't be too pleased if you do." He has the even, relaxed tone of someone walking down a beach.

"My fr— What?"

But I know what.

Annie.

"Pretty simple situation," Robert says. "She's with some of our buddies. I have to make a call every fifteen minutes to keep them happy. I don't make that call, and well . . . " He shrugs. "Drop the trash can, honey."

Behind me, Nic has gone dead still. Very slowly, I set the bin down. The clunk as it touches tarmac is way too loud. At my sides, my fists are balled tight enough for my nails to cut into my palm. I don't care how much bad blood there is between me and Annie, if they've touched her . . .

Robert's smile gets wider. "Good girl."

"Eat shit, grandpa."

He actually laughs, then gestures to his right. "Our ride is this way. Come on."

"What do you want?"

"Nothing to do with me." He sucks his lip. "Pop wants to talk."

"And just who the fuck is Pop?"

"The boss." His eyes bore into mine, and despite his smile, there's zero humour in them. "And trust me, by the time this is over, you're gonna know exactly who the fuck Pop is."

TWENTY-NINE

Reggie

It takes Reggie a good few minutes to get the story out of Africa.

He is almost incoherent with rage, yelling into the phone. "An electric boy," he keeps saying, using the words like the most searing insult imaginable. "He touch me and *ba*! Throw me ten metres back. And Teggan is helping him!"

Reggie's breathing too fast, her breaths too shallow, her diaphragm clenching. It takes everything she has to slow it down.

Thank Christ Moira can't hear her. Africa's on a cellphone connection, while Moira speaks to Reggie over an open comms line, currently muted. Since Reggie can't type messages, only dictate them, she has to mute the comms line whenever she speaks to Africa. And the longer she mutes it . . .

As if on cue, Moira speaks into her ear. "Ms McCormick – we're getting a lot of National Guard chatter. Something's happened at Dodger Stadium."

There's a horrible moment where she thinks Moira is going to ask Africa for an update too. It doesn't come. " . . . Um, yes, Roger that. Looking now."

Reggie long ago built backdoors into the communications

networks of the Coast Guard, LAPD, fire department . . . and
the National Guard. She finds it quickly, eyes narrowing as
she listens. The voices on the channel are urgent, panicked,
talking over each other, dissolving into bursts of static, but
Reggie can still pick up on a few words. *Lightning strike. Four
dead. Six . . . no, seven injured.*

Reggie closes her eyes for a moment. Between what happened at the storage unit, and the garbled story coming from
Africa, she'd guessed most of this already – if not the specifics,
then definitely the broad outline. But to have it confirmed . . .

Teagan, what in God's name are you doing?

But of course, Reggie knows that, too. The girl doesn't
want to let the child – whoever the child is – fall into Tanner's
hands. Or hers.

Reggie hadn't really thought about it until now – she'd
spent so long as head of China Shop that the idea of not being
included was almost completely beyond consideration. And
yet, Teagan – and Nic Delacourt apparently, God knows how
he's involved – have gone off on their own. Maybe Annie too,
although Africa says he hasn't seen her. Reggie has worked
hard to build her relationships with her team, and to be frozen
out like this . . .

"I need solutions now, Ms McCormick," Tanner barks in
her ear. "Is this related to the incident at the storage facility?
I'm seeing plenty of weather activity over the LA area – can
we confirm whether this was just a normal lightning strike?"

"I . . . I don't—" Reggie clears her throat. "I don't know yet.
I'm going to send the team down there, and I'll see if there's
any camera footage from around the stadium."

"What about the communication issues with Ms Frost and
Ms Cruz? What's our status on that?"

"Working on it."

"Maybe we should get some more boots on the ground. Navy SEAL headquarters are in San Diego – they're not who I usually use, and I'd have to fast-track their security clearances and do some serious arm-twisting, but—"

"No." Reggie's voice sounds a lot calmer than she feels. "It's under control. We've got this."

"A SEAL team might—"

"Right now, we don't even know if what happened at Dodger Stadium is linked to the storage unit," Reggie says. The lies come easily, far too easily. "We could be deploying them for nothing. At least let me do some more digging."

Tanner digests this. "You have one hour. And keep existing communications open."

A thought flashes across Reggie's mind. "I'm going to shut down all comms and reboot. It might be some kind of kernel panic that hasn't resolved."

On any other night, Tanner would probably have detected the note of bullshit in Reggie's voice, but not tonight. She has a million things on her mind, and doesn't have time to process the reasoning. "Fine. Get it done."

With a sigh of relief, Reggie shuts down all comms systems. Then, raising the phone to her ear, she says, "Did you get all that?"

"Uh-huh." Africa still sounds furious. He sniffs loudly. "Is OK. They will not have gone far."

"Right. Look, we need to strategise. If—"

"No." He coughs, harsh and hard, almost like a roll of thunder on its own. "Before, I did not know what was what. Now I know exactly what to do."

There's something in his voice that chills Reggie to the bone.

"This boy is dangerous," he continues. "He already kill many people. It's just like before, with the one who can cause the earthquake. What is this boy going to do if we let him keep going for too long?"

"You can't . . . " She licks her lips. "We can't *kill him*."

"You not have a problem with killing the other boy. The earthquake one. What is different here?"

"Matthew Schenke," Reggie says, through gritted teeth, "was a clear and present danger. Whoever this boy is, he doesn't—"

Africa speaks over her. "I not get surprised this time. Not for this one. I will follow them, I will find them and I will do what I have to."

"Africa. *Stop*." Reggie's diaphragm clenches again as she raises her voice. She's working herself too hard, her frail body starting to protest. "Think for a second."

"I am thinking," he says. "And this is what Mrs Tanner would ask me to do, if she knew. I tell the lie to protect you Reggie, because I respect you, but I am not going to pretend this boy will live. Whether I do it or someone else does it . . . "

"You are way, way out of line."

He sighs. "I will protect you for as long as I can, Reggie. But you are the one who is out of line here." A rustle of fabric over the phone, as if he's getting to his feet.

"Listen to me. This isn't like before. Teagan is *with* this boy. She's helping. She wouldn't do that if—"

"She help him because he is like her. Teggan is my friend, I never be with China Shop if not for her . . . but I also know that she does not think straight. She thinks she can fix anything. But she cannot fix this."

Reggie opens her mouth to tell him no, he can't do this, how could he even be thinking about it? But the words won't come. And even if they did, what difference would they make?

Africa pauses, as if weighing his words. "I am sorry you

cannot see what I see, Reggie. I did not want any of this. We should all be working together. But if I am the only one who can do what has to be done, *yaaw*, then I will."

"Africa. Africa!"

But he's gone. And when Reggie tries to call him back, the line goes to voicemail.

She sags back in her seat, suddenly aware of just how much pain she's in. The space between her shoulder blades, at the base of her neck, feels as if someone has jammed a red-hot poker into it. Her diaphragm is actually twitching now, sending helpless little coughs up her throat. The sensations are familiar, but she can't remember a time when they were this bad.

Africa on his own mission. Moira wanting updates, threatening to send in the SEALs. National guardsmen, dead. Teagan and Annie, AWOL. Another child with extranormal abilities. And Reggie, at the middle of it all, unable to do a damn thing.

Walk away.

She half-smiles at the turn of phrase, one she's been unable to stop using. Walk away. Let it all go. Submit the audition tape to Darcy Lorenzo. If it bombs, well, she'll still be able to look herself in the mirror. And whatever happens, she won't have to do this any more.

She actually gets as far as moving the chair back, getting ready to spin round, exit the office. The freedom – the *release* – is so close.

And yet, even as she heads for the door, for a life that doesn't involve Moira Tanner and Idriss Kouamé and people with abilities, she's working the problem. She can't stop it – it would be like trying to stop a speeding train by sticking out your foot.

Where would Teagan and Nic be going?

They're heading south ... but why? They're obviously trying to get this boy somewhere, they wouldn't just ...

Suddenly, she's back in Nemila. Not in the room with the fists and feet and the child's crayon drawing of flowers on the wall. But after, in the forest, with Moira Tanner pulling her along, branches whipping at her face and mud spattering her calves, her jelly-legs threatening to up and quit. The sky through the trees turned orange by the burning farmhouse behind them, the screams and the choking smoke that followed them even as they lurched up the hill.

It was only when they crested the ridge that Reggie realised Moira had been hit. Blood soaked the sleeve of her khaki shirt, and when Reggie had pulled the collar down to look, Moira had *hissed*, biting her lip to keep from screaming.

Reggie's body was a mess of aches and bruises, of horrid, rolling pain that made her think of waves in a tidal pool, washing back and forth. She could barely walk. And now here was her rescuer, her shoulder turned into ground meat.

At that moment, their natural states were almost exactly reversed. Moira had torn through the farmhouse and the guards like a hurricane. But now reality was setting in, her body going into shock. Meanwhile, Reggie, who had existed for the past day in a pain-soaked, half-conscious haze, was suddenly fully alert, awake, her vision and hearing sharper than they'd ever been. To her, the night seemed alive with smoke and ash and crackling flames, and her partner was sagging against her, and Reggie could not have that.

Reggie had ripped a strip off Moira's shirt, bound it tight around her shoulder. Then she'd gotten her arm under Moira, hefted her, even though she herself was starting to go loose and fuzzy again.

"We're not done yet, bitch," she'd said.

She doesn't remember most of what followed. They'd spent six days in the forest. Reggie was unconscious for much of the time, and when she was awake, she burned with thirst and infection.

Moira must have been the same, but every time Reggie opened her eyes, she was there. Somehow, despite her horrific shoulder injury, Moira Tanner had gotten them to Zenica, to a hospital.

The debrief had come later. Moira wanted to know about the list – the one detailing the people the Serbs wanted to take out. And when Reggie was finally done, when she'd told Moira everything, the woman had stood. And in one of the only times Reggie could remember her doing so, she had smiled.

"We're not done," she'd said simply.

In Moira Tanner's world, they were never done.

Before she can stop herself, Reggie moves back to her monitors, pulling her trackball towards her. The intelligence community still hasn't found a way to improve on the simplicity of Google Maps, so that's where she goes. She finds the storage unit, then navigates down to Dodger Stadium. Could Teagan be trying to get back to her apartment in Leimert Park? No – she's not even heading in that direction. Come to think of it, her new place is in Pasadena, very far to the north-east. Nic's apartment in Sawtelle is similarly far-off.

Could she be coming to Carson? To the China Shop office itself? No. Why would Teagan go AWOL, only to come right back here?

The river.

Reggie can't believe she didn't see it before. She navigates down the map, moving along the storm drain from the Glendale Narrows past Dodger Stadium, past the collapsed Main Street Bridge. Further south, tracking the river's meandering path. Arts District, Pico Gardens, Redondo Junction, South Gate, Lynwood. Nothing jumps out at her.

She keeps an ear on the National Guard channel. Most of it is confusion, garbled shouts, requests for medical assistance. But she hears other things that worry her. Words like *pursuit* and *can't have gone far* and *heading south.*

Morton. Lynwood Gardens. Hollydale. Reggie is about to give up and dive deeper, maybe see if she can run some facial recognition on any camera footage she can dig up, when something Africa said tugs at her memory.

And this boy, this person, Leo Nguyen, ya, he put his power into me, throw me back a hundred metres!

Leo Nguyen. Africa had been speaking so fast, his accent so heavy, that she'd thought it was a word in Wolof or French that she didn't know. But it's a name. It may be a false one, but . . .

For normal people, trying to find a particular birth certificate in the United States would take days, involving a search of fifty states' Vital Records Offices. For Reggie, who can cut through the systems like a peregrine falcon diving for prey, it takes minutes. In the past six years, there have been 3,659 Leo Nguyens born in the United States.

What if he's not American?

No time for what-ifs. Chances are good that this boy is as old as Matthew Schenke was. Four or five. That narrows the Leo Nguyens down to around 800 or so. Of those, 732 are currently registered for Pre-K schooling throughout the country. Reggie concentrates on the remainder, diving deeper and deeper.

Her diaphragm loosens up, her breathing slower now, almost effortless.

She starts with New Mexico, which is where Matthew Schenke came from. There are eight Leo Nguyens who aren't currently registered for Pre-K. One is a long-term patient at the New Mexico Cancer Centre in Albuquerque. That leaves seven unaccounted for.

Reggie pauses, biting her bottom lip.

None of the Nguyen families she's found are particularly wealthy. It's not likely they'd have additional homes in Los Angeles. That means they needed a place to stay. A motel, an Airbnb, a friend, a family member.

It's this last one she tackles, pulling up the details of the parents, and digging deep into the records to trace any relatives in the Los Angeles area. The fourth Leo Nguyen's mother has a cousin in Santa Clarita, which makes Reggie's heart leap – but only for a second. Santa Clarita is to the north, in the *opposite* direction to where Teagan is headed.

But the sixth Leo Nguyen's father, Clarence, has a relative in LA too. A brother, with an address in Compton.

And Compton sits just to the west of the LA River.

Got you.

In moments, she has an address for the uncle. Now what the hell does she do with the information?

Giving it to Africa is out of the question – Reggie is not going to help him murder a child. So what, is she planning to go on down there herself? *And do what, exactly, Warrant Officer McCormick?*

She could go down to the address in Compton, all right, and wait for Teagan and the boy to show up. But if they were coming on foot down the LA River, she'd be waiting a while – if they even let her in the building. And that's assuming Africa didn't get to Teagan first. Or the National Guard, who are clearly on the hunt.

Reggie licks her lips, running her tongue gently over them.

There might be a better way.

The problem is: it's completely insane.

If they're heading where she thinks they are, they probably won't get off the river before Rosecrans – the long east–west avenue that marks the border of Compton. If she can get to the river there, they'll come to her.

Reggie pulls up the map, squinting. The 710 runs west of the river, and is going to be hell to get across in her chair. But to the east, there's a park, running alongside the river for maybe a mile before it becomes a golf course. If she can get to that park . . .

The thought is intoxicating. It feels urgent, somehow – a call she couldn't ignore if she tried.

And when she gets down to it, what else is there left to do? She's lied to Moira, and that lie is going to collapse on her at any moment. Her team is unresponsive. She is sick to death of this office and this horrible apartment.

So why not dive in? Why the hell not?

It'll be hard. Getting around LA when you're an incomplete quad was tricky even before the earthquake. But Reggie McCormick once had to learn to breathe again, months on a machine struggling to take the tiniest sip of air unassisted. Getting around in her chair? It's nothing. She'll deal with it.

She reaches for her phone, wavers.

What is the endgame here?

If she actually does find Teagan and Nic, meets the boy they've stolen . . . what then? Is she going to persuade them to hand the child over to Moira Tanner? Help them find a safer place to hide him? What?

She honestly doesn't know.

China Shop has folded in on itself, splitting into factions. Teagan and Nic – and, she presumes, Annie – want to save the boy. Africa wants to kill him. Moira doesn't know about him yet, but when she finds out – and she will – she'll want the boy for herself. Reggie still isn't sure where she fits in all that, but as her fingers hover over the phone, she thinks there's a way to find out.

If she goes into the field, intercepts her team, she can act as a peacemaker. She can bring everyone together: be the calm, cool centre, help everybody find a way forward. Before anyone else gets hurt.

Right now, this entire day has turned into what Teagan, with her delightful mouth, would call a clusterfuck. Reggie may not be with China Shop for much longer, but if she's going to go out, then she'll go out the right way. Not sitting here, cowering behind a screen.

She steels herself, then picks up the phone. In the past, her regular cab company was one that was specifically friendly to the disabled community, but they're gone now — another victim of the quake. She doesn't like having to use someone else, but she doesn't have a choice right now.

"Hello? Yes, I'd like a cab please. Biggest one you got. Going to Ralph Dills Park. Yes, for right now."

THIRTY

Teagan

Every so often, throughout this whole insane day, I've let myself fantasise about what I'd do when it was all over.

A really hot bath, with more bubbles in it than actual water. A beer. No, *three* beers. All lined up neatly. So cold the glass is frosted over. And a sandwich – nothing too fancy, maybe some pastrami and brown mustard on really good bread. With a pickle. Then sleep. At least twenty hours of deep, dark, dreamless sleep.

The most enticing part of this fantasy? Being alone. I haven't been by myself since I was flying my makeshift hoverboard around an electrified storage unit, while coming down off a meth high. That did not, shall we say, recharge my introvert batteries.

I'm alone now, and I feel like I should be able to take *some* pleasure in that. Even just a little. Problem is, I've been separated from Nic and Leo, and locked in the grimmest room I've ever been in.

I mean that, by the way. It's a concrete cube with a single bare light bulb hanging from the ceiling, and a single battered wooden chair. The concrete has some *very* suspicious stains on it. There are metal brackets bolted to the walls, as if this used to be a storeroom, but there are no shelves in sight. A cigarette packet lies crumpled in a corner.

It's kind of ridiculous, actually. I didn't exactly expect plush couches and complimentary fruit bowls, but I also didn't expect Robert and his friends to hang out in a movie cliché. You know the ones I'm talking about, where the bad guys always have their lair in a warehouse filled with hanging chains and flickering lights and grimy, unwashed corridors? Well, the Legends clearly saw those movies and thought, *Hey, we should get some of that action!*

After they took us, I figured they'd bring us back to the hotel – the one with the meth lab. Turns out they've got a few spots, and the one we're at now is an old train depot in Chinatown. They didn't bother blindfolding us on the way over.

Which worries me. A lot.

The depot is a cavernous, echoing space, filled with silent train cars and lengths of rotting track. There's trash everywhere, along with stacks of mouldy crates. There's a big, rectangular central shed, sets of tracks running in and out of it. On the long sides of the rectangle are storerooms and offices, two floors of them on each side, with grimy windows looking out onto the main part of the shed. There's a smell to the place, a sick tang: crack smoke and ozone and, weirdly, a hint of jasmine flower.

I didn't dare fight back. Not even when they separated me from Nic and Leo. We still don't know where Annie is, if she's even in the same building.

Leo, thank fuck, was still out of it. Conscious, but super-woozy, and unable to walk. They didn't make Nic put him down, but they did pull him to a different part of the depot. I told Nic to relax, that we'd figure this out. Charitably: I don't think he believed me.

And now I'm just sitting here. Trying to figure out what the fuck I'm going to do.

I've sent out my PK energy a dozen times, and there are plenty of things I could use it on. Hell, it would take me about half a second to open the door. The lock is a piece of shit.

Problem is, if I do that, then Annie dies. Also Nic.

So I sit. And try not to freak the fuck out. Try not to focus on my hunger and thirst and my leaden, aching tiredness and how deeply fucked I am.

I actually drift off a couple of times – microsleeps, the kind where your dipping head makes you snort yourself awake. Come to think of it, why am I actually staying awake? I'm not doing anything. I could probably take a nap right now, and—

My house has doors that open but never close, and it lies, oh it lies it lies.

I shudder, suddenly fully awake. Fucking Zigzag prick. What the hell does he want? Well, OK, he wants Leo . . . but *why*?

And I still can't shake what he did to me. That fantasy world that he put me in felt so real. Like Jonas Schmidt was right there, ready to take me away from all of this.

He must have pulled that from my subconscious. I guess I really do still hold out hope for a hot German billionaire to swoop in and save the day. I don't know whether to be appalled or just sad.

Footsteps. Shuffling noises outside the door. Low voices. I snap out of my thoughts, blinking, trying to look both relaxed and supremely pissed off.

The door opens, and a tiny woman comes in.

No, seriously. I thought I was short, but this woman is a good foot shorter than me. She looks like she'd disintegrate if you blew her a kiss. At least, that's what I think until I see her face, the sour twist of her mouth, the hard lines around her even harder eyes, which look like chips of flint. Blow this woman a kiss, and she'd take your head off your shoulders.

Like the other Legends, she's wearing a black motorcycle jacket with patches everywhere. The jacket is open over a grey shirt, buttoned at the collar and open at the bottom. Enormous black shades sit propped on her forehead, and she's rocking thick dreads which go all the way down to her waist.

She moves to close the door. As she does so, one of the guards outside turns towards to her, his eyebrows raised, as if questioning her decision to be alone with me. She doesn't even look at him. Just shuts the door, then leans against it, arms folded.

Studying me.

I don't happen to like being studied. "And just who in the fuck are you?"

"I'm Pop," she says.

I blink. "I'm sorry, what?"

She shrugs, as if she's used to this reaction. "It's short for poppet." She has the faintest hint of accent – Haitian, maybe, or Jamaican. Annie would know, for sure.

I grit my teeth. If they've hurt her . . .

"Where are my friends?" I say.

"We'll get to that."

"Now would be good."

She scratches her chin. It's a quick, precise movement with the index and middle fingers of her right hand. *Scratch-scratch.* Arms back to folded. Her eyes never leave mine.

The silence goes on for a little too long. I'm about to speak again when she says, "So. Superpowers, huh?"

I'm about to deny it, the reaction automatic. But fuck it. It's not like she doesn't know already.

I reach out with my PK, grab her glasses off her head, and float them over to me. Slipping them on without touching them.

I expect her to jump. Snatch at them. She doesn't move. Instead, as the glasses settle onto my face, she gives me a single nod. "Nice."

"You're welcome," I say, feeling like I told a joke where the punchline didn't land. It doesn't help that wearing dark glasses in a dark room is a dumb idea – there's a reason Pop had them propped on her forehead. I have to stop myself from taking them off.

Pop's wearing a watch – a big chunky Casio. It beeps softly, and she glances at it, then reaches behind her and raps on the door, still looking at me. Robert sticks his head in, and she whispers a few words to him. I'm guessing they're along the lines of, *So far so good, make the call with the codeword that prevents everybody getting murdered.*

Man. Why couldn't my parents have given me super hearing?

Robert shuts the door behind, and Pop turns back to me. "How is it you do what you do, exactly? Where'd you learn that?"

"Where are my people?" I say.

"Was it gamma rays or something?"

The sunglasses are getting to me. I reach up, prop them on my forehead. A petulant thought: *You're not getting these back.* "Where. Are. My people?"

"And you're like a crime fighter? LA's finest?" *Scratch-scratch.* "What I don't understand is what you're doing returning to the scene of . . . well, not the crime, but you get what I mean. We had people all over the city looking for you, but I didn't exactly expect you to come back to the bridge. I put a couple of the boys there just as a precaution, and then your friend walks right past us. And what's with the kid?"

"Touch him and I'll tear your face off."

Her expression doesn't change. In a weird way, she reminds me of Tanner.

"Just so you know," I say, putting a confidence into my voice that I absolutely don't feel, "I work for the US government."

She says nothing.

"All hell is about to come raining down on you. But I tell you what. You let me go right now, me and my people, and we walk away. I've got bigger shit to fry than your little biker club."

Pop laughs. It's a genuine sound, almost sweet, like a little girl's laugh.

"Something funny?"

"No, I just like the fact that you called us a club. Most people talk about motorcycle *gangs*."

"Did you not hear the part about the US government? I'm serious, man. I'm talking special forces, Black Hawks, extraordinary rendition. Fucking drone strikes. Your day is about to get a lot more complicated."

"So the US government is going to let someone like you get taken by people like us? Where are these special forces, exactly? Where are the men in black, coming to take us to Guantanamo?"

"Probably on their way."

"Maybe. But then, if I'm the government, why am I letting someone like you just wander around the storm drains? *Especially* after what you did to us before."

"You can ask them when they get here."

Pop sighs. Then she walks towards me, footsteps reverberating in the tight space.

I blink at her. "What do you think you're—?"

I don't get the rest out, because she slaps me.

It's not a hard slap. Just deliberate, precise. And here's the thing about slaps: a punch will make you bleed, but a good slap will make you cry. You can't help it. It's a blunt strike to the sinuses, and your eyes will water a little no matter how much you try to stop it. Punches hurt your body. Slaps hurt everything else.

I snarl, grab the first thing my PK touches – a loose metal bracket hanging on the wall. Then I rip it off, and send it hurtling towards Pop. Before it can touch her, she slaps me again, backhand. Stars explode in my vision, and my grip on the bracket goes fuzzy. It bounces off Pop's shoulder, and she doesn't even flinch.

"Do that again," she says. "See what happens to your friends."

I sniffle like a little kid. I can't help it – my sinuses have swollen up, my cheeks hot and stinging. I glare at Pop, hating how small I feel.

"Your story doesn't fly," she says. "Either you don't work for the government, or you do, but you're trying to go behind their backs. Doesn't matter to me – you can talk all you want, but we're still gonna do business."

"*Do business?*" I get out. My voice feels thick, foreign, like it belongs to someone else.

"Why not? If everything were just a business transaction, the world would be a better place."

"So killing people, selling drugs and guns and shit . . . just business, huh?"

She sighs again, as if the conversation bores her. "You know, in Haiti, people's lives are bought and sold all the time. For almost nothing. America, you try to pretend you are better, but what is the prison system here? The healthcare system everybody has to pay for? How many lives go in and out, in and out, and it's *legal*?"

A half-smile. "Maybe it's because you are white. You don't see what's right in front of you."

It's hard not to think of Nic – of what happened back at Dodger Stadium. I want to spit something back in Pop's face, but everything I can think to say feels wrong. And then there are all those people lined up at Dodger. A queue of weary, sick faces, knowing that the food they're getting will have to be enough. How many of those faces were black, Latinx, Asian? How many were white? I don't know. I don't think I looked.

She goes on. "And after the Big One, here in LA – you think the US government treats people *fairly*? They don't give a shit. They never have. Now, we –" Pop taps her chest "– me and my brothers – we do way more than the government ever will."

"What does *that* mean?"

She ignores me. "And at least we are honest. We don't pretend to be something we are not."

"And what sort of *business* do you see us doing?" I ask the question before I can stop myself, knowing I'm being led down a particular path, and helpless to stop it.

"Simple." She digs in her pocket, pulls out her phone. Aims it at me, tilting her chin upwards. "Move something."

"Sorry?"

"Do what you do. I want a record of it."

Oh. I see what's going on here. "You think you can make *money* off me?"

"Of course." She shrugs, like it's the most natural thing in the world. "A lot of money."

"Yeah, OK." I'm aiming for contempt, but can't quite get there. My cheeks are still on fire.

"You know, it's a funny thing. You go apeshit on us in the middle of LA, throw around a bunch of shit with your powers, whatever they are, and not a single video or photo makes it online. Not one. Plenty of chatter, plenty of talk, but no evidence. Nothing."

"Yeah, that was on purpose."

"I thought as much. But you got people interested, all this talk on the streets now about this superhero who took down the Legends. Now there are a *lot* of people who will pay money for evidence of what you do."

"Wait, hold on, just so I get this straight. You're going to just put out this clip of me using my ability—"

"No," she says, faintly offended. "I'm not putting it out anywhere. I'm just selling it to the highest bidder." She pauses, as if thinking. "And maybe showing it to some of the people we run with. Can't have them thinking we've gone soft."

" . . . Whatever. You think they're actually going to *believe* it? It's amazing what you can do with CGI these days."

"I only have to find one person who believes it. What they do with the video after is none of my concern."

"And after? You just let us walk out of here?"

She at least has the good grace not to lie. "I don't know. Maybe you and I can work something out, maybe not. We'll see."

"Uh . . . no," I say. "I'm good. Thanks."

"Maybe I need to explain how business transactions work." She doesn't lower the phone. "I'm offering fair compensation for your services. I keep your friends alive. Oh, and I'll get you some food and—"

Which is when she does lower the phone.

Tilts her head. Looks more closely at me.

"Hm," she says.

"What?" I snap.

She ignores me, backtracking to the door, having another hushed conversation with Robert. She has her back to me, head out the door, completely unbothered at exposing herself. I can't do anything but sit there and fume.

This isn't just a don't-kill-anyone safe-word moment. One or two other bikers join the conversation, which gets more heated. Pop keeps her voice too low for me to hear, but she's clearly insisting on something. After about a minute, one of her buddies puts something in her hand.

Pop pulls her head in and locks the door, still with her back to me.

"OK," I say. "This has been a lot of fun, but how about we get to the part where—?"

Pop has meth.

I realise it before I've even finished speaking. She's holding a small Ziploc bag of it: greasy, crystalline powder. No: it's not as fine as the stuff we stole before. There are chunks in there, bigger rocks of the stuff. It hasn't been cut yet. It's pure. Even a tiny, tiny bit would do the trick.

Pop's mouth is moving. Words coming out. You could make a bag that size last for ever, taking no more than a little bit every day. How much does it cost anyway? What are they selling it for? They must have more here, too, bags and bags . . .

Pop registers that I'm not listening, snaps her fingers. "I thought I recognised it."

My mouth has gone very dry. "Recognised what?"

She smirks. "The comedown. You're feeling it aren't you? Riding the old dragon. The stomach. The head." She taps the back of her skull. "How are the hallucinations? Are you seeing the shadow monsters yet?"

"The . . . what?" But I know what. The little flickers at the corners of my eyes. The dead certainty that someone is walking up behind me.

"Your pupils aren't huge any more," Pop goes on. "But I bet they were, weren't they? That's why I didn't spot it before. I figured the jitters you had on you were because of this." She waves her hand at the room. "Robert says you weren't like this before, so what was it? Did you decide to experiment? Take a little taste of what you stole? Good shit, isn't it?"

She's still holding the bag casually in both hands. God, there are even bigger rocks in there, crystalline chunks. Put one on the counter, crack it with the heel of a knife. Scoop up the smaller fragments, pound them into clean, shimmery powder . . .

"You only need a tiny bit." Pop taps the bag, using the same two fingers. "Then the pain? The hollow stomach? All of that goes away. You'll just feel good, all the time. And by the way, you should see what my lab boys are doing to this stuff. It just gets better and better. That gun shipment you tried to mess with? That was just the last batch I wanted to offload. Forget firearms – who needs the hassle, when the profit margins on this stuff are so high? It's *that* good."

"What . . .?" I clear my throat. "What do you want?"

She shrugs. "We're still gonna make a little movie, but I'll keep it for myself. Little insurance policy in case anybody says we can't control our spot. But other than that . . . you come work for me, and I keep you in top shape. No more shadow monsters. Oh, and your friends stay breathing."

And that's when I know what I have to do. There's no choice.

"All right," I say. It's barely more than a whisper.

"What was that?"

"I'll do it. I'll do what you want."

The smile eats up Pop's face. "I knew I could count on you." She points the phone at me, still grinning. "Maybe ... how about you move the chair you're sitting on? Should be a piece of cake for you."

"Yeah," I say, not looking at her. I get to my feet, unsteady, exhausted. Wishing there was another way. Feeling the burn and the ache and the horrifying, hot paranoia.

I raise my eyes to look at the camera. Behind it, Pop's grin gets even wider.

"One thing," I say.

"What is it?" Pop replies.

I grab the phone with my PK, rip it out of her hands, and jam it into her open mouth.

THIRTY-ONE

Teagan

Pop staggers backwards, clawing at her face. She makes a strangled, gagging sound like a trapped animal. The top corner of
the phone smashed a couple of her teeth in, and as she gasps
for air, one of her shattered canines falls to the floor. Blood
smears her chin.

She tries to pull the phone out, gripping it in both hands,
fighting it even as it worms its way deeper. To be fair, I don't
actually want to kill her, so I give her an assist. I rip the phone
away from her mouth, and before she can react, I snap it at
her face. Her nose explodes, spraying blood. I step back neatly,
eyes never leaving her.

Pop staggers, clutching at her ruined face, finally looking
up at me. "*You—*"

I pull the phone towards me, then send it flying at Pop's
forehead. She puts a hand up, trying to stop it, doesn't get
there in time. It hits dead centre, snapping her head back. She
crumples like she's been shot.

The phone is wrecked, its screen destroyed. I let it drop,
bouncing off Pop's chest. Her eyes have the same unfocused

look that I saw in Nic's. I don't even think she knows where she is right now.

Hmm. Maybe I hit her a little too hard.

Fuck it. Slap me? I slap back. And I slap a lot harder.

I rip the door open with my PK. Robert's there, along with a balding, heavyset gentleman with a huge beer gut and terrible tattoos. They both spin around, gawping at me.

The dude with beer gut reacts first, bursting into the room. He gets brained by the chair I was sitting on, and collapses on top of Pop, who lets out a heavy *whuf* as he crushes her.

Robert, to his credit, is a little smarter. He whips the phone up to his ear, turning, trying to run so he can make the call. I take the phone away from, snapping it against the wall. In response, he swings around and sprints headlong into the room, like a running back going for a tackle, hurdling Pop and coming right at me. I whip the chair up, holding it between us, intending to have him smack right into it. He comes to a stuttering halt, fury on his face, and grabs at the chair legs. For a second, he's engaged in an awkward wrestling match with the thing, his eyes flicking back and forth between me and it, like he can't believe his life has come to this.

Pop has a knife in her jacket pocket. It's not a killing-people-knife – or at least, I hope it isn't. It's a regular Swiss Army penknife. I have it out of her clothes and in the air in seconds, the blade flicked open and just touching the soft spot under Robert's chin. He freezes, still holding onto the chair.

The room goes woozy for a moment. I have to focus very hard to pull reality back. If I'm not careful, I'll lose control. That would be all kinds of bad.

"Where are they?" I snarl.

"Fuck you," Robert snaps back.

"Sorry, I don't know where *fuck you* is." I dig the knife in just a little more.

He lets go of the chair, tries to back up, getting away from the knife. I make it follow him until he's right up against the wall. He keeps looking at the door, like he's expecting backup.

"I'll feel them long before they get here," I say.

He grins. "You ain't gonna kill me."

"You sure?" I say.

But of course, he's right.

I've killed before. When my life was in danger. It messed me up good, gave me some banging nightmares. I really don't want to do it again. And it's as if Robert can see the indecision in my face, because that's when he reacts. He snatches the knife out of the air, using my distraction to pull it away from his throat, then dives at me, arms outstretched.

A dive that ends when I hit him in the head with the chair.

Yes, OK, fine, I should have tried to take him with me, gotten him to show me where Nic and Annie are. I have no idea how I would have pulled that off, but that was, in fact, the plan. Then he got inside my head, and I reacted . . . poorly. Hey, just because I've been trying to think through my decisions doesn't mean I'm perfect, OK?

He crashes to the ground at my feet, out cold, legs twitching.

Right next to the bag of meth.

I drop to my knees to grab it. It's surprisingly heavy in my hands, like it's filled with wet sand. The rocks crumble ever so slightly under my fingertips. I can't look away.

Sensing inorganic objects is incredibly difficult for me – I have to be in absolute fight-or-flight panic. But when I ingested that meth this afternoon . . . it was easy. Not just to sense organic matter, but to move it, with almost no effort.

If I took some of this meth now, if I snorted it, it would

supercharge my PK beyond anything I'd ever felt before. I'd be able to find Annie and Nic and Leo in seconds – in fact, not only would I be able to know where they were instantly, but I could take care of anybody guarding them. Probably without being seen. And then fly us right out of here. Just lift us up and take us all the way to Compton. And the pain, the twitchiness, the shadow monsters? Gone, gone, gone.

This little bag in my hands could make all my problems go away.

I fumble at the Ziploc strip, actually getting a finger inside the bag, wondering what I could use to crush the rocks ... when I realise my hands are shaking.

Trembling.

I stare at them, willing them to stop. They don't. They shiver, like I'm an old woman with palsy.

It's impossible not to think of Jeannette. Africa's girlfriend. Did her hands shake like this? Did she feel this same burning *need*? Did she feel it as her teeth came loose in their sockets and her shoulders began to hunch?

Even now, even with the horror and the paranoia and the sheer *revulsion* blooming in my mind like ink in water, I can't let go of the bag.

Can't? Or won't?

I make a noise that is a kind of hitching sob, and let the meth go. Put my head in my hands. No. No fucking way. I'm not doing it again. I don't care how powerful it made me feel, how potent the high was. The crash was – *is* – one of the most awful things I've ever felt. Like a million spiders were crawling over every inch of my body, inside and out. And yeah, the meth would make it go away ... for a while. But for how long? And if it became permanent ...

God, I wish Africa were here right now. He'd know what

to do. He could *help*. I crouch there, shuddering, paralysed. I'm desperate to run as far away as I can from the meth . . . and I can't bear the thought of leaving it behind.

OK. OK. We can be smart about this. Meth is awful, horrible shit, but the clarity I felt this morning . . . I can't just ignore that. I don't have to take some now, and I don't have to get addicted. When this is all over, I can . . . experiment. Maybe a tiny dose gets me all the advantages, without any of the downsides. If I do the drug in a controlled situation, as opposed to, you know, inside a burning car under a collapsed bridge, or in a biker hideout . . .

I can deal with the effects of the comedown for now. So far so good, right?

Before I can second guess myself, I drop the meth into my pocket. I don't need it now. I don't. I'll just . . . hold onto it, figure out what to do with it later.

I stick my head out into the corridor. There's nobody coming – I would have felt them by now – but I take a look anyway. I jam the door shut behind me, scrunching the lock mechanism with my PK, then head towards the central part of the depot. Annie and Nic could be anywhere, true, but I feel like I could wander the corridors for ever and not find them. I need to see if the bikers are guarding a particular spot.

And yes, before you ask, causing a ruckus and escaping was absolutely the right call. Whether I went for the meth or not, I don't believe for one second that Pop would have let me any of my friends live. You don't become the head of a motorcycle club – gang, cabal, whatever – without being ruthless as fuck. And if you're a four-foot-tall Haitian woman, you'd better have a double helping.

Nic and Annie were dead the second I gave in to Pop. Maybe Leo too. Now? I have about fifteen minutes to find them. Less, actually, because it's been a few minutes since Robert made the call, but . . .

I can still make that work.

The corridors are a warren of discarded trash, flickering lights, disused filing cabinets, bins full of rusting parts. Broken glass, too. I can't even see where it came from – there aren't any windows or anything. It's as if the Legends scattered it around, thinking it might make the place a little more homely.

I have to get out into the main part of the depot, which is on my right. As the thought occurs, the world goes so woozy that I almost fall over. I have to grab the wall to keep myself upright, stay still for a second, a second I don't have because it's already been at least a minute since I left my little holding cell, and the twelve-or-so minutes I thought was enough time is looking tighter and tighter.

Soft, sprinting footsteps. Coming up behind me. I spin round, breath caught in my throat, almost over balancing. A shadowy figure rushes at me – Pop, or Robert, or one of the others, I can't see. I react, snarling, grabbing whatever trash I can get my PK on and hurling it at the figure. Bottles and lightbulbs and shreds of plastic wicker through the air, a storm of jagged edges, slashing right through the figure, which—

Isn't there. It's gone. My projectiles clatter to the ground, ricochet off the walls. The only sound is my breathing, hot and harsh and harried.

There was someone there, I know there was, I heard them . . .

The slightest sound from my right. The crunch of a foot on broken glass. The slight click of a switchblade. My reaction is almost involuntary, like twitching your foot when the doc hits your knee during a reflex test. Everything in the corridor not nailed down goes flying, turning the air around me into hurricane.

There's nobody there. Of course there's nobody there. There never was.

Gotta get some Howlin' Ray's. Best fried chicken in LA. You won't even need the drugs any more, just some hot sauce and—

I put the knuckle of my right middle finger in my mouth. Bite down hard. Keep it there until my breathing slows down. Until my shoulder stop shaking.

Jesus Christ. What if I do that when I'm with Annie? Or Leo? What if I hurt them? What if I mistake them for someone else, and end up hitting them with a broken bottle, shards of glass sticking out of . . .

Just take a little bit. Just a tiny hit. A tiny little grain, that's all I need. No more pain. No more seeing things. Just clean, clear power.

A dot of blood wells up from my knuckle, touching my tongue. I pull my finger out of my mouth, spit, grimace, my head a little clearer.

Fuck that. Not happening.

Twenty seconds later, I slip out a door into the main depot. There's a big flatbed train car near the door I came out of, its bed sitting empty, but with conveniently huge wheels to hide behind. I scoot down next to it, eyes closed, sending out my PK in a wide arc – or as wide as I can manage without passing out. The headache pounds at me, as if furious that I didn't give it what it wants.

Lighting in the depot comes from huge, widely spaced banks of fluorescents, most of which are burned out, leaving the space in twilight. There are low voices from somewhere nearby, along with the clinking of metal on metal.

My heart starts to hammer. What seemed like a smart plan when I was kicking ten shades of shit out of Pop and company is looking less smart by the second. It would be pretty simple to take out most of the bikers on the floor, especially if their guns didn't work. But I can't stop them shouting, and I'm almost certain that whoever is holding Nic and Annie would hear them. I *cannot* let that happen.

Of course, there's a whole other side to the depot, opposite the end I came out of. More offices, more winding corridors, a whole open section that looks like a machine shop. I have maybe six or seven minutes, and I don't think it's going to be enough. I have no idea where my guys are being kept.

Somewhere outside the depot, thunder rumbles. The rain's starting to come down a little more heavily now. It's full dark now – I have no idea what time it is, though. 7 p.m.? Eight?

OK. Maybe if I get closer to the other side, I can use my PK to track down Nic and Annie. All I have to do is use it to locate a couple of guns close together. Guns means guards, and guards mean prisoners.

I hope. I'm kind of winging this.

I take another look over the top of the car, then scoot round it in an exaggerated roadie run, moving on the balls of my feet. At any second, I'm expecting a startled yell, thundering footsteps. I'm so wired for them that I almost lose my footing on a slick patch, cursing under my breath as I nearly trip over a rotting sleeper. Somehow, I manage to keep my feet, ducking behind a stack of plastic boxes. They're identical to the ones you'd rent for an apartment move.

Someone clears their throat around the corner of the boxes, no more than ten feet away. "I still say the eighty-one point game was the best."

"Are you serious?" The second speaker has a voice like charred gravel. I can already feel his gun, as well as his partner's. "You think that's better than Game Seven at Boston?"

"Game Seven? No way. Kobe was the ultimate selfish player. I mean, he went six of twenty-four—"

"And won a championship, so who cares?"

"I miss the Mamba though, man. For real."

A few seconds of silence, followed by a resigned sigh. "Shit, me too."

I lick my lips, trying not to think about time ticking down.

The last time I spoke to Nic, we were yelling at each other. And Annie . . . that argument we had. I can't let that be the last time I speak to them. I don't care what we were fighting over – it doesn't even matter. I'm going to find them again. I *won't* let them die.

And Leo . . . Christ, if they've hurt him, I will tear this fucking building down with them inside it.

I risk a peek over the top of one of the boxes. The bikers are twenty feet away – one bent over a Harley, the other leaning idly against a train car. He's the one with the gravelly voice, and looks like a sasquatch dressed up in human clothing. I flash back to Pop – four feet tall, female, Haitian. How in the name of blue fuck does she hold sway over a man-bear like this guy? Who *is* she?

I duck back down. Whatever. These two are distracted, not looking in my direction – I can sneak past them, get behind the next train car over.

Just use the damn meth.

My determination melts away like ice cream on a Venice Beach afternoon. Because if there was ever a time to supercharge my PK, it's now, right? I don't have time to play find-my-friends. I don't have time to deal with imaginary attackers creeping up behind me. A single wrong turn, a single minute spent looking in the wrong place, and they're done. And there are so many places to search.

The indecision paralyses me. For a few seconds, I quite literally can't move. All my attention is focused on my pocket. A few moments later, my hand moves on its own, feeling out the shape of the meth crystals. A tiny bit, just a couple of grains, enough to at least boost my echolocation. That's all I need right? That's—

"Oh shit," says a deep, gravelly voice from above my head.

I look up – right into the face of the sasquatch.

THIRTY-TWO

Teagan

I grew up on a ranch in Wyoming.

OK, yes, part of it was a giant genetics lab belonging to my parents, where they created me and my brother and sister. But a ranch is a ranch, and that means we spent a lot of our childhood playing with guns.

Nothing crazy – my parents weren't cult members, or militia psychopaths. We didn't spend time drilling with AR-15s. But we had a fair few pistols and hunting rifles lying around. We spent a lot of time popping varmints and aiming at tin cans.

Adam and I couldn't hit a damn thing, but Chloe was a natural. It might have been part of the genetic ability my parents gave her: the ability to see infrared radiation. I told her she was good because she could see the targets better than we could, and she just rolled her eyes and said that wasn't how it worked. Then I may or may not have dumped a bottle of water over her head, and she may or may not have chased me around the yard with a giant stick while Adam howled with laughter.

Point is: my idyllic American childhood means that while I might not like guns, I know how to handle them.

Sasquatch's pistol is a big one. A Glock, maybe. He is very startled when I take it away from him with my PK and jam it under his chin. He jerks in place, and his mouth snaps shut.

I hold a finger to my lips, not looking away from him. Yes, I am short and not too fit and having one of the worst days ever, but I can be fucking scary when I want to be.

"Minnie?"

It's the dude fixing his bike. I glance over quickly – he's up on one knee, but hasn't looked over his shoulder yet. That situation's going to last about three seconds, after Minnie here – and what the fuck kind of biker name is Minnie? Is it short for something? Minneapolis, maybe? – doesn't holler back.

I reach out with my PK, snatch up the other biker's spanner, and give him one hell of a whack on the noggin. He grunts, slumps against his bike.

Do I feel bad about hitting so many people in the head? Leaving a trail of concussions and possible brain injuries? Sure. But they started it. And besides, no one gives Batman shit when he beats up a warehouse full of the Joker's goons.

Minnie looks like he wants to pass out, and tear my head off, all at once. His left hand quivers, starts to reach for the gun under his chin.

I move it upwards, lifting his head. He actually goes up on his tiptoes. "Bad idea."

He stops, glowering at me. His gaze keeps flicking over my shoulder, as if expecting Pop and her goons to come to his rescue.

"Hey." I snap my fingers. "Focus, Minnie Mouse. You've got two of my friends. Tell me where they are."

He starts to speak, but I cut him off with a raised finger. "Just point. Jesus."

After a few seconds, he does, indicating one of the train cars about a hundred yards away, towards the middle of the depot.

Only one end of it is visible. It's a flatbed, like the one I hid behind ... only this one has a shipping container plunked on top of it.

There are probably a few more bikers standing guard – I can't tell from here, they're a little out of my range, but it's a sure bet. Well, that's OK. I don't have to go over there myself. Not when I have Minnie to do my dirty work for me.

Quick as anything, I zip the gun around to the back of his head, jamming the barrel into the fold of fat at the back of his neck. I certainly don't plan on killing him ... but he doesn't have to know that.

When I tell him what I want to do, the sour look on his face gets even worse.

He slowly turns, starts walking ... then looks back. "Who the hell *are* you?"

I show him my teeth. "I'm Batman. Get moving, jackass."

As he turns, a thought occurs to me. "Wait. Give me your phone."

He stares blankly at me. I have to snap my fingers at him, like an entitled customer at a restaurant. "Come on. Give."

He hands it over. I didn't think it was possible for the look on his face to get even more sour than it is already, but it does. I wink at him, pocketing his iPhone. Can't have him sending texts for help while I have him under the gun, can we?

I gesture to him to start walking. He threads a path between the trains, heading for the shipping container. I follow, keeping my distance – far enough to be out of sight, but close enough to keep my grip on the gun. When we're within about fifty feet of the container, I duck behind a stack of rotting wooden railway sleepers, eyes closed, focusing as hard as I can. There can't be more than a few minutes left on the clock, if that. Unless ... unless I'm too late. They might have already ...

You would have heard the shot. Focus.

Quickly, I explain to Minnie what I want him to do, ignoring the violence being promised by his eyes, then use my PK to get a picture of the area around the shipping container. Three bikers outside, their rifles and pistols and piercings and wallets showing up clear in my mind. Inside the container, two more. Other objects too – a set of keys, a ring, a thin chain. Nic? Annie? Maybe . . . but none of those objects are moving.

I swallow, let out a breath, move the gun down to Minnie's back, keeping it pressed tight to him. He can approach, and the other bikers won't even know the gun is there.

"Yo," he says, his voice distant.

One of the other bikers says something I can't catch.

"Pop wants 'em. Get 'em out here." He's doing a solid job, his voice not shaking at all. *Good boy, Minnie.*

Another inaudible response. Then someone else says: "Why'd she send you down, bro? She's supposed to call."

Oh, thank fuck. They're still alive. *I made it.*

"Beats me." Minnie says. "She's in with the other one. The one with the powers."

Laughter. "That's some wild shit."

"Got that right. Anyway, let's go, time's a-wastin'."

There's the groan-clunk of a shipping container door opening up. More voices. I sneak a look over the top of the sleepers, but I'm at *just* the wrong angle. I can't see shit.

I should move. Get a closer look. The objects in my PK field are moving though, the ones that I think belong to Annie and Nic starting to make their way out of the container.

Man. It can't be that far to Compton, can it? Maybe Leo's family will have some food for us when we get there. If they're Vietnamese, then chances are somebody in the house has some phở broth socked away. Maybe I could ask them nicely to heat it up. Throw in some thinly sliced beef, some noodles, a few crunchy beansprouts. I can actually taste it – hot and sour, the fat in the broth coating my lips, the beef only just cooked, maybe even a couple of tendons in there, the hit of chilli sauce and lime as—

From somewhere near the shipping container, there's the clatter of something falling to the floor.

My head snaps up – was I asleep? Was that a *microsleep*? Did I actually drift off, now, in the middle of—

One of the bikers says, "What the hell is that?"

Another: "Is that a gun?"

Ah.

Fuck.

"*She's here!*" Minnie roars. "Kill 'em! *Do it now!*"

I do not let them *do it now*.

Here's thing about microsleeps – and I believe I speak from experience here. When you snap out of them, you get a little burst of energy. Your brain goes, *Holy smokes, that was close, I'd better be extra vigilant from now on.*

It only lasts about a minute before you're drifting off again, but that's OK. In my case, the energy burst even gives my PK a little boost. And in one minute, either we'll all be free, or we'll all be dead.

"China Shop!" I yell. "Get down!"

And then I go to work.

I grab all the guns with my PK, rip them out of the hands of whoever is holding them, and hurl them away. Then I do the same thing for all the knives – and good Lord, do these people like their knives.

It's not going to be enough. So I focus, grit my teeth, ignore the headache and the hollow in my stomach, and grab one of the railway sleepers I'm crouching behind. Yes, they're made of wood, but they're covered in convenient metal brackets and rivets. I lift one up, and send it whipping through the maze of train cars.

Imagine you're an outlaw biker. You know you're facing off against someone with psychokinesis, so you're not totally surprised when you can't hold onto your weapons. But you probably *aren't* expecting to be suddenly attacked by a giant block of malevolent wood. In fact, if the sudden shocked screams are anything to go by, it would be safe to say that their gast is totally flabbered.

I don't bother with precision. I just zip the sleeper into the area around the shipping container and start thrashing it back and forth. The air fills with shouts, yelps, the heavy thud of thick wood colliding with thick biker. Jesus, I *really* hope Annie and Nic heard me when I told them to get down. I stumble towards the fight, nearly tripping a dozen times.

Nic and Annie lie in the dirt. Nic is face down, and Annie has curled into a ball, knees to her chest. They are surrounded by bikers, most of them unconscious. Minnie is crawling away, dragging a broken leg. A guy with a fully tattooed face is literally trying to fight the sleeper, throwing wild punches at it as it whips past him.

It's not going to be long before reinforcements arrive – there's no way others won't have heard this commotion. Then again, shouldn't they be here by now? Of course, I took out a good-size group of them after Pop's little interrogation, and I've wiped out an even bigger group here. There might be stragglers here and there, off in different parts of the depot, but this isn't a videogame. Pop doesn't have an infinite supply of henchmen.

Nic and Annie have their hands cuffed behind their backs. Not a problem. *Snap.*

The tattooed biker ducks under the sleeper and runs at me, arms outstretched, fingers hooked into claws. I raise an eyebrow, swing the wooden block around, and knock him on his ass. "Go to sleep," I say. Which, all things considered, is actually a pretty good line.

Nic raises his head to look at me, and my breath catches. His face is a bruised, bloody mess, his lips split and bleeding.

And yet, despite everything, he manages to smile.

I don't get a chance to return it. Because that's when Annie, who has also gotten unsteadily to her feet, catches sight of the crawling Minnie, and goes fucking nuts.

In two strides, she's over to him, and plants a gigantic kick in his chest. Full wind-up, running start, driving-from-the-hips *pow*. He gasps, mouth working like a goldfish as he tries to comprehend his snapped ribs, and the gasp becomes a horrid scream when Annie stomps down hard on his leg.

"Hey." Nic's voice is slurred, mushy.

"Annie!" I shout.

Annie doesn't hear us, or doesn't care. She drops to her knees, straddling Minnie's body, and starts punching.

You *never* want to take a punch from Annie Cruz. Minnie's face just . . . disintegrates. He tries to push Annie off, but he may as well be trying to lift a car. Each hit sounds like a watermelon being dropped onto concrete.

And throughout the assault, Annie doesn't say a thing. Not a word.

Nic gets there before I do, but it's only when I jump in to help that we pull Annie off – and even then, it takes every ounce of strength we have. Minnie has passed out, which is good, because his face looks like it's been forced through a meat grinder.

Annie is crazy strong, twisting in our arms. She doesn't speak, doesn't even look at us. It's only after I get in front of her and make her eyes meet mine that she starts slowing down, like a wind-up toy running out of juice.

"It's OK," I say. "You're OK."

Her shoulders rise and fall, rise and fall. She blinks . . . and then wraps me in a huge hug. The kind of hug that crushes the air from your lungs.

"I thought you were . . . " She trails off, buries her face in the top of my head, taking a shaky, trembling breath.

Then, abruptly, she lets go, leaving me gasping for air and wondering what the hell just happened. I was expecting her to say, *Hi, thank you, good to see you.* I wasn't expecting . . .whatever that was. She hugged me as if I would vanish if she didn't.

When I look up, she's staring daggers at the unconscious Minnie.

A hand on my shoulder. Nic, pulling me into a hug of his own. It feels really freaking good. Like we never argued. Like *this* was how it was meant to be.

After a long moment, he squeezes, and releases. I have to fight the urge to keep holding on.

I keep an ear open for any running footsteps, any other bikers coming to check what all the fuss is about. There's nothing. Just the steady patter of the rain outside the depot, the occasional rumble of thunder.

Guess I was right. This group, plus Pop's goons, equals most of the bikers.

"Leo?" I ask.

"They took him that way." Nic points over my shoulder, towards the north-west corner of the depot.

"They say what they want with him?"

He shakes his head. I can't help but glance down at Minnie – or what's left of him. He might have been able to lead us to Leo. Christ, if only Annie hadn't . . .

I bite down on the thought. That's not going to help any-body right now.

Together, we make our way over to the far wall. I take the lead, using the little PK I have left to scan for any enemies. None appear. Even when we get to a door leading to the main corridor that joins all the offices, there's no one around. This section of the building is identical to the one I escaped from: same grimy corridor, same flickering fluorescents.

The little spurt of adrenaline I felt is fading fast, another microsleep dancing at the edges of my mind. I bite my lip, using the jolt of pain to focus. It works for about half a second, and then my thoughts run away from me. I can't do a thing to stop them.

It's only when Nic grabs me that I realise I'm about to walk right into a wall. "Easy," he says, pulling me upright. "You OK?"

"Nothing a few thousand hours of sleep won't . . . Hold up, what is that?"

"What?" Annie says.

I close my eyes, listening hard. Yeah, there it is again. It's laughter.

A child's laughter

Nic and Annie have picked up on it. They push past me, a new urgency to their movements. I hustle to keep up.

I'm still alert for the appearance of any more bikers. I am very much running on empty, and I'm not sure I have what it takes to deal with another group of them – even with Nic and Annie backing me up. But as we make our way through the office area, following the sporadic laughter, none appear. This place is deserted.

It doesn't take us long to find the source of the laughter. It's coming from behind a closed door on the second floor of the office area. There are grandiose gold letters on the door, now faded and chipped: ACCOUNTING AND RECEIVING. There's a small window set above them, but it's got a blind pulled down behind it on the other side.

I find Nic's eyes. He flicks them at the door, and the meaning is clear. *Anybody we have to worry about?*

I concentrate, scanning the room with my PK. There are no guns in the room, nothing like that. There's plenty of *stuff* in there ... but it's not what I expected. The shapes are unfamiliar. I run my mind over them, trying to understand what I'm feeling. Metal rods, bending in strange ways. What feels like a blackboard, or an easel. And is that a ... plastic toy plane?

At that moment, there's a delighted, childish shriek from behind the door. A little girl's shriek.

Whoever was speaking in the low voice raises it. "Anastasia! *Silencio, por favor, ya te dije.* OK?"

In response, there's more laughter. From *other* children.

What the hell?

Slowly, very slowly, I open the door.

THIRTY-THREE

Teagan

There are children there. Obviously.

And not just one or two. A good twenty of them. The youngest looks about three, and I'd put the oldest at maybe six.

The room itself used to be an office, a place where accounts would be accounted. It's been transformed into a classroom by someone on a real budget. There's a pile of hand-me-down children's toys in one corner; the metal frame I felt was one of those gizmos where you move beads along a curved, looping track. A stack of puzzle boxes and books sits next to the toys, along with a couple of thick foam mats. There's no blackboard – just an easel with a thick pad of plus-sized paper hanging from it.

The kids are sitting on the floor, cross-legged, giggling at something. In front of them is a middle-aged woman with a messy ponytail, dressed in jeans and a green zip-up hoodie. She's holding a book – one of the *Captain Underpants* stories.

And in the middle of the group of kids: Leo.

His black hair is messy, sticking up in all directions. There's a giant grin on his face, a grin which turns to laughter as one of the other kids pokes him in the ribs. His arms are still twitching – something which doesn't seem to bother the other children – but he's awake. Alive.

The woman in front turns to look at us, her eyes going wide. One by one, the kids follow her gaze, all of them going silent as they spot us framed in the doorway.

Leo is one of the last to notice. When he does, his whole face lights up. "Nic!" He tries to get to his feet, but his legs aren't working right. His left eye has started to twitch, too, jumping and spasming.

Annie strides into the room. She grabs the woman by the hoodie, and slams her against the wall, ignoring the children's screams.

The woman shakes her head frantically, trying to twist away. Annie won't let her, jamming a forearm against her throat. She cocks back an arm, fist clenched. Her knuckles are already caked in blood. Apparently, beating Minnie to a pulp didn't do enough to drain off her anger.

Nic and I sprint after Annie, yelling at her to stop. I don't know what's going on here either – I'm just as confused as everyone else. But it isn't some kind of kiddie torture chamber. I have no idea why there's a school or a daycare or whatever the fuck this is inside a biker hideout, but these kids clearly aren't in immediate danger.

This has been the roughest of rough days, but somehow, Nic and I have mostly managed to keep it together. Annie . . . it's like she's wandered off the edge of the map. Like her pain has taken her somewhere the rest of us can't go. She's reacting to everything like it's a threat, meeting every situation with raw emotion.

"No." Leo is still trying to get to his feet, helped by one of the other kids, a little girl with cornrows. "She's nice! Don't hurt her!"

Nic gets to Annie first, jamming his hands in between her and the woman. I have to stop two of the kids in the front row, stepping into their path. "Chill," Nic is saying to Annie. "Just chill, all right?"

Annie grunts, like she's been punched. Then abruptly, she lets go of the terrified woman, stepping back. She turns away, hands laced against the back of her head, shoulders heaving.

By now, at least half the kids are pushing past me – there's no way I can stop them all. They get between Nic and the woman, shoving him away, yelling at him to stop even though he hasn't touched her. Some of the other children are sobbing, the rest staring open-mouthed at us. The noise builds and builds, filling the room.

"*Hey!*" Nic yells, making me jump.

It's loud and sharp enough to stop the kids shouting. As they simmer down, he levels a finger at the terrified woman. "Start talking. What is this?"

"We're just reading," one of the bigger kids says.

"Yeah," says another. "Go away."

"Why are there children here?" I say to the woman. "Who are you?"

She swallows, starts speaking very fast. "*Lo siento, soy Gabriela Garcia, solo estoy aquí para enseñar a los niños—*"

Annie snaps her head around, still looking venomous. The teacher – if that's what she is – actually flinches.

"*¿De dónde vienen?*" Annie says. "*¿Qué hacen éstos aquí?*"

They go back and forth in rapid Spanish for a few moments, then Annie turns to us. "These kids lost their parents in the quake. Or they're Dreamers."

"What?" I ask.

"Children of immigrants. Mexican, Salvadoran, Haitian. She says Pop came to her, asked her to help out, teach the kids."

"She was reading to us," Leo says.

The woman's fear gets the better of her. She dissolves into hacking sobs, burying her face in her hands.

It starts the kids off again. Several of the bolder ones get right in Annie's face, even try and push her. The room fills with angry little voices.

Somehow, Leo – with the help of the little girl holding him up – manages to squirm his way to the front, between Annie and the others. He turns to face them, a determined look on his face. "No, guys! They're my friends!"

Annie looks down at him, blinking in astonishment.

Leo's bravery doesn't seem to help matters. The bigger kids step around him, continuing to yell at Annie. Shit, if we don't calm them down soon, the noise might bring some more goons . . .

"*Tranquilo*," Annie says. "*¡No vamos a lastimar a tu maestro!*"

We're not going to hurt your teacher. I think. Annie keeps talking, patting the air, raising her voice over Leo, who is still trying to get a word in edgeways. And slowly, the mob of kids quietens down, although they still look restless.

Pop's words, coming back to me. *After the Big One, here in LA – you think the US government treats people fairly? They don't give a shit. They never have . . . Me and my brothers – we do way more than the government ever will.*

It doesn't make sense. Pop and her *brothers* sell drugs. Weapons. They're a fucking cancer, a tumour worming its way through my city. They came in here to take advantage after the quake, to make *money*, not to help kids.

The woman is lying, she has to be. Whatever Pop has planned for these kids, it's not good. Human trafficking is definitely a thing – maybe she's planning to sell them to factories, or . . .

Except: what possible reason could Pop have to set up a classroom like this? To bring in — let's not sugar-coat this — a school teacher? If she wanted to put these kids to work as some kind of fucked-up slave labour, she wouldn't be spending time getting someone to read to them.

"*Solo intentábamos ayudar,*" the sobbing woman says. Then: "We were just trying to help. Please."

"Annie," I say. "Watch the door."

No response. Annie is taking deep, steady breaths.

"Annie. Watch the damn door. *Now.*"

She glances at me, her expression unreadable. She takes a quick look at Leo, then does as I ask, heading over and poking her head out into the corridor. I cross over to Nic, threading my way through the kids, most of whom are giving me confused, wounded looks.

"What did we just walk into?" I mutter to Nic when I reach him.

"I mean ... " He bites his lip. "It's possible. Nobody says these biker dudes can't help a bunch of kids if they want."

"But they ... they sell guns, Nic. Like, actual assault rifles. Why would they ... ?"

But I'm starting to understand.

You're probably shocked to hear this, but I listen to a lot of hip-hop. Rappers idolise drug dealers — hell, some of them even steal their names. Rick Ross, Noreaga, Freeway. Rae from Wu-Tang. You can't listen to rap without getting to know a little bit about the people these artists took their names from. The dealers. The hustlers. The real-life bad guys.

Those same bad guys gave out free turkeys on Thanksgiving, used their profits to build community centres, paid rent for struggling friends and relatives, coached youth basketball teams. They'd spend the day flooding the streets with dope, and then head on over to the local church to help out at the homeless soup kitchen. Part of it was about image, sure ... but not all of it.

Who's to say Pop isn't the same? Who's to say she doesn't see herself as the hero here? The woman getting these kids off the streets, helping them out when the government won't. Can she really justify doing that, while turning around and selling guns and drugs to everybody else?

It doesn't matter whether she *can* justify it or not. In her mind, it's totally fine.

"Nic," I say quietly. "Go get Leo."

He gives me a worried look, then makes his way over. Leo holds out his arms eagerly, and he doesn't catch Nic's slight hesitation, the same look on his face that he had when we were coming down from the stadium – like he's being asked to carry a bomb. But all the same, he scoops the kid up.

"What do we do with the rest?" I say.

Nic looks over Leo's shoulder at me. "What do you mean, what do we do?"

"About the kids. About ... whatever this is."

"Teags – we don't have to do anything. We just take Leo and go."

"We can't just leave them!"

"Why not?" He nods to the woman. "They're supervised. Annie did a number on her, but she's OK."

There must still be some worry in my expression, because his own softens. "Look, I know we don't always agree on this stuff, but there's nothing we can do for these kids. We can't take them with us."

He's right. Of course he is. He might not have handled the situation with Africa at Dodger Stadium well, but he's still one of the sharpest people I know.

He hefts Leo, adjusting the boy's position in his arms. "We can find Leo's dad. We can do that much. Right, buddy?"

"I don't wanna go," Leo says.

"I know, my man. But we can't stick around for ever."

"I wanna hear the rest of the story!"

I bite my lip. We don't have time for this. Any second now, Pop's goons are going to burst through the door.

I'm expecting the kids to protest as we take Leo away, maybe to demand the return of their friend. They just watch us, clustered around the still-sobbing Gabriela Garcia.

I didn't really look at them before, but I'm doing it now. And what I see is trauma.

I've been around it enough to know the look, even in little kids. There's a coldness in the eyes, a mistrust. A way of standing, with slightly hunched shoulders, as if bracing for a hit. These kids ... they've all been through something. And here we come, busting into their one safe space, taking their friend away.

It's not like that. Stop it.

All the same, I can't help turning to the teacher and saying, "I'm ... we're real sorry."

"Just go. Please."

I put an arm around Annie's waist. She resists me for a second, then follows.

I'll come back for these kids, when this is all over. Make sure they don't have to live in abandoned train depot/drug den. I'll get the authorities involved – somehow – make sure the kids can ... can ...

Can what? Go into foster care? Be placed with new parents? Do I even have the *right* to make that decision? And if I do, do I actually trust the US government to do it properly?

I have no idea.

We head back into the main part of the depot in silence. I scan for anybody approaching, but there's nobody. We pick our way between the trains, hopping over the disused railway sleepers. A sudden surge of guilt — should we call an ambulance or something for the bikers I beat to shit? I could use Minnie's phone. But what if Reggie ... what if she's monitoring 911 calls?

Fuck me, what a day.

Amazingly, this place has exit signs. We end up slipping out on the west side of the building, into what used to be an employee parking lot. It's raining more heavily now, dots of chilly rain spattering my skin.

There are no cars there. Instead, there's a messy line of Harleys — or whatever type of bikes theses jackasses ride — lined up against the fence. This time, there *is* a biker standing guard, a youngish dude sitting on one of the bike seats. How did he not hear all the shit that went down in the depot? But he's nodding to himself, and there are white dots in his ears. AirPods. This idiot is listening to music. He hasn't even heard us approach.

I don't give him a chance to cause us trouble. I grab his pistol out of his waistband, wave it in front of his face. He's so startled he actually falls off the bike, landing ass-first on the concrete. I root around in his pockets with my PK, which makes him squirm even more — trust me, having someone use their mind to investigate the area close to your genitals can be quite startling. His cellphone pops out, along with a metal money clip, and a set of bike keys. Those could be handy. Seeing the cellphone makes me realise that I still have Minnie's, jammed into my pocket. I debate throwing it out, but fuck it: it could be useful.

"Run," I snarl at the biker.

He doesn't argue, scrambling to his feet and taking off towards the boom gate separating the lot from the street. Halfway there, he trips, the wet surface sending him flying, and does an almost acrobatic recovery, leaping to his feet and running even faster.

I let the gun drop. Just in time. I am *very* close to running out of juice completely, fatigue and hunger and sleep deprivation burning holes in my ability. I put my hands on my knees, making myself take deep breaths. Ah, shit – we should have looked for food in there. Why the hell didn't we?

"Where are we gonna go?" Leo says, sullen.

Annie cranes her chin, looking south. "We're not far from the river. We can take the bikes. It's all concrete storm drains from Dodger onwards, so it should be a straight shot down."

She's speaking too carefully, as if she doesn't trust herself.

"We only got one set of keys," I say, jingling them. "We're gonna need two bikes, surely?"

"*Stop right there!*"

It comes from the entrance to the parking lot. There's a group of people there, led by a man with wraparound sunglasses and a very big gun.

The National Guard have found us.

THIRTY-FOUR

Teagan

They must have been tracking us since Dodger Stadium. Maybe they saw Pop's guys take us, followed us all the way here. They were probably figuring out how to get inside when we strolled out the front door.

Perfect.

And once the soldier with the wraparound shades starts yelling, they all do.

There are about ten of them, spread out, moving in the rifles-up–knees-bent way that soldiers do when they're looking for someone to shoot. This time, it's not just a group of scared kids. Shades has got himself a new posse. The National Guard might not be our finest fighting force, but these particular soldiers look like they didn't get the memo.

I try to lock down their guns now, the same way as before. But as soon as I do, I lose my grip. My PK just slips right off. I grit my teeth, trying to force it ... and a whammer of a headache blooms at the base of my skull.

"We got a problem," I hiss at Nic.

"Yeah, I can see."

"No, their guns, I can't—"

"Who the fuck are you people?"

Pop.

She's pushing through the door we came out of, with about ten very angry bikers flanking her. They are bloody, bruised and very, very angry. The look on her face could give God a heart attack.

Actually, her face itself could give God a heart attack. Man, I beat the *shit* out of her.

There's a second where I think we're going to have an actual Mexican standoff. Everybody wanting to kill everybody else, but nobody wanting to actually start shooting.

That doesn't happen, because without warning, the bikers open fire on the National Guard.

Yeah. Come to think of it, they probably weren't going to talk this out like grown-ups.

The world erupts with gunfire. We hit the deck, Nic rolling to protect Leo. I clap my hands over my ears as someone scrabbles at my shoulder – Annie. She rolls me towards her, pulling me onto all fours, hustling me behind the line of bikes. I get a split-second glimpse of Pop, down on one knee, no cover at all, pulling the trigger of a huge pistol again and again, the kickback so intense that it's miracle she can even stay upright.

Annie yells right in my ear, her words inaudible over the gunfire. I gape at her, thinking, *This is a dream. I didn't wake up this morning. This entire insane day is happening in my mind.*

The bikes. If we can get them going . . . and I have a key! One I took from the dude on guard duty! If we could—

Oh, yeah, I have a key all right. *A* key. Singular. Four of us are not going to fit on one bike – and on that note, how the hell am I going to find out which keys fit which bikes? It's not like I can call a timeout here.

I'll have to start them manually, using my PK. It can't be

that difficult – after all, a key just pushes tumblers into line. And as long as these bikes don't use complicated electronics, I can get it done. Assuming my PK actually plays ball.

I grab hold of Annie. "I'm going to start that bike!" I shout, waving my hand at the closest one.

"*What?*"

Ah, fuck. We could spend the rest of the night trying to hear each other, and it's not going to be long before either Pop's people or the National Guard remember who they *really* want to kill.

I am going to have to dig deep. Comedown be damned, there's got to be *some* PK left in there, and I am damn well going to find it.

I close my eyes. Clench fists, which doesn't really help, but feels like it should. Concentrate. I send the PK out, slipping into the nearest Harley, finding the key mechanism. The tumblers inside.

There. *Got you.* Pushing the tumblers up and holding them. One . . . at . . . a . . . time . . .

The bike roars to life. Even with the gunfire, the *blat* of the engine is so loud that it nearly takes my head off.

"Yes!" I yell – right as the bike explodes away from us, wobbling wildly, the engine roaring. The back wheel actually fishtails, very nearly smacking Annie in the head.

I stare in horror as our noble steed rips right into the middle of the gun battle, bullets already *spang*ing off the metal frame. The bike crashes onto its side, bodywork screeching. As I watch, goggle-eyed, it takes out one of the bikers at the ankles. He didn't see it coming, too focused on his targets, and it hits him so hard that he actually somersaults.

I have no idea why the bike leapt forward like that, and I don't have time to find out. Or the PK to do so: I really have drained the tank. Nothing but grey static and that awful, thundering headache.

Annie grabs me, pulls me in close. Hunches around me, as if her body can stop bullets.

I try again, but there's nothing. Nothing we can do but wait for it to be over.

I'm expecting a calm. This isn't the first time I've faced death, and I know what it usually feels like. It's an acceptance – an awful, languid acceptance. There's nothing more you can do.

This time, it's different. I'm not calm. I'm fucking *furious*. Furious with myself: a hot, embarrassed anger.

A while back, when I was seriously looking into going to chef's school, Tanner asked me a question. If I had to give up my dream of being a chef, but doing so would save countless lives, would I do it? I hated the answer. Hated how simple and clear it was, with no wiggle room.

Now, though? Seconds away from having a bullet rip through me?

I should have given her another answer. I should have told her to get fucked. I should have found another way. Because it's not anger I feel, not really. It's something much worse.

It's regret.

I don't know how much time passes. I go deep into myself, the bitter feelings pulling me in. It's only when Annie pushes away from me that I come back, blinking.

Before I can ask why we're not dead yet, Annie grabs me by the shoulder, turns me to face her. Her eyes are huge with worry. "Are you hit? Come on, baby girl, tell me if you got hit."

" ... What?"

"Are you hit?"

"I ... I don't think so?"

Before I can ask her what she's doing, she pulls me roughly to my feet. My instinct is to duck back down, get out of the firing line. Only ... nobody's shooting any more.

No – that's wrong. The gunfight has just moved. It's inside the depot now, the Legends retreating, the National Guard pushing up. As I turn to look, a guardsman sprints towards the depot entrance in a roadie run, one of his buddies close behind him.

"Are you OK?" It's Nic. He's holding a terrified Leo, the boy clutching him so tightly that it's a wonder he can still breathe.

"Yeah, but—"

Annie crouches a short distance away, next to a biker. A very dead biker, a pool of blood spreading out from his head. She's holding something aloft – a set of keys. She must have gone through the dude's pockets.

"Quick," she says, jogging back to us. "Match the bikes to the keys. Before they come back."

I goggle at her, still not a hundred per cent sure this isn't a dream. "But—"

"*Let's fucking go.* Nic—" She tosses him the key she grabbed. "You and Leo take one bike. Teags and I got the other. Do *not* turn the ignition on without engaging the clutch."

"Which one is the clutch?" Nic snaps.

"Should be a lever on the left handlebar." Annie digs in my pocket without asking, snagging the key I grabbed before.

There's still gunfire coming from the entrance to the depot. Angry shouts, screams of pain. The air stinks of cordite. How in the name of blue fuck did we slip through the cracks here? *How are we not dead?*

I am not a fan of standing around doing nothing. No situation has ever been improved by staring stupidly at it. But right now, as Annie and Nic zip between the bikes trying to find the ones that work, it's the only thing I can do.

Annie and Nic find the right bikes at almost exactly the same time. Annie's is an enormous black Harley, with one of those silly little raised passenger seats on the back. Nic's is a few bikes down the line: a sleek, neon-blue ride with a bulging gas tank. Annie is holding on tight to the handlebars, her left hand wrapped around a thick lever.

I have an absurd urge to tell them to find one with a sidecar. I've always wanted to ride in a sidecar.

"Get on!" Annie yells at me.

I snap out of my stupor, jogging across and clambering aboard, perching on the passenger seat and wrapping my arms around Annie. The seat is one of the most uncomfortable things I've ever sat on, way too small, finding the bony parts of my ass in seconds. Nic jams Leo down in front of him, the two of them chest to chest. An odd thought bounces through my mind: *We should have helmets. You shouldn't ride bikes without helmets. It's dangerous.*

Yeah, you know what's more dangerous? Hanging around a gun fight. The sooner we get the fuck out of here, the better.

"Turn left out the gate," Annie yells at Nic. He doesn't reply, just pops the kickstand, and takes off. Or tries to. The bike immediately stalls, wobbling like crazy. Nic has to jam his feet into the concrete surface to keep it upright.

"Work the clutch," Annie snarls at him. She takes a deep breath, visibly calms herself. "It's just like a car. Pop the clutch and accelerate at the same time."

"I've never driven manual!"

"Are you serious right now?"

I open my mouth to tell her to ease up, and then Jonas Schmidt walks out of the night, sauntering towards us.

THIRTY-FIVE

Teagan

Jonas wears the same outfit as before – same suit, with the white T-shirt underneath it. His hands are in his pockets, and the smile on his face is gentle.

"Hello again, Teagan," he says.

This isn't real. It's not real, it's the Zigzag Man, he's here, he—

But these thoughts come from very far away. It's as if they belong to someone else.

I blink – it seems to take ten years to open and close my eyes – and I'm no longer outside the train depot in Chinatown. I'm in a hangar at an airport, standing alongside a sleek private jet. Slanted rectangles of sunlight paint the floor, coming from windows set high in the rear wall. Jonas is at the bottom of the plane's entry stairway, which leads up to a door filled with warm, beckoning light.

And I can't believe how calm I feel. It's as if the light coming through the plane door is inside me, too, blooming inside my chest. I can't look away from Jonas, can't look away from that easy, welcoming smile.

I don't want to.

It's happening faster this time, you're much more exhausted, he's inside your head—

"I'm here to help," Jonas says.

The others are in trouble, Leo, Annie . . .

"Isn't this what you want?" Jonas's eyes crinkle in amusement.

"I—"

"Just come with me, and everything will go away. You won't have to make any more decisions. I'll do it all – all you have to do is come into my house."

The calm light fills every part of me. I take a step towards him, a smile of my own breaking out of my face. As I do so, there's a strange sensation on my shoulder, as if someone is gripping tight, shaking. I reach up, brush it away, and the feeling vanishes.

"You can do whatever you want," he says. "And I will be there. I will always be there."

No, this is wrong—

Except: I do want him. I want him so badly.

I want what he represents. Freedom. The ability to make my own choices without having to worry if the consequences will hurt me, or hurt others. I want to make choices that I will not regret.

And I want someone I can be with. I *burn* with that want.

Someone to listen to me, and to hold me, and to make love to me. I want to make love without thinking, to have it be as natural and as easy as the light that fills me up.

Jonas can offer me that. He can help me. He can protect me. He can love me.

"I'm ready," I say, reaching out to him.

His smile grows wider. "I never had a doubt."

He takes my hand. His skin is warm, and dry, his grip firm.

"Come into my house." He gestures to the door of the plane. The light is so bright that I can't actually see the interior. "Come into my house, and be safe."

The same irritating sensation on my shoulder – both shoulders now. I shrug deliberately, trying to get past it, walking towards the plane.

But something holds me back. Locks my feet in place.

Jonas turns, frowns. "Isn't this what you want?"

It is. It's what I want. What I can't understand is: why, as Jonas says those words, does his face became Nic's?

There was no mistaking it. At least . . . I *think* there was no mistaking it. My thoughts are slow, mired in the warm light.

I open my mouth to tell Jonas that this *is* what I want, but the words don't come. When I try to speak, I can't hear myself.

"My house is close," Jonas says.

Emergency blink. Emergency blink now!

"We can spend all the time you like inside it. It goes on for ever."

I let go of his hand.

Let my eyes slowly close.

"Teagan." Jonas's voice is different now. Changing. For the first time, a tiny needle of fear pierces my chest.

"My house does not lie," Jonas says.

I squeeze my eyes shut, then open them.

And scream.

The hangar is gone. The plane is gone. Jonas is still there, but his skin is melting, running off his face like slow-moving lava. The light is everywhere, but it's no longer warm. It's hot, burning, searing, and there are flames and smoke and the needle of fear has become a knife, twisting, and Jonas . . .

He's not Jonas any more.

He's Carlos.

Carlos Morales. A man I've tried very hard to forget. My old China Shop teammate. My friend. The person who betrayed me, who tried to frame me for murder.

The man I left to die.

To *burn.*

The fight I had with Jake, the only other psychokinetic I've ever met, left Carlos impaled on a steel pole. A wildfire was approaching and I couldn't get out in time and I was so scared, and I—

"*Hola, mi hermana,*" Carlos says. His grin is the most awful thing I've ever seen, a white slash in a blistering, burning face. "It's been a long, long time."

I blink, again and again, but it doesn't work. Carlos takes a step towards me, still smiling as the fire ravages him, and I topple over backwards. I'm sobbing, screaming at him that I'm sorry, but the words are silent. I can't look away. In desperation, I try to reach out with my PK, but there's nothing. Not a single thing, not even fuzziness. It's like it's gone for good.

"There's a fire in my house, *mi hermana.*" Carlos raises a burning hand, examines it, as if surprised at the scorched, peeling skin. The flames have burned a hole in his cheek, exposing his jaw. His face changes, Jonas one moment, Nic the next, all burning, all grinning. "There's a fire in my house, and it's your fire, and it is going to eat you alive."

I can't scream any more. I can't breathe. And I can't look away.

I'm going to burn. Just like before, in Wyoming, when Adam burned down our ranch and killed Mom and Dad and Chloe and—

There is another sound, a screeching, grinding bang. All at once, Carlos vanishes. So do the flames.

I'm on my back, in front of the depot, the wet concrete soaking through my clothes. Annie is close by, on her knees, retching, as if trying to bring up something foul. The Zigzag

Man must have hit her, too. Nic is still holding Leo, but the bike he was on—

I don't really understand what I'm seeing. As I turn my head, I catch sight of the bike, which is roaring across the parking lot – just like before, when I turned the key with my PK. And dancing out of the way, cursing, nearly getting creamed by it—

The Zigzag Man.

He only just dodges the charging bike. As it crashes to the ground, his head snaps towards us.

He's dressed in all-black, like before. Same black bandanna, tied over the lower half of his face. Above the bandanna, below the thick mane of straggly black hair, his eyes radiate pure hatred.

"Leave us alone!" Leo screams.

The Zigzag Man tilts his head. "It's time to go, little bug."

"Back off, asshole," Nic snarls at him.

Get up. But I can't move. I feel like I'm waking up from a deep sleep myself, my movements sluggish and uncoordinated, my PK a distant memory. I don't know what's happening here. Where did the Zigzag Man come from? Did Nic attack him with the bike? How—?

"*Motherfucker!*"

Another bang. This one much closer. Then two more.

Pop. She's coming out the front of the depot, a glare on her mashed face, a big-ass assault rifle held tight to her shoulder. I can't see her eyes from here, but it's as if she doesn't know where she is. She's just shooting, firing at anything that moves.

The Zigzag Man looks at her, and she stumbles. The rifle clatters to the concrete, Pop swatting at the air, like she's being attacked by a swarm of flies. She twists her face away, cowering . . . and screams.

In one move, Annie reaches down, scooping me up and dropping me onto the back of the bike. I didn't even see her get off the ground.

"Hold on!" she barks at me.

Somehow, my hands find her waist, hold tight.

Then she guns the throttle, and shoots right towards the Zigzag Man. For the second time, he tries to get out the way, but the edge of the handlebar just catches him across the waist. He grunts, knocked sideways. Pop is still firing, and I swear one of the bullets passes an inch from my face.

Nic's got hold of his bike again, lifting it up, hoisting a screaming Leo onto it and desperately twisting the key. The Zigzag Man reaches for him, fingers hooked into claws, but then the throttle catches. The bike kicks into life, and then all of us – me and Annie, Nic and Leo – thunder across the parking lot.

The Zigzag Man's eyes meet mine. The fury in them is almost beyond words. There's a horrible, fleeting moment where he's Carlos again, burning, blistering before my eyes—

Then we're gone.

THIRTY-SIX

Reggie

The cab driver won't load Reggie's chair.

It's a problem she's had before, many times. On a normal day, it would be exasperating, another insult to be endured. Today, it makes her want to spit lava.

She's on the curb outside the China Shop offices. It's full dark now, about 9 p.m., drizzle falling from a leaden sky. She's wearing a rain jacket, a thick one with decent padding. Putting on her own clothes is hell – most days, she needs Annie's help to do it. But if she has to, she can get her arms into a jacket, even if it does take her ten minutes.

"It won't fit," the driver protests. He has the build of a linebacker gone to seed, with messy red hair and a pencil-thin moustache.

"You think this is my first rodeo?" Reggie snaps. "Pick me up, put me in the back, then put the chair in the trunk. Why do you think I ordered a bigger ride?"

The driver sniffs. "It's too heavy to lift anyway."

"So it *will* fit. You just don't want to put your back out."

"I don't have insurance. I don't wanna get sued if something happens. And besides, if I pick you up ... I mean, you're a woman and all ... "

None of this is new to Reggie. Anybody with a disability has gone through it – hell, it was a running joke in her theatre troupe, that they'd miss their performances because they couldn't get cabs or ride-sharing. If only her regular cab company was still around. It would have saved her having to deal with this fool, and his problematic beliefs.

God, she loathes the word *problematic*. It's an academic's word, one trotted out by the speaker to show how erudite they are. A look-at-me word, never deployed to correct a wrong, just to extract attention. Or, more often, simply to indicate something the speaker doesn't like, and doesn't think anybody else should like either.

It's not that it was wrong to use, in terms of the strict definition, but it carried so much baggage. And it was absolutely useless in getting other people to change their ways. Telling someone what they said was *problematic* was like throwing a tennis ball at a wall. You'd entertain yourself, for a while, but you were never busting through.

In Reggie's experience, most people aren't deliberately evil. They just don't always think about their words. In most cases, she's happy to set them straight. Not tonight. Tonight, she does not have time to put up with whatever nonsense this ignorant asshole is sending her way, or to wait an hour for another cab to show up

She fixes him with a sweet smile. "Honey, let me tell you something. You know what I do for a living?"

"I don't really—"

"I'm a hacker."

He scoffs. "OK."

"You don't believe me?"

"I mean . . ." He's looking around him, as if trying to find an excuse to get out of this conversation. "I don't mean no disrespect or nothing. But I mess around with computers a little bit too."

"*Mess around with computers*. That's adorable."

"It's not that hard, like ... Anyway, what are you gonna do? Steal my identity or whatever? Empty my bank account? Come on."

Reggie tilts her head back, rolls her tongue around her mouth. "Stealing your identity never causes as much trouble as you think. Places like banks and government agencies know about it, so they take precautions. No, I'm not after your money. If you drive away without me and my chair in your cab, I'm going to do things to you that will take months to entangle. And there won't be a fraud department or case officer in the world who can help you.

"For starters, I'm going to dig up your details, sign you up to every free trial on every bogus health cure website and multi-level marketing scam I can find – and I'll tell your inbox to mark them all as priority. I could probably write a program to do it automatically, while I have a cup of tea."

"Hey—"

"After I get done destroying your inbox, I'm going to use my corporate credit card to order as many large appliances as I can, and get them sent to your house. And not just kitchen appliances, either. I hope you like industrial water pumps, because you're going to build up quite a collection of them. From multiple companies. All of them with different returns policies."

He stares at her, his mouth open.

"*Then*, I'm going to gain access to your cab company's system. I'm going to start sending false pickup information to your dashboard screen. Not very often – just often enough that you'll never be quite sure if it's a real pickup or not. Of course, you could call your dispatch to check, but how long do you think they'll put up with *that*? And then—"

"Are you threatening me?"

"Oh yes. Very much so. Because understand this: I do not have time for your petty hang-ups today. I don't care what you think about people in wheelchairs. I am not interested in your opinions on women. In the grand scheme of things, little man, your opinions mean zip. What I have to do is far more important. So let me be absolutely clear on this. Let me put it in words of one syllable, so you can get it through your head. On this night, right now, *do not fuck with me*."

The curse word is a jolt, like a zap of static to a finger, a not-quite-unpleasant sensation. Overdramatic? Perhaps. But what the hell – Reggie always did enjoy chewing up the scenery a little.

It's the same dramatic streak that led her to bring a knife.

Reggie has a set of modified cutlery – forks and knives and spoons with rings on the handles, so she can slip them over her fingers and eat without having to grip them. She even has a serrated steak knife, because there's nothing quite like a medium rare rib-eye – she doesn't eat it often, it's heavy on her stomach, but when she does she likes a sharp knife.

It's this she has in her pocket. No point kidding herself – if she's in a situation where she has to use it, she'll probably be dead before she can get it out. But it makes her feel better having it, a little more secure.

The cab driver bites his lip, looking sullen. But he doesn't move.

"Fine." Reggie spins her chair around. "I'll get started on those emails, while I wait for another cab." But she can barely muster enough venom to get the words out. Damnit, she *needed* this ride. By the time another one bumbles its way to her, Teagan might be—

"Wait."

She stops, doesn't turn around.

"I'm sorry. I'll ...We can try load the chair in the back. I just meant ... It wasn't like I was saying ... "

"Well then." Reggie can't stop herself beaming. "Let's go."

Five minutes later, she is in the back of the cab with her chair in the rear trunk space. The driver had to wrestle with it to get it in there – it is, Reggie will admit, pretty damn heavy. She even felt a little bad for him. Only a little though – his feelings probably hurt worse than his back does. And in the scheme of things, she has much bigger things to worry about. Like what she's going to say to Teagan if (*when*) she finds her. How she's going to defuse Africa. And what on earth they're going to do about the boy.

All the same, as they head up South Wilmington Avenue, Reggie can't help but feel a lightness. For the first time in an age, she's away from the China Shop offices. She's out in the field. Sure, it's not under the best of circumstances, but she'll take it.

And she *can* pull this off. She can be the peacemaker, get everybody – Teagan, Africa, Moira Tanner – on the same side. She can bring China Shop – the organisation she's devoted years to – back together.

And wouldn't that be sweet? To pull off a win at the last second? To not have what might be her final China Shop job end in disaster? To show Moira and Teagan and everybody else *why* they need her, and to do it in the field, not parked behind a desk.

And when – *if* – she decides to leave, it'll be on her own

terms. If she actually does decide to pull the ripcord, then she'll go out under blue skies, floating free. She can move onto the next phase of her life, knowing she gave this everything she had.

Or are you just looking for an excuse to stay? For Moira to fall at your feet and tell you how much she needs you?

Reggie forces herself away from the thought, watching LA slip by out the window.

THIRTY-SEVEN

Teagan

So it turns out, you can totally fall asleep while escaping from a gunfight on the back of a really loud motorcycle.

We're not talking deep, restorative sleep here. What I get are microsleeps, pulling me into unconsciousness for a second or two at a time even as Annie guns the engine and we zip through the deserted streets.

You want to know the really weird part? I dream. I didn't think you could dream with this kind of sleep, but it turns out that's not true. All you have to do is take copious amounts of meth, get into fights with a motorcycle gang, have a mysterious enemy plant horrific visions in your head — something I'm probably going to have to go back into therapy to process, by the way — all while transporting a superpowered child through LA.

In my dream, I'm back in Wyoming, on my family's ranch. It's one of those rare days when my mom and dad aren't testing our abilities — I don't know how I know this, but I do. No endless hours in the barn behind the house, where I attempt to precisely move metal rings with my PK while Chloe uses her infrared vision to identify objects behind a screen. She and I are out in the woods, on horseback, riding through rivers and winding our way through dense groves of lodgepole pines.

Keep up, Chloe says. She turns to look at me, but I can't see her face.

Strangely, this doesn't bother me. I'm happier than I can ever remember being. Every sensation – the wind in my face, the rough leather reins in my hands, the piercing blue of the cloudless sky beyond the pines – is crystal clear.

Where's Adam? I ask. All of a sudden, it's important to know where my brother is, although I can't for the life of me explain why.

Chloe smiles. I know this, even though I still can't see her face. She can be cold sometimes, going into her own head and freezing me out for days if I do something she doesn't like. But not today. Today, she loves me, and she's my sister and we—

Right then, I snap awake, jerking up into the real world so fast that I nearly topple off the back of the bike. My arms are still wrapped around Annie's waist – God knows how I even managed to hold on while I slept. I reflexively squeeze harder, causing her to grunt in alarm.

We're somewhere in Chinatown. The roads are clear of cars and debris, but the actual surfaces are cracked and pitted, uneven. The damage slows us to a crawl. The bike headlights cast the streets in an eerie glow. Every so often, I'll spot a face peering out at us from an alley or broken window, gaunt and suspicious. But nobody stops us.

If my haywire sense of direction is to be trusted, we're heading back to the river. As we turn onto Spring Street, the road drops sharply. It's become a huge sinkhole, with a massive puddle of water at the bottom, maybe fifteen feet across. Yellow plastic barriers cordon it off on either side, as if approaching cars would somehow miss the gigantic gap. Then again, this is America. You can't trust people to see what's right in front of their faces.

The edges of the hole, where the sidewalks are, look OK. They dip sharply, but then rise again to the level of the street, narrow but driveable. Or rideable, I guess. The surfaces look damaged, but stable.

Annie takes it slowly, expertly tweaking the throttle, keeping us dead straight as we head down the steep slope, then up the far side. She pops us up on the far side of the sinkhole, turning us sideways so she can check on Nic. Turns out, he's not doing as well as we were.

Nic's into extreme sports. Rock climbing, surfing, snowboarding. He's pretty good at them too. Apparently, that doesn't translate to riding a motorcycle. He got to the bottom of the dip OK, but looks like he's having trouble getting back up the slope. He's taking it a snail's pace, the engine revving in uneven bursts.

"Lean forward!" Annie shouts, hands cupped to her mouth. "Use your legs to grip the tank!"

Nic doesn't appear to hear her. His gaze stays locked on the front wheel, his knuckles white on the handlebars. All at once, his bike accelerates, roaring up the slope. Leo yelps, squirming as he tries to hold on tighter.

"Brake. Brake. *Brake!*" Annie jumps backwards, swinging her long arm into my path, like I'm about to step into traffic. All I can do is watch, blinking stupidly.

There's a moment where Nic almost makes it – where he seems to get things under control, stabilising the bike. The moment vanishes almost as quick as it arrived. He crests the top of the dip, front wheel up in the air. Then he comes back down with a bang, and dumps the bike.

Nic's howl of pain even louder than the impact. Leo goes tumbling, bouncing across the cracked concrete.

Annie and I sprint across to them. Visions of shattered bones and concussions flicker in my mind, but as we get to the bike, Nic shoves it off him, then springs to his feet like a boxer jumping up off the mat. He has the wild-eyed, jittery look of someone who still isn't quite sure if he's OK or not.

Leo is on his feet too. His hands are scraped up something bad, but otherwise he looks unhurt. He totters across to us, his eyes almost as wide as Nic's.

I don't know who to go to first. So I choose the third option, which is to stand there gawping like an idiot.

Nic's right elbow is messy with road rash, bits of grit and dirt embedded in it. He taps at it, winces, then flexes his legs. "That was fun," he says, his voice way too high-pitched. Amazingly, he holds out a high-five for Leo. Even more amazingly, given his shredded hands, Leo grins and returns it.

"What the hell?" Annie growls. "I told you to lean forward."

"I *was* leaning forward," Nic says, absently patting his legs.

"So you're OK?" I say, my voice just as high as his.

"I think so. Yeah. It hurt but . . . yeah. How 'bout you, little man?"

"I'm fine," Leo says. He holds up his hands, blinking at them, then holds them out to us. Like he wants them graded. "Ow."

"Damn," Nic says, leaning down to lift the bike. "I was finally getting the hang of gears, and then the slope just . . . damn."

Annie bends down, helping Nic right the bike. "Yeah, well, it's flat from here on out." She glances back at the sinkhole, as if expecting Pop to reappear like the damn Terminator. "Let's go."

Nic and Leo might be fine, but their bike isn't. Twenty minutes later, as we rumble down Alameda, it gives a sputtering,

gurgling noise, and dies. Nic and Leo coast to a stop, and
Annie has to pull back, driving in a wide circle. I'm micro-
sleeping again, this time without any weird dreams, and wake
up with a snort.

"I think it broke," Leo says.

Nic dismounts. "Can we fix it?"

"We'd better." Annie jogs over. Halfway there, she turns
back. Studying me. "You're OK, right?"

Her sudden concern knocks me off balance a little. "Um.
Yeah. I'm fine."

She looks me up and down once more, then heads over to
Nic. "Keep an eye out. Watch our backs."

I don't have the heart to tell her my PK energy is pretty
much at zero right now.

Nic and Annie fuss with the bike for a few minutes – well,
Annie fusses with it, Nic just tries not to get in the way. I
wander over to Leo, still not a hundred per cent sure this isn't
a dream. I'm awake now, at least, my brain given a nice little
jolt of energy.

"No go." Annie gets to her feet, wiping oil-stained hands
on her jeans. "Dead."

"Sorry, man," Nic says. "It must have happened when I
dumped the bike."

"So what do we do now?" I ask.

"Guess we walk," Annie says.

"Um, Annie?" I point to Leo. "Maybe walking isn't
the best—"

"I'm OK," Leo says, rocking from foot to foot. "It feels
weird and stuff but, but the wiggles are gone"

"We still got one bike," Nic points out. "You could go
ahead with Leo, and—"

"No." Annie's voice is harsh. Harsher than she intended,

because almost immediately, she draws into herself, as if telling herself to chill the fuck out. She glances at Leo, tries again. "I'm not splitting us up again. That didn't work out so well last time."

We're in DTLA now, west of the river. Compton is to the south – the far south. A whole lot of walking. After everything that's happened today, I feel like I've walked for years. Decades.

Looking around, I'm pretty sure I'm not the only one who feels this way. Leo's wiggles might be gone, but he's exhausted. Nic and Annie too. The bruises and cuts are still fresh, and their bodies are probably screaming for rest.

"Can we just stop for a few minutes?" I say. I'd prefer a few hours. Ideally, a whole month. But even sitting down for a little while will help.

"Bad idea." Annie shakes her head. "We gotta keep moving."

It would be a lot more convincing if she didn't look like she was about to fall over.

For a long moment, nobody says anything. Annie keeps glancing back up Alameda, as if looking for anyone chasing us.

"Maybe it's not such a bad idea," Nic says. Leo punctuates this with a massive yawn.

Annie shakes her head. "We have to—"

"Annie, come on," I say. "Ten minutes. We take ten minutes, catch our breath, then we keep going."

"They're probably coming after us right now. You know that right?"

"OK, so we hide. They're not gonna search every single building."

She wavers. She's as exhausted as I am, and probably in real pain from the bruises. Her lip has started bleeding again, a thin trickle of blood on her chin.

"We gotta get the bikes off the street anyway," I point out. "Can't just leave 'em for the Legends to find."

"OK, genius." Annie rubs the back of her neck, wincing. "Where should we ...? What is it?"

I happen to be looking over her shoulder as she speaks. I hadn't noticed it before, but there's a strange building behind her – one that isn't a rectangular office block, or line of stores, like most of the buildings you see in this part of town. It lies at the other end of a short plaza, which is now a graveyard of toppled palm trees. It's an odd shape – like a church, with a tall tower at one end.

Nic squints into the darkness. "Teags, what do you see?"

"Son of a bitch," I murmur, a smile cracking my face.

Annie spreads her hands, eyebrows raised.

I straighten up. "Come with me." Without waiting for them to agree, I march off, heading for the strange building, ignoring the protests from Annie and Nic.

Eventually, I'm far enough ahead of them that they have no choice to follow. They wind the heavy bikes through the fallen palm trees, and by the time we reach the front of the building, Annie looks like she's going to fall over.

OK – maybe I should have gone back and helped with the bikes. But as the details of the building coalesce out of the downtown darkness, I decide not to be too hard on myself.

When Annie sees what I see, she lets out an exhausted laugh. "Unreal, man. Unreal."

Nic frowns. "Is that—?"

"What does it say?" Leo asks, pointing. There's a wide awning that projects out from the building entrance, big metal letters bolted onto the front edge, looking out over the plaza.

I grin. "It says, *Union Station*. Come on, little dude. I got something amazing to show you."

THIRTY-EIGHT

Teagan

God, if he or she or they actually exist, is a gigantic prick.

No, for real. Take one look at the world today, and tell me that God isn't out to mess with us. But every once in a while, you get a freebie. And right now, on this, the most fucked up, weird, hallucinatory night of Teagan Frost's wild life, we've just gotten a gigantic freebie from the Big Dickhead in the Sky.

Getting inside Union Station is not easy. It's still standing – obviously – but it's been closed off, the windows and doors covered by thick, heavy wooden boards. Annie and Nic try to persuade me that it's a non-starter, that we can't get in, that we should go somewhere else.

The glass doors under the awning are sealed off with the same boards. They're secured with a horizontal steel bar, locked in place by two of the biggest, toughest padlocks I've ever seen. Goddamnit, I was really hoping there'd just be a basic lock – one I might even be able to kick in. Then again, whoever owns Union Station probably didn't want that happening.

"Locked," Annie says, as if that settles the matter.

For a second, I waver, not sure if I can do this. Then, I take a deep breath, gather what little is left of my PK, and go to work.

It's hard. Brutally hard. The headache comes roaring back, the lock greying out in front of me. I have to have a very serious talk with myself as I force my dregs of PK energy into the lock. *Come on, dude. You can do it. All you need to do is move a couple of latches. You don't have to deal with guns, or motorcycles, or shift slabs of concrete. Just a couple of tiny latches. That's all. Come on.*

Nothing happens. A horrible, slimy, sweat breaks out on my forehead. I grit my teeth, doing everything I can to ignore the headache. I am going to make this work. I am *not* going to look like a punk, not after getting excited about finding Union Station. I *want* what's inside.

I want something good for us today.

"Teags . . . " Nic puts a hand on my shoulder.

Click.

It happens so suddenly that I almost gasp. Just like that, the lock is open. I reach out with a trembling hand, pull the big glass door open with a squeak of disused hinges.

"There," I say, my voice shaking. Like I totally knew that was going to work.

"We can't just stop here," Annie says, although not even she sounds convinced. I flash ten fingers at her, as in: *ten minutes.* Then, without waiting for a response, I step inside. Like I know exactly what I'm doing.

The station interior is pitch-dark, dead silent. Nic and Annie follow, shaking their heads, sending drops of water flying everywhere. Leo, however, hovers on the threshold, hugging himself.

"What's wrong?" I ask – then immediately see the problem.

I pull out my phone – well, the phone I stole from Minnie. Maybe there's a way to turn on the flashlight without unlocking it. But when I open it up, I'm mildly surprised to find that the dumbass didn't activate password protection. I guess when you're a badass leather-clad biker, you don't sweat about people stealing your phone. Pop would probably tear him a new one if she found out.

I'm tempted to mess around on the phone a little, maybe see what weird photos he's taken, but decide against it. I am not in the mood for biker dick pics right now. I activate the flashlight, noting the time: 21:53.

I also note the background: a smiling Latinx woman, holding a swaddled baby. It's hard not to think of Minnie, beat to shit by Annie, his face mashed hamburger. I swallow, looking away from the screen. Nothing we can do now.

The flashlight isn't super-strong, but it pushes back the darkness a little. Leo swallows, then limps inside. I smile at him, thinking how crazy it is that a kid who has seen as much as he has could still be afraid of the dark. Then I feel bad for thinking this, then reach out and take his hand.

Union Station is not your average train stop. It's this amazing art deco building, with high, vaulted ceilings and little filigrees and details on every pillar and doorway. Of course, it's less amazing now: silent as a tomb, and clearly damaged. One of the many chandeliers lies in a smashed pile in the middle of the lobby.

"Teags." I don't think Annie means to whisper. "Y'all know there might be other people here, right?"

"Yeah? So?"

"Don't pretend like you don't know what I'm talking about."

"I can't feel anybody with my PK." That's a blatant lie, I can barely feel anything with my PK right now, but she doesn't have to know that. I don't care if the devil himself lives here; we *have* to rest, if only for a few minutes.

And there is no better place to do it, in the whole of LA, than Union Station. I grip Matthew's hand, and lead us deeper into the building.

Our footsteps echo off the high ceilings as we head into the main hall. Annie did manage to plant a tiny seed of doubt in my mind – I don't know if we have the energy to fight off yet more people who want to mess with us, for whatever reason – but there doesn't appear to be anyone around. It doesn't look like people have been here at all; the inside of the station is musty, but there's no trash, no signs of life. Figures, given the heavy-duty security.

Maybe it's the darkness, which the phone flashlight only pushes back a little way. Maybe it's the silence. But I can't stop thinking of the Zigzag Man.

I don't feel like I have a choice – like if I ignore the thought, it'll swell and swell until it pops the top off my head. Both times, the Zigzag Man used his ability on two of us. The first time, it was me and Nic, and the second, me and Annie. Why would he stop there? Why not take us all out? Put us all in his fantasy world? Unless . . .

My ability has limitations. I'm stronger that I used to be, but unless I'm high on meth, I still have a limit to my range and strength. Maybe the Zigzag Man has limits, too. Maybe he can only affect two people at once, and no more. Maybe we can use that. Somehow.

It's strange that he didn't use his ability on Leo when he first tracked us down. Maybe he thought he didn't need to – that Leo would be tapped out, his wiggles preventing him from fighting back.

The idea of someone with the ability to make you see things that aren't there isn't as far-fetched as you'd think. When you can move shit with your mind, your notions about what is possible and what isn't are very flexible. But where did the Zigzag Man come from? How does he exist?

And both times we've run into him, we only barely escaped.

Sooner or later, our luck is going to run out, and I still don't have the first clue how to actually stop this guy.

More than that: if he comes back, and makes me see Carlos again, puts me in the fire . . .

"My fingers hurt." Leo squints down at them. His left eye is still twitching like crazy.

"Leo," I say, keeping my voice steady. "The Zigzag Man . . ."

"Huh?"

"Is there anything you can tell us about him? Anything at all?"

Leo bites his bottom lip. When he finally speaks, it's as if he hasn't heard me. "Me and Olivia and Lucas would use our powers, and then we'd get to play, but—"

"Who's Olivia?"

"She could do math and stuff."

Math. I want to ask Leo more, but before I can, he says, "Sometimes the Zigzag Man and the other lady would watch us."

"The other lady? Who's she?"

"I don't know. What's gonna happen to the other kids? Are they gonna be OK?"

For a second, I think he means the other kids at the School. Lucas and . . . Olivia, was it? But no – he's talking about the Legends' Daycare for Wayward Orphans. I want to tell him not to worry, that of course they're going to be OK. In the end, I can't do it. I don't have the energy to lie. "I don't know. But Mrs Garcia seemed nice, so . . . "

He ponders this for a minute. "Where're your mom and dad?"

It takes me a couple of seconds to form the words. "They . . . aren't around any more."

"Did they die?"

" . . . Yes."

"Oh." He thinks about it. "That's sad. I would miss my dad if he died."

"Your dad's ... We're gonna do everything we can to find him, OK?"

"Hey," he says, "did your mom and dad know about your powers?"

The smile I give him feels forced. "Yeah. Actually, they ... they kind of gave me my powers. Me and my brother and sister."

"They had your same powers?"

"No. Chloe could see heat – she could see how hot and cold things were. Adam – my brother – he never needed to sleep."

"He could stay up all night?"

"Pretty much."

"Cool!"

It was very much not cool. Turns out, having no sleep your entire life turns you into a psychopath. Adam was the one who killed my parents, and Chloe. He would have killed me too if I hadn't booked it the fuck out of there. I'm not shy about my past – I came to terms with it a long time ago – but that doesn't mean I'm going to give Leo the details. He hasn't exactly had a normal childhood himself, and I probably shouldn't make it any worse with horror stories.

God, Chloe ... I miss my parents the most, but I miss Chloe too. What girl wouldn't miss her big sister? Especially when she's the source of so many good memories. Like riding through the woods, the wind whipping against our faces, both of us laughing.

At that moment, I spot what I'm looking for. Nic does too, and bursts out laughing. "I forgot these were here," he says, grinning at me.

I can't help but smile back. Because yes, I am a genius.

Union Station isn't just an architectural masterpiece. It has the greatest waiting room known to man. If you think that sounds lame, then I want you to imagine yourself and your buddies relaxing in giant, puffy armchairs while you wait for your train. That's right: armchairs. Dozens of them, aligned in neat rows across the waiting room, each one a miracle of squashy leather upholstery and smooth mahogany.

LA is a dirty, messy, chaotic place, but there are some spots that stay pristine and untouched, against all odds. No graffiti, no vandalism. And it appears that despite the quake, despite everything that's been thrown at my city, the Union Station waiting room is one of them.

I turn to Annie, raising a hand for a high five. She stares at me, shaking her head in wonder.

"Don't leave me hanging," I say. I make it sound light, but I really do want her to high-five me. I want her to be OK with this.

After a few seconds, she gives my hand a weak slap. A moment after that, we crash down into the chairs.

The leather is old and slightly cracked, dusty as hell, not as comfy as I remember. You wouldn't want to sit in this chair every day. But right now, at this moment, it's the best thing I've ever felt. It is all I can do not to go to sleep right here. I wink at Leo, who sits with his legs dangling off the chair opposite. Against all odds, he's grinning too.

We sit in silence for a few minutes. Just ... being. Yes, we're being chased by the Legends and the National Guard and Africa and the goddamn piece-of-shit Zigzag Man, but it feels like we've called a time out in this little game. Not to say that we can totally relax yet. We won't be able to for hours. But resting for a little while here will make those hours more bearable. And as grouchy as Annie and Nic were about coming in here, they're also sinking into the leather seats. Welcoming the cracked, dusty embrace.

It's only after another microsleep almost takes me that I remember the meth in my pocket.

My hand jumps to it, half wanting to check it's still there, the other half hoping it isn't. But there's a muffled crackle of plastic under my fingers.

Come on. You took the meth for a specific reason, remember? I have this bag so I can test it later – find out what very small amounts do to my PK. I didn't plan to get high this morning, and it does *not* mean I'm going to become addicted. In fact, this is probably a smart way to treat the urge I'm feeling. It acknowledges it, doesn't try to force it away, gives it a healthy outlet.

Leo speaks, jerking me out of my thoughts. "Nic, do you have powers too?"

When there's no response Leo leans over, and tugs on Nic's sleeve. "Hey."

Nic jerks his arm back, as if Leo had shocked him. He stares down at the boy, as if seeing him for the first time, then gives his head a little shake. "Sorry. What?"

Leo repeats the question.

"Oh. No. I'm normal."

I raise an eyebrow.

Nic realises what he just said, and gives me an embarrassed look. "Well, I'm ... I mean, no, I don't have powers."

Leo doesn't appear to notice that Nic just called him and me abnormal. "Annie, do *you* have them?"

Annie shakes her head.

Leo huffs out a dramatic breath. "It's like we're in a movie," he says.

"Yeah," says Nic. "*The Avengers*."

"I don't really like superhero ones," Leo says quietly, as if admitting he did something bad.

"What? Why not?"

He little-boy-shrugs. "I dunno. They're not fun."

"Same," I tell Leo. Well, that's half true. Batman isn't bad. Mostly because he's just a normal guy with a ton of money and cool gadgets. Technically, anyone could be him.

"Wait, what?" Nic squints at me. "You've never seen *Avengers?*"

"Well yeah, obviously I've seen it. It's just really unrealistic."

There's a part of me that can't believe we're actually talking about this shit. Superhero movies we've seen, in the middle of everything that's happening? Then again: why not? We've all been through the ringer, and if talking about random movies lightens the load, then why the fuck not? I'm down.

"It's a *comic book movie*, man," Nic says. "What did you expect?"

"I have insider knowledge of what it's really like." I nudge Leo. "We both do. Besides," I tell Nic, "you like that arthouse stuff, don't you?"

"Hey, *The Graduate* isn't an *arthouse* movie, man. It's a classic."

"What's *The Grad-jit?*" Leo asks.

Nic and I exchange a worried look.

"Um . . . " says Nic.

"It's boring," Annie says. "You wouldn't like it."

"How about you Annie?" Nic asks. "You watch Marvel movies? I know you don't have powers or anything, but you're in the business. Sort of."

Annie shakes her head. "I'm not really into movies."

"Oh come on."

"They're annoying," she says. "Especially if they're set in a real place. The ones set in LA always get stuff wrong. I hate that."

"They don't all get stuff wrong." Nic actually sounds offended. "What about . . . like, *Mulholland Drive*?"

"Never seen it."

"*What?*"

"Dunno what to tell you. I'm more of a book person."

"Never?" He actually gapes at her.

"Do you realise how many great movies you're missing out on?" I ask. "*Die Hard* was set in LA."

"So was *Training Day*," Nic says. "*Boyz n the Hood. The Big Lebowski. Nightcrawler. Collateral.*"

"Yes!" I snap my fingers at him. "Everybody always forgets *Collateral*. That is a goddamn amazing movie."

"Right?"

I deadpan a cop's voice. "Hey, is this blood up here on your windshield?"

"I, uh . . . " Nic can barely keep a straight face. "I hit a deer. On Slauson."

And together, grinning stupidly at each other: "A South Central deer?"

"I've never seen that movie," Leo says. He does it in such a prim, offended manner that I can't help but break out laughing again. So does Nic.

We look at each other – and it's like the argument we had before, after Dodger Stadium, suddenly leaps to the front of our minds at exactly the same time. It's a look that says, *No amount of movie references or dumb superhero jokes is going to bridge this gap. Maybe nothing will.*

All at once, I desperately want to tell him that that's bullshit. I'm still trying to untangle what we said to each other, but I'm not going to let what we said define our relationship. Not a chance.

I don't get a chance to process it. Right then, my PK gives a *ping*.

I'm very far from being at full capacity. But my ability to sense stuff has come back, a little. And right now, I'm sensing a bunch of wallets and cellphones and coins and glasses heading towards us from deeper inside the station. A second later, there are voices.

My eye's meet Annie's. She's halfway out of her seat when four bobbing lights come into view. Cellphone flashlights, or actual torches. It's impossible to see who's behind them.

"Who's that?" says a male voice.

"Thought you said this place was empty," comes another voice. A woman this time.

"You have gotta be kidding me," I mutter.

"Teagan, we good?" Annie says, not taking her eyes off the lights. Nic steps protectively in front of Leo. I can just make out the dark shapes behind the floating lights now – it looks like there are five figures there. My first thought is that they're city officials, come to clean any squatters out of the station. But there's something in the way they're standing that tells me otherwise. They're not the Legends, or the National Guard – I can't feel any weapons. And I'm pretty sure they weren't conjured by the Zigzag Man.

"How y'all doing?" one of them says. His voice is deeper than the others.

"We're having a great night," I tell him. "A legendary one, actually."

"Is that right?" The man's torchlight jerks. "Time for y'all to move on. We got here first."

Were they here already? Deep in the station where we couldn't see them? They must have been ... but then, why are they the *only* ones here? There is no possible way we got here at exactly the same time as a bunch of dudes who suddenly remembered the existence of Union Station, and decided that it was a primo camping spot. Not even we can be that unlucky.

And how the hell did they get in here, anyway?

"We were just going," Nic says.

I flick an annoyed glance at him. "Uh, no we're not. We'll go when we're damn good and ready."

"We're claiming this spot for the camp," says someone else. "And we don't know you. Get outta here."

Annie tugs at my arm. "Let's go," she hisses.

I swing my arms wide. "Who the hell *are* you? *Ow.*" There's a sudden burst of pain at the base of my skull, my shoulders protesting at the movement. I recover quickly. "You do realise this is a public building right? You can't just—"

"You know what?" rumbles the man with the deep voice. "Y'all being disrespectful. Empty your pockets. Then you can go."

Are these jackasses trying to *mug* us? Of all the shit that's happened today . . .

Fine. They're about to find out that I'm not that easy to roll on. Except . . . I don't know if my PK is going to help this time. There's not enough of it. And even as the thought occurs, I'm weighing the odds, not liking what I see. Five of them. Three of us – four if you count Leo, who is as much out of gas as I am. We're already bruised, bloodied, exhausted.

If they want to mug us, who the hell is going to stop them?

"I said," the man repeats. "Cough it up. Go on. Or—"

"Woah, hold on!"

It comes from my right, a spot I haven't even looked at yet. There's a sharp, delighted bark, and Bradley Cooper bursts out of the darkness.

The dog jumps up on Leo, yapping and licking at him, almost knocking him over. His owner steps into view, a huge smile on his face.

We all stare at him, open-mouthed. It's Nic who speaks first.

"*Grant?*"

THIRTY-NINE

Teagan

I'd heard a lot about the homeless camp on the storm drain, even before this whole crazy night kicked off. It's one of those things you see in the news or on social media, and kind of just skim by. Or at least, I do.

I pictured a few tents, maybe a FEMA outpost or two. On the scale of one to shit-I-had-to-think-about-tonight, a homeless camp somewhere to the south didn't even bump the needle.

And I certainly was *not* expecting it to take up an entire freeway interchange.

The first things we see are the winking lights of cook fires. A hundred of them, it looks like, glimmering in the darkness like stars. The sound comes next: an almost subsonic hum, the noise of a thousand voices laughing, shouting, grumbling. The hum is mixed with the hammering of metal on metal, the thin crackle of cooking fires. It swells into the night, amplified by the concrete corridor of the river.

And then the camp coalesces out of the dark, and all I can do is gape.

LA is known for its traffic, and almost all of that traffic

happens on our gigantic freeways. Those freeways have even larger interchanges: giant spaghetti junctions, where freeways loop over and around one another, multiple levels of them, creaking under the staggering weight of cars and trucks. Or that *was* the case, before the quake. There are plenty of interchanges that got damaged, declared very-much-not-safe to drive over, and the 710-105 is one of them.

It's a gigantic, concrete Celtic cross where the two freeways intersect. The whole interchange is almost half a mile wide, most of it positioned just to the west of the storm drain. The section that crosses the drain has to be seven hundred feet wide, easily, multiple layers of freeway piled on top of one another.

But it's not the size of the interchange that gets me. It's the size of what's underneath it.

Most of the interchange supports are propped up with heavy-duty steel scaffolding – a huge nest of it, bars and platforms and catwalks holding the entire edifice up. There are tents everywhere – and I do mean everywhere. Not just on the concrete channel, but on the scaffolding platforms too, *and* on the actual freeways themselves. Some genius has actually hung rope ladders, turning the whole camp into something a little kid would dream up. The river itself cuts right through the middle of the camp, the channel vanishing into the maze of scaffolding.

The whole thing looks like a catastrophe waiting to happen. Here and there, the scaffolding has been bolstered by lengths of bamboo, the stalks lashed to the existing steel, strengthening the structure. There's a crew of men levering another set into place, they themselves standing on a makeshift platform positioned under the lowermost freeway loop.

Both sides of the storm drain are lined with flood barriers, right up to the freeway. A lot of them look like fresh repairs, or replacements. I can't tell if the city did it, or the people in the camp.

"We're getting dozens of new people every day," Grant says. Turns out, he was the reason these people were in Union Station. When his new buddies mentioned how full the camp was getting, he had an epiphany: why not occupy the station? It was, after all, just sitting there, sealed off but empty. When he was told it was impossible to get inside, he happened to mention that he was a former electrical engineer for the railways, and he happened to know a few ways in that were probably a little less secure . . .

They actually arrived some time before we did, and were just leaving as we got there.

"How many people here now?" Nic asks him.

He whistles. "Must be over two thousand, easy."

Honestly, it looks like more. They crowd between the tents, shuffle in a long queue around makeshift kitchens, crouch in small groups playing dice or dominoes, sit alone with their phones. Some of them give us curious glances, and a few shout hello to our little honour guard, but most just ignore us.

There are business suits, tattered nurses' scrubs, overalls, crisp white Ts with red and blue bandanas – the Crips and the Bloods, for once not appearing to give a shit about their beef. Men, women, kids, dogs, cats. Birds in cages. The air smells of weed and charcoal, sweat and rotting garbage – which is everywhere, piled up in stinking, tottering heaps.

"Did you know about this?" I ask Annie.

She shrugs. "Sure. It's gotten a lot worse since I last saw it, though."

"Worse?" The man with the deep voice – Grant introduced him as Alvin – kisses his teeth. I'm still not sure I've forgiven him for trying to rob us. "Please. We doin' just fine."

"Clearly," I say, eyeing a piece of makeshift scaffolding that looks like it's going to fall down if I raise an eyebrow.

"Oh, y'all think just because we out of work, we don't know what we're doing?" Alvin points, indicating an older man with a neat beard, fussing over a bamboo support. "See that dude? He worked construction for thirty years – built Tom Cruise's spot. He's been helping build this place up. We got a bunch of other dudes too."

"He put up the scaffolding? The metal stuff?"

"Nah. Government did that shit, then they left. Y'all know how it is. Don't matter though, we got all kinds. We got doctors, construction guys, Uber drivers, chefs, all of it."

Alvin sees the incredulous look on my face, and gives me a weary smile. "Twelve million people in the Greater LA area, y'all think a couple thousand didn't get screwed by insurance after the quake? Probably a lot more than that. Blue collar, white collar, all of it."

"I can help rig up some lights, by the way," Grant says. "I'm an electrical engineer. We could tap into the power grid, and—"

"Dude, I told you, we got it under control," Alvin says. "All that shit was done before you got here."

"Right," Grant says, a little crestfallen.

"Your house gone, maybe your car," says the woman next to Alvin. "Insurance company won't pay cos you didn't take out special coverage or your property taxes were overdue or whatever. Government supposed to help, but they can't agree on what to do, or whether they should accept aid from other countries or what not. Where you gonna go?"

"Lucille's right," says Alvin. "I mean, to be fair, some of us still got jobs to go to, you know? We got cars, but we gotta park them way away from here." He waves at the dark, interlocking freeway above us.

"I don't get it," I say. "If you're still getting a salary then why not rent, or . . . ?"

"Like there's so many properties out there to rent," says Lucille. "Most of us ended up with bad credit too. You know what I used to be? A prop designer. Eleven years. You think they're making movies here any more? All the big studios moved their shit. Someone told me the other day to go live in Vancouver, find work there. Fucking Vancouver! You know how many people from California tried to move to Canada? Take me years to get up there." She sniffs. "I'm LA born and raised. I'm never leaving."

She glances at Leo. "Oh, sorry, little man. I didn't mean to swear in front of—"

"It's fucking OK," Leo says, with a shrug.

I swear everybody takes a step back from him, wincing and hissing and telling him to mind his language. He blinks at us. "You guys say it all the time."

"Is that right?" Alvin fixes us with a pointed look.

I quickly change the subject. "Isn't it dangerous here? This is literally a storm drain. Aren't you guys worried about . . . ?"

I trail off, thinking about the blockage upriver, at the broken Main Street Bridge. All that water, building and building.

We used to get flash floods in Wyoming sometimes – I never got caught in one, but I know a little bit about how they work. We'd get them on dry creek beds and up in the canyons. They're nasty all right, big swells of water carrying a shit-ton of debris: broken trees, snapped branches, even boulders. They don't just appear from nowhere. You have some warning – you can hear them coming – and if you have a clear enough viewpoint, you can actually see them too.

I squint up the sides of the concrete storm drain, wondering if we'd be able to get out in time if a flash flood *did* chase us down. There are more flood barriers on either side of the camp, many of them looking brand-new, without graffiti. That confuses me, but only for a second. Some of the barriers were probably knocked down in the quake, and what I'm seeing are the ones the city replaced. The barriers are wall-to-wall on either side of the channel, with only a few gaps here and there for bridges, or maintenance worker access.

Not good if you happen to be living here.

"Sure." Lucille nods. "It's crazy dangerous."

Alvin sighs, like this isn't the first time he's had to explain this. "You think this is the only homeless camp in LA? Ever since those skyscrapers came down in Skid Row, bunch of people been looking for places to live. You got all these camps springing up everywhere, and one by one, the government comes in and shuts them down."

"Why?"

"Who the hell knows? Different reason every time. Safety, security, bringing down the tone of the neighbourhood, whatever. But then some people started camping here, and nobody was hassling them. Word got around, more and more people moved in . . . " He grimaces. "Even this place is getting to full. S'why we were scouting other spots, ones where folks wouldn't really get hassled."

Annie raises an eyebrow. "Like Union Station?"

"Why not? Trains aren't running. Place looks boarded up from the outside. Nobody's checking it. Why the hell not?

"What *do* you guys do if there's a flash flood here?" I ask Grant, trying to sound casual.

He looks bewildered. "A flash flood?"

"It's when water—"

"We'd get out of here," Alvin drawls. "No problem. If there's water coming, we'd see it way before it hit."

Lucille points up the channel. "Probably hear about it too. Data's a little sketchy here, but we still got some."

Alvin grimaces. "I mean, you think about it, we get swept away in a flood or whatever, it's probably a good thing for the government. Less people to take care of. Maybe that's why they've left us alone."

Ugh. And I *work* for the government. I'd love to say that Alvin's crazy conspiracy theory is just that, but I can totally see it happening.

I have to remind myself that it was the Legends who smashed us into the bridge supports in the first place. Without them, the bridge would never have collapsed. *I can't take on responsibility for everything.* All the same, the thought doesn't sit easy.

"Over here." Grant ushers us through the maze of scaffolding, to a spot close to the sloped edge of the channel. There's a cookfire, a big one, blazing in a sawed-up metal half-barrel. Two dozen people are clustered around it, some with blankets over their shoulders, talking quietly in small groups. A few kids, even a couple of newborns. Sleeping bags and camping cots and blow-up mattresses everywhere.

"Yo," Alvin barks. He claps Nic on the shoulder. "They're good. I checked 'em out."

Grant winks at me. I really want to ask him how on earth he hooked up with a group of half-assed stick-up artists. But I am way too fucking tired right now.

"Sit down," Alvin rumbles. "Yo yo, clear a spot for 'em! Make yourselves comfortable. We got heat, we got some water. *¿Juan, vato, queda algo de comida?* Maybe some of that steak?"

"I'm sorry." I raise a finger. "Did you say *steak*?"

"Don't expect the Four Seasons." He snickers. "But yeah, Juan —" he indicates a short, stooped man near the fire "— he found a butcher shop that was going out of business. We pooled cash, bought a bunch of stuff. Y'all are welcome. Won't even charge you – you know, to apologise for trying to jack you before."

"I love you," I say. I mean it, too. Juan has already slapped the meat on the grill over the fire, the sizzle as sweet as angel trumpets.

"Can I have some?" Leo says.

Nic shakes his head. "Look, thanks for the offer, but we gotta keep moving."

"I dunno." Annie frowns. "We could use some food."

"What about the Legends?" Nic asks. "Or – you know. Mr Zigzag Guy?"

"We gotta eat," I tell him. To be honest, I don't care how much he protests. I probably wouldn't care if Pop herself came bursting into the circle waving a bazooka. I am eating that steak.

All the same, I get a little jolt of worry. It's not just the Legends, or the Zigzag Man, or the National Guard. It's Africa, too. His network of contacts isn't as deep as Annie's Army, but it's still extensive . . . and it's a sure bet that he knows at least a few people here. I'm almost certain he's still in play – Leo hit him pretty hard, but then again, Africa's pretty hard himself. He's out there, right now, maybe hustling connects in Skid Row for info. Maybe he already knows where we are, is on his way down here . . .

At that very second, my gaze happens to land on a dude off to the side, talking on his cellphone. He's long-term homeless, it looks like, shirtless despite the rain, his body a mess of bruises and track marks, his face pinched and sour. His eyes meet mine, and he looks away quickly.

I shake my head, irritated. Not every person on the phone will be calling Africa, or even know that the big guy is looking for us. All the same . . . we shouldn't stick around any longer than we have to.

Food first, though. We all get a piece of steak, the silent Juan doling them out. They arrive on paper plates, still sizzling, with two slices of white bread on the side already soaking up the juice.

It's only steak in the sense that it's a cut of meat from a cow – we are not, as Alvin said, talking dry-aged rib-eye here. But . . . dear God and all her drunken angels. I've eaten some amazing things in my life, but I think this piece of mystery meat between two slices of Wonder Bread may be the very best. It's gone in four enormous bites.

Leo grins, juice running down his chin. "Thank you," he tells Juan.

I raise a hand. "Seconded. And thirded."

Annie and Nic nod their thanks – Nic might have been dubious, but his sandwich doesn't last much longer than mine. By now, most of the people around the fire have forgotten about us, going back to their own conversations. Given everything we've been through tonight, it's cool to be around people who *don't* want to murder us – who, in fact, don't give the tiniest shit about who we are, and what we're doing.

As I lick the last drop of juice off my lip, Leo points. "What's in there?"

We follow his finger. He's pointing to a gap in the storm drain's sloping side, just visible through the mess of scaffolding. The gap looks like an entrance to a passage, cut into the concrete. Two people are vanishing into it as we look, a couple of teenagers, one laughing at something the other said.

"Oh." Alvin takes a swig of water from a bottle, wipes his mouth. "Sewers."

"What, they come out here?" Nic says.

Alvin shrugs. "Sure. Convenient spot for crews to access, right under the interchange. Or it was, anyway. Beats going down a manhole."

Another group emerges out of the gap – this time with two kids in tow. "What are you guys doing in there?" Annie says.

"*Doing?*" Alvin cocks his head. "Man, relax, people just posting up in there, you know? Sleeping bags or whatever."

"Wait, wait, wait," I say. "You have people sleeping in the *sewers*?"

"Look around you, man. Not a lot of space left here." He waves a hand at the scaffolded mess of the interchange.

"The sewer tunnels are pretty wide here," Grant says. "And there're plenty of catwalks and storage areas you can find a spot on."

"What about the smell?" Nic asks.

It's Lucille who replies. "You get used to it. I was in there, for a while."

"It's good we can get in there," says Alvin thoughtfully. "Lotta people here who can't climb up on the scaffolding. Or don't want to."

"Hey." Annie taps Lucille on the shoulder. "There a bathroom round here?"

"Nah. We just sort of find a free bit of ground and squat."

Annie stares at her.

Lucille guffaws again. "I'm messing with you. We got the sewers, honey! It doesn't smell great, but there are some spots in the tunnels with privacy. Even got toilet paper, *and* some bottled water to wash your hands. Come on, I'll show you."

"Can I come?" Leo says, getting unsteadily to his feet. "I wanna see."

"No." Annie gets to her feet, not looking at him.

There's something about the way she says it, a vicious edge

to her tone. Fucking amazing. After everything we've been through, she *still* thinks Leo is the Antichrist.

But this time, she surprises me. She makes herself look at the kid, take a deep breath.

"It's more of a, uh . . . a ladies thing," she tells him.

"But I wanna see the sewers!"

"Ah, it'll be fine," Lucille tells Annie. "I'll watch him while you do your business. Give him the grand tour."

Annie tilts her head, looking at Leo. It's far too serious a look for something as everyday as a trip to the bathroom – even if that trip happens to take you into the sewers themselves.

"You know what?" she says. "Sure, what the hell. Come on."

"Yes!"

I should probably use the bathroom too. But then I discover that I have no desire to stand up, or possibly move from this position ever again.

I watch them go, my mind returning to the build-up of water behind the collapsed bridge. Some of it was draining through, I'm sure it was – that would relieve the pressure. Maybe there won't be a flash flood – or if there's going to be, the people in charge of LA's roads will actually have enough warning to get off their asses and do something before it happens. Even if they don't, it's hard to believe these folks wouldn't get some warning. God knows what the flood will do to the camp itself, but at least they'll be able to get out in time . . .

It takes me a few seconds to realise that I'm alone with Nic.

FORTY

Teagan

He glances at me, then looks away, taking a swig from a bottle of water someone must have given him, staring into the distance. The conversation has drifted away from us, Alvin and Grant moving over to hover by the fire with Juan.

I clear my throat. "I'm glad we got to eat."

He nods. "Mm."

"That was probably the best steak of my life. Better than the one we had in Pasadena – you remember that one time?"

"I do, yeah." He puts the water bottle down carefully, still not looking at me.

I close my eyes, irritated with myself. We've got a long way to go before we get Leo to safety, there's already plenty of bad blood between Nic and me and trying to fake being friendly isn't going to help. I should shut up, get some water of my own, rest and recharge.

That's what I want to do. What happens instead is me leaning forward and saying, "Look, about earlier . . . I really didn't mean it in a racial way. I'm super-sorry. I was just . . . "

"Just what?" He picks up the water bottle, toys with it.

Well, no point stopping now. "I was angry. I wasn't thinking straight. And if you'd told me that you felt this way . . . "

"Told you?" *Now* he looks at me, anger flashing in his eyes. "I shouldn't have to tell you not to treat people like that. Talk to them about fuckin' *laws*."

" . . . I'm sorry."

"I'm not a spokesman for black people, Teagan. It's not my job to explain race to you, or anybody. That shit gets exhausting real quick."

"I know."

"Do you?"

Even I am smart enough not to answer that question. Problem is, I have no idea what to say next. It feels like every response is a hand grenade.

"Look, man," Nic says, after a long moment. There's no more anger in his voice – just weariness. "I know you're not racist. I get that. I've seen how you treat other people. But that doesn't mean you aren't *capable* of racism, you know what I mean? Unconsciously. The background you come from, the privileges, there are certain things you just take for granted.

"I never had that. When I was growing up . . . I didn't grow up in the hood or anything, but shit, even now, the law doesn't treat me fairly. Me, and everybody like me."

"I totally get that. I'll be better. I promise."

It sounds lame, even as I say it. And on the heels of it comes a flash of anger. Not at what Nic said, which is right on the money. It's about what he did at Dodger, the way he intervened with Africa – how he got those National guardsmen killed when Leo went nuts. However dumb I was afterwards, how can he not understand that he screwed up?

Of course, I don't have a clue how to voice this without coming off as a colossal asshole.

Fortunately, I don't have to, because right then Nic says, "I messed up, didn't I?"

"Uh ... OK?"

"I didn't mean for all that shit to go bad. At Dodger. Africa was ... I just thought that under the circumstances, I was doing the right ..."

He trails off, drops his head, as if searching for the words.

"I didn't mean for anybody to get hurt."

The words come very slowly, carefully, as if one wrong move will break them. "Those people ... if I hadn't ... If I hadn't gotten up in Africa's face, they might be—"

"No." I'm surprised at how firm my voice is. "Listen to me. That is *not* your fault. I don't even think it's Africa's. *No one* knew Leo could call down fucking lightning bolts like that – not even him. That was a bad situation, and yeah, people died—"

Saying it like that, just stating it, makes my voice catch. Up until now, I hadn't really had a chance to think about those dead National Guard soldiers. Now ... it's like I've ripped the scab off a fresh wound.

I swallow. "People died, but it was an accident. That's all."

"Does Leo know?" he says, his voice dull.

"I don't think so. He passed out pretty much straight away."

"Should we tell him?"

It's a long time before I answer. "I don't know."

"Shit."

"Yeah."

Because think about it: how on earth are you supposed to put that on a child? *Especially* when you've only known him a short time? How can you possibly have that conversation?

Nic clears his throat. "Just ... just watch what you're saying sometimes, OK? With the race stuff, I mean."

"I will. I promise."

He nods, still not looking completely satisfied. And the silence that falls is still hella uncomfortable.

Nic makes a strange sound – a kind of bemused *hmf*. When I look across, he's shaking his head.

"What?"

"Just a weird fucking night man. The race thing is probably the only part of it I actually *do* understand."

I don't really know what to say to that, so I settle for an answering *hmf*.

"Yo, what kind of fucking name is *Zigzag Man*, anyway?" he says.

"I dunno. Leo never really said how he got it."

"We should ask him again."

"Honestly, at this point, I don't actually care. I just want this done with."

"Got that right."

We're both trying to sound light, just two friends having a chat by the fire. But there's an undercurrent to our words. A worry. No: a *fear*.

Fear that the Zigzag Man, stupid name or not, might come back.

"What did he make you see?" Nic asks.

The question catches me off guard. "Huh?"

"When he got in your head." He looks away. "I mean, if it's not too personal. You don't have to tell me if—"

"No, it's OK." And it is. Weirdly, it's kind of a relief. I'm not going to tell Nic about Jonas – that's mine, something I want to keep very close. But Carlos and the fire have been preying on my mind since I saw them. That's an experience I thought I'd dealt with, and it wasn't a lot of fun to have to relive it. Nic knows about what happened, and maybe talking about it will take away its power.

When I tell him, he grimaces. "*Fuuuuuck.*"

"Yeah."

"Jesus, I'm sorry, Teags. He just pulled that out of you? How?"

I shrug. "Like I said before man, we don't have a WhatsApp group. I don't know how this dude does his voodoo." I stop, surprised at my use of Annie's term.

"Well, still. Sorry you had to go through that again."

"How about you?" I say.

It's a long time before he answers – long enough that I start to wonder if it's me who should be apologising for asking personal questions. But then he says, "I saw us."

"What you mean?"

"That's why I was so surprised you saw Carlos. Because that's a bad thing, right? And what I saw wasn't bad at all. It was just . . ."

"You guys doing good?" Grant says, over from the other side of the fire. I didn't even see him come by.

Nic flashes him a thumbs-up. After Grant goes back to his conversation, Nic says, "You remember the time we went to that beach bar up in Malibu?"

"The whitest bar on earth?" I smile, appreciating the irony.

"That one. It was a good day though, right? Good food."

"Please, those tacos were meh. But I did have fun though."

"So did I. And that was the point. I didn't want to leave this . . . dream or vision or whatever that the Zigzag dickhead made me see. I wanted to stay there for ever." He pauses, chuckles. "In the whitest place on earth."

"Yeah."

He side-eyes me. "That's it?"

"What do you mean, that's it?"

"No comeback?"

"What do you want me to say? It's a nice memory."

"Nothing. Never mind."

"I'm not always going to make a dumb comment. I know I do it a lot, but I'm trying to take things more seriously, and . . ."

And then it all spills out of me, the words almost tripping over one another. "I'm trying to be better. OK? And . . . and make the right decisions, like everybody tells me to. But half the time I have no fucking clue what I'm doing, and it always feels like there's no correct answer, for any of this. Every single thing I do, there's going to be somebody who gets pissed off, or some fucking *thing* that's going to go wrong."

My voice cracks, tears pricking the corners of my eyes. Christ, I'm tired. It's a feeling that drills right down into my bones.

"I'm making myself think. That was what Reggie, and Annie, and everybody always told me to do. Stop just reacting, and actually *think* before you do shit. But it doesn't help. It just makes things worse."

"Welcome to being an adult."

The silence this time isn't comfortable . . . but it's not uncomfortable either. It's like it gets out the way, the space filled by the crackle of the fire and the soft murmur of conversations, the distant hiss and burble of the river.

"You just . . ." He thinks for a moment. "You gotta just fall back on logic. A, then B, then C. No matter what, there's always an answer that makes sense."

"OK, Spock." I wipe my face.

He rolls his eyes. "Well, so much for no comebacks."

"Answer me this then. What should I have done when I found Leo? What was the *logical* choice?"

"I—"

"I'll tell you. Logically, I should have handed him over to Tanner."

I force him to meet my eyes. I want him to *understand*. "But you know what? That wasn't the *right* decision. That kid doesn't deserve to get locked up in a facility, like I was. He doesn't deserve any of it."

"I get that," he says. "But it didn't have to be that simple. We could have found a way to hand him over *and* keep him safe. Tanner's not above the law, and—"

A frustrated groan hisses out of me. "You still don't get it."

"Oh, come on. If—"

"No." I talk over him. The tears are on my face now, warm against my skin. "You're so convinced you're right that you don't even consider the possibility that you might not be. You say you're sorry for what went down at the stadium, but I don't think you really get it. It's like after the quake, when you told me I was selfish for not helping out."

"Teags, I apologised for that."

"You're sorry for how you said it, sure. But deep down, you still think you were right. Don't you?"

He's about to protest – his leg muscles actually tense, like he's about to leap to his feet. But then he subsides, looking away. Hands knotted in his lap.

Lucille returns, Leo at her side. Annie must still be doing her thing. Nic flashes him a questioning thumbs-up, which Leo returns with a grin. "I saw a 'gator!" he says.

"Lizard." Lucille rolls her eyes.

"But it was a really big one."

She and Leo shuffle over to the fire, both of them arguing good-naturedly. Nic stares at Leo's back, his jaw clenched.

He sighs, tilting his head back and massaging his neck. As he does so, the light from the fire catches his face, highlighting it.

I'm not big on nostalgia. There's a lot I miss about my life pre-Tanner – I miss riding with my sister, talking with my brother, eating my dad's cooking and getting hugged by my mom – but I don't spend all my time missing it, if that makes sense. It could never last, and I think I knew that, even before the government scooped me up. Those memories are like keepsakes on a shelf. I can take them down whenever I want them, turn them over in my hands, put them back knowing they'll always be there.

What I do miss – and I didn't really understand it, not until this second – is Nic.

I miss getting dinner with him, both of us diving headlong into whatever weird Cambodian or Peruvian or Japanese dish gets put in front of us. I miss his laugh. I miss how he looked at me, before he knew about my ability: the contentment in his eyes, because I was his friend and he was mine.

And I want us to be more than that. I always have.

The Zigzag Man keeps making me see Jonas Schmidt. I don't fully understand how his ability works – it's as if he reaches into your mind, and makes you envision your innermost thoughts. Let's not sugar-coat this: clearly, I have major feelings for Jonas. But I have major feelings for Nic, too. And when you get down to it, really get down to it, *he's* the one I want to spend my life with.

There's so much that's happened between us. It's piled up and piled up, stacking a mile high between us, all of the shit we've been through and all of the shit we've said to each other. We have *both* acted like douche-nozzles.

Well, no more. I'm tearing that fucking pile down. I'm setting it on fire, then bulldozing it into the Pacific. As a rapper wiser than me once said, you don't try to find the needle in a haystack; you burn the haystack down and pick the needle from the ground.

And shit, wasn't that whole song about leaving the past behind? Seth Sentry. *Langolier's Banquet.*

I never played it for Nic. Maybe I should. I think he'd understand.

"Let's start over," I tell him.

"Huh?"

"When this is done." I nod to Leo. "When he's . . . when he gets to where he needs to go. Let's just start from scratch."

"What does that even mean?"

"Dinner. You and me. Somewhere with really good food – like, *really* good food."

"Is there even anywhere left in LA for—?"

"And we take everything that's happened with us, and we just pretend it never did. Like we're meeting for the first time."

"How would we even do that?" he says, laughing.

I hold out my hand. "Hi. My name's Teagan. I can move shit with my mind, but I like eating, and listening to rap music, and . . . and lying in bed on the weekends with a cup of coffee. I drive a shitty old Jeep and I love living in LA, even though the traffic sucks ass. What's your name?"

"Come on, man. *Start from scratch?* I don't even . . . How would it work if . . . ?"

I don't say anything. I don't know how it would work, not really. But it feels like the right decision.

He looks down at my hand – and suddenly, I'm not sure I've done the right thing.

Because I can guess what he's thinking. He's looking at all the things I'm trying to draw a line under. All the shit we've been through together. The horrible things we've said to each other. The wrecked apartments and gunfights. The text messages that were never answered, the calls that weren't picked up.

He's thinking: can we really pretend all of that never happened? Is this person genuinely suggesting we just ignore it?

My hand hangs in the air, trembling.

His eyes meet mine. Hold my gaze.

And then, slowly, his fingers wrap around mine.

"Hey, Teagan," he says, still kind of laughing, like he can't believe we're doing this. "I'm Nic. Nic Delacourt. It's nice to meet you."

I squeeze his hand. He squeezes back.

And neither of us let go.

FORTY-ONE

Reggie

The cab drops Reggie at the dead end of San Carlos Street, just south of Rosecrans. There's not much there. A few sad-looking houses, some of them boarded up and lifeless. A pick-up parked at the end of the street, dusty with disuse. Beyond the cul-de-sac, there's an expanse of hard-packed dirt bordered by scrubby trees, with nothing in it but an old merry-go-round. As if someone wanted to build a playground, but ran out of money halfway through.

Beyond the dirt, the ground rises sharply, plateauing after perhaps fifteen feet of elevation. *The river must be just over the hump.* If she can get down there, intercept Teagan and Annie . . .

Well, she'll figure that part out later.

There's just enough ambient light here to see by. The rain has let up a little, which is good, but the ground is already muddy as all get out. Reggie eyes it, suddenly unsure. Is her chair going to be able to get through it?

All at once, she feels very alone. There really is no one around – not a single sign of movement from the dark houses. The cab turns left at the closest intersection, dropping out of sight. *Probably glad to see the back of me,* Reggie thinks bitterly.

"Come on, old girl," she mutters, pushing the chair's joystick. "Let's keep it moving."

The kerb doesn't present much of a problem – it's nothing more than a thin lip at the edge of the tarmac. The chair tilts as it clears the bump, the wheels digging into the mud on the other side. *Moment of truth.*

The motor whines, ratcheting up a notch. For a horrifying half-second, the wheels spin – and then catch, jerking forward. The ground looks muddy, but it isn't quite deep enough to stop Reggie moving. Not that it's easy; she bounces in her seat, rocking back and forth. Her shoulders ache, and the familiar tightness in her diaphragm is worse than usual.

As she passes the merry-go-round, a sound reaches her. The crackle of old leaves being stepped on. She snaps her head in the direction of the noise, off to the right. But there's nobody there, no figures emerging from the trees.

Get it together. Reggie pushes the joystick even harder – she's going to have build up a little speed to get up the slope ahead of her. Shouldn't be too difficult. Her chair isn't top of the line, but it's powerful enough. Once she clears that, there should be a flat section where she can catch her breath, rest a minute. The river should be visible from there, too. She's pretty sure she won't actually see Teagan and Annie – that would be ridiculous – but at the very least, she can get a sense of the lay of the land. And once she's on the concrete storm drain surface, things should be a lot easier.

Reggie's chair eats up the muddy ground, the motor whining harder. She makes contact with the slope, lurching back in her seat as the chair tilts upwards. It's a lot steeper than she thought it would be – for a horrible second, she's sure she's going to keep tilting, topple right out of her chair.

But no. She's steady now, the motor rising to an angry pitch as it digs in. She slows right down now, inching forward, but that's OK. All she has to do is keep moving.

Except: not even *that* is happening. The motor is going at full bore, and she's come to a dead stop on the slope.

"Damn it, no." She's got the joystick as far forward as it can go. "Come on."

Is there a setting she can change? An extra gear for her to engage? If she had a half-decent chair like she'd asked for, this wouldn't be a problem.

The motor sounds wrong now – like it's on the very edge of blowing something important. Cursing, Reggie lets the joystick go, engaging the brake. She'll let the motor cool down, but she'll be damned if she loses any ground.

A moment later, she starts to tilt backwards.

Her centre of gravity is too high. Without the forward motion to compensate, the front wheels are starting to lift off the ground.

Reggie teeters, breathing hard, frozen. In the split-second before the tilt becomes too much, spilling her out of her chair, she releases the brake. The chair coasts backwards, wheels rumbling as she hits the mud, rolling to a stop a few feet from the slope. The wheels and the bottom half of the chair are spattered with mud. Her legs too, brown and gunky up to the knees. For once, Reggie is grateful she can't feel them.

She presses her lips together, trying to control her breathing. There are tyre tracks on the slope – Reggie barely made it three feet up before the motor started to struggle. Three measly feet.

Well, fine. She'll just try it again. Take another run at it. She has come way too far to be defeated by a little hill.

Come way too far? That's a laugh. All she did was call a cab, have a little fight with the driver. She's barely gone fifty feet under her own steam.

Don't you dare. Don't you dare do this to yourself. Not now.

A minute later, she tries to climb the hill again. This time, she doesn't even make it three feet. The motor starts complaining the moment she hits the slope – and this time, there's the added smell of burning. Reggie is forced to drop back before it goes. The only thing worse than falling out of the chair would be the chair itself catching fire.

There has to be somebody she can call. But who? Africa? He's off on his own mission, won't even answer the phone – and if he did, there's no guarantee he want to help her. He has gone way off the edge of the map. And – Jesus, what if he's caught up with Tegan and Annie already? What if he somehow managed to stop them, or bring them in? The entire team could be back at the office right now, or en route to a pickup point to meet with Tanner's people. She should have left a message at the office, something to let them know where she's heading.

She tries Africa's number anyway, but of course, he doesn't pick up. The burning smell has dissipated, a little, but there's no point taking another run at the hill. If she can't get more than a couple of feet up, she's not going to make it all the way to the top.

It occurs to her to try moving further along, to the north or south – perhaps there'll be a shallower slope. But the trees, while thin and scrawny, are tightly packed on either side of the makeshift playground. It's possible that she could navigate her chair between them, but she's more than likely to get stuck. She'd be in an even worse position than she's in now.

"*Goddammit.*"

It comes out louder than she intended – but then again, it's not as if anyone is around to hear it. She spins her chair around, pointing back towards San Carlos Street. Nothing for it. She's going to have to head back the way she came in, follow the river to the south. Perhaps there will be another way onto it. Of course, she could always call another cab. *And how long is that going to take? Another hour? Two? Where do I even tell them to go?*

"Are you OK?"

A startled grasp almost jumps out of Reggie. Her hand snaps to her pocket, where the knife is. Except: it's going to take far too long to slip her fingers through the holes on the handle, far too long to lift it out and—

"Sorry," the speaker says, hands up. "Didn't mean to startle you."

Reggie's hand slows, then stops. The speaker is a woman in her mid-twenties, dirty blonde hair pulled back in a ponytail. She's slight, but clearly in good shape, wearing a brown leather jacket and tight red sweater over jeans and Doc Martins. Reggie can't help thinking there's something a little off about her appearance. Mostly it's her eyes, which are a little too big for her face.

"That's OK," Reggie says, glancing back towards San Carlos Street.

"Saw you trying to climb the hill." The woman nods towards the slope. "Don't know if there's much of a view at the top."

"I'm—"

Trying to get to the river. But how on earth does she say that without sounding like a complete lunatic?

The woman tilts her head. "Would you . . . ? Do you need a push? I'm sorry if that's not, you know, the right thing to say here . . . "

"No, no." On a normal day, Reggie would resent someone trying to help. But since she's not getting up that hill on her lonesome, she'll take all the assistance she can get. "That'd be great. Please."

"OK, sure. How should we—?"

"Just push me. I'll disengage the motor."

"You got it."

The woman moves behind her, out of sight, grasping the handles on the back of the chair.

Finally, Reggie thinks. *A little luck.*

FORTY-TWO

Teagan

Five miles. That's it. That's all we have do.

It'll be an hour's walk – maybe even less, if we hustle. A straight shot down the river around Alondra Boulevard, then through Compton to Leo's uncle's place. Then we just hope to hell his dad is actually there – or if he's not, that Leo's uncle is in a welcoming mood.

Plenty can happen in five miles. But as we head south from the interchange camp, I'm feeling ... surprisingly good. Not in top shape, no way – not on a meth comedown, not after the night we've had. But we've had food, and water, and a chance to sit for a little while. No ambushes or gunfights in the past hour. Nic and I made nice. There is a chance we might actually make it through this – a small chance, but I'll take what I can get.

Also, I didn't have to spend long in the sewers under the freeway, doing my business. Maybe the people hanging out in there – and holy hell, a lot of people decided to set up shop in the tunnels – have gotten used to the smell. Not me. I can't think about it without wanting to retch.

The storm drain is wide and empty, the river a straight channel right down the middle. There are still unbroken lines of flood barriers on each side, but Annie says there'll be a few gaps the further south we get.

My PK isn't back to normal, but the rest and the steak have helped. My little gas tank is probably back up to twenty-five per cent. I keep my PK alert for anybody approaching, but aside from a few homeless folk heading north to the camp, pushing shopping carts loaded with their belongings, there's nobody we need to worry about.

Leo still can't walk without limping, but he barely seems to notice. He sticks close to Nic, a few feet behind me and Annie. "Are we gonna be there soon?" he says, speaking so fast he almost trips over the words.

"Yeah, I think so," Nic says breezily.

"I'm gonna make sure you can stay with, with my uncle." Leo nods to himself, like he's made a difficult decision.

Nic gives a noncommittal grunt. Then he says, "How're the ... wiggles right now? You good?"

"I'm OK!" Leo grins up at Nic, who returns it.

"No using your zaps," I say over my shoulder. "I don't want to carry you the whole way. You're heavy."

"I am *not*!"

"Hey, who's done most of the carrying tonight anyway?" Nic says.

Leo looks worried. "But what if the Zigzag Man ...?"

"Tell you what." I slow down, so I'm walking beside him. "I'll make you a bet. Whoever uses their powers first ..." I falter, then it comes to me. "Gets a big, sloppy kiss from Nic."

"Ugh!" Leo makes a disgusted, delighted face. I wink at Nic, who is trying very hard not to laugh.

"You guys done messing around?" Annie says. "We got a ways to go yet." There's an amused look on her face though, as if she too can't help but feel a little lighter.

"OK, OK," Leo says. "But I wanna show you something."

"No, Leo," I say. "I said no zaps."

"Yeah but just one thing, OK?"

A few feet to our right, there's a puddle of dank water, pooled on the concrete. A pigeon waddles along one edge, beak idly tapping at the water. Like all city pigeons, it gives precisely zero shits about us.

Leo crouches down, putting a hand on the concrete.

"Come on, dude," Nic says. "Don't—"

There's a sharp *bzzt* – more felt than heard – and the pigeon explodes upwards with a panicked squawk. It flaps in place two feet off the ground, feathers flying, wings beating so hard that it nearly turns itself upside down. Somehow, it rights itself, and flies away, wobbling wildly, almost crashing into the side of the storm drain.

"*Leo!*" Annie gapes at him.

I collapse, howling with laughter. I can't help it – Leo might have just committed a heinous act of animal cruelty, but I can't stop thinking about how the pigeon wobbled and bobbled and flapped its wings at a million miles an hour.

I clutch my stomach, tears streaming down my cheeks. Leo is grinning like a fool.

"You can't do that." Annie is literally shaking a finger at Leo, a horrified expression on her face.

"I just gave it a little—"

"It doesn't matter! That bird was just minding its own business!"

Oh God. My lungs are going to disintegrate. I'm down on my knees now, hands on the concrete, and I'm laughing so hard my face hurts. Everything we've been through tonight, all the insane shit . . . it's all coming out. Even Annie is struggling to keep the disapproval on her face, shaking her head and grinning to herself.

But Nic . . . Nic isn't laughing. Not even a little bit. "What the hell is wrong with you?" he says to Leo.

"I was just—"

"You think this is a joke?" It's like something has given way inside Nic, an impulse that he can no longer control.

Leo falters. "I just wanted to show you something."

"You could hurt people. You could hurt yourself. You could—"

Abruptly, Nic snaps his mouth shut. Looks away. Neither Annie nor I are laughing now.

Leo looks down, scuffing the concrete with the toe of a dirty sneaker. "I'm sorry."

"Yeah, well." Nic still won't look at him.

"I didn't hurt myself." Leo waves his hands in the air. "And the bird's OK!"

And the pigeon is indeed fine. It's giving the puddle a wide berth, but it's back on the concrete, pecking for scraps at the edge of the slope.

For some reason, that makes Nic even angrier. "From now on," he tells Leo, "don't use your power. Not ever. You keep that inside you."

"Nic, ease back," I say. What the hell's gotten into him?

"Yeah, man, relax," Annie mutters, which surprises me a little bit. She's not exactly a fan of Leo, or what he can do.

Nic looks between us, then takes a deep breath. "You're right," he says. "Sorry. Things are just getting to me." It doesn't escape my notice that he's not looking at Leo when he says it.

Annie runs a hand through her hair. "Come on. Still a ways to go yet." She marches off, setting the pace.

We resume walking in silence, Leo between Nic and me. The boy walks with his head down, dragging his feet a little.

"You are evil," I tell Leo, although I make sure I'm smiling when I say it.

"It was just a bird," he mumbles.

"Yes, it was. It's OK this time, but maybe don't do it again, huh? Or we'll tell your dad."

Leo blushes. "Nooooo."

"Yeeeees."

"Do you think my dad'll be there?" Leo asks again. He looks worried all of a sudden, the pigeon forgotten.

Nic clears his throat. He speaks quickly, as if ashamed of his little outburst. "He will. And if he's not, for whatever reason, we'll find him, OK?"

"What if we can't?"

"We will." I nod towards Annie, who by now is a good fifty yards ahead of us. "Come on. We gotta keep up."

"But ..." And all at once, there's panic on his face. "But you don't know what he looks like! What if we saw him, and I didn't see him, and you did, but you didn't know?"

Following that particular burst of little-boy talk takes some doing, but I manage. "I'm pretty sure he would have seen you," I say, hustling him along.

"Maybe you can show us a photo of him," Nic says.

Leo skirts the edge of the puddle, and as he does so, his face lights up. "*I* know what he looks like!"

"All right," I say. "That sounds good. Fire away."

Leo thinks. "He's really tall. He's got black hair, and ... and glasses."

"Cool," I say, exchanging a look with Nic. A look that says, *We'll be sure to keep an eye out for a bespectacled Asian man with black hair. Very few of those in California.*

"When he left me at the place, he had a jacket like the people who work there. He's got blue pants, and red shoes. Like, really red."

As he talks, I come to a dead halt. Just stop cold.

"Thanks," Nic says. "Got it. We'll keep a look out, won't we, Teagan? . . . Teags?"

He had a jacket like the people who work there.

Red shoes.

Back in the storage unit, before I found Leo . . . I found a body.

A man wearing exactly what Leo described.

No. No way. You're imagining it.

But I'm not. I wish I was, I wish to God I was, but . . .

Leo's dad left him in the storage unit. Hid him. Told him he was going to get help, that he'd be back soon. He told him to use his ability if he had to – if anybody came, and tried to take him. What if . . .?

What if Leo got scared? What if he was alone and worried and he got scared and used his ability—?

Before his dad had left the building.

My eyes meet Nic's. His forehead creases with concern. "What is it? What's wrong?" Leo looks between us, puzzled.

"I just . . . " I lift a hand to my face, let it drop. "I'll be back in a second."

"Um, OK. What—?"

I push past them, moving into a jog, heading for Annie. I don't know what I'm going to do – I have to tell someone, but it can't be Nic. Not right now, not when Leo is right there.

Annie has come to a stop, her back to me. She's staring down at a piece of trash – a piece of furniture or something, I don't know. I skid to a halt next to her. "Annie – we've got a big fucking problem."

She doesn't respond.

"Leo's dad, he . . . I think he might be—"

"That's Reggie's chair," Annie says. Her voice is barely a whisper.

"I – what?"

Annie points to the piece of furniture. Except, it's not a piece of furniture. It's a motorised wheelchair, turned on its side.

My brain short-circuits, Leo's dad temporarily forgotten. "What? No. It's just a chair. Why would it be Reggie's?"

"It's hers." That same dead tone. "I recognise it. It even has her little bag." She points to the back of the chair, where a small, multicoloured cloth bag hangs from a strap.

"What's going on?" Nic says. He and Leo have come up behind us.

I don't know what's going on. I don't know how our little straight shot down the river went so bad so quickly. But I'm putting a stop to it, right now, because this? This is some bullshit.

"The chair can't be Reggie's." I say firmly. "There's no way. How would she even have gotten down here?"

"Woah, wait, what?" Nic says. "What does Reggie have to do with this?"

"Who's Reggie?" says Leo.

"Annie, think. I know it looks like her chair, but . . . "

Annie isn't listening. She bends down, plucks at something embedded in the chair's mechanism. Something I hadn't noticed before – a slip of paper. She unfolds it, her hands hardly shaking it all.

The writing on the paper is in block capitals. As heavy and direct as a shotgun blast.

HOLLYDALE PARK. WEST OF THE
BASKETBALL COURTS.
MIDNIGHT.
BRING THE BOY.

FORTY-THREE

Teagan

I hate the phrase *I can't even.*

Every time somebody says it, I want to yell at them: *Can't even what? Finish the sentence, you lazy fuckwad!* Usually I couldn't care less about other peoples' little sayings and vocal tics. But for whatever reason, that one is my kryptonite. If you say it around me, I may express a desire to punch you in the dick.

Well, I get it now. Standing over a wheelchair that I'm really starting to believe belongs to Reggie, in the middle of a storm drain, while we're trying to track down a man who I just found out was accidentally killed by his own son ...

I can't even. I have lost the ability to even.

"Let me get this straight." Nic has his hands on his hips. "The Zigzag Man took your boss?"

"Who else could it be?" Annie's still talking like she's been tranquilised.

"The Legends? Or—?"

"They wouldn't know about Reggie," I say.

"They could have found out!"

"Why is this so hard for you?" Annie says. "The dude tried to hit us twice. When that didn't work, he found another way."

"It's him," Leo says. He scuffs the concrete with his shoe, not looking at us.

I'll have to tell him about his dad, sooner or later – and do I feel guilty about how relieved I am that it's not the most pressing issue right now? You bet your sweet ass I do.

"I mean ..." Nic falters. "OK, let's say that's right. Somehow, he got your girl Reggie, and *somehow* got her chair down here. How'd he know we'd even see it?"

"Good point," I murmur. Not that it's one I have an answer for.

"And why not just hold her hostage here?" Nic goes on. "Why make us go all the way back to ... what was it, Hollydale Park?"

Annie makes a helpless, disgusted sound. "He wants to do it somewhere quiet, not where anybody can walk by."

"But the river is quiet," Nic says. "I mean we've seen a few other people, but mostly it's just been us, right?"

"He wouldn't know that. And even if he does, why take the chance? And he must have figured out we'd come this way."

I grind the heel of my hand into my forehead. The Zigzag Man's been trying to get ahead of us this entire time, striking at the worst possible moments. Looks like he finally did it.

Who the fuck *is* he? What do these people *want*?

Annie looks at her watch. "Just past eleven now. Hollydale Park's back past the camp, east of the river. We can make it if we hustle."

"Wait, I'm sorry." I say. "Are you seriously suggesting we go back the way we came?"

"Are you seriously suggesting we *don't*?" Annie stares at me in disbelief.

"I just think—"

"He's got Reggie. If you don't think he'll kill her, you're an idiot."

"We should just think about it, is all," I say, feeling more lame by the second.

Annie's right, of course. We have to go back, because there is *no way* I'm letting Reggie get hurt. But if we do . . .

It means handing over Leo.

Can we do that to him? Betray a four-year-old boy, for one of our own? Hand him back to the Zigzag Man, to the one person in the world that scares him the most?

How would that be any better than letting him fall into Tanner's clutches?

I know what Reggie would say. I can even hear her words, that honeyed Southern accent. *Hell no, darling. Don't you worry about me. You keep going. Get that boy somewhere safe.*

And I have no idea how to tell Annie that. Not a clue.

"If we hand Leo over," Nic says, eyes never leaving Annie, "then a lot of people are going to get hurt."

"Says you."

"Says him." He points to Leo, who actually flinches.

"I'm not trying to hear that. Don't even talk to me about that."

"Annie." You can hear the patience wearing down in Nic's voice – the razor thin edge of it. "You might be willing to risk thousands of people, but I don't know if I am."

"Oh, OK. Sorry, Reggie, we bailed because we *maybe* thought a kid with abilities was—"

"There's no maybe. We know exactly what'll happen if we don't keep him safe."

"*We don't know shit!*"

He gets in her face. "Well then tell me, Annie. Go on. We go save Reggie, we hand Leo over, then what? You think nothing happens? What are you gonna say to Reggie when Leo . . . ?" He swallows. "When they make him overdrive a power plant? Or put a million volts through the Pacific Ocean?"

I don't even know if that's possible. Then again, until today, I didn't think any of this was possible. I badly want to tell Nic that this isn't the place for logic, and reason, and cold-minded arguments. Problem is, the alternative isn't much better.

As if sensing my thoughts, Nic looks over at me – a look I almost flinch away from. "Teags, back me up."

I shake my head, my mouth open, the words stuck in my throat.

Now Annie is staring at me too. "You cannot seriously be considering this."

"I—"

Annie grabs me by both shoulders, makes me look her in the eyes.

"It's Reggie," she says through gritted teeth. "The woman who's always had your back. Since China Shop started, she's been the wall between you and Tanner. And you just wanna, what, throw her to the fucking wolves?"

"No! Annie, I never said that—"

"Then why aren't you telling your boyfriend –" she jabs a finger at Nic "– to get the hell on?"

"Hey, that's enough," Nic says.

Annie ignores him, letting go of my shoulders "I don't believe you, Teagan. I really don't. After all this, you just roll over?"

"He's four years old!" I still don't have a clue what to do, but I feel like *someone* should point this out.

"*It doesn't matter.*" Annie's hands are balled in tight, bloodless fists. Abruptly, she jabs a finger at Leo, who flinches. "He's just like that Matthew kid, the one who killed—" She takes a deep breath, looks away. "I can't believe you're protecting him, still, after everything that's happened."

"He's not Matthew," I shout back. "Jesus, Annie, think for a second. Matthew was a . . . a . . . a psychopath. Leo's just . . . he's a normal kid."

"He's from the same place."

"He doesn't want to hurt anybody!"

"Oh yeah? What about at Dodger Stadium? Nic told me all about that shit."

Nic gives me a helpless shrug.

Annie isn't done: "He's dangerous. I'm done protecting him. Not when Reggie might get hurt."

I don't believe this. I thought Annie had finally come around – that she'd stopped hating Leo for what he is. For the past couple of hours, she'd actually been treating him like a real person. Turns out, that was a thin scab over a very deep wound.

"It's like Nic said. If we hand him over, they'll make him hurt a lot more people than Reggie." The words spill out of me, like they were there all along. "Annie, I know what happened with Paul was hard—"

"Don't you say his name." Spat through gritted teeth.

"Why not? He was my friend too. I hated what happened to him, but Leo didn't do it. None of this is his fault, and the way you talk to him, it's not fair. You can't hate him like that. He's *not* Matthew."

"*Both of you,*" Nic steps between us. "Enough. Let's just talk this out. If—"

"I'll go," Leo says.

He has to say it again, louder this time, before we turn to look at him.

"Leo," I say, disbelieving. "No."

"It's OK." He smiles. The damn kid actually smiles. "I don't want anyone to get hurt."

"But . . ." I walk over, crouch down so I'm at his level. "The Zigzag Man *wants* you to hurt people."

A hardness comes into his expression then. One I haven't seen before. His lower lip juts out slightly, defiant.

"I won't let him," he says. "Even if he tries to make me. I won't do it."

"Leo," Nic says. "Buddy . . . we can't ask you to do this. It's too much."

"I wanna help," he says simply.

Annie is nodding to herself, arms crossed tight over her chest. She at least has the good grace to stay silent.

"Are you *sure*?" Nic says to Leo, crouching down next to me. "Because nobody here is going to make you do it."

"I'm sure."

Nic looks like he wants to throw up. "Please," he says. "Please, Leo. Don't do this."

Leo takes a tentative step forward, then another. Then he wraps his arms around Nic's shoulders.

I look away. Eyes closed. I want to hug Leo, and hit him, and scream at him, and then scream at Annie.

Most of all? Most of all, I want to find the man who took Reggie. That's the one bright spot here. After all this is done, maybe, just maybe, I'll get my shot at him. Make him regret the day he fucked with us.

Leo lets go of Nic. "Come on," he says, a little too brightly, turning and heading back the way we came.

Nic and I exchange a look. *Are we really doing this?*

Behind him, the LA River stretches away into the darkness. A flat, beaten-up slab of concrete. An easy walk. And no more than a few miles away, less than an hour . . .

We were so goddamn close.

"Come on," I say to Nic and Annie, turning to go. Then, quietly, making sure Leo is far enough ahead of us: "Let's go punch this dude in the dick."

FORTY-FOUR

Teagan

This must be what it feels like to almost-but-not-quite reach the summit of Mount Everest. The failing isn't even the worst part. It's the descent. Going aaaaaall the way back down, covering the same ground, knowing you didn't make it.

Back we go, back up the river. Back towards the camp, towards Pop and the Legends, towards Africa, if he's still out there.

If? Who am I kidding? He's probably tracking us down right now, and chances are he'll show up at exactly the worst time.

Every so often, Nic will cast a dark look in Annie's direction. She ignores him, focusing on the way ahead. Leo is walking with us, on Nic's left. Our footsteps on the concrete are dull, like they're coming from inside a soundproofed room.

Eventually, the silence gets to me. "Maybe we could have our cake and eat it," I say, which is a poor choice of words, because now I want cake.

"What do you mean?" Nic says.

"Well, we've got *some* time, right?" It's around eleven-fifteen, a little under an hour from the deadline. The rain has picked up now, plastering my hair to my forehead. I have to keep wiping drops out of my eyes. "Maybe there's a way to get Reggie back without losing Leo." I cast a guilty look at him, and he just shrugs.

"Maybe." Nic sounds unsure.

"I mean, it's not like this Zigzag guy is bulletproof." I say.

"You got a gun hidden somewhere we don't know about?" Annie says.

"I don't mean *literally* bulletproof. I'm not saying shoot him. But it seems like it's tough for him to hit more than two people at once, so maybe we could . . . I don't know, ambush him somehow . . ."

Nic gives me a dubious look.

"Besides," I continue. "He's not all there – did you hear what he was saying? All that *my house is a lie and the walls go on for ever* and blah-blah?" I try to say it like it's no biggie, but truth be told, even repeating the words sends a horrid little shiver up my spine.

"If he took Reggie, and set all this up," Nic says, "then he's obviously not a complete fruitcake. Plus, he knows how many of us there are. If we don't all show at the same time, he'll figure out something's up. It's not worth the risk."

"We . . . we wait until we've made the exchange, till we've got Reggie back. Then we can hit him. He can't take all of us at the same time."

"Good plan," Annie mutters.

A group of people – homeless folk from the camp, it looks like – move past us on the opposite side of the river. They're arguing about something, angry voices reaching us.

A brainwave. "Hey." I snap a finger at Leo. "You've still got some juice, right? You didn't blow it all on that pigeon?"

"Um," he says. "I think so."

"Perfect!" I spread my hands. "So we zap him the second we see him. Boom. We all go home."

Nic shakes his head. "Nice idea, but I'm guessing he'll take that into account. He obviously knows what Leo can do."

"Stop bursting my balloon, man. Take it into account how?"

"He'll probably keep hold of Reggie until they make the exchange." Annie's voice is as dead as our footsteps. "He'll dose Leo with something, *then* let Reggie go."

"If he does it at all," Nic mutters.

Annie glares at him. "Got something you wanna say, *vato*?"

"Chill, both of you," I tell them. Last thing we need is to have some bystander come find out if we're OK. And there *are* bystanders now – groups of people pushing their belongings in shopping carts, loners toting backpacks. One of them, a crusty old guy with a unibrow, glances in my direction, gives me a sour look. I have to resist flipping him the bird.

"Why are there so many people?" Leo asks suddenly

"There aren't that many ... " I trail off. He's right. It's not just a few small groups here and there. The bend of the river is up ahead, curving back around to the west, and in the space between the bend and where we are, there must be a hundred people. There's a little more ambient light here than there was further up the river, so they're not difficult to spot. I was so wrapped up in my own thoughts that I genuinely didn't notice.

There's the roar of a motorcycle engine, making me jump. *The Legends – they found us.*

But it's not them. On the other side of the rushing water, a beat-up old Triumph zooms past. The bike has a sidecar, and the person in it – a bearded man holding a baseball cap down on his head – is yelling something at us. Impossible to hear over the roar of the engine. The man's windbreaker has come loose, flapping out the back of the sidecar like a superhero cape.

"OK, hold up." Annie strides over to the nearest group

on our side, a cluster of teenagers – two girls, three boys, all of whom look worried. "What's going on?" Annie points upriver. "Why's everybody heading out?"

I don't quite hear the response, which comes from one of the older boys, a kid with a dirty Clippers hoodie about ten sizes too big for him.

Annie snaps her head in the direction of the homeless camp. "For real?" she says.

"The hell is happening?" Nic asks me. All I can do is shrug.

Annie jogs back to us. "We got a problem."

"Yeah, I figured." I nod to the kids. "What's up?"

"Flash flood."

"*What?*" Nic says.

"What do you mean, a flash flood?" I blink at her. "From where?"

It's dumb question. I know where.

A certain collapsed bridge further upriver. A mess of concrete slabs and burned metal. A nice little barricade for the storm water to pile up behind.

My stomach gives a sickening wrench – *technically* the bridge collapsing wasn't my fault, but . . .

But it wouldn't have happened at all if we didn't steal that meth. And whose idea was that?

"What's a flushflood?" Leo asks Nic. Nic ignores him, straightening up, craning his neck to spot an exit from the river. There isn't one. It's wall-to-wall flood barriers, because of course it is. Before the quake, the 710–105 interchange was major. It makes sense that the LA City Council would want to protect the areas around it first.

When you're raised in Wyoming, you get pretty good at reading the weather, staying out of the creeks and the ravines. Apparently I forgot it after I left the state, mostly because it's not something you have to worry about while cruising for tacos down Sunset Boulevard.

We have one thing going for us. Flash floods are scary, but they don't move all that fast. Ten feet per second is pretty normal, which sounds awful, but isn't actually that bad.

"How long?" I ask Annie. "Did they—?"

She's gone pale. "Forty-five minutes. Maybe."

Well, shit.

"What happens when the flash gets here?" Leo says, his eyes huge.

Nic puffs out his cheeks. "Then this whole place is underwater, bud."

"But . . . but what about the people? At the place where everyone was? The camp place?"

"They know it's coming," Nic tells him, "so they're already getting out of the way." He points to the groups of people streaming past us. "See?"

"But where are they gonna go?"

I'm thinking the same thing. Staring at the group of kids Annie spoke to, at the other people around us. Maybe I can help them. Maybe I can use my PK, bust down one of the flood barriers, clear a path or—

"*Hey.*" Annie grabs me by the shoulder, makes me look her in the eyes. "They are not our problem right now. Reggie is our problem. There's not a thing you can do about no damn flash flood, and it looks like everybody got the message anyway."

"But the bridge. Annie, it was us who—"

"Nope. You didn't crash us, and you didn't make the bridge collapse. That's not on you."

I'm about to argue with her, but she's got a point. The flood will be bad . . . but it doesn't look like it's going to hurt anybody. It'll wreck the camp under the freeway interchange, cause some damage, but that's all.

Reggie's in danger. As long as the people in the camp hustle, they're not. Stopping to help . . . it won't make any real difference.

"All right," I say. "We double back. Find the first gap in the flood barriers, then—"

"Nah." Annie points upriver. "We're going that way."

"You literally just told us there's a giant flash flood coming from that direction."

"I think . . ." She bites her lip. "No, I'm sure. The nearest flood exit to us is actually past the camp. I'm positive."

"Then why is everybody else heading away from it?"

"Beats me. Maybe it's bottlenecked – too many people trying to get out at once, so folks're looking for alternatives. Doesn't make a difference for us though. We go through the camp, pop out the river first chance we get. OK?"

It sounds crazy. It *is* crazy. But if Annie's right, then it gives us more of what we need: time. Time to plan, to maybe scope out the park where the Zigzag Man wants to meet, plan . . . something better than the shitshow of a strategy we have now. If we double back, who knows how much time we'll lose?

"You still want to do this?" Nic says to Leo.

Leo bites his lip, then nods. "I think so."

"All right." Annie starts walking. Fast. "It's not far. Let's move."

FORTY-FIVE

Reggie

When Reggie opens her eyes, she's back in Nemila.

She is sitting in a wooden chair, jagged splinters digging into her legs. Plastic zip ties bind her wrists to the arms of the chair, digging into her skin. Two more at her ankles. There is no other furniture in the room – just a single bulb, hanging from the roof. The room is deep in the basement of the farmhouse, the air stale and still.

No. It's not real. It can't be. We got out.

But she can taste the air, feel the splinters, the rigid hardness of the chair back digging into her spine.

I was going to the LA River. I was chasing Teagan. I wasn't—

But she's already turning her head to the right. She doesn't want to, but she has no choice. And on the wall, just visible beneath the grime: the drawings. Ancient crayon, flowers and boats and castles, something that might be a bird floating free.

A scream begins to claw its way up Reggie's throat, moving far too slowly, as if it knows it has all the time in the world. And oh, there are the footsteps outside the door, the heavy boots, the door creaking open, the men bringing jumper cables and fists as heavy as anchors, and the scream is in her mouth now and this time there will be no Moira Tanner coming to save her, not this time, she's going to die here, she—

A woman's voice, calm, speaking almost right next to her. "Clarify."

Reggie snaps her head towards the sound, her breath coming in horrified gasps. The door is still opening, slowly, slowly.

"Rhetoric. Parallel. Window. Prospect."

The colours in the drawing are starting to run together, the light from the ceiling bulb flickering and flaring.

"Triangle. Altitude. Zigzag. Zigzag. Zigzag."

For the second time, Reggie gasps, choking awake, her eyes flying open.

She's in an open space under a dark night sky, absent of stars. There's the sense of clouds hanging low, and a very gentle drizzle is falling, the drops almost kissing her skin. Oh God, her *head* – it aches, throbbing with a sick, horrible pain. And she's cold, too, her skin prickling and sensitive.

Grass underneath her. Dry, crackly. She's desperate to roll over, get her bearings, but her body won't cooperate. Where's her chair? Where the hell is she? And what happened to Nemila? She was *there*, back in that room, the terror as fresh and clean as a scalpel cut.

"I'm sorry about that," the woman says. "Sometimes, I don't even know he's doing it."

Reggie snaps her head to the side. She can't see the speaker from where she is. Instead there's a man, sitting cross-legged a few feet away from her. He's dressed in black, his face almost hidden underneath a gigantic mane of scraggly grey hair. Underneath his beard, his mouth is moving silently. Eyes closed, his head bowed, as if in prayer. His left hand rests on his knee, but the other slumps in the grass at his side.

The voice comes again, from somewhere behind her head. "I can sit you up, if you'd be more comfortable."

The speaker is a woman – the woman who offered to help her, and who (the memory comes reluctantly, as if it doesn't want to be pulled into the light) stuck something in her neck as they were approaching the slope.

Comfortable? Reggie has to bite down on the urge to yell at her, to scream. It won't get anything done – and if she's sitting up, if she could just see where the hell they are . . .

Before she can respond, there are hands under her armpits, pushing her upright. Something with a few soft edges – a pack or bag, maybe? – is pushed under her upper back.

They're in a park, on what looks like gentle slope. The slope leads down to a wide expanse of grass – a soccer field, Reggie realises, currently empty. There's a basketball court beyond it.

"What the hell did you do to me?" she croaks. "What was that?" There are so many other questions she has, but right now, there's nothing more important. She was back in Nemila, back in that room, and she *knew* it was real. How did—?

The woman sighs. "I can't control what he makes people see. I can barely control him. I'm glad I caught you when I did – if you stay in the worlds he makes for too long, it's much harder to get out."

She has a soft voice, almost delicate. "Are you cool enough?" she asks.

"My – I'm sorry, what?"

"Your body temperature. I'm aware that differently abled people sometimes have trouble with—"

"*Differently* abled?" Reggie snarls. Whatever's happening right here, she's not about to let whoever this is pull out that old chestnut. "I'm disabled."

"I . . . apologise. I meant no disrespect."

Reggie's awareness is coming back now, along with a dose of righteous fury. That man – these people – put her back in the worst memory of her entire life. She has no idea how the hell that is possible, but she feels ... violated. Unclean.

"Listen here," she says, "you plan on putting a blanket on me, you better keep that pretty nose clear, 'less you want it bitten off."

"Do you need any water?" the woman says, as if Reggie hadn't spoken. "The sedative might make you thirsty, I think."

Reggie's throat is a barren wasteland, the headache still blaring in her skull. She yet again tamps down on her anger, grunts an assent. A water bottle is held to her lips, and she sips delicately. It helps, a little.

She thought the man's lips were moving silently, but that's not quite true. He's whispering to himself, very quietly, and very quickly.

"Why are we here?" Reggie asks.

"We won't be bothered, even when Teagan joins us."

Teagan. Reggie closes her eyes, helpless anger flooding through her."

Just like that, Reggie remembers the knife. She glances down at her pocket – it's still there, the handle tenting the fabric ever so slightly. The woman didn't frisk her, probably didn't think she needed to.

Except: there's no possible way she can find it, slip her fingers into the handle, pull it out and use it – not before the woman takes it away.

No matter how far Reggie turns her head, she can only catch a glimpse of the woman from the very corner of her eye.

"This is about the boy?" she asks. "Isn't it?"

"You could say that."

"Why'd you send him? What is it you're trying to—?"

"Send him?" The woman makes an irritated mouth noise. "I didn't send him anywhere. He wasn't even supposed to be here."

"You're not doing very well then, are you?" Reggie spits. "This is the second enhanced child you've lost in a year."

"Enhanced." Amusement in her voice now. "I suppose you could call us that."

Us.

"In any case," the woman goes on. "Matthew certainly wasn't lost. He did exactly what he was supposed to."

"What, nearly destroy the whole damn west coast?"

Another pause, as if the woman is weighing up whether or not she wants to talk to Reggie. "You couldn't possibly understand."

"Try me."

"No. I don't think so. This isn't a comic book. I'm not just going to explain everything while we wait for Teagan. Especially not to someone who works for the intelligence services."

"There is no end," the man whispers. "Only the black only the walls and halls and lights—"

Reggie closes her eyes, trying to shut out the insane words. Whoever this woman is, she was planning to make use of the two boys – Matthew Schenke, with his power over the earth, and the boy who can control electricity. More than anything else, what Matthew did caused chaos. It destabilised Los Angeles, fractured it. It changed the status quo.

She's trying to do the same to the whole country. She wants to take over.

But that's absurd. You couldn't *take over* the United States. Even for somebody in command of enhanced individuals, it was too big. Too many people, too many balls you'd have to keep in the air, too much ground to cover. At best, you could hold a small section of it, but even that wouldn't last long – not when you'd face resistance within and without.

So what, then?

Maybe she wasn't trying to take over. Maybe she was simply trying to destroy, bring the country to its knees. But that didn't make sense either. What did that even mean? In real terms? The United States isn't a single thing. It's towns and cities, people and ideas, scattered across thousands of miles. Trying to destroy it in any meaningful way is pointless – and Reggie has the sense that this woman, whoever she is, would know that.

Reggie is hurting, but she's awake now. The pieces whirl in her mind. The two boys. The woman. Teagan. The School. Round and round they go.

And then just like that: they snap together.

What was it the woman said? *You couldn't possibly understand.* This isn't about power, or destruction.

This is about survival.

"Money," Reggie says, breathless.

The woman doesn't reply. But Reggie could swear she shifts slightly, her clothing rasping against the grass.

"All of this . . . you're doing it for money." Reggie speaks quickly, trying to keep up with the torrent of thoughts. "What did you do, short the markets before the quake? Invest in construction?" It sounds so boring, so *mundane* – but what else could it be? "You're trying to buy your way out. You want people – *your* people, enhanced people – to be safe. You're trying to protect them from the government. From everybody."

It made sense. If you controlled disasters, if you could make them happen on a whim, you could make incalculable amounts of money. Enough to buy or create a safe haven for any number of enhanced individuals. Reggie doesn't know what that would look like – it's almost too big for her to wrap her mind around – but she's already figuring out the rest.

"I'm impressed," Reggie continues, almost spitting out the words. "Money's one thing, but it only gets you so far, doesn't it? Sooner or later, the government would find you, and they'd move in. They'd destroy you. Unless, of course, you made it almost impossible for them to do so."

All at once, Reggie is back in Afghanistan, tasting the dust and the heat. She doesn't even need the psychopath in black to get her there – she can see it clearly in her mind.

There was a term the military used when battling insurgents: asymmetrical warfare. Regiments of trained soldiers with their guns and tanks, powerless against random roadside bombs, RPG attacks, suicide strikes. A war they could never win, because they could never see the enemy.

What this woman is doing is the ultimate in asymmetrical warfare. How could you fight a war when the consequences of the attack left you completely unable to function? When you couldn't even be sure that it was an attack at all?

And that was the genius of it. Sending children with abilities out into the world to wreak havoc was just the kind of thing that would draw unwanted attention . . . but to everyone else, an earthquake would just be an earthquake, no matter how deadly it was. Reggie had only discovered the existence of Matthew Schenke through a lot of digging, and not a small amount of luck.

She still has nightmares about what would have happened if she'd let it go, if she'd listened to the rest of China Shop and ignored her instincts. They would have written it off as just an earthquake. And when Cascadia was triggered?

The even larger fault line, running up the west coast? Same thing. They wouldn't ever have known it was an attack at all.

The woman didn't need to destroy the United States, or capture it. She just needed to keep it on the back foot, always reacting, unable to respond effectively. Unsure if the attacks even *were* attacks. She can turn an enhanced individual lose any time she wants, and it'll make her money. And every time it happens, it becomes even harder to stop her.

It's Moira Tanner's worst nightmare. *Everyone's* worst nightmare. If she lets this woman take back the boy, the one who could electrify entire buildings, rain thunderbolts . . .

Dear God.

"I am sorry, by the way," the woman says.

Reggie's voice is cold fury. "There is nothing you could say right now to—"

"I tried to do this without hurting anybody," the woman says, talking over her. "If Leo's father hadn't run—"

"Leo? The boy?"

"Mm. But he did, and I'm tired of chasing down Teagan and her friends. So I had to bring you in. Don't worry – if everything goes to plan, we'll all make it out of here alive."

"Alive." Reggie almost laughs. "That's rich. How many people did you kill when you sent that boy Matthew to California? He was a monster, you *knew* he was a monster, and you still turned him loose."

Before Reggie can continue, the woman says, "You use that word so freely. I would have thought someone like you would be more . . . understanding."

"What word? Monster? Honey, that little boy hated everything and everyone. All he wanted was to do was burn the world down and spit on the ashes."

The woman sighs. "Matthew – Lucas, I should say, that's his real name, by the way – is . . . " She pauses. "Complicated."

"Wrong. He was—"

"Is."

"I'm sorry?"

"Not was. Is. He's back with us now."

Reggie's heart stops beating. That's what it feels like. Just frozen cold in her chest. The thought of that . . . no, goddammit, she *will* call him a monster. The thought of him still alive is abominable.

"He's complicated," the woman says again. "But he's also one of us. He's like me. Like Leo. And like Teagan, although I'm not sure she'd appreciate the comparison. And I suppose I shouldn't be surprised that you'd use the word *monster* after all – it's what I'd expect from someone who doesn't have what we have."

"Teagan's no monster."

"That she is not," the woman says, a strangely warm note in her voice. "But she'd be called one, if people knew what she could do. All of us would be. We'd be seen as freaks."

The seated man has stopped whispering. He's humming now, a single tuneless note, almost inaudible. He hasn't opened his eyes.

Reggie says, "The people I work for—"

"Moira Tanner."

"So you do know her. Then you know how she operates, and you have to know that she'll find you. *We'll* find you." Saying the words before she can stop herself, aware that she may no longer be part of the *we*.

"Good luck," the woman says.

"And don't, don't, by the way, pretend like you're so noble. Wiping out thousands, just to protect a few individuals?"

"Your point?"

"My p—? Jesus Lord, honey, if I have to explain, you're *way* off the edge of the map."

"If there were another way to do it, I would." The woman's calmness digs at Reggie like an itch.

"Whatever you say."

"I don't really mind if you believe it or not. Protecting myself, and those like me … it's the only thing that matters." Her voice hardens, just a little. "If the public knew what we were, we'd be dead. All of us. I'm simply making the first move. And if a few people die, well … "

"You do realise that you're not making it out of this?" Reggie coughs suddenly, sharp and ugly, her diaphragm hitching. "The … *hhhrm* … the boy. Leo? He doesn't want to follow you, does he? He wasn't even supposed to be here – that's what you said, right?" She laughs, a mad sound that feels like it comes from somewhere far deeper than the cough did. "This is a kid who can turn a whole building into a live wire. He'll fry you the second he sees you."

It's a long moment before the woman replies. "You may not believe this, but I hope you don't have to die today. It'd be such a waste."

"What do you mean?"

"I'm well aware of what Leo can do. But I do know him, and I don't think he'd be willing to get you killed."

"Please. He can hit you with a lightning bolt faster than you can pull the trigger."

"Who said anything about pulling a trigger?"

The woman steps into view then, looming over Reggie. Against the still-bright sky, her face is a dark silhouette.

She's holding something in her hand, and Reggie has to let her eyes adjust before she gets a good look at it. When she does, she stops breathing.

It looks like the plastic remote control for the Scalextric race car set she had when she was a kid – like a pistol without the barrel, an oversized trigger protruding from it. It's a remote detonator. Reggie's seen plenty like it before. The woman's finger rests lightly on the trigger.

Reggie has gone cold again – and it has nothing to do with the woman's ability.

The woman taps the bottom of the detonator. There's a small box bolted onto the body, one no bigger than a thumb. Like the dot at the bottom of an exclamation point.

"Accelerometer," the woman says. "Thirty dollars off Amazon, and a couple of hours to wire up correctly. If it detects sudden movement – if I drop the unit – it activates. Sends the same signal as if I pull the trigger." She shrugs. "I don't really know what would happen if I was electrocuted, so I hedged my bets."

The woman nudges the object she placed underneath Reggie's shoulders.

Another cough bursts out of Reggie again, painful and frail. She can't look away from the woman's eyes. She expects them to display madness, insanity, but what she sees scares her even worse.

Determination.

Clear, defiant purpose.

"They'll be here soon," the woman says, letting the bomb trigger drop to her side. She looks towards the distant basket-ball court. "Let me know if I can make you more comfortable."

FORTY-SIX

Teagan

Something's wrong.

I'm not talking about Reggie's kidnapping. Or the flood. Or the number of people tonight who want us dead. All of that is seriously messed up, but that's not what I mean.

I'm talking about the homeless camp under the freeway.

We're hustling our way through the maze of scaffolding, alongside the river channel. The camp isn't empty, far from it – despite the dozens of groups we passed on the way, there are still plenty of people here.

They *are* packing up their stuff: clothes hurriedly being shoved into bags, shopping carts filling up, people darting back and forth under the shadow of the freeways. But I expected everyone to have cleared out already, because what the fuck else do you do when there's a huge flash flood inbound?

"Annie?" I say.

"What?" she snaps. She's already irritated, mostly because every single person we passed has tried to tell us about the flash flood.

"Can we stop for a sec?"

"Kind of on the clock here, Teags," Nic says, stepping over a steel scaffolding pole, turning to help Leo.

"Yeah, I know, I just need a second."

We have to keep moving. There's not a lot of time to fuck around here. But it's like a cut on the roof of your mouth, one you can't stop tonguing.

So despite our little situation, I take a look around me.

A real good look.

A woman strides across our path, a mane of scraggly red hair framing a panicked face. She wears a grey tank top over a long, flowing skirt, edged in mud, and she's shouting: "Casey! *Has anyone seen Casey?*"

Two men to my left, one of them sitting propped up against part of the scaffolding, the other bent over him. The sitting man is passed out, a thin slick of drool on his chin, his hands splayed on the concrete, twitching in a way that reminds me of Leo. His pal shakes him, yelling at him to get up, that he can't carry him. Since he has a crutch under one arm, that's probably true.

A dog zips past, barking hysterically. It vanishes into the network of scaffolding, only to reappear a second later. Its eyes are wild, panicked.

A man at the entrance to the sewer tunnel, where Annie and I went to use the bathroom. He's hanging out, yelling directions at a friend. "—torches or anything? The lights went out and—"

Another man, down on his knees, desperately trying to get two crutches underneath him. His dirty jeans are cut off at the right knee, and the leg below is a mess of crusty bandages. As I watch, he almost gets himself upright, loses it, comes crashing back down.

A panicked group of people over to our right, milling around one of the makeshift platforms lashed to the bamboo scaffolding. There are people on the platform, but the ramp they rigged to get up there has collapsed. Next to them, a short distance away, some insane jackass is playing a guitar, staring blankly into the flames of a cookfire, like everything is just dandy.

People. Everywhere: people. And not just a few. Hundreds. *They aren't leaving. Not nearly fast enough.*

Maybe it's because I came in here with Grant and Alvin and Lucille, but I had this idea that there were people in charge at this place.

Alvin sounded so sure about this place having some sort of order. Like it was a coherent community that would look after itself no matter what. But that's not true. It's not even close to true.

"*Teagan.*" Annie is furious now. "What the hell are you doing?"

I slowly look back at her. "Annie ... these people ... "

"What about 'em? We—"

She's interrupted by a tug at her sleeve. It's a little girl, ten or eleven, with neat braids hanging down her back. She's wearing an old red hoodie over jeans and a pair of light-up sneakers. Only one of them is working, blinking a frantic red.

"Have you seen my mom?" the girl babbles.

"Uh ... " Annie just stares at her.

"Her name's Shonda. She looks like me but with long hair. Have you seen her?" She looks around, craning to see behind us, as if we're purposefully trying to hide her mother. "She went to get some water, and then everybody started running, and I went to the water place but she wasn't there."

"We haven't seen her," Nic says, sounding dazed.

"Maybe the Zigzag Man got her." Leo claps a hand to his mouth, like he knows he's said something he shouldn't.

The girl's eyes meet mine, just for a second. Before I can say anything, she bolts, yelling out for her mom, zipping between scaffolding.

Is it possible to have an awkward silence in the middle of a panicked crowd? Why yes. Yes, it is.

"Can we find her, find her mom?" Leo asks.

"I don't think we have time," Annie says, more gently than I would have expected.

I take a deep breath. "Actually . . ."

"Actually . . . what?" says Nic.

"Well . . ." I spread my hands. "Look, it won't take long. I can echolocate, remember?"

Leo screws up his face. "What?"

"The thing I do where I can sense objects with my PK." I look up at Nic and Annie. "If the kid's mom is wearing jewellery or whatever, maybe I can find her."

"Stop." Annie holds up a finger. "Don't you dare."

"Don't I *dare*? You're seriously suggesting we just leave that little girl to—?"

"*Yes.*" But she can't stop herself glancing at the little girl, who is just visible off to our right, her back to us, still yelling for her mom. "We have to move, or we're not going to get out of here before the flood—"

Fuck this. Before any of them can stop me, I dart away, heading for the girl. "It'll only take a second," I yell over my shoulder.

"Teagan!" Nic yells. "Wait!"

The girl zips off before I can get there. I have to sprint after her, nearly tripping over the scaffolding a couple of times, almost knocking people over. But eventually, I catch her, swinging myself in front of her with my hands up. She goggles at me, like she's never seen me before.

"Your mom," I say. "Shana?"

"Shonda."

"Right. Does she have any jewellery on? Like a necklace or a bracelet?"

Someone bumps me from behind, nearly spilling me right into the girl. Annie and Nic are just making their way over to me, Leo in tow. They look somewhere between pissed off and *really* pissed off.

I speak quickly. "Kid. Jewellery."

The girl gapes at me. "You can't rob my mom!"

"What? No, I—"

"She's trying to rob my mom!" The girl yells this out, jabbing a trembling finger at me. Fortunately, the place is in such a panic that nobody pays any attention. Behind the girl, Annie is staring at me in absolute wonder.

"No!" I wave my hands, bringing the girl's attention back to me. "I'm not, I promise, I—"

"Then why do you want her jewellery?"

"I ..." *Shit.* "Look, it doesn't have to be jewellery. It can be anything. Keys, or a cellphone, or ... "

A cellphone? *Brilliant, Teagan.* Let's try and track this kid's mom by finding objects also owned by probably every other person here.

The little girl tilts her head. "Are you a crazy person?"

"I promise I'm not. But I think I can find your mom."

"How?"

For a moment, the words defeat me. "Please, hon. Just tell me if she has anything on her."

Seconds tick by. Seconds we don't have. God, this was a stupid idea, this was—

"Um ... she's got this, like, bracelet she wears," the girl says. "It's not real gold or anything ... "

I almost gasp with relief. "Does it have links? Is it a solid piece of metal?"

Now the kid looks even more confused. "I dunno? It's got this thing hanging from it. Like a little charm."

"What kind of charm?"

"It's in the shape of a frog," she stammers.

I'm not at what you call peak performance here. But my little echolocation trick doesn't take much energy – I'm not lifting anything, I'm just sensing it. So even before the little girl has finished speaking, I send my PK out in a wide circle, as far as it will go. Sampling the pieces of jewellery I find, each one lit up in my mind like a glittering star in an inky black sky. Necklaces, chains, rings. Zeroing in on the bracelets. Metal ones, plastic ones, links, bronze, gold, until—

"Wait here," I tell the girl.

"Who are—?"

"Wait here. Do *not* move."

Annie makes a grab for me, but I duck underneath her arm, zipping away into the crowd. Telling myself that this won't take long, that they can't possibly be angry at me for this.

I keep my mind locked on the bracelet, my PK wrapped around the tiny little frog charm hanging off it, swinging wildly as its owner moves back and forth. Someone has put a makeshift bridge over the channel of water, a big sheet of reinforced steel, and I bolt across it, ducking under yet more scaffolding. *Where are you?*

I'm so focused on my PK that when I finally locate the bracelet, it takes me a second to spot the owner.

I grabbed her arm. "Shonda, right? I've seen your daughter."

She does indeed look like her kid, just with longer hair. She's in a full panic, but the word *daughter* is like a signal flare, locking her attention in.

"You have?" she says. She has a Southern accent, reminding me of Reggie – something I could do without right now. "Where is she?"

I point back in the direction I came from, describing the spot where the kid was standing. Hoping she hasn't moved, because if she has, I don't know what I'm going to do.

Before I've even finished talking, Shonda is moving. She turns back, awkwardly, confusion fighting the need to be with her daughter. "How did—?"

"Never mind. Just go. Get your daughter and get the hell out of here."

I watch her go, stuck in my own mind for a second. Which means I get one hell of a shock when Annie and Nic appear in front of me, both of them speaking at the same time.

"OK." Nic has his hands up. "This isn't the best time to—"

Annie talks over him. "—don't have time to mess around with your damn—"

"—this wasn't what I meant, and I really don't think this is the moment for—"

"—always do this, always getting in the way, why can't you listen just once—?"

"*Hey!*" I yell.

Amazingly, it works. It startles them both into silence. I really didn't expect it to, but I'll take what I can get. Behind them, Leo gapes at me. He doesn't look angry. If anything he looks impressed.

I turn back to Annie and Nic. "How long before the flood gets here?"

Annie pinches the bridge of her nose. "Teagan—"

"Annie. How long?"

She glares at me, but the gears are turning. "Half hour. Maybe less."

"OK," I say. "Hear me out—"

"*Dios mio.*" Annie shakes her head, An expression of total exasperation on her face. "You are unbelievable, man."

"I just think that—"

"What about Reggie? You're just gonna leave her hanging while you help out kids you don't even know? Is that it?"

"Of course not!"

"Then what is it? Because if I remember correctly, you *agreed* to come with us. We don't have time for you to start having second thoughts, so you stow that shit, right now, or I swear I will rip your damn arms off."

"What the hell is your problem?" I roar at her. "Do you not see what this place is—?"

Nic shoves himself between us. I hadn't actually realised it, but we had gotten right up in each other's faces. And not in a good way. The kind of getting-up-in-your-face that results in somebody getting knocked the fuck out.

"You know what?" Annie jabs a finger in my face. "We don't need this. You wanna be a selfish prick, you go right ahead. Come, don't come, I don't care. But we're leaving." And with that, she turns and stalks away, following the line of the channel.

Selfish prick? Does she not see what I just did?

"The girl and her mom found each other," Leo says, popping up behind Nic. I didn't even see him leave to go check on them. *We should keep a closer eye on him.*

The thought makes me woozy, the world swimming in front of me. Annie has stopped about fifty feet away, her back to us, shoulders trembling with rage.

"Are we done here?" Nic says. He doesn't sound irritated or angry any more – just exhausted.

"I—"

"All right then." He turns to go, only to stop and look back when he realises I'm not following.

For a few seconds, we just stare at each other. People mill around us, shouting for their loved ones, yelling instructions, gathering their possessions.

The corners of Nic's mouth twitch. "When I said you should use your ability to help people, this wasn't really what I had in mind."

"Nic ..."

"We need you, Teags. Reggie needs you."

"I think ..." I swallow. "I think these people might need me too."

"Just—"

"Look around you." I hold my hands out, like I'm telling him to come at me. "Let's be generous. Let's say we really do have thirty minutes now. Do you really think that this place is going to be empty by the time it's underwater?"

"That's not on you. None of this is on you."

"Look, I get it. The bridge wasn't totally my fault. But that doesn't mean I get to just walk away from *everything*. I can't."

I'm sweating now, despite the chill air. "Before, when I didn't want to go help people in San Bernadino ... there were already people helping out. Here, there's nobody else. Nobody's coming. No cops, no fire department. The government isn't sending people. The city doesn't give a shit. If I don't get involved, what do you think is gonna happen?"

Leo comes and stands next to Nic, his face knotted, as if thinking hard.

Nic laces his fingers behind his head. "They're not just gonna listen to you out of the blue."

"They don't have to." I lick my lips, thinking back to how

I found Shonda. "I can help people find each other. If they're trapped, I can get them out. Hell, maybe I can create an exit." I look towards the underside of the freeway, where it meets the top edge of the storm drain. It's a sheer wall of concrete, but . . .

"I don't wanna hear this," Nic says. "I don't wanna hear this shit, Teags. Just think for a second."

A frustrated, angry howl bursts out of me. I'm not expecting it, even as it starts to happen. It's so loud and so sudden that both Nic and Leo take a step back

I spent most of today fighting a losing battle against confusion and exhaustion. The meth comedown, the people chasing us, the ridiculous number of times we've almost died. Twice today, I have literally been trapped in horrific hallucinations. The rest of the time, I've been seeing things my own mind has put there, little flickers and feelings that someone is coming up behind me. For the first time today, maybe for the first time in years, I know *exactly* what I have to do.

"Think?" I lock eyes with Nic. "Think. OK. I'm getting mighty tired of that word. I've had people telling me to think before I do shit for . . . well, pretty much for ever. Everybody has this stupid fucking *idea* in their head that I'm just this little kid who doesn't know what she's doing.

"But here's the thing, dude. I *did* start thinking. I *did* start acting like a grown-up, even if nobody noticed. Tanner told me I needed to focus on the job and help catch the bad guys, and that's exactly what I did. You know what it all got me? Using my abilities like I was told? It made me miserable. Being an adult about everything made me fucking *miserable*."

I probably shouldn't getting into this now – no, scratch that, I definitely shouldn't be getting into this now – we are running real short on time. But I don't have a choice. It's all there, and at this point, it's coming out no matter what I do.

"All I ever wanted was to cook." Tears prick at the corner of my eyes, but my voice stays steady. "I just wanted to work in a kitchen and go home at the end of the night knowing I made people happy. I had to give that up, because everybody acted like it was this stupid, childish fantasy. And I thought they were right, and I did what they asked me to, made the adult choices, and Nic? Guess what? *It wasn't enough for people.* You, Reggie, Annie, everybody. I'm still just a little girl, I don't take responsibility, I'm too reckless. It's never gonna be enough, no matter what I do, no matter how grown-up I act."

"I don't get why you think that—"

"If you say that word one more time I'm going to take your car keys out of pocket and jam them up your nose. I *am* thinking. I'm looking around me, and I'm seeing people that are going to die if I don't do something, and I'm doing it. *Don't* tell me I'm not thinking, and *don't* tell me I'm not acting like an adult here."

"I never said that!"

True, he didn't, but there's no chance of stopping me now. "Everybody wants me to use my power to save lives? OK. I'm gonna save lives. Maybe giving up chef school was the right thing to do, but that doesn't mean I have to give up everything else. Adulting means making your own decisions, and I'm making this one. I've thought about it, and I've made a call. This is happening."

He's slowly shaking his head. I can't read the look on his face; it's as if awe and disbelief had a baby, and that little baby expression was then adopted by exasperation and raised to be pissed at just about everything.

"I don't want you to do this," he says, after a long moment.

"I know. But I have to."

He looks away then, eyes shining. Fixed on the middle

distance. As if he's trying to process what he's feeling, and can't quite do it.

Annie is still there, twenty feet from us. Arms folded, impatient, not looking at me. I want to call out to her, but I have no idea what to say. Maybe I can convince Nic – maybe – but there's no chance with her.

"What if the water gets here and you're still helping people?" Leo says. I'd almost forgotten he was still there. He hasn't said a word.

I force a smile onto my face. "I can fly, little man."

"You can *fly*?"

"Well, sort of. I can make other stuff fly, and then just stand on top of it." I turn to Nic. "If the flood gets here and I'm still around, I'll levitate myself up onto the freeway. Promise."

"What about Reggie? What are we going to do if—?"

"You got this." I can't help but glance at Leo, still kind of amazed that he's okay with everything. "There's still time before the meet. Between you and Annie, you can figure something out."

"What if we can't?" His voice is a croak.

There's no answer to that. Nothing any of us can say, or do.

After a long moment, Nic steps forward. He wraps his arms around me, and pulls me close.

"If the flood gets here, and you're still around, you get the fuck out," he says. "I don't care how many people are left. I want that date, Frost," he says.

I smile into his shoulder. "Wouldn't miss it for anything."

"I'm serious. First date. You and me, good-ass food. No earthquakes or electricity powers, or saving the world. You better not miss it, you hear me?"

A sound comes out of me, and I don't know if it's a laugh, or a sob.

We stand there for a few seconds, clutching each other tightly. When I finally let go, I get an immediate urge to go back in, just hug him and hug him until the whole world burns.

Instead, I crouch down, and wrap my arms around Leo.

"I'm sorry," I whisper. And this time, there's no mistaking the tears rolling down my face. "I'm so, so sorry."

"It's OK."

"We'll . . . we'll figure out a way to keep you safe. From the Zigzag Man, I mean. Nic and Annie, they'll . . . "

The look in his eyes feels as if it should be coming from someone much older. "I know."

Annie still hasn't moved. She's just standing there, twenty feet away. A still form in the middle of the chaos.

Is she just going to walk away? Without saying anything?

After all we've been through, I hoped . . .

I don't know what I hoped.

Leo takes Nic's hand, and Nic looks back at me, one last time.

Then they're gone.

I close my eyes, just for a second. Centre myself as best I can – which is hilarious, since I've never been very good at that. But I've got a lot of work to do, and not a lot of time to do it, so I'd best figure this shit out fast.

Best thing to do would be to create an exit, a way out under the freeway on either side. But I'm not sure I could do it without completely revealing my ability – or at least, without scaring the hell out of people. Then again, who gives a fuck? I need to get these people out *now*.

Problem is, if I start moving things around – even if nobody knows it's me – it might start a panic. Just because I create an exit doesn't mean anybody is going to go near it. And looking around now, I'm already seeing ways I can help – confused people I can assist. If I can get a critical mass of them moving, then the rest might follow. *Just start small. Help one person, then another. Then another.*

Heavy footsteps, coming up behind me. I whirl, just in time for Annie Cruz to put her hands on my chest and shove me.

It's not a big shove. She doesn't knock me over or anything. But it still makes me stumble back a few feet, arms out behind me, feet slipping on a wet patch of concrete. "Annie, what the f—?"

"You piece of shit."

It come through Annie's gritted teeth, more hiss than words, and that's when I see just how angry she is. This isn't regular angry. This is nuclear reactor angry. This is burn-the-world-down-and-dance-on-the-ashes angry.

I look past her, hoping that Nic will save me. But he and Leo are nowhere to be seen.

"Annie – Jesus Christ, enough, OK? We don't have time for—"

"Fuck you." She jabs a finger into my chest, Flexing and un-flexing her other hand, like she wants to slug me. "You're not a . . . a . . . a fucking superhero. I don't care what powers you got and shit, you don't have to save the world every time."

"Please stop," I say.

"No, no, you don't get to—"

"Annie, please, I don't—"

"Because I'm tired of having to keep your ass out of trouble. You do this shit over and over, and you think you're gonna live for ever and—"

"*Stop it!*"

My voice cracks so hard that the words are barely understandable.

"You don't get it—" she starts.

I cut her off. "No. *You* don't get it. Don't pretend like you didn't hear what I told Nic – you know exactly why I'm doing this. It's my decision. Nic understands it, Reggie will probably understand it too; hell, even *Tanner* might understand it. Why can't you?"

"You wanna know what I saw?" she says. "When the Zigzag Man hit us that last time?"

She's barely holding it together. Under the rage is raw, brittle terror. "I saw *you*," she says. "Dead. Just like Paul. Under the fucking ground."

I put a hand on her shoulder. She smacks it away. "Don't you fucking touch me."

"But Annie . . . I made it. *We* made it. You pulled me out of there, right?"

"I can't lose you again." Hissed through gritted teeth. "If you go, there's nobody else. Nobody who's got my back."

"I—"

Her words come in a sudden rush. "You're the only one who gave a shit, you know that? After Paul. You were the only one who kept asking how I was doing. Reggie tried, but she had so much to deal with already. Africa, he's a good dude, but it's not as if he . . . He doesn't know how to say it. Even my mom, she misses Paul too, I know she does, but she never wants to talk about him. It's like she wants to pretend it never happened. Like we're all gonna be fine. Same thing for everybody who came to that memorial service we had for him. They were just there for the party. They don't care about us. So yeah, when you get down to it, you're the only friend I've got."

I am completely at sea in this conversation right now. Way beyond sight of land. What she's saying doesn't make sense. More than that: I'm not just confused, I'm angry.

"I don't get it." My throat feels too tight, furious tears

pricking at the corner of my eyes. "You've been pissed at me for weeks now. Fuck it, *months*. No matter what I do or say, you just yell at me. Or make snarky comments. Or tell me I'm being . . . being stupid. Don't pretend like you—"

"*Because you keep trying to get yourself killed!*" She roars in my face. "You keep putting yourself in these situations, and you do it over, and over, and over, and for what? For people who don't care about you? Who don't even know who you really are? And if they did know . . . Teags, if they knew, they'd . . . "

She trails off, closes her eyes. I'm about to interrupt, but she starts speaking again before I get there.

"You keep risking your life and you pretend like it's no big thing because you got your voodoo. Like the rest of us don't have to watch it happen. Like we don't count at all."

Her voice cracks. "What if this is the one time it doesn't work? What if you're gone, and I'm still here?"

And all at once, it's like she shuts down. Like she grabs her emotions, and locks them in place. Her eyes go dead.

"No more," she says. "I can't deal with this shit any more. If you stay here? If you don't come with me right now? We're done, you and me. I'm out of China Shop, out of all of it. You will *never* see me again."

I'm not just lost at sea, I'm getting hit by wave after wave. This is . . . *insane*. Where is this coming from?

But of course, I know the answer to that, even if she doesn't.

It's coming from a place of confusion.

A place of grief, and loss, and fear.

It's twisted the way she views the world. Made it impossible for her to think straight. She's so terrified of losing me that she's blocked out everything else, focused all of her anger on me because in her mind, I won't *listen*.

What would happen if the situation was reversed? If it was

Annie who might die, and not me? How would I feel if she kept putting herself in danger?

I don't know.

And that's the scariest thing of all.

"Last chance," Annie says.

There's a moment where I almost go with her. Take her hand, let her lead me out. Away from all of this. Let her take me to a place where we save Reggie, save Leo. And a place where I can save her.

But around us, the chaos hasn't stopped. The people are still here, still not leaving fast enough. Soon, the flash flood is going to be here. And if I go with Annie . . .

I don't want to make this choice. It's worse than anything I've experienced today. Worse than the meth comedown. Worse than splitting up the team.

I meet her eyes. A part of me expects her to soften, to finally understand how irrational she's being, how she can't possibly ask this of me. Instead, she just shakes her head. Slowly. Side to side.

"Annie," I whisper. "Don't."

She steps back, like I slapped her.

Then she turns, and runs.

FORTY-SEVEN

Teagan

There is nothing I can do.

Not a damn thing.

All I can do is watch her go. Running through the conversation in my head, trying out a million different imagined responses, a million ways that it could have gone differently.

The urge to chase after her is almost overpowering. Chase her, stop her, *demand* that she explain herself. *You don't treat friends like this. You don't give them ultimatums.*

And what would you say if someone you cared about kept putting themselves in harm's way? What would you do?

She never told me. She never told me how she felt about me.

But is that true? Or did I just ... miss it?

I don't know.

What I do know is this. I have to survive. I have to stop the flash flood. Because there is no way I'm letting that be the end of it.

So I push everything that just happened to the back of my mind.

In twenty-five minutes, this place is going to be underwater.

Unless I figure this out pretty fucking fast, everyone here is going to be in the middle of it.

First things first. Let's make an exit.

I move as fast as I can, winding my way through the scaffolding. I keep having to dodge around people, yelling at them to move.

I pop out the southern end of the camp, scanning the side of the channel to my right. It's wall-to-wall flood barrier at the top, but I think I can change that. I hope.

I'm already breathing hard, my chest burning. The second I get in range, a little way up the slope, I wrap my PK around the supports of one of the barriers – the big metal brackets holding it in place. I grit my teeth as I pull them upwards, tearing the bolts out of the concrete.

The barrier gives a screeching, groaning sound, starting to tip forward. There are panicked yells and shouts below me, but they are focused on the tipping barrier, not on me, which is good. The problem is, the barrier isn't going down easy. It resists me, forcing me to push more energy into my PK.

Use the meth.

My hand is on my jacket pocket, over the little baggie inside. *Being supercharged would make this easy.*

I jerk my hand away. I don't need the meth to do this. I *don't*. I took that little bag so I could experiment later. That's all. I definitely didn't bring it with me so I could snort from it whenever I needed to use my PK.

As if validating this, the barrier suddenly comes loose. It tips forward, slamming onto the slope, turning sideways as it slides down the concrete. I have to skip out of the way, and it crashes onto the flat part of the storm drain.

Now there's a gap. A big empty spot at the top of the slope, like a missing tooth.

It doesn't look like anyone knows that it was me who created it, and more importantly, it doesn't look like they care how it happened. They are already scrambling up the slope to my left and right, yelling at others to follow.

That's a good start. But there's no guarantee that the people under the freeways will even know there *is* an exit, especially if they were at the far end. The camp is a big, confused, buzzing mess.

The problem isn't the people currently on their feet, moving around, trying to track down lost family members or friends. They know what's coming, and they know they probably don't have much time. The problem is the people who *aren't* moving. The ones who are passed out, drugged out of their minds, disabled, injured. There's nobody coming for them, nobody to hustle them along. This place might have had some loose organisation, once upon a time, but it's gone to shit now.

The people leaving or getting ready to leave don't know about the ones who are still here. They probably aren't even aware they exist. But I am. Because I can feel the objects they carry with them. I can pick up their cell phones and watches and chains, their backpacks and wallets and money clips. All I have to do is look for the objects that aren't moving.

And as I sprint back into the chaos of the camp, that's exactly what I do.

I don't let myself think. I don't let myself consider anything else, especially not Nic and Leo, especially not Annie, not my friend, not my—

Fuck you. Focus.

There's the man with the injured leg, the one with the crutches. Or should I say crutch — somehow, in the chaos of the last few minutes, he's managed to lose one of them. I don't even know how that's possible. Did someone steal it? Who the hell would do such a thing?

As I watch, he wobbles to a halt, then sits down with a thud, his chest heaving.

The sight of him blows a fuse in my mind. Because even if I can get people moving, what about the ones here who *can't* move? I could pick them up and carry them with my PK – somehow – but I have no clue how to do it without revealing my ability and causing a panic.

I shouldn't have sent Nic and Annie away. I should have asked them to help. Doing this on my own is insanity.

Except: if they didn't leave, then Reggie dies.

I'm breathing too fast, the sheer weight of what I'm trying to do settling on me like a heavy blanket. I claw in my pocket for my phone, thinking that maybe I can call someone, anyone. I'm pretty sure the cops or the fire department won't respond in time, but it might be worth a shot.

It takes me a second to realise that the phone isn't mine. I stare down at it, completely blanking, until I remember. It's the phone I took from Minnie, the biker Annie beat the shit out of back of the train depot.

Whatever. A phone is a phone. I don't even need to unlock it to dial 911 – although it wouldn't matter, because Minnie was a badass biker who thought passwords were for losers. My fingers punch in the number and are about to dial when I stop.

What if . . .?

No. I can officially say that is the dumbest idea I've ever had. It could blow up in my face in so many spectacular ways.

I raise my eyes to the injured man, the one with a single crutch. He's trying yet again to get moving, and it's not working.

And then I'm opening the phone, navigating to the contacts.

It takes me no more than a few seconds to find what I'm looking for.

Phone calls and data are hit and miss in LA right now, but for once, the telecommunication gods are in a good mood. Robert's voice comes through the connection loud and clear: "Who the hell is this?"

FORTY-EIGHT

Teagan

I can't help but smirk. Just a little. "I'll give you three guesses but you're only gonna need—"

"You made a big mistake."

"Don't ruin my line. Dick."

"You're fucking dead. You hear me? When we find you—"

"I know, I know, hung, drawn, quartered, remains scattered to the four winds, whatever. Listen—"

All at once, there are those muffled scratching sounds you get when two people trying to fight over one connection. Then there's another voice in my ear. One belonging to someone I thought was dead.

"*Ma petite*," Pop says. I knocked a couple of her teeth out, back when I escaped the train depot. Broke her nose. Her voice is very slightly mushy. "You had better run very, very far."

I recover surprisingly quickly, given the circumstances. "Howdy, Pop. Glad you made it."

She laughs – a surprisingly innocent sound. "You think your little soldiers cause me trouble? Your little soldiers are *dead*."

A nauseous little hitch of guilt grabs hold of me. If tonight had gone differently, those soldiers would still be alive.

I push past it. Guilt can come later. *If there is a later.*

I need to move a lot of people very quickly, and I can't do it if I have to spend that time helping people who can't help themselves. A squad of bikes – hell, even three or four of them – would make a massive difference. They can zip in and out of the camp, getting the injured to safety.

"What you did to me?" Pop says. "What you did to my brothers? It will follow you for ever."

"Shut up."

"What?"

"Fucking zip it. You need to listen, and you need to do it right now."

As quickly as I can, I tell Pop about the camp, and the flash flood. I tell her what I need her to do. Amazingly, she doesn't interrupt.

I haven't looked at a map, so I don't know for sure, but it should be a quick fifteen-minute bike ride from Chinatown. That's more than enough time for them to get down here, and give me a hand giving people out.

Assuming I can convince them not to murder me.

"You want to do some good?" I say. "Beyond just helping out a few kids? Get your ass down to the 710 where it crosses the storm drain. You've got about twenty minutes."

"Is this a joke?" Pop says.

"I wish."

"If you think we're just going to—"

"Come help out, or don't," I snap. "I don't have time to convince you, so you make up your own mind."

With that, I end the call.

And get to work.

There's a man frantically looking for his dog, who refuses to leave until he finds him. I close my eyes, zero in on the plastic buckle on the dog harness. I don't stick around to enjoy the reunion, yelling at the man to get the hell out, already looking for the next target.

I rouse two drunks sleeping in a makeshift tent – two dudes snuggled up, spooning, one of them with his arm wrapped tightly around the other. When it turns out they are still drunk, and not inclined to move, I collapse their tent on top of them. They scramble to their feet in a panicked daze, taking in the chaos around them.

I dive into the sewers. The cavernous dark is lit by a dozen waving cellphone screens, and I use my PK to create a map of the rest, ignoring the burning headache at the back of my skull. I find the people without cellphones, without any source of light. A man who has lost his wheelchair. Three kids stoned out of their mind on God knows what. Some jackass trying to find a way out through the sewers, stumbling around with his hands out in front of him like a zombie. I send them all out towards the storm drain exit, ignoring their shouted questions.

No sign of Pop and the Legends. How much time do I have left? Ten minutes? Fifteen? I scramble back out into the storm drain, suddenly terrified of being caught unaware by the flood. But it hasn't appeared yet in the channel to the north of us. I put my head down, focus on my PK and keep going.

There's a steady stream of people heading towards my improvised exit now, but it's not enough. Nowhere close to enough. It takes all the self-control I have not to scream at everyone around me, the dumb motherfuckers who are *still here*. I come across two more kids, hunting for their parents, and it takes me way too long – a whole two minutes, maybe three – to find them, zeroing in on an engraved money clip in the dad's pocket. I don't give them time to enjoy the reunion, slapping the mom on the ass as I run past, making her jump. "Go," I say. "Right now, *move!*"

Right then, my exhaustion goes from a bubbling five to a screaming eleven.

I come to a shuddering halt, hands on my knees, the stitch in my side so powerful that it feels like it's going to burn my torso to ash. The headache is bad now, as bad as it's been all day. It's astounding that I've managed to keep going as long as I have.

And I can't stop. There are still people here. A quick check with my PK shows at least two dozen wallets and cellphones and chains that just aren't moving. Some abandoned, for sure . . . but how many are still attached to their owners?

Pop and the Legends still haven't shown up. I don't think they're going to, either. My great plan came to nothing. I didn't spend too much time on that call – perhaps no more than a minute. But when you only have around twenty or so to play with, a minute is a lot.

Unprompted, my PK latches onto something I can use to fly: a wooden pallet, leaning up against a scaffolding pole a few feet away. It has metal brackets, so I already know I can lift it, use it to levitate the safety. Still no sign of the flood. I make a mental note of where to find the pallet, telling myself that I'll wait until the last possible second to use it. Then again: if I wait until the last possible second, if I'm still telling people to get the hell out of here, then it's too late. They're toast. Even if they head for the exit right then, they won't be able to get there before the flood sweeps them away.

I have to survive this.

I can't let Annie lock me out of her life. That shit is not gonna happen.

"Get it together, bitch," I snarl at myself, pushing the thoughts away, and the headache with them. It works, a little, so I double down. "Cock womble. Asshole. Cookie Monster. *Fuck*."

My motivational cursing session stops when the damnedest thing happens.

A van appears, a big white one, screaming down the storm drain towards the camp from the north.

My first thought is that the Legends have arrived, that they decided not to come on bikes. Except: I know that van. I should. I spend a lot of time in it during China Shop missions.

"You have got to be fucking kidding me," I murmur.

The van screeches to a halt a few feet from where the scaffolding starts, rocking on its suspension. The cabin is turned slightly away from me, the driver flailing his limbs inside, as if fighting with the seatbelt. A moment later, the door explodes open, and Africa levers himself out onto the concrete storm drain surface.

He's still wearing that stupid, oversized FBI windbreaker over the dark suit and red shirt. The collar of the shirt has gone skew, sticking up like a flag caught in the wind. I have a sudden, half formed urge to hide, but I cannot convince my exhausted body to move.

Africa looks at me, looks away – and then his eyes snap back. He lifts a giant arm, levels a shaking finger at me.

"*You!*"

"Me," I mutter.

He marches towards me, finger still pointed, like it's a magic wand he can use to turn me into a frog. All the same, it's a wary approach, his eyes flicking left and right. It takes me a second to realise that he is looking for Leo. Once electrocuted, twice shy, I guess.

"They're gone, dude," I say. "Reggie's—"

"Where is he?" His eyes aren't just darting, they're practically rolling in their sockets.

I pinch the bridge of my nose. "Not here. Obviously." *I don't have time for this.*

He barks a laugh. "You lie. Of course he is here. You are here, so he must be."

"Africa," I say, with frankly a lot more patience than he deserves. "It's just me. Reggie's in trouble, and Annie and Nic—"

"I think you come here." The arm sweeps to the side, gesturing at the camp. "I think, hmm, Idriss, if they are going south, what is the most direct route? And I see the river, and then I know. And of course, you would come here sooner or later. To the camp under the freeway."

It's then that he appears to notice just how chaotic the scene is, pick up on the dozens of people gathering their shit and getting the hell out.

His eyes swivel back to me, as if deciding that he has to stay on track. "Teggan, we must talk." The outstretched arm falls to his side, sliding into the pocket of the windbreaker. I didn't really pay attention to it before, but he's exhausted, same as I am. Run ragged. A man at the end of a very long tether. "This boy is dangerous. He kill those people at the stadium. I know you want to help him, but please, you must *listen* to me."

I've had enough of this. I take two strides towards him, and get right in his face.

"Here's what's happening," I snarl. "Remember our little crash at the bridge? Well, turns out, if you put a lot of debris in a storm drain, there'll be a flood. It's gonna be here any minute, and if we can't get these people out –" I jerk a thumb over my shoulder behind me "– they're all going to die."

"Teggan—"

"And Leo isn't here. The kid. Neither is Nic, or Annie. You know where they are? They're going to help Reggie, who has been kidnapped by . . . I don't know who he is, but he has abilities too. There's a lot of shit going on, and I do *not* have time to deal with you right now."

He stares at me, horror falling on his face. "Reggie is in trouble?"

"Yes. But listen – there's nothing we can do for her right now. If you want to help, then you need to get these people out."

He's shaking his head, as if he doesn't believe me. And is that a distant hiss of rushing water I hear? I'm pretty sure it's just my imagination, but . . .

"You wanna know what makes Moira Tanner's dick hard?" I say. "The one thing that gets her up in the morning? Saving lives. If people die, all she wants to know is how many people actually made it out OK."

I jab him in the chest. "The best job you can do right now is to help me. Get in that van, wait until I've filled it up with people, then drive like hell. I think we can squeeze ten people in, and it probably won't take that long either. Injured people only. There are exits up the sides of the storm drain now, but there'll be too many people for you to get through. You'll need to drive like hell downriver, away from the flood. Find an exit with enough space for the van."

He doesn't want to believe me. He's spent this entire day thinking I'm the enemy, and I'll say this for Africa – he always finishes what he starts. But at the same time, he can't deny what's happening right in front of him – the panic, the hordes of people, the distinct lack of Leo, or Nic, or Annie.

Seconds tick by. Seconds we don't have. I've already wasted way too much time talking to him.

Eventually, he gives a single, grave nod, his eyes never leaving me.

"I park the van over there," he says, pointing to the nearest piece of scaffolding. "We open the doors, and then I help you find people. Then we both get in, and we both go, and then we go and help Reggie."

I don't have the energy to tell him that I'm going to stick around for as long as possible. I just nod back, my eyes never leaving his.

At some point, we are going to have to figure out how we ended up on opposite sides of this. Africa and I haven't always seen things the same way, but I get the feeling today would have been a lot easier with him on my side.

I thought I was good at making and keeping friends. I don't know if that's true any more. And I don't know how much of it is down to me, and how much of it is the fault of others.

I was friends with Carlos. He betrayed me. Sold me out.

I was friends with Africa. But I kept pushing him away.

I was friends with Annie, and—

No. We weren't friends. Not with the way she treated me. The way she got angry with me, for the smallest things. The way she forced me to choose between her, and saving lives. You don't do that to people you call *friend*. Fuck her.

So why do I keep seeing her face? Why can't I get rid of the horrible, sick pang in my stomach that I felt when she walked away?

Africa drives the van right into the middle of the camp, navigating his way through the scaffolding. It's tough going, and takes way longer than I would have liked, but it looks like there's going to be just enough room for him to drive out of the camp as well.

I keep moving, forcing my exhausted legs to walk, then run, as I hunt down the injured. The van is a stopgap at best – we won't be able to make more than one or two trips before the flood reaches us. But it's better than nothing.

And all the while I'm waiting for the distant sound of rushing water. The feeling of the ground rumbling under my feet.

Africa collars people to help gut the van's interior. Tool kits, duffel bags, boxes of old electronics. Everything Paul installed in the van is taken out, set aside. It's a strange thing to watch. The van was an extension of Paul's mind, ordered in a way that made sense to him and him alone. It's where he'd be during our ops, running comms. Where he'd meticulously store and label everything we needed.

All of it. Tossed onto the surface of the storm drain. Not even looted – just left there. Ready for the flood to sweep it away.

In the end, we get way more than ten people into the van. Closer to twenty. The vehicle is so overloaded that the tyres almost touch the wheel arches. I have to turn people away, telling them to get the hell out through the exit I made. My voice is hoarse now, my throat burning, the meth comedown back in full force at the worst possible time.

I stop for a second by the side of the van, under the China Shop bull logo. *If nothing else, at least we get some good PR out of this.* The thought is so out-of-place that I actually laugh at it, an exhausted snort-chuckle that makes my throat ache.

Africa claps me on the shoulder. "I think we can get one more. Climb on board."

"No."

"Of course we can." He gestures to the van, annoyed. His own voice has started to suffer, the boom robbed of its bass. "Even if you have to hang out the door—"

"I'm not done here."

I don't even know how it's possible, but there are *still* people in the camp – I can feel the objects they're carrying, moving around. Almost everybody has gone, the two thousand people here reduced to a couple dozen. But those couple dozen aren't moving, for whatever goddamn reason, which means it's on me to get them out of here. The Legends aren't going to show.

The van's sliding door is still open. The guy with the crutches – well, crutch – and the fucked-up leg is inside, looking like he barely knows who he is, let alone where. There are dudes holding their folded wheelchairs to their bodies, a woman with what looks like a nasty head injury, her hair matted with blood. A teen girl catches my eye. "Are we going or what?" she shouts, her voice edged in terror.

Africa hovers, his jaw working, glancing between me and the van.

"Dude, I'll be fine," I say.

"Teggan, you must not stay."

"Just go. *Please.*"

And still he doesn't move.

I raise my eyes to his. "I did not just run my ass ragged so you could hang around and *not* drive these people out of here." I nod downriver. "Go."

With a lingering look back at me – a look filled with doubt and worry and desperation – Africa climbs behind the wheel. The van roars to life, the engine straining as Africa accelerates. I catch his eyes in the side mirror one last time, and then the van lurches forward, wheels screeching. It almost collides with one of the scaffolding poles, just misses, nearly hits a second. Africa gets it under control, and the van rumbles away, heading out into the open air beyond the camp. I have a sudden, desperate urge to run after it, climb on the back somehow, leave this mess behind.

Instead, I straighten up, ignoring my aching muscles and the pounding throb at the base of my skull and the bone-weary, leaden exhaustion. *Almost there.* Two dozen people left, maybe even less. Ten minutes should do it. Ten minutes, and I can get the hell out myself.

Which is when I hear it.

An almost inaudible hiss. The sound of a radio in another room, tuned to a dead station. The sound of someone exhaling directly on a microphone, the soft breath distorting and crackling ever so slightly.

Very slowly, I turn around, and look upriver.

I don't have ten minutes. I may not even have five.

The flood has found us.

FORTY-NINE

Reggie

Reggie spots Annie first, crossing the field at the bottom of the slope. There's a man walking next to her – with a start, Reggie realises it's Nic Delacourt, Teagan's old . . . crush? Friend? She still isn't sure, and she's even more confused about what Nic is doing here. Teagan must have called him, or . . .

A tiny figure emerges from behind them.

Objectively, Reggie knew that the boy couldn't be more than four. And yet, seeing him here, she's struck by how small he looks. Like a strong breeze could simply lift him away.

Behind her, the woman gets to her feet. Silent. Waiting. The seated man continues to chant.

Reggie has a sudden urge to shout a warning, tell Annie and Nic to stay away. But her strained, trembling diaphragm won't push the words out.

There's a long moment where the world holds its breath. There's no sound but the distant rumble of thunder in the north. The very slight rustle of fabric as the woman who holds her captive shifts from foot to foot. The clouds have covered the sky above them now, dark and heavy.

Reggie has already felt one or two tiny, spitting droplets on her forehead.

How much pressure on the trigger would it take to set off the bomb? It's all too easy to imagine the sudden kick in the small of her back, the searing pain, the bright light obliterating everything, wiping her from existence.

The approaching trio are close enough that Reggie can pick out more details now. Annie's shoulders are tense – her upper body hardly moves at all as she walks, her arms barely swinging. Nic is a little looser, but not by much, and his face is pinched with worry.

The boy between Annie and Nic is Asian, with a black fringe and enormous, terrified eyes. He wears a dirty, sodden T-shirt over torn jeans. Reggie feels a renewed surge of hate for her captor – how can she treat this boy, this *child*, like a tool? Like a weapon?

Then again, he's not just a boy. He has the ability to call down the lightning.

"Reggie?" Annie calls out, when she's around twenty feet away. Her voice is as tense as her shoulders.

"I'm all right," Reggie says. Or tries to. It barely carries, nothing more than a croak. A wave of shame rolls through her, at Annie seeing her like this. A pawn in a bigger game.

Reggie has always thought of hostage negotiations as taking place on a larger scale – a building surrounded by strobing blue and red from patrol cars, the FBI getting ready to breach, even though she knows it's an image taken from the movies and that most stand-offs are nowhere near as dramatic. But this feels like it's gone too far in the opposite direction – it's too calm, too quiet. The insanity of the situation is at odds with the calm soccer field, the distant basketball court, the hillside with the grass hissing gently in the breeze.

"That's close enough," the woman says. Then: "Hello, Leo."

Leo flinches, and Reggie expects him to step behind Nic. He doesn't. He holds his ground – trembling, but steady.

"I wish you hadn't run away," the woman says. "If your father—"

"My dad hates you." Leo's voice is tiny, but still carries. "*I* hate you, and the Zigzag Man too." He cuts a look at the seated figure, rocking back and forth.

Reggie does too. *Zigzag Man*, she thinks, and shivers.

Nic's eyes meet Reggie's. He looks drawn and tired, like it's been weeks since he slept. The last time Reggie saw him was during the incident with Jake, the other psychokinetic.

She has a sudden urge to apologise to him, tell him she's sorry he got mixed up in this. What was the saying? *I wish we could have met under better circumstances.*

"Don't come any closer," she says. This time, her voice carries. "There's a bomb."

In half a second, Annie's anger goes from simmering to boiling. Her eyes dart to the shape underneath Reggie, then back up.

There's another rustle of fabric – the woman lifting the detonator, no doubt. "You see this, Leo? No games now. If I let go, or squeeze too hard—"

"I know." The boy sounds exhausted too, his voice that of someone much older.

"This is going to be very simple," the woman says. She sounds reasonable, even gentle. "You're going to come with us. I'm going to give you something – a little jab, just like a flu shot. It won't hurt, I promise, and it'll make you sleep."

Leo nods. He looks sick.

"Look at me, bitch." It's as if Annie rolls the word around in her mouth, tasting it. "There's gonna be a lotta scary dudes coming for you after this. I'm not even talking about the government, although you'd best believe they'll be hunting too. I'm talking about every soldier in every hood in LA, every gangster, every shooter, every contact I got. I'm putting the word out. They're gonna be coming for your ass."

The woman ignores her. Barely even looks at her. "Where's Teagan?"

"She couldn't come," Nic says.

"She's here somewhere, isn't she? I do hope *she* understands what will happen if the pressure on my trigger finger changes. It would be a shame if she sprung a trap, only to kill her colleague." She raises her voice. "Come on out, Teagan."

"She's not here," Annie says, through gritted teeth. "She . . . " But it's as if she can't get the words out. She snaps her mouth shut, hands balled into fists.

She's not lying. Reggie can tell. Teagan really isn't here. Reggie feels a mix of hurt and pride – hurt that Teagan didn't come anyway, and pride and relief that she was smart enough to stay away.

"There's a homeless camp," Nic says. "Upriver from where you left the . . . " He clears his throat. "The chair. Regina's chair. There's a flood coming, in the storm drain, and Teagan's helping get people out."

This time, the woman does laugh. "Is that right, Teagan?" she says loudly, as if hoping her voice will carry to wherever the girl is hiding. "Wherever you are, it's best if you stay there. I see anything moving in a way it shouldn't, and . . . " She raises the bomb trigger, holding it high.

The steak knife. Reggie still has it, tucked into her pocket – her special knife, with the rings on the handle to slip her fingers into. If she could just . . .

Just what? She doesn't dare stab the woman, doesn't dare

do anything that would make that trigger finger squeeze. Especially not now, with the others so close.

"Come on, Leo," the woman says.

Leo doesn't move. He's not looking at the woman. Instead, he's looking at the figure he called the Zigzag Man. As Reggie watches, the boy starts to shake his head back and forth, slowly at first, then faster and faster. "I don't wanna."

"Yes you do," the woman tells him. Reggie has never wanted to hit someone so badly. From the look on Annie's face, she isn't the only one.

Leo bows his head, wiping at his eyes. "I'm sorry, but I don't wanna," he says, the words coming out in a rush. "I know I said I'd go but I don't wanna be with the Zigzag Man, please don't make me go!"

He reaches for Nic, who scoops him up in a hug. Reggie has never seen a man look so wretched.

The woman mutters something, which sounds to Reggie like the word *Pathetic*. "Leo," she says. "Come here. Now."

"He's scared," Annie spits at her. "Can't you see that?"

For a second, a different expression flickers across the woman's face. One that might be something approaching concern. But it's gone almost as soon it appears, replaced by steel-hard resolve. "Last chance," the woman says, raising the bomb trigger.

Slowly, ever so slowly, Nic puts Leo down.

The boy doesn't want to let go. He keeps stealing glances at the Zigzag Man, and Reggie can't help but do the same. The man is lost in his own world.

Nic and Annie both talk quietly to Leo. Both of them crouch down, holding his hands. They too seem to be in their own world . . . and all Reggie can do is silently watch, fuming, hating how helpless she is. Hating that she's a bargaining chip.

She expects the woman to get more and more impatient, but surprisingly, she stays silent. Why wouldn't she? She's won. *She's won.*

And eventually, Leo turns around. He still crying, but his mouth is set in a thin line now. He's not looking at the Zigzag Man, just at the woman with the bomb trigger. Nic watches as Leo starts to walk, shaking his head. Neither he nor Annie move.

The woman must have a vehicle nearby – how else would she have gotten Reggie to the park? By the time Annie and Nic get Reggie off the explosives and give chase, both she and Leo will be long gone.

And then . . .

More dead. Maybe thousands more. Hundreds of thousands. Leo forced to use his ability to help carve out a new world.

Reggie's hand is in her pocket now, fingers slotting into the holes of the specially designed handle on the steak knife. Except: what good will it do? Even *if* she gets the knife out in time, and even *if* she stabs the woman, what on earth would it accomplish?

The woman might squeeze the bomb trigger, or drop it entirely. If it were just the two of them, Reggie might consider doing it – pretty hard to carve out a new world if you're vaporised. But it's not just them. It's Leo, who is way too close to the bomb.

And Reggie cannot murder a child.

They planned to do so before, when Matthew Schenke was on course to set off the Cascadia fault line and kill millions. Taking him out seemed like their only option. But Matthew was a sociopath, and he knew exactly what he was doing. Leo doesn't deserve this, any of it, and Reggie isn't prepared to take his life.

"That's it," the woman murmurs. "Come on."

"Leo." The desperation and despair in Annie's voice cuts Reggie's heart in two. "We'll find you, OK? We're not gonna stop looking, no matter what. We'll get you out, just . . . just stay strong, you hear me?"

Leo looks as if he wants to say something, but he just nods. Never stopping his slow, steady walk.

"We'll find your dad," Nic is saying. "We'll tell him you're OK."

Reggie happens to be looking at the woman right then, and the oddest thing happens. The woman's expression changes. It goes from cold control to absolute shock, just for a microsecond. Then it's as if the woman gets a hold of herself, slams the mask back down again.

"We know the way to your uncle's house." Reggie gets the sense that Nic is not even talking to Leo now, that he's just talking to keep himself sane. "We're gonna head straight there after this, find your dad, figure this all out."

"Don't listen to them, Leo," the woman says. "Your dad's with me. We've already found him. He's waiting for you."

Leo comes to a halt. Looks up at her.

"He's with you?" he says.

The woman nods. "He's in a safe place. He wants me to bring you to him."

It's the wrong thing to say. Reggie understands that instantly. Leo tilts his head, biting his lower lip.

"He hates you," he says.

A half-smile crosses the woman's face. "Maybe he does. But I don't hate him, and I certainly don't hate you. Now come on."

"Where's my dad?" Leo says quietly. "Really?"

All at once, Reggie doesn't want to know. Doesn't want to hear it.

"Like I said." The woman sounds irritated now. "He's nearby. Somewhere safe."

"*No*." Leo actually stamps his foot. "He wouldn't go with you. He wouldn't."

There's a sudden rumble from the dark clouds above them – a rumble that goes on far too long. Lightning flashes in the clouds, leaving glowing afterimages.

"Leo." Nic starts moving towards him, his eyes huge, ignoring the anger on the woman's face. "Buddy, listen to me, you have to control it. Don't do this."

Reggie sucks in a horrified breath. *The lightning strikes at Dodger Stadium.*

"Get back," the woman spits at Nic, her voice nearly lost in another boom of thunder.

"Where is he?" Tears are rolling down Leo's cheeks. "*What did you do to my dad?*"

"Leo, take it ea—" Nic gets out.

And then the world fills with white.

It's a flash so bright that it sears itself into Reggie's mind, obliterating all thought. It's followed a split-second later by a massive, cracking *bang*, and a shockwave that rumbles up through her body.

The lightning struck twenty feet from them, not far from Nic and Annie. The woman sprints towards Leo, dives for him, just as Nic does the same thing. But right then, a second bolt hits the ground. Reggie actually gets a look at this one: a jagged spear etched in a white so bright it's almost yellow. It lands between her and Nic, and although it doesn't hit him, he staggers sideways, losing his balance. Leo is screaming, his face raised to the sky, mouth open in a terrified little boy howl.

Annie sidesteps around Nic, lunging forward. And at that moment, the lightning strikes for a third time.

It hits right next to Annie.

No more than two feet from her.

And in the frozen moment of the strike, Reggie sees the electricity leap to her body. Crackling across it in jagged, spitting arcs, moving up her legs and chest and jaw.

Annie's arms fly out. Her back arches, her head snapping up. It makes her look like a dancer, contorting herself in mid-air. The edges of her jacket are smouldering.

The bolt of lightning vanishes, and Annie crashes to the ground.

This time, it's Reggie who screams.

FIFTY

Teagan

There's a great meme that did the rounds online a few years back. It's called "The Last Great Act of Defiance".

As memes go, it's pretty simple. It's a drawing of a mouse, standing on hind legs, watching as a voracious, razor-beaked owl dives down on it, talons outstretched. The mouse is sticking an exhausted middle finger up at the owl.

You can probably see where I'm going with this.

Problem is, as the flash flood grows on the horizon, filling the storm drain from end to end, I don't have any strength left to raise a middle finger. I just stand there, shoulders sagging, watching the end creep closer.

My brain, however, is a goddamn hornet's nest. *I've got to everybody out. Now. Right fucking now.*

But what if the flood gets here before I can? And it will, because that thing is moving at ten feet per second, and I have four or five minutes before it hits. If that.

OK. Just think. What if I . . . fuck, I don't know, got everybody still here onto a big platform and levitated them out of here? It might work – but it might just as easily go horribly wrong. People might fall off. They might freak out – and I do not have time right now to explain who I am and what I can do. They might simply refuse to get on the platform, which means we'll still be arguing when the wave hits us. That's *if* I have the PK energy to lift that much weight.

And – *oh, shit* – that's not even the biggest problem. There are still some people downriver, looking for an exit. The China Shop van is probably still in the storm drain, Africa hunting for an exit. Ditto for the Legends. When the flood hits the homeless camp, it's going to sweep everything away. All that scaffolding, everything not nailed down. The wave will obliterate it all.

The distant radio-static hiss has gotten much louder, even in the thirty seconds or so since I spotted it. It's deeper, more thunderous, and that little line of water on the horizon has grown. It's bigger now, big enough that it isn't just a little line of water. It doesn't look that high – six feet, maybe eight – but it's *violent*, a massive, boiling mess of dirty white foam.

It's not just water. There's debris, too. I can't make the details out from here, but I have a good idea of what's in there. Concrete and rubble. Wrecked cars. Trash. Bamboo stalks.

The LA River is taking revenge on us for hiding it. For lining it with concrete and pretending it didn't exist. For building on it and pissing in it and trying to prove that we were better. It's an absurd thought, pointless and stupid. But as I watch the torrent approach, as the sheer rage of it becomes clear, it's a thought I can't get rid of.

And it's raining hard now. Bucketing down from black clouds. The storm letting loose, all at once, frigid wind whipping the drops left and right. As if the sky has decided that it wants to help the river wipe us from existence.

I'm too late.

No. Fuck that. It's not too late. There are a hundred things I could do here to get everyone to safety. It's just that . . .

It's just that all of them have massive problems. And if I get it wrong . . .

I turn to look at the camp around me, refusing to believe I'm out of options. There are *still* people at the bottom of the slope, near the exit I made – I have to get these assholes moving. But what am I going to do about the people who, unbelievably, are still in the camp?

The dude over there, fussing with his bag, desperately trying to pack his possessions because apparently saving your prize collection of bowling trophies or whatever is super-important when a tsunami is coming. He'll be easy. But even as I think this, a woman stumbles past, high off her mother-fucking tits, screaming for somebody called Derek. I've hadn't seen her before now. It's like she's been waiting this whole time to show herself.

And – holy shit, is that guy *drawing*? Yep. This happy asshole is kneeling on the ground and muttering to himself and drawing something with a piece of chalk. He's facing the flood, and either doesn't know it's there, or doesn't give a shit.

I'm not going to be able to get them all out. Not in the three or four minutes I have left. Not even with the assistance of Africa, or the Legends. And even if I did, even if I somehow managed to clear this place in time, it wouldn't help the poor fuckers downriver.

My hand strays to my jacket pocket, and my eyes go wide.

And immediately squeeze shut. No fucking way. I promised myself I wouldn't. And in any case, we are not talking about a few random organic objects here. We are talking about a mass of raging water. I don't even know for sure if I'll be able to affect it.

I have to try.

I squeeze my eyes shut, the consequences of what I'm about to do bouncing around my mind like ricocheting bullets.

There has to be another option. There *has* to.

There isn't.

I turn, and step into the storm.

Face the flood.

It's much closer now. Huge chunks of concrete tumble end over end, carried by the sheer force of the water. The cars in the torrent spin, almost lazily. The bamboo stalks bounce and crash, moving in and out of the sick-looking foam.

Here we go.

It's a thought that's supposed to give me confidence, and it doesn't work.

I wipe rain out of my eyes, blinking hard. Then I reach into my pocket, and pull out the meth.

Such a small thing. A little plastic pouch, filled with crystalline white powder.

I shouldn't have this. I told myself I took it so I could *experiment* — so I could figure out if there was a way I could use it safely.

What a crock of shit. That little story I told myself was just that: a story. I got high on meth, and I wanted more, and I had a chance and I took it. That's all.

Maybe — just maybe — I could have gotten past the addiction. Not going to happen now. I can't microdose here, not with the flood bearing down on me. The only way I'm going to stop it, the only way I save the people still in the homeless camp, is by getting a good-size hit into my system.

As I look down at the baggie, the want swells up inside me. The *need*. The awful feeling that I'm holding the only key to true happiness in my hands.

I'm not an idiot. I know what happens to meth addicts. I know how bad it can get. And those thoughts make me recoil, because there is no way – no way in hell, not ever – that I'm letting myself become one of those people. I'll cold turkey this motherfucker, check into rehab, do whatever I have to—

Except: if I don't take this meth, right now, people are going to die.

Not me. I can fly the fuck out of here. Grab my little pallet with its handy metal bracers, and magic carpet my ass up onto the freeway. Watch the flood sweep by underneath me. Then go and find the woman who took Reggie, and beat the shit out of her.

And then never be able to look at myself in the mirror again.

I laugh. It's a desperate, pathetic sound. My whole big speech to Nic about making adult decisions, doing the right thing, and it turns out that doing the right thing in this case involves taking a shit-ton of hard drugs.

There's gotta be another way. Something you haven't thought of.

There isn't.

And I am out of time.

The baggie is your basic Ziploc. I pop the seal, letting out a tiny puff of white powder. I'll have to snort it, properly this time. How long will it take to kick in? If the flood gets here before it does . . .

I cup my palm, and tip some powder into it. It looks like heaped, white sea salt.

Having this shit, this salt-looking drug, in the palm of my hand is like a mirror image of the life I wanted. As if somewhere, an alternate-universe me is in a kitchen somewhere, holding a small pile of sea salt. That version of me turned her back on China Shop, decided to be happy and live her life on her own terms. She *made* it work.

I wish I was her. Instead of the Teagan who acted like an adult, and is now facing down a raging flood using a bag of meth as a weapon.

I stick my face in the pile of meth, and take a quick, hard *sniff*.

It's like somebody letting off a firecracker in the middle of my head. A piercing, burning, jagged pain explodes across my face. I jerk back, yelping, blinking back acid tears. The rest of the meth in my palm scatters into the air, and I almost drop the whole bag.

I make a sound that is halfway between *ugh* and *argh*. Hell, my entire face feels halfway between *ugh* and *argh*. I shake my head, snorting, like a horse shooing away a fly. God fucking dammit. Wow, I am *not* doing that again.

I take a deep breath, hoping that maybe I've been sucked into that parallel universe where I'm a famous chef and not trying to stop a flash flood in a storm drain. No such luck. The water is closer now, a boiling mess of froth and debris.

I'm still terrified, still exhausted . . . but the burning in my sinuses acts a little like a slap in the face to a drunk, clearing things up for a minute. I stuff the rest of the drugs back in my jacket, hating myself for doing it, but knowing I might need them.

I send out my PK in a wide arc, looking for any phones pointed in my direction. I can't find any, and the phones that I do find get a quick *crunch* on the internals. When the meth kicks in, I'll have to do a wider sweep, just like I did when I fought off the Legends. I'm under the cover of the freeway, out of sight, so I shouldn't have to worry about being spotted — although there are probably a few people still in the camp who are going to get one hell of a shock.

I have to be ready. I flex my fingers, focusing on my PK. I *think* it's stronger, but if so, it's not by much.

"Come on," I whisper. "Hit me."

It doesn't. The flood keeps coming, and my PK stays very much as it always has been. The front edge of the flood is a rolling nightmare, and the concrete underneath my feet is starting to vibrate.

"Any minute now . . . "

Shit, what if I didn't take enough? I'll have to do another dose, and even then it might not kick in before the flood gets here.

I would give anything right now to reverse time. Fuck my conscience, fuck anybody stupid enough to still be in the storm drain with the flood coming down on them. If I could turn back the clock, I'd throw that fucking bag of meth as far as I could and get the hell out of here. I wouldn't let this poison anywhere near me. But I did, and it's inside me now, and I put it there. This is one little doodle that can't be undid.

I need another hit. I paw at my jacket pocket, hating that I have to do this, knowing that there's no choice. I'll have to hope that there's time for—

Oh.

Oh, *shiiiiiiiiiiii*

FIFTY-ONE

Teagan

I exhale.

It takes a thousand years.

My PK range doubles. Triples. Quadruples. Goes further than it's ever been. I'm at the centre of a sphere of burning, clean, white light. A light that burns away fear, my doubt, everything. A light that leaves nothing behind but stillness.

The air tastes of damp wood, burning trash, the sour tang of urine. Bad smells all – but strangely, they don't bother me. I note them, acknowledge them, let them be.

I can move anything with my PK. Anything. Organic, inorganic, it doesn't matter. Right now, in this moment, I'm stronger than I've ever been.

I take a few hundred years to appreciate the sensation. Letting it wash over me. There's no pain any more. No hollow stomach. How could I have wanted to take this back? I can't even remember what I was scared of. It's miraculous.

Slowly, oh so slowly, I turn my eyes to the flood.

Three hundred feet away now. Maybe thirty seconds from impact. Carrying so much debris that the water itself is boiling up the sides of the channel, tendrils of raging white froth reaching out for me.

I smile. It's lazy, easy-going, like I'm strolling through the park and have come across a piece of litter on the ground, one that I can pick up and dispose of without a second thought.

Park. Wasn't Reggie in a park? Wasn't that where Annie and Nic went? Wasn't Reggie in some kind of trouble?

It doesn't matter. When I'm done here, I can go save her.

I roll my shoulders, take another gentle breath. Stare at the giant torrent coming to sweep me away. It's two hundred feet away, closing fast.

A sound reaches my ears from behind me. That's what it feels like – a noise that swims through the air, languid and easy, alighting on my ears with the softest touch. Engines. More specifically: motorcycle engines.

I look over my shoulder, and smile.

The Legends are here.

There are four of them, winding their bikes through the maze of scaffolding. There's Robert, on one of the biggest bikes I've ever seen, a monster Harley Davidson with handle-bars you could do pull-ups on. He's with two goons I don't know . . . and Pop.

She's not riding a bike. She's riding a gigantic, four-wheeled ATV that looks like a runty monster truck, painted bright green. She is staring in absolute horror at the approaching flood, her mouth open.

A second later, she locks eyes with me.

I have a sudden urge to yell that I'm high on meth – and not just any meth. *Her* meth. Instead, I give her a little wave. I'm glad she's here. I don't need her, because I'm going to stop the flash flood all by myself, but she might come in handy later on.

I don't think she's going to shoot me – not now, not when she actually sees what's happening here. And if she does, so what? I'll stop the bullet in mid-air.

I turn away, and Pop and the Legends fall from my thoughts.

Wait. What if there are people on the other side of the flood barriers? That's where the water is going to go, after all. But a quick check with my PK shows nobody in range. There's a section of freeway on the west side of the storm drain, which is wrecked enough that there no cars at all driving on it – none that I can sense. To the east is a section of vacant lots, plus a few destroyed homes. Nobody around. No one to get hurt.

It's perfect.

I'm humming now. The opening bars of "The Next Episode". Dre and Snoop, backing me up. And as I hum, I bring my PK inwards. Marshal the invisible energy in front of me. My ability – the weird, fucked-up thing that makes me different from everybody else, that I'm still nowhere close to understanding.

A hundred feet away. Ninety. It's possible that I could stop the water now, even at this distance – the meth hit has made me that powerful. But I want strength, not range. I want to grab the entire flood – water, debris, all of it – and send it up and outwards. I want to look it right in the face before I send it on its way.

Fifty feet. Forty. Driving rain soaks my clothes, drenches the skin on my face. Thunder cracks the clouds above. I smile through it all.

A tiny grain of doubt. My PK may not work on water. I've never tried it before. But the water is thirty feet away now, and there is no time left to doubt myself.

I grab my PK, wrap it around the flood. Every tree branch,

every bamboo stalk, every car, every piece of rubble, trash, concrete, wood, dirt.

And water. Every individual molecule of water, each atom of hydrogen and oxygen. A billion of them. No, a trillion. Uncountable. I wrap my PK around all of them—

And *push*.

FIFTY-TWO

Teagan

It's like a wave breaking against a sea wall.

The flood *explodes* upwards, a torrent of water bursting into the air, tossing concrete rubble and destroyed cars into the sky like they're made of packing foam. The water balloons upwards and outwards, cascading over the flood barriers. The noise is incredible: Krakatoa getting hit with a meteorite.

And I am not ready.

Even with the meth boosting my PK, I am just not prepared to grab a million tons of rushing water carrying half a million tons of debris, and stopping it in its tracks.

It's like getting punched in the stomach by God. I grunt, ferocious tears squeezing out from my closed eyes. I actually slide backwards, my shoes scraping across the concrete, nearly toppling over. The water isn't like other objects. It doesn't have boundaries, or a shape. It's everywhere, and keeping hold of it . . . I have to force each individual molecule to listen to me.

And of course, it's not just the water. It's everything *in* the water. A thousand objects, some big enough to give my PK trouble on a good day.

I lean in, like I'm walking into a strong wind. I've never

concentrated this hard in my entire life. The focus is total. I channel everything I have towards the raging torrent. I'm not even sure I'm breathing. The world's worst headache is back, growing at the base of my skull.

The rain actually *bends* around me. The drops flying away. I didn't even realise I was controlling them.

The water and the debris crash down on the flood barriers. They crumple, collapsing under the onslaught. A chunk of concrete the size of a small car rips one of them in half. The sound of the flood buries the noise of tortured metal.

And I can't get the water out of the storm drain fast enough. It just keeps coming, piling up. It gets higher and higher in front of me. Twenty feet. Twenty five. I grit my teeth and roll my shoulders and *make* it do what I want, putting everything I have into it.

You shall not pass, I think, the thought wild and uncontrolled.

Except: it's too much. The sheer force of the flood is too much to contain. My PK was a wall before, grabbing the water at a specific point and not letting it past. But the water and debris at the edges are starting to find their way through, the flood creeping in on either side of me, rolling down the sloped side of the storm drain. Before I can blink, it soaks my ankles, climbing towards my knees.

"Not today, *fucker*."

I dig deep, pulling in even more PK energy, refusing to acknowledge the screaming, horrifying headache rolling up from the back of my skull. I plug the gaps, forcing the water back. Holy shit, how big is this damn flood?

A car nearly crushes me. It must have gotten high enough to escape my PK. It comes rolling over the top: a mangled wreck that used to be a Prius. I yelp as it crunches into the concrete, jumping backwards, and for a half a second, I lose focus on my PK.

The flood explodes towards me. I snap my PK back on it, once again refusing to let it pass. It's now ten feet from me, barely under control. Cold, dirty, spitting water hits my face, my eyes.

I don't know if the camp behind me has cleared. I don't dare look. I don't know if anybody can see what I'm doing, or if anyone is filming on a cellphone I missed. There's nothing I can do about it now. I don't even know if my exit plan – grab the metal-and-wood pallet, and get the hell out – is going to work any more, or if I'll have time to do it. All I can do is push the flood back.

And it keeps coming. Every time I think I've got a handle on the water, a fresh surge pushes me backwards. It can't have been more than thirty seconds since the flood met my PK, but it feels like thirty years.

Even with the meth, I'm running out of gas. My arms are made of lead, the headache turning my vision grey. There's a curious metallic taste on my lips.

Blood. That last one is blood. My nose . . . it's gushing, and I don't know if it's from the meth I snorted, or the raw energy flowing through me.

As the flood inches closer, as more water slips through the cracks, I start to scream.

Not in pain, or terror. It's a scream of rage: a furious, determined howl that comes from the very deepest part of me.

It builds and builds and builds, and with it comes another surge of PK, an explosion of it, the most energy I've sent out at once, ever. It hits the wall of water like an invisible fist, punching a hole in the flood, pushing it back.

But every action has an equal and opposite reaction. And this time, the opposite reaction is like nothing I've ever seen.

The concrete around me *cracks*, the fissures spiderwebbing

out in a dozen directions. The cracks form a loose circle around me, leaving me standing on a small, whole section. And that section . . .

With a crunching, grinding sound, that section tears loose of the concrete around it. Lifting itself, and me, into the air.

I don't even know how it's happening. I could swear I'm not controlling it with my PK – it's just *flying*, all by itself, like it's defying gravity as a side effect. I waver, struggling to keep my balance, as I rise before the flood.

Dark lights flicker at the edge of my vision. I'm going to black out. I'm still screaming, and as my throat contracts in agony, the concrete slab I'm on tilts towards the flood, like I'm on a seesaw, the front dropping while the rear rises upwards. I have to bend my knees to stay upright. The surge of PK energy starts to fade.

Get out of here. Get above the water!

But I can't. At any second, I'm going to lose my hold completely, and then I won't even have solid ground to stand on.

Holy fuck: my blood. Droplets of it float into view, hovering in the air in front of me.

I go to one knee on the concrete, driven there by the raw power. In desperation, I throw a hand out, like I can direct my energy, channel it. But it's never worked in the past, and it sure as hell doesn't work now. There's a cascade of water bucketing down from above, more and more of it flooding the camp, and I am going to lose. I am going to be swept away.

I claw at my pocket for the meth, but it won't work. By the time the extra dose kicks in, it'll all be over. No matter what happens, I'm not going to have enough energy to make it out of here. I'm trapped.

The concrete beneath me starts to drop. Somehow, I am still screaming, but it's no longer a human voice. It's something raw and jagged, an animal sound, and I've got almost nothing left. There's no extra surge of PK coming this time. I am about to drain the tank for good.

The flood rears over me like a striking tiger, held in place by the very last dregs of my PK. I close my eyes, and rise up off my knee, onto my feet.

In the last instant available to me, I'm expecting to see my friends. Annie. Nic. Africa. Reggie. They are what I want to hold onto. Instead, it's my sister I see: riding ahead of me, through the woods, looking over her shoulder and laughing.

And I find, at the very end, that I want to hold onto that, too.

FIFTY-THREE

Reggie

As the lightning rains down, as the world fills with noise and thunder and searing light and drenching rain, Reggie does the only thing she can think of.

She reaches out, stretching as far as her body will allow. She forces herself to keep her eyes open as she wraps an arm around Leo, and pulls him in close.

He almost gets away from her. He's squirming in shock and terror, little legs lashing out. But somehow, Reggie keeps hold of him. She grips him as tight as she can, his back against her side, the lower half of her face nestled in his hair.

"It's all right," she whispers. Leo's screams drown out her words. She has lost track of Annie and Nic, can't see her captor. All she can do is hold the boy close, whisper calming words to him.

"Easy, baby." She can't rock him back and forth, it's beyond her – her torso and hips just don't have the ability. His eyes have rolled back, the whites showing under fluttering lids. Reggie doesn't even know if he can hear her, but she keeps talking anyway. "I know you're scared, but you have to stop, please, baby, just ease up. It's all right. Everything's going to be all—"

A bolt of lightning strikes so close to her that Reggie is certain she's been hit. It leaves a burning trail in her vision, and it's followed by a dozen other strikes, the boy's rage climbing.

Everything in her wants to push the boy away, make herself smaller, protect herself from the onslaught. The terror of being struck is as raw as an exposed nerve ending.

"And it's nowhere as bad as her fear that her captor might be hit. Her, and her bomb trigger. The backpack under Reggie's body feels like it's made of a super-dense material, a metal from a distant star with a giant gravitational pull, sucking everything towards it.

And still, Reggie keeps talking, because there is absolutely nothing else she can do. "Shhh, baby. Shhh. I know you're scared, but you have to listen to me. We're going to finish this together, we're not done yet, we have to keep going . . ." Tears are pouring down her cheeks, but Reggie barely notices. "You and me. All you have to is breathe, and we're not done yet. It's OK."

The boy's screams have turned to sobs. His legs are still kicking out, but the kicks are different now – more like heavy muscle spasms.

The ground is smouldering in a dozen places, actual flames in others. The sky above them is nothing but black clouds. But there are longer gaps between the lightning strikes now. Slowly, ever so slowly, they start to ebb.

Reggie keeps talking. "That's it. Let it go."

Annie lies sprawled on the ground a few feet away – Reggie has to force back a soft moan of horror when she spots her. She can't be dead – it's simply not an option. Reggie won't let it happen.

Nic curls in a tight ball nearby – did he get hit too? But as Reggie watches, he gets unsteadily to his feet, flinching as a lone bolt strikes a short distance away.

"Nic," Reggie says. "Just—"

She doesn't get the rest out, because at that moment, Nic sprints past her. Heading right for the woman.

Reggie tries to yell at him *no*, the woman still has a grip on the bomb trigger. She can't get the word out – her throat has locked up, horror freezing her in place.

The woman is up on one knee. Nic's attempt to take her by surprise does not go well, because the Zigzag Man gets there first.

Reggie is expecting him to use his ability. He doesn't bother. He uses Nic's own momentum against him, grabbing the back of his shirt and hurling him forwards. Nic's feet tangle up and he goes sprawling, grunting in pain.

Reggie keeps whispering, not daring to stop, until she realises that the boy is no longer listening. He's gone completely limp.

Nic hauls himself upright, throws a wild haymaker. The Zigzag Man blocks it easily, then whips a cupped palm around and onto Nic's ear.

Reggie's seen the move before, in combat training. The pressure can pop the eardrum. Nic stumbles backwards, streaming eyes squeezed shut.

The Zigzag Man steps into his space, and lands a flat hand on Nic's nose, which breaks with a sound that reminds Reggie of crunching ice cubes. Nic goes down hard, arms wheeling.

There are no more lightning bolts. No sound but the howling wind.

The woman straightens up, takes a shaky breath, and turns towards Reggie. The look in her eyes is pure fury. Rain plasters her hair to her forehead.

"It's OK, baby." The boy is beyond listening now, but Reggie doesn't care – if she stops talking, she'll crumble.

"We're going to fix this, don't worry about it, you just stay with me."

Somehow, Nic is still conscious. He reaches out for the Zigzag Man, trying to grab his ankle. The man sidesteps, barely glancing at Nic.

"Let me have them," he says. There's a wheedling, pleading note in the Zigzag Man's voice that Reggie finds more horrifying than anything. Above his beard, his eyes are wild. Vicious. "Let me take them into my house. Let me hide them in the walls."

"Program," the woman spits. "Captain. Tournament. Disorder."

"*Please.*" It's a growl: an insane animal noise.

The woman steps between Reggie and the Zigzag Man, her voice suddenly urgent. "Photograph. Skeleton. Zigzag. Zigzag. Zigzag."

He subsides, his face slipping into a perfect blank. A slave once more.

Reggie meets the woman's eyes. "You can't have him."

In response, the woman simply bends down, hooks a hand under the boy's armpit.

And with every ounce of strength she has, every inch of mobility her arm will give her, Reggie swings her modified knife at the woman's throat.

She'd taken it out her pocket the moment she realised what Leo was about to unleash, hidden it under her body. Her fingers slotted in the rings built into the handle. The blade slashes through the air, and Reggie knows, *knows*, that it will find its target. The woman underestimated her, and Reggie's going to make her pay.

The woman snaps her left hand up faster than Reggie would have thought possible. She catches Reggie's wrist, stopping the blade an inch from her throat.

"Really?" she says, contemptuous. "You thought that was going to work?"

Reggie would give anything to snap back at her: *No. But this will.* And then attempt something else, surprise her, knock her off balance . . .

But there's nothing else. She has nothing left to try.

The woman plucks the knife from Reggie's hand, almost tenderly slipping it off her fingers. Then she hurls it away.

Reggie tries to pull her arm back over Leo, but the woman stops her. She lifts the boy out, then stands, hefting his unconscious body. Leo's legs are twitching badly now.

"We'll find you," Reggie says to the woman, knowing it's not a good idea to provoke her, and not caring. Raindrops fall into her mouth, cold and somehow slimy. She spits them out, snarling. "Do you understand that? You are about to bring the wrath of God down on you and yours."

The woman turns, and walks away. The Zigzag Man follows, like an obedient dog.

Reggie sucks in a deep breath. "You don't get it. It's like Annie said: there's nowhere you can go." She raises her voice, as loud as it will go. "It's not just her contacts who'll come after you. Every special forces squad, every investigator, every single intelligence operator employed by the US government: they are *all* going to be looking for you. There'll be nowhere left to run."

"We don't have to run," the woman says over her shoulder. "We won't even have to hide for much longer."

She lifts the bomb trigger, glances at it. Then casually, almost as an afterthought, tosses it away.

FIFTY-FOUR

Teagan

"Teggan!"

The voice reaches me from what feels like a very long way away. Another galaxy, maybe. Or from the afterlife.

"Teggan! *Under you!*"

I don't know how I do it, but I get my eyes open. Turn my head. Still not convinced what I'm hearing is real.

The flood is still being held at bay, although that's going to change in maybe five seconds. The concrete slab I'm on is now twelve or fifteen feet off the deck. And *on* the deck, wheels almost submerged in the rushing water . . .

The China Shop van.

With Africa sticking his head out the window. Yelling my name.

What in the name of fuck is he doing here? Does he not *see* the enormous flood?

Reality slaps me around the face. The stupid son of a bitch came back for me. He actually thinks he's going to drive me out of here.

I open my mouth to tell him to get the hell away, and then I see the most wondrous thing.

No people. The homeless camp is finally, finally empty.

There's no way to know for sure ... but somehow, I do. Everybody is finally safe. Africa and the Legends got the last of the people out.

As if hearing my thoughts, the pressure of the flood gets even worse, almost punching through my PK completely.

I lean back on the slab, willing it to move down towards the van. It doesn't listen to me at first – but then it starts to move. Slow, sluggish, but moving. To my right, a section of scaffolding collapses with a clatter, forced off its foundations by the rising torrent.

"Come come come!" Africa slaps the door with a massive palm. "On the roof. Get on the roof!"

I'm right at the end of my tether, so what he's saying doesn't register at first. What the fuck is he talking about, the roof? Does he not—?

Which is when the last of my PK drains away completely. And the flood, freed from its shackles, comes roaring down towards us.

I topple off the concrete slab onto the roof of the van, landing on my back, hard enough to knock what little wind is left out of me.

Africa punches the gas. There's a horrible second where the wheels do nothing but spin in the water. Then the tires catch, and the van leaps forward.

The water hits the concrete, right behind us. The impact is so powerful that it actually jolts the van, bouncing me up off the roof. I shriek, coming back down with a thump, numb hands scrambling for purchase on the slick metal, as the roaring waters explode upwards again. There's the insane clanging of a hundred scaffolding poles giving way at once, wrenched away by the force of the water. The concrete slab I was on vanishes under the raging torrent.

We pop out from under the freeway, wheels sending up

great gouts of spray, being chased by an enormous, frothing wall of water and debris. Africa swerves to avoid – well, actually, I don't know what the fuck he swerves to avoid, but it sends me sliding sideways. I throw my hands out, grabbing the edge of the roof closest to my head, fingers scrabbling at it.

There's a metallic *whang* as a piece of scaffolding bounces off the van, hitting right where I was a second ago. *Christ, that was close.*

We're not moving fast enough. Not even close. The flood has ripped through the homeless camp and is right on our heels. If it hits us, it'll lift the van right off the concrete, send it tumbling.

And there's not a damn thing I can do except hang on, and hope.

He can't keep this up for ever. We have to get out of the storm drain. Only, how the hell are we going to do that, when there are flood barriers for ever? Come to think of it, where are the people Africa drove out of the camp? Surely he didn't drop them off in the middle of the—

There's a gap. One of the flood barriers on the left is down – a different barrier to the one I knocked over. I have no idea how they did it, but someone managed to rip the brackets out of the ground and send it sliding down into the storm drain.

I let out a scream of triumph as Africa swerves towards the gap. If we can just keep our speed up . . .

A second later, we hit the slope, and that's when everything goes *really* wrong.

The slope is at an angle. Obviously. That means the wet, slippery roof of the van is suddenly no longer flat.

If I'd been in a better state of mind, I might have foreseen this. But I'm so out of gas, and so desperate to get the fuck out of the LA River and never, ever come back, that I just don't think about it until it's actually happening.

This time, my palms can't get enough friction. I have enough time to let out a single strangled, panicked yell, and then I'm off the roof.

Time goes very, very slow, and everything in front of me gets crystal clear. The van. Africa's panicked, desperate face in the side mirror. The slick concrete of the storm drain. The drops of water in the air.

My shadow on the ground, growing bigger by the nanosecond.

I throw out my PK in one last, desperate burst, trying to find *anything* that will help—

I snag the van's side door. Without even realising what I'm doing, I rip it open, nearly tearing it off its slide mechanism. At the very last instant, with my arms stretched as far as they will go, I grab the handle.

If this were a movie, I'd just hang there, disaster miraculously averted. I do not hang. I bounce.

The van takes my weight so suddenly that it almost pulls my arms out of their sockets. My feet smack the concrete, skidding wildly, the laws of physics doing their best to rip me off and flay every inch of skin from my body. Oh, and you know how it feels when you catch your fingers in a door? Imagine that, only the door wants to kill you. My howl of pain turns into words: "*Fuck fuck fuck fuck*—"

There's the *blat* of another engine, so close it nearly splits my head in two. Then the most miraculous thing happens. Someone grabs hold of me. A huge, meaty arm covered in tattoos wraps itself around my midsection, and pulls me close.

I don't know what the hell is happening, or who's got hold of me. All I can do is let go of the door handle and hold on. As my feet judder against the wet concrete, as freezing water peppers my face and the flood makes one last, desperate lunge for us: I hold on.

We crest the edge of the storm drain. The van goes

airborne, all four wheels leaving the ground as it roars into the open air. Whoever has me, and whatever goddamn vehicle they're driving, does the same. For a split-second, I'm weight-less. Completely free.

Then we come down with the biggest bang I've ever felt.

Whoever is holding me is strong, but the impact is enough to wrench me from their grip. There's a tangled, panicked second where I'm still weightless, and then I hit the ground. Hard.

I roll, tumbling sideways, the sky and the van and the dirt spin-ning around me. I don't get knocked unconscious. Exactly the opposite. There's so much adrenaline and methamphetamine and terror burning in my body that I come out of the roll and stumble to my feet, hyperventilating, spinning in wild, jerky circles.

The skin on my hands has been ripped away, the raw flesh stinging. My left knee is sending up *very* urgent signals of pain, and every breath feels like it's going to burn through the walls of my lungs.

It's not just my knee, or my lungs. My whole body is a distant forest fire of pain, glimmering on the horizon but growing closer by the second. I don't know if it's the meth keeping me upright, or the adrenaline, or both. The world goes wavy for a long moment, tilting so badly that I almost fall over anyway.

I'm in a vacant plot of land bordered by the storm drain on one side, and warehouses on the other. It's so similar to the place I first entered the storm drain with Leo that for a second, my poor, addled brain makes me think I'm actually back there.

The difference is that this time, there are people here. A *lot* of people. A hundred, maybe more. Dirty faces with soaked skin. And all of them staring at me. They're not silent – there's a hum of voices, rolling like waves across the crowd. Almost drowned out by the flood waters rushing past below us.

Almost, but not quite.

There's a squeal of brakes, followed by a grinding blast of tyres on dirt. The China Shop van comes to a rocking, shuddering halt, Africa stumbling out, head snapping side to side, looking for me.

And just beyond him, screeching to a halt: a motorcycle. A big, red Harley-Davidson, and on top of it . . . Robert. He was the one who grabbed me when I came off the van.

He saved me.

Just beyond him are the other bikers. Pop is there too, soaking wet, her hair a mess, clambering off her gigantic ATV.

Someone in the crowd cheers.

It's an exhausted, almost desperate sound. But it kickstarts something, and then the whole crowd is going nuts. Cheering, clapping, punching the air. Men and women, kids, dogs barking. The crowd surges forward, and for a moment, I have this absurd idea that they're going to pick me up and drop me back in the river.

They don't. They surround me, Africa, the bikers. They clap us on our backs, shoulders, grab our hands and pump furiously. Every touch sends bolts of furious pain through my insulted body. Through the chaos, I spot Alvin, of all people, hooting and hollering even louder than everyone else.

I just stare, my mouth hanging open. I don't know what I expected, but it wasn't this.

They know what you can do. They saw.

I don't know what that means yet, but the crowd gives me a little bit of a preview. Because not everyone is cheering. Most people are . . . but there are others who are just gaping at me. The emotions on their faces are not just relief, happiness, excitement. There's awe there. Fear. Disbelief.

And yet somehow, in this moment, in this hurricane of

handshakes and back pats that make my body jangle with pain, it doesn't matter.

"Thank you," I murmur, as my hammering heart starts to slow, just a little. "Thanks. I . . . thank you."

I'm still not completely sure I'm not dead. It feels like I've stepped into another universe. One of those places where everything is almost, but not quite, exactly the same.

In that instant, I lock eyes with Pop.

She is in the middle of a crush of people, but somehow, I have a clear line of sight right to her. And despite the fact that she just about everyone is congratulating her, she ignores them. In that moment, I am the only one she's paying attention to.

You know the phrase *balanced on a knife edge*? I've never liked it. I know knives, and let me tell you, most of the ones in your kitchen right now are so blunt you could do a handstand on the edge and not draw blood. But I do think there are moments when everything hangs in the balance. When a situation could turn out fine, or go completely to shit, and the difference between the two scenarios is barely the thickness of an atom.

And as Pop looks at me, I can't help but think of all the times we've clashed today. The meth I've stolen, the people who died, the gunfights and car chases.

But I also think of what we just did. The dozens – no, *hundreds* – of people we saved. She may have gotten there at the very last minute . . .

But she still came.

Pop looks at me. I look back. And for a few seconds, it's just her, and me.

Then she shakes her head. Once to the left, once to the right, back to the centre. The very tiniest smile blinks onto her face, just for a moment.

And then, incredibly, she flips me a lazy salute.

In a daze, I return it.

Then she climbs back on her ATV, gesturing at Robert and the others to follow, and guns the engine. The crowd scrambles to get out of her way, and in seconds, the Legends are gone.

Africa is standing head, shoulders and chest above the crowd. He has the strangest expression on his face. A queer mixture of horror, pride and disbelief. He shakes his head, his eyes never leaving mine.

I fight my way over to him. He's only about twenty feet away, but it seems to take for ever to get there. Everybody wants a hug, a fist bump, to give me a shoulder squeeze or a pat on the back. Someone starts chanting – the chorus of DJ Khaled's "All I Do Is Win", if you can believe that – and in seconds, half the crowd is singing along, wildly off-key, drunk on it.

I get within a few feet of Africa, and he reaches out for me, pulling me into a crushing hug.

It hurts. A lot. Every muscle aches, from my toes to my eyelids. All the same, it's so, so tempting to just stay there, in the deep, warm circle of his arms, but I can't. *We haven't won yet*, I think. Because no matter how many faces there are in the crowd, no matter how happy they all are, I don't see the faces I really want.

"Reggie," I say. Thinking: *Nic too. And Annie. And Leo.*

"Huh?"

I pull away so my words aren't muffled by his chest. "Reggie. We gotta go."

He nods. "Ya, we go find her. Together."

There's no mistaking the question mark at the end of that word, hanging just out of sight.

I reach out, grip his arm.

"Always."

FIFTY-FIVE

Teagan

There's a lot Africa and I have to say to each other.

We need to talk about Leo. About everything that's happened over the past few hours. We need to talk about whether or not we can actually work together any more: the ground beneath us was always a little shaky, from the moment he joined China Shop, and now it feels like it's split into a huge chasm. One I have no idea how to cross.

Oh, and we also need to talk about how, exactly, we are going to deal with the goddamn fucking asshole known as the Zigzag Man. Personally, I'm in favour of holding him down and hitting him in the face until he stops moving, but I'm open to suggestions.

The problem is, I am finished. Done-zo Washington. I have passed somewhere beyond the point of total exhaustion. I pushed my body and my ability to the absolute limit, and as much as I want to have all of these conversations, I am completely unable to talk. The moment Africa drives the van away from the noise and chaos of the crowd, I pass out. There's no slow slip into unconsciousness, either. One second, I'm awake. The next, it's goodnight, Teagan.

At one point, I become aware of Africa trying to talk to me, his voice growing more and more frustrated when I fail to respond. It's like a half-remembered dream. One filled with noise, bright bursts of distant lightning. Like I'm lost in the depths of a thundercloud.

Faces keep drifting in and out. Sometimes they look at me, but most of the time, they just pass me by. Nic and Leo. Africa. Reggie. Carlos, grinning at me, his face blistered and blackened. Jonas, with that enigmatic smile.

And Annie.

Africa is the last one. It takes me a minute to realise that unlike the others, he's real. And then it takes me even longer to realise that he's talking to me.

"Wake up. We are here."

Even then, it's not enough to pull me out of the darkness. It's only when I hear the next sound he makes – a horrified intake of breath – that I finally force myself awake.

The van comes to a shuddering halt, Africa clambering out the door. We're in a muddy field, lit by the van's headlights. There are people visible in the light. And not all of them are on their feet.

I make a noise that is unlike anything I've ever heard. A sick, desperate, animal gasp. I don't care how done-zo I might be – I dig deep, find enough strength to clamber out the van myself. It's a lot harder than it should be. My knee is in agony, jeans taught over swollen flesh. Dried blood crusts my face. It's still pounding with rain, although I barely notice any more.

I don't know where to look. Nic, Annie and Reggie, all down; no Leo, no Zigzag Man. *Please, no. Please.*

Reggie is closest. She's propped up on a backpack, and as I skid to my knees next to her, she says, "She took him."

"I—"

"Annie. Help Annie."

"Is everyone OK?" Africa shouts. My breaths are coming quick and fast, as if I can't quite get enough air into my lungs. The rain is falling thick and fast now, and it makes the air feel too thick, almost soupy. Nic is slowly sitting up, blinking hard, bald head shining in the wet. There's something wrong with his face. It's covered in blood, and his nose—

"Teagan." Reggie lifts her arm, gesturing. "Get Annie. Go."

That's when I see her.

Really see her.

The awkward way she is lying, with her legs cocked out, as if broken. The strange angle of her head.

She's not moving.

I don't even register the run to her body (*it's not a body, she's alive, she has to be*). I'm simply *there*, as if I teleported away from Reggie. I can't breathe. It's not just her body position, bent and awkward and wrong. Her shoes are gone. Parts of her clothes are smoking.

Behind me, Nic is saying, "The backpack bomb – it was fake. They—"

Reggie: "Doesn't matter. We need to get out of here."

Africa, thundering: "What is happening? Who did this?"

I barely register any of it. I kneel beside Annie, my hands hovering. We need a doctor. We need—

Africa moves me aside. Almost gently. Then he reaches down, and lifts Annie off the ground. In his arms, she looks as fragile as a baby bird.

I can move things with my mind. I can lift cars, shred concrete, throw people through the air. I can stop an entire flash flood in its tracks.

And I have never felt as powerless as I do right now.

FIFTY-SIX

Reggie

There is video.

It's not very clear, the footage jerky and amateur. It doesn't show Teagan's face – whoever took it was standing some way behind her, at the bottom of the storm drain slope on the south side of the homeless camp.

Teagan told Reggie she'd taken care of the phones, but she must have missed one. The video captures her standing alone, facing down the flood.

And it captures the moment when she stops it.

Unseen spectators yell in disbelief as it happens, their voices failing to be drowned out by the roaring of the flood. The camera tilts sideways, drops, as if the person filming can't keep it steady. Then it refocuses, zooming in on the wall of water. Reggie watches it in silence. On the other screen, Moira Tanner stares at her. Her face expressionless.

It's now almost 2 a.m. The video is already spreading. Hundreds of thousands of views already, increasing by the second. It's on every platform. The first news stories have begun to appear. The memes. The hot takes.

Reggie isn't sure if Teagan knows yet. She suspects not. The poor girl could barely stay awake.

Annie is still alive. Just. *Small mercies*, Reggie thinks.

After Teagan and Africa found them, they loaded Annie into the back of the van, and drove like hell for Cedars-Sinai Hospital. Reggie called Moira on the way. Give her this: the woman acted fast. She didn't ask questions, just told them to drive faster. By the time they got to the hospital, there was a full team waiting for them at the ER entrance.

They whisked Annie away. Nic was admitted, although a cursory check from an ER doc showed that nothing he'd suffered was life-threatening. Africa insisted on having Reggie checked out, but aside from exhaustion and a fuzzy hangover from the drugs, there's nothing wrong with her.

Nothing physical, anyway.

She and Africa gave Teagan a ride home. The girl nodded absently when Reggie said she was going to speak with Tanner. She kept passing out, her head tipping forward onto her chest.

The office in Carson is the same as before. Unchanged. It feels wrong – China Shop, the world it operates in, has been turned upside down. Such a series of events demands chaos, broken walls, physical damage. But there's none.

Well, except for her chair. Another one gone, she thinks bitterly. Moira had acted fast there, too. Reggie doesn't have the faintest idea how she managed to conjure up a motorised chair from the other side of the country at one in the morning, but she did. It's not nearly as nice as any of Reggie's previous chairs, but she's certainly not complaining.

The video ends. An invitation to watch multiple reaction videos pops up. Reggie grimaces, closes the window. Africa stands behind her, silent, body as tense as steel wire.

"What's our play?" she says quietly.

Moira's voice is as calm and still as a frozen lake. Never a good sign. "We have assets in Moldova and Macedonia. They're already working to spread as much confusion as they can online – it's surprisingly easy to muddy the waters. In a way, I suppose we got lucky – there's the just the one video, for now, and Teagan's face doesn't appear on it. Also, I wouldn't call the eyewitnesses exactly . . . reliable."

Reggie wants to tell her that just because the people under the freeway were homeless does not mean they're unreliable, but she holds her tongue. Right now, that would be less than helpful.

Moira says, "Tell me everything."

Reggie takes a deep breath, and does.

The Legends. The Main Street Bridge. Leo. Teagan and Annie dropping off the radar. All of it. The only part she leaves out is how Africa lied to Moira – she can read the coldness in the woman's face, the lack of emotion, and she has a sense of what's coming. Throwing him under the bus would not help anybody.

When she's finished, Africa clears his throat. "Mrs Tanner – that woman, the one who took the boy. They cannot have gone far. I will take Teggan and—"

"You will do no such thing." Tanner's voice is a deadly whisper. "As of now, Teagan Frost is off the board."

Reggie's blood turns to ice.

The deal Tanner had – *has* – with Teagan is brutal in its simplicity. Teagan works for Tanner, and Tanner does not hand Teagan over to the government departments who want to cut her open and see what's inside – the departments run by people who think she is more useful to them dead than alive. Teagan is not supposed to reveal what she does, to anyone, ever. Especially not on video.

"You can't do this," Reggie says.

For the first time, a flicker of annoyance crosses Tanner's face. "For heaven's sake. I said she was off the board, not in custody. Although it's going to take every ounce of political capital I have to keep it that way – every subcommittee and review board in Washington with security clearance will want to burn me alive. And until I can pacify them, I don't want Ms Frost near any sort of operation. At all."

"What will you tell them?" Africa asks.

Tanner appears to weigh her words carefully. "That she's an asset. That she saved lives. That she is the one individual with extranormal abilities who we *can* control, and that that means she will be more useful in the field. And she should consider herself damn lucky. If this had happened a year ago, she would already be on a plane to Texas. But things are different now."

Her eyes find Reggie's. "There's a very good chance my intervention may not be enough for my superiors. They may want to take a different route."

Reggie lifts her chin. "Those people, the ones in the camp – they're *alive* because of Teagan. If she hadn't—"

"It doesn't matter. Don't you understand that? We are fighting a war here, and right now, Ms Frost has made it exponentially harder for us to do so.

"As it is, her actions must have consequences. From now on, she will be continuously monitored. Location, communications, all of it. And in ways she cannot disrupt or remove. I have given her far too much leeway, and that ends now."

It hasn't escaped Reggie's notice that Moira has yet to mention her, or what she did. And as if picking up on this thought, Tanner says, "Ms McCormick, you lied to me. You compromised the integrity of our operation, at the worst possible time."

"I—"

"I am removing you from your post, effective immediately. You are no longer head of operations for China Shop."

And there it is.

Africa sucks in a breath, grips the back of Reggie's chair, as if steadying himself. Reggie knew it would happen quickly, but it still hits her like a punch to the gut.

"I understand," she says, amazed at how calm she is. "I assume you'll want me to continue to act as the systems expert for—"

"No. As of now, your clearances are revoked. You are not to participate in or advise on any missions conducted by this government. Your services are no longer required."

This time, it's Reggie who sucks in a horrified breath.

A demotion was expected. A punishment of some sort. But *this* . . .

She should argue. She should fight this. She is one of the best hackers in the country, and China Shop can't possibly run itself without—

And yet even as the thought occurs, she's questioning it. What good would protesting do? Even *if* she could convince Moira to let her keep her position, it wouldn't last.

Nemila was one thing. There was a time when Reggie would have called the bond between her and Moira unbreakable. The six days they spent in that forest had forged them in steel. They were closer than friends. They were sisters.

But it's been a long time since Nemila, and both of them have changed. She knew this, even if she didn't want to think about it. The bond between them had become as fragile as spun glass, and the last twelve hours have shattered it. From now on, every briefing Reggie gave would be suspect. Questioned. Interrogated.

Doubted.

That's how Moira thinks. Why continue with her, when they could hire someone almost as good – and who, more importantly, will play by the rules? Moira is nothing if not a pragmatist, and what could be more pragmatic than that?

Tanner's face softens almost imperceptibly. "Your medical insurance with the federal government will continue for the notice period, per your contract. Your final pay cheque will still arrive. And you have your settlement from the Army, of course. You can remain in the office quarters until you find suitable accommodation. But you are not to take part in any operations, in any capacity. Am I clear?"

She does not, Reggie notices, mention that this is the third destroyed chair in two years. Her version of being generous, she supposes.

"Mrs Tanner . . . " Africa's face has gone grey. "This . . . I don't think . . . "

"Mr Kouamé." Tanner's attention snaps to him. "You are the only person in China Shop who obeyed orders, and worked within mission parameters. As of now, you are the acting head of operations."

Reggie can't stop a stunned gasp from slipping out. *Africa. Head of China Shop.*

But why not? Why the hell not? China Shop as it stands is finished. Paul is dead. Annie may soon follow him. Teagan is . . . not herself. Reggie is no longer part of anything. So why not have Africa run things? What harm could he possibly do?

She finds herself embarrassed at the thought. As if he's an imbecile, an amateur. She has to remind herself just how far he's come, how seriously he's taken his new role. He's a long way from the damaged homeless man Teagan first made contact with. He has a life now, a steady relationship, a home, a job he clearly cares about and wants to be good at.

But this isn't what he wanted.

Africa has always lionised Moira Tanner. Why wouldn't he? She gave him everything he ever dreamed of. But as she looks him, Reggie is more sure than anything: he never saw himself doing it at the expense of the team. He probably thought that he might one day take over when Reggie retired. Not when she was pushed out, in the wake of a failed operation.

A spiteful part of her – a part she would have utterly ignored yesterday, but which is heard far too easily today – wants him to throw it back in Moira's face. To say no, that is unacceptable. That he will work with Reggie, or he will not work at all.

But of course, he doesn't. He straightens, and with only the barest glance at Reggie, says, "I understand."

Reggie tries to be angry, but she can't do it. Can't even fake it, mostly because what she feels is relief.

Cold, calm relief.

A worrying thought tugs at her. Before she can get there, Africa voices it. "But so I am clear: you are saying I am *acting* head. Who is—?"

"It will take time to wrap up my commitments in Washington, and to meet with the various stakeholders to give them answers on what happened today." There's no hint of emotion from Tanner now – it's as if she's reading from a script. "Until I can relocate, you will take point on our operations."

Until she can relocate?

"You are coming to Los Angeles?" Africa says.

"China Shop has not been as effective as it should. And given recent events, it's clear that that is a situation I cannot allow." She narrows her eyes, very slightly, as if steeling herself to begin an unpleasant job. "I will be taking command of the operation directly."

FIFTY-SEVEN

Reggie

"Mr Kouamé," Tanner says. "Your mandate is simple. You are to gather as much intelligence as possible on the man who attacked your team today, and his handler. Who they are, what they are planning, where they are located. If they were in Los Angeles, then they will have left a trail – accommodations, vehicles, supplies."

Africa seems to be struggling to take this all in. "What about Annie?"

"If she recovers, Ms Cruz can join you. She will be subject to the same restrictions as Ms Frost, in terms of monitoring and communications. I will be sending additional staff in due course to implement that, and assist you in your duties."

"*If* she recovers?" Reggie stares at Tanner. "That is a member of your staff. She put herself directly in harm's way—"

"Enough." Tanner's voice is barely a whisper. "She is as much to blame for this as Ms Frost. But do *not* think that I am leaving her to fend for herself. She is receiving the finest medical care possible, but my understanding is that her injuries are severe. We have to plan for what happens if she does not survive."

"And that doesn't bother you?"

"It doesn't matter whether it bothers me or not. It is simply the situation we find ourselves in."

Reggie has to fight to keep her face neutral. You couldn't argue with Moira Tanner on things like this. It would be like trying to drill a hole in a stone wall by giving it an evil look.

"Any questions?" Tanner asks.

Plenty, Reggie thinks. But Moira wouldn't be able to answer a single one of them.

"I . . . " Africa swallows. "Yes. I have some. But I would like to think about them, if that is all right."

"Very well. I will be in touch tomorrow."

Her gaze lingers on Reggie, as if she's about to say something else. Then she looks away, and kills the feed.

A silence falls over the office. Reggie can't believe how calm she feels. And the *relief* – the guilty, delightful relief.

"Reggie," Africa says slowly. "I never wanted—"

"It's OK," she says, privately amazed she can still speak.

"This is not right. You are the boss."

"Not any more. You listen here, honey. You've got a lot of work to do, and not nearly enough time or resources to do it. The only way you keep this ship floating is if you focus on what you're good at. Don't—"

The coughing comes out of nowhere, her diaphragm going taut as a snare drum.

"I will get water." Africa is seven feet tall, so big that he almost fills the tiny office. But at this moment it's as if he's shrunk to half his size.

"I'm all . . . " Reggie has to fight to get the coughing under control. "I'm . . . *hrrrrm* . . . fine."

"Reggie . . . "

"No, just *listen*. Don't do what I did – don't spread yourself too thin. You've got connections the rest of us could only dream of – hell, even Annie doesn't know some of the people you do. Go talk to them. Find out where that woman came from, get some solid intel." She forces herself to smile. "Prove you're as good as Moira thinks you are."

After a long moment – a very long moment – he nods. "*Ya*. OK."

"You'll be fine," Reggie says, placing a hand on his. Truth be told, she has no idea if that's true. But she can be one hell of an actress when she puts her mind to—

Actress. In all of the chaos, she'd almost forgotten about the audition. She has to force herself not to start laughing. After all that agonising over it . . .

"What will you do?" Africa says quietly.

Reggie finds her voice. "I'd like to be alone for a while." The very slightest tremor in her voice – she clamps down on it hard. "Go home, go see Jeannette, get some food. I *am* going to need a little help later, with getting into bed and such. Annie normally does that for me, but . . . well."

He nods. "Of course, yes. If you are sure, then I will come back. Of course I will help."

"Great. You can start by fixing me a cup of tea."

He does. And still, he leaves reluctantly, asking again if she's all right, if she'd prefer him to stay. Reggie practically has to yell at him to get him out. But eventually, he leaves, and Reggie is alone.

For a long time, she simply sits there, staring at nothing. Quietly amazed at just how good she feels. She's no longer guilty about the relief – she lets it overtake her, wallowing in it, the sheer bliss of knowing that no matter what happens, she won't have to deal with any of the shitty details. No more invoices. No more ordering equipment and uniforms. No more trying to find the right brand of coffee.

Moira was right about one thing: Annie *is* getting the very best possible care. The ICU at Cedars-Sinai is one of the best in the country – the hospital took a hit after the quake, but the departments that are still running know their stuff. There's not a lot that she can do for Annie that the doctors aren't doing already.

Annie has to recover. She has to. No, she *will*.

God, Reggie is going to miss her. She's going to miss all of them. She won't miss the drudgery of running China Shop . . . but she will miss having Annie looking after her, the quiet conversations they'd have. She'll miss Teagan – even though her life will probably be a lot less stressful without her. She'll even miss Africa. She doesn't bear him any ill will, just hopes to God he knows what he's getting into. Moira Tanner isn't the devil, but dealing with her does have some similarities.

She's surprised to find she isn't bitter. She's not sure she would have done anything differently.

The rest of her life stretches before her.

She reaches for her trackball, pauses, half-wanting to postpone it. Wait until tomorrow, when she's mentally ready for—

Screw it. At the very least, she can read the script the agent said she was going to send over. She can start there.

But there's nothing from the agent on her personal email. She refreshes, glancing at her connection indicator, even though she knows the internet is working fine.

Ah well. Agents are busy. Chances are that Darcy Lorenzo – that was her name, wasn't it? – simply forgot to send it over. Not to worry. It can wait until tomorrow.

A thought enters her mind then, one that she had before, but never actually paid attention to. How, exactly, did Darcy Lorenzo of DCA Talent get her number?

"What does it matter?" she says, irritated with herself. She refreshes her email again, then closes the window. She'll watch a show or two, take her mind off things. If she really can't stop thinking about it, she can find some test scripts online, or pull up some of her old ones from the Playhouse.

And yet, the thought won't go away. She gives an annoyed cluck, opens her browser and locates DCA Talent's website. She should probably read Lorenzo's bio – it might prove useful later.

Only: the DCA Talent site doesn't list Darcy Lorenzo as an agent. Reggie scrolls through the list of names, mouthing them: *Andy Goldstein, Larissa Schrambling, Sarah Yuan . . .*

The tiny drumbeat of worry in her chest kicks up a notch. *So she's not listed. So what? It doesn't mean anything. They might not have updated their site. She could be new at the agency – hell, she probably is, if she's calling up an old theatre hack like you—*

"Enough. Don't do that," Reggie says to herself.

But it doesn't stop her from calling Darcy Lorenzo's number. Belatedly, she realises it's a cellphone number. Wouldn't Lorenzo have called her from an office phone? The landline at the DCA offices?

Her earpiece is silent as the call connects. Jesus, what the hell is she going to say if Lorenzo answers? *Hi, sorry to call so late, but I just wanted to see if you really are an agent?*

In her ear, there are three gloomy beeps. Then: "The number you dialled has been disconnected."

Reggie barely registers hanging up.

She's replaying everything that's happened in the past twenty-four hours, running through it in her mind.

How someone tipped off the Legends about who Teagan, Annie and Africa were.

How their communications systems were compromised.

How the woman who kidnapped her knew where she, Reggie, was going to be. How she must have been watching the offices, ready to follow Reggie if she left.

"Uh-uh," she says. Then again, more strongly: "Uh-uh. No."

But that doesn't change the fact that someone has been messing with China Shop. Trying to disrupt their operations.

What if a part of that was getting inside their heads? Splitting their focus, making it so they wouldn't be as effective in their decision-making? So they'd be too fragmented to operate effectively?

Reggie's mouth is very dry. There's no way. And yet: didn't that call plant the seeds of doubt in her mind? Didn't it help push her to make the choices she did? She can't stop her mind connecting the dots, even as a sick nausea blooms in her stomach. The call from Darcy Lorenzo was probably part of a coordinated strategy, a plan to disrupt China Shop, the one group in Los Angeles who might be able to—

Do what?

But oh, Reggie knows. Because she's remembering Darcy Lorenzo's voice now. And the voice of the woman who held her hostage.

They're the same.

Only China Shop could retrieve Leo Nguyen. Only they would be able to take him off the board. And so China Shop would have to be disrupted. Distracted. Split. Taken off the board themselves.

There's no agent. No audition.

There never was.

Reggie's arm drops. Her fingers slip out of the rings on her cup handle, the vessel smashing on the floor. The sound makes her jerk in her chair, tears an awful cry out of her chest.

"God," she says, and then she's sobbing, raising her hands to her face. Her body shakes with hurt and embarrassment – no, not just embarrassment.

Humiliation.

For a few hours, she thought she could do it. She had an

opportunity, golden and bright, and she meant to take it. But it was never there. Of course it was never there. How could she have ever thought that someone like her would get to . . . to . . .

She has always been the calm centre of the storm. The peacemaker. The professional, the one who gets the job done. The one who holds everyone together. Her job was to lead a team: to be the quiet, still ground that everyone around her could stand on.

No longer. In her pain, in the very depths of her misery, alone in an office she is no longer allowed to work in, Regina McCormick finds something else.

Anger.

Rage.

Slowly, oh so slowly, it dries up her tears. It tightens her chest and shoulders and kills the nausea in her stomach and leaves her light-headed, breathing in and out, focusing on one thing. The face of her captor. The woman who did this cruel, monstrous, hateful thing.

Reggie may not work for China Shop any more. She may be on the outside. But Moira Tanner cannot take her knowledge. She cannot take away the fact that Reggie is one of the most competent hackers on the planet. Someone who can cut through systems security like a katana through paper. Someone with the power to end worlds.

It doesn't matter whether she helps Teagan and Africa, or does it by herself. She's not done. She'll never be done.

Reggie makes herself picture the woman in even more detail. Her face, her voice. And she makes a solemn, calm, quiet promise.

I'm coming for you.

FIFTY-EIGHT

Teagan

I'm supposed to be back at home. Or what passes for home these days – my tiny-ass temporary apartment in Pasadena.

I should be sleeping. The deepest, darkest, cousin-of-death sleep, after this unbelievable, monstrous hellstorm of a day.

And at first, that's what happened. Physically I'm OK – I think. They strapped my knee in a million miles of athletic tape, but the doc who looked it over said there wouldn't be any permanent damage. Then he looked me up and down, sniffed and told me to get some Adderall from the pharmacy downstairs. Then he gave me a pamphlet for a drug counselling service.

Awesome.

But by the time Reggie and Africa dropped me outside my front door, the meth comedown was back, and it was the entire world. There wasn't a single part of me that wasn't in agony. I had no stomach left – it had been sucked into a black hole. Iron railway spikes had been driven into the base of my skull. I was shaking, hyperventilating, doing everything I could not to vomit all over the China Shop van.

I have no idea how I managed to get inside. Africa helped me, kept asking if I was all right, even wandered around tidying the place. Like it would help, somehow. It took a lot of energy I didn't have to assure him that I'd be fine, to get him to do the one thing I really wanted: to be left alone.

When he finally left, I crawled into bed, not even changing into my PJs, just kicking my shoes off. Not caring. Fuck the world. Fuck everything. Just let me die.

I slept. For about ten minutes. And then I was wide awake, horribly alert, twitching and grinding my teeth. Every nerve in my body vibrating with electricity. All I wanted to do was sleep . . . and I couldn't.

I don't care if it jacks my ability. Meth is the fucking *worst*.

I didn't have my phone any more, but I did have Minnie's. So I called Nic. Hoping he'd distract me, clear my head. He was at his parents' place – God knows what he told them. He was also hopped up on mucho painkillers.

We didn't talk for long. I had to bite down on my nervous energy. "I'll call you tomorrow, OK? Promise."

"You'd better." He was practically slurring his words. "Glad you're OK."

I shake my head, still not sure that's true. "You too."

"Love you."

I don't think he meant *love you* love you. Like I said: high as fuck. But it didn't stop a strange, queasy feeling from rolling through my body.

Sleep was out of the question, so I did what I always do when I need to calm myself down. I started cooking.

Initially, I think I just planned to cook myself dinner, but it kind of sort of got out of hand. A quick tomato sauce for pasta became a ragu, which became a *lot* of ragu. I made a huge salad to go with it, clearing out my fridge, throwing in every little odd thing I could find: anchovies, a bag of half-finished croutons, a hastily made vinaigrette. I realised that I didn't want to eat any of it, couldn't even *imagine* eating any of it. I just needed to occupy my fritzing, tortured body.

Somewhere along the way, I baked chocolate chip cookies, burning through the last of my expensive sea salt as garnish. The tiny-ass kitchen with its wonky oven didn't even phase me. My apartment filled with warring smells, my sink vanishing under a growing pile of pots. I used practically every perishable item in my fridge, every can in my cupboards, and I was still fizzing with energy. My thoughts wouldn't stay off Nic, and increasingly, they wouldn't stay off Annie.

Which is how I ended up driving back to the hospital.

Back to Annie's room.

Thank fuck she's not in the burns unit. There were *some* burns, sure, most of them on her torso, but apparently not enough to put her in isolation. Just the regular ICU. Like that's any comfort. Apparently, what happened to her is known as splash damage, where a bolt of lightning hits the ground and travels outwards from the point of impact, going through someone on the way. If she'd been hit directly . . .

As it is, her heart stopped twice after she got to the ER. She has a ruptured eardrum. Burst blood vessels. She's in a coma.

I can't get over how small she looks. Annie is tall – six feet, easy. But under the snaking network of tubes that criss-cross her chest and cover her face, under the strips of medical tape and the wristbands and the bleached hospital sheet, she looks tiny. She's in critical condition. I don't remember much of the conversation we had with the doctors, but . . .

There's not a single thing I can do to help my friend. I can't even offer her one of the cookies I baked.

Friend.

Is that what she is?

I'm not supposed to be here – it's way outside visiting hours.

But the advantage of turning up at a hospital with snacks is that you can bribe the nurses. And besides, I don't think an Army could have kept me away. A couple of nurses gave me the stink-eye, but so far, no one's moved me – maybe due to Tanner's influence, I don't know.

Tanner. Christ. I haven't even thought about how I'm going to deal with her. With everything. It's all a problem for tomorrow.

Right now, I just want to sit in this chair, in this private hospital room, and be with Annie.

It's all I can do.

Drawn curtains. Dark, silent TV. The lights are up, but there's no sound other than the gentle beeping of the machines keeping Annie alive. The chair I'm in is on the window side of the bed, pushed up against the corner of the room. It's old, but comfy. I'm half expecting to fall asleep, because surely it has to happen at some point. But the meth has plugged my body into a nuclear reactor. There's too much energy, and nowhere for it to go. My teeth feel electrified, like they're actually vibrating in their sockets.

The very last of the meth is still in my pocket. A tiny pile of it, no bigger than the hole between finger and thumb when you make the OK sign. It's kind of amazing that the little baggie survived . . . Well, everything. But it did. I was adamant that I was going to throw it away, or leave it at home. I didn't.

I don't plan on taking this goddamn drug ever again. That's the truth.

It has to be.

"Whooooo," I say, tilting my head back, stretching my arms overhead. "What a day, man. What a fucking day."

Yes, I am talking to myself. You try being on the run for twelve hours and then snorting half a bag of meth. The horrible comedown seems to have bottomed out now – I can hold a thought in my head, at least.

"I have to hand it to you, Annie," I say. "You had me worried. I thought you were ..."

I sniff hard. Look away. I will *not* say the word dead. I will not put that awful, fucked-up nonsense into the universe.

"You know," I say, turning back, speaking without really meaning to, "apparently people in a coma can actually hear what's going on around them. Maybe you can actually hear me right now. Who knows?" I clear my throat. "It's 5 a.m., and this is your local news bulletin for the Greater Los Angeles area. A surprise flash flood was stopped in its tracks today by a masked superhero, saving hundreds of lives. Well, she wasn't masked, but whatever. Also, a boy with electricity powers was stolen by a lunatic who can make you see things that aren't there. The world may be ending, but sources tell us that local psychokinetic Teagan Frost still makes the best chocolate chip cookies."

I take a bite to confirm my information. "We'll be back with more after these messages," I say, through a full mouth.

As if in response, the public address system in the hall bleeps, paging a doctor to head to the ER. Someone yells something in response, and there's distant laughter.

"I did stop the flash flood, by the way," I say. "Stopped that shit cold. Although I ..."

Fuck it. "I had to take another hit of meth to get it done. I'm still pretty blasted right now actually. If blasted is actually the way to describe it. Stoned, maybe? I dunno. Let's stick with blasted. Either way, you didn't have to keep my ass out of trouble like you said. I got into and out of it all by myself, like a big girl. Well, OK, Africa helped. He showed up, by the way. So did the Legends. I ... well, it's a long story."

A car honks on the street outside, the driver revving the

engine, cutting through the quiet night. Raindrops beat a tattoo on the windowpane, and somewhere in the distance, there's a peal of soft thunder.

"You're a total bitch, by the way," I say.

I mean it to sound light-hearted. A cute little joke. It doesn't come out like that.

"You were pissed at me because, what, I kept putting myself in danger? I was going to get myself killed and leave you alone, and I was a bad friend? You know how crazy that is, right? Not to mention unfair, and irrational, and . . . Annie, you can't just do that to someone. You can't put that on them. How the hell did you think that was OK?"

I rub my face, standing up out of the chair. Start to pace, moving mindlessly back and forth. I have no idea if she can hear any of this, but it's not like it matters. It's all coming out, boiling out of me like water from an overflowing pot.

"Let me tell you something. Ninety-nine per cent of the time, I have no idea what I'm doing. I'm making all of it up as I go along. Every part of my life. But here's something I do know. Here's something you can take right to the fucking bank. Back at the homeless camp, you told me – you literally told me, right to my face – that I'm the only friend you've got. Well, friends don't treat each other this way. They don't get angry and shut each other out and act like one of them is a little child, you *asshole*."

The crazy thing is, even as I say this, I realise who does treat people this way. Siblings. Brothers and sisters. My sister Chloe could be amazing, the best big sister anyone could have. Someone I could talk to for hours and go on long horseback rides with and pull pranks on our brother. But she could also be cold. Hurtful. It was like the flick of a switch. She'd turn into this . . . this *robot*. Looking at me and sizing me up like an insect, especially if I didn't do what she wanted me to. She could freeze me out for days sometimes. It hurt like hell, but what was I supposed to do? You can't choose your family.

So what, is Annie my sister now? A replacement for Chloe? Fuck that. I had a sister, and I'll never have another, and I'm not gonna sit here and pretend that Annie and I have that kind of relationship. We never have. She is *not* my sister.

It's wrong to have her be so silent. To have this conversation be one-sided. What would I have said to her if she wasn't unconscious? Would I have had the guts? I have no idea.

"You lost Paul," I continue, my voice thick with unshed tears. "I get it. You were hurting, and somehow, you got it into your head that this was the correct response. That it would make you feel better to push me away. Well you know what, Annie? It isn't, and it won't.

"I've lost people too. My whole freaking *family*. Mom, Dad, my sister and brother. All gone. I'm not perfect. Believe me, I know. But what happened happened, and I would never take it out on someone else the way you did to me. Especially not someone I considered a . . . "

A friend.

I grip the edge of the bed so hard that my knuckles turn white. "Fuck you. How fucking dare you? You say to me I'll never see you again? If I stayed to help the people in the camp? OK. Got it. Message received. You get your wish. I'm out."

That's it.

I'm going to stand up. I'm going to walk out of here.

The anger is gone. What's left behind is a bitter resentment, one I can't help but luxuriate in. In the time I've know her, I've gotten *snatches* of what Annie would be like as a friend. Little moments here and there where we weren't fighting, where we really connected.

Talking on the roof of Paul's Boutique, the old office in Venice Beach, after the whole Jake thing blew over.

Inviting me for dinner at her mom's house, which happened before the big quake. When Paul was still alive. She tried to pretend like her mom was making her do it, but you could tell she was kind of excited.

Singing the goddamn *A-Team* theme song in the van with me as we drove to one of our missions.

The links she'd send me on WhatsApp a couple of times a week. Cool songs and videos from hip-hop artists. Never any commentary, never a *Hey, saw this and thought of u* ... but a steady stream of links nonetheless. Like the one time I talked about how awesome Benny the Butcher was, and she somehow found this old, super-rare pre-Griselda freestyle from like 2005. Sent it to me out of the blue. Shrugged when I thanked her, like it was no big thing.

Her surprised smile when I made the team chocolate brownies. Her sincere nod of thanks, mouth full, as she worked her way through two or three of the things, one after the other.

No. I am not doing this to myself. Those little moments are like brief snatches of sun behind dark clouds. They don't make up for the unrelenting, endless wave of shit she's sent my way. The anger, the contempt, the disgust. Maybe we could have been closer, but she pissed it all away. And for what?

So yeah. I'm going to leave. Right now.

But I don't.

For a long minute, I just stand there, looking down at her.

Then I take her still hand in both of mine.

"I don't want you to go," I whisper, soft as a prayer. "Please. Stay with me."

If the powers behind the universe had any sense of justice,

this is where Annie would open her eyes. Say my name. This is where she'd squeeze my fingers in hers.

Instead, there's only silence. Her hand, unmoving, under my own.

After a minute, I let it go. I sit back down in the worn chair in the corner, put my elbows on my knees, drop my head between them.

The door to the suite opens. One of the nurses maybe, or a doctor – and they're probably going to give me shit again for being here. Well, that's fine. Maybe it really is time to go.

I lift my head, and the Zigzag Man is right in front of me.

Standing in the doorway. Silhouetted by the bright lights in the corridor.

I blink. It can't be him. There's no way. He'd never just walk in here. It would be Jonas stepping through the door, or Carlos, or . . .

But there's none of the same dreamlike feeling from before. No sense of unreality. Just this man, standing before me. Same leather jacket. Same heavy black boots. Same wild beard and insane, staring eyes.

Turns out, I do have a little PK left.

There's a tray of surgical instruments against the wall. Scalpels. Scissors. Forceps. I snap them into the air in front of me, business ends pointed right at the Zigzag Man.

"Where's Leo?" I say, through gritted teeth.

He smiles at me. He's not wearing his bandanna any more— for the first time, I can see his whole face. And a little radar pings in the back of my mind starts to send a signal.

I ignore it. "I'm gonna count to three. Then all of this –" I gesture at the very sharp pieces of metal in the air between us "– is going right in your fucking eyeballs. One. Two."

But I'm doing more than counting.

I'm *seeing*.

This whole time, I never really got a good look at the Zigzag Man. It was always in the heat of the action, masked by the insane visions he planted in my head. This is the first time I'm actually getting to look at him properly. And as I do so, my mind is making connections, putting together pieces of the puzzle.

I know this person as Harry. A scruffy, silent homeless guy who used to hang around my old apartment in Leimert Park. He never said a word to me, always kept his distance. He was a fixture on the street, a local figure, but one I didn't pay much attention to.

But I'm looking past that now. And it's not Harry I'm seeing.

My ability has evolved over time. I've gotten stronger. I've gained the ability to manipulate organic objects, not just inorganic ones. If my ability has evolved, then it makes sense that others' abilities would work the same way.

The Zigzag Man has the ability to make you see things. He has the ability to make you . . . dream. The kind of ability that might have evolved from . . . from . . .

From someone whose ability was to never require sleep.

I'm fighting it, even as my lips form the word *Three*. I'm reaching. It doesn't make sense. It's a logical leap too far, my exhausted brain jumping to conclusions and—

—and I'm looking into the eyes of the Zigzag Man, and I'm seeing Adam.

My brother.

Harry. The Zigzag Man. My brother. They're the same person. This whole time, all these years, and he was right in front of me.

My words fade. Choked off. I can't speak.

A woman steps out from behind the Zigzag Man. She's

older, with a look in her eyes that speaks of hard miles and tough journeys, but there's no question. It's a face that looked back at me from atop her horse as we rode through the Wyoming wilderness. A face that I'd see when we hung out in her room, listening to music and reading magazines. A face that could turn cold and dark in a nanosecond if its owner was unhappy with me. A face that I thought I'd never see again.

The face of someone who should be dead.

My sister.

My *real* sister.

The surgical instruments clatter to the ground. I take a step back, and when my legs bump the chair behind me, I sit down hard.

My brother and my sister step into the room, and stand side by side before me.

"It's good to see you, Emily," Chloe says. "We need to talk."

ACKNOWLEDGEMENTS

Hey. Teagan here.

Jackson Ford is currently passed out drunk on the couch behind me after only his second pineapple daiquiri. I've drawn a dick on his face. He had it coming.

Unfortunately, we are on deadline, and he hasn't done his acknowledgements for the third book in a row. So once again, it's up to me. I'm kind of hungry right now, so I may or may not end up comparing everyone in these acknowledgements to food. Sorry not sorry.

Ed Wilson, Jackson's agent, is a grilled cheese sandwich. There isn't a single situation that a grilled cheese sandwich can't fix, and the same could be said for Ed. However, he's English, so he'd probably serve the sandwich with Branston pickle or something. I think we'd all agree that's a crime against nature. Don't do it, Ed.

Anna Jackson and Nadia Saward are peanut butter and jelly. The perfect combo, the ultimate editorial tag team. Together, they made this book thousand times better, and they even managed to remove the time-travelling unicorn samurai from eighteenth-century Japan that showed up half-way through. Oh, and since the last book, Anna Jackson has actually transcended the editorial world and become the literal head publisher of Orbit Books. And she hasn't even reached her final form yet. Go, Anna, go.

Bradley Englert, editor at Orbit US, also had a hand in this. He's a New Yorker, so clearly he is pastrami on rye. If there's one thing that New York can do better than Los Angeles – and there aren't many – it's deli.

Joanna Kramer, managing editor at Orbit, is Maldon sea salt. A super-crunchy, delicious garnish that brings a dish together, finishing everything up nicely.

Nazia Khatun and Ellen Wright, publicity, are another great combo. I'm going to go with salt and vinegar, the greatest potato chip flavour known to man. On their own, they are both great. But put them together, and you've really got a party.

Madeleine Hall, marketing, is one of those really yummy garnishes you get on plates at five-star restaurants. Deep fried garlic chips, maybe. Or glazed carrots. Something that helps sell the whole meal.

Sophie Harris did the cover. Which makes her an onion. Don't knock onions, man. Without them, the whole kit and caboodle falls apart.

Saxon Bullock is a clove of garlic. Garlic is an annoying ingredient. It's irritating to peel, and a pain in the ass to chop. It makes your fingers all sticky. And yet, without it, things just wouldn't work. You can never have enough garlic, and Jackson can never have enough of Saxon's copy-editing. He might swear and rage and threaten to sue, but ultimately, he does what Saxon tells him to. Because Saxon is brilliant. A pain in the ass, but brilliant.

All right, you know what? Now I'm starving, and I just realised that I have a whole lot more people to thank. My world has gotten a lot bigger over the past couple of years, which means more people had a hand in making it awesome. So I'm going to go grab a snackie and pick this up later, without the awkward food metaphors.

OK, back. Made myself a grilled cheese sandwich in the end. Never mess with the classics.

A big fist bump to the Hachette Audio Division, for making my audiobooks so incredible. Louise Harvey, Pavel Rivera, Lauren Patten and Jesse Vilinsky. If you haven't heard them yet, you are missing out on some of the best audiobook reads ever recorded. I'm a totally unbiased observer obviously.

While he was writing this book, Jackson relied on several experts to help him get things right. Chances are he screwed it up anyway. It's his fault, not theirs. Wyatt Turney helped out with the science of electricity, and Michael Atkins talked at length with him about the LA River. Ross Howard helped with Spanish translation. Dr Vee Wilson used her experience as a spinal rehab specialist to help Jackson get the details right for Reggie's disability, and used her experience as Jackson's mom to repeatedly remind him that she brought him into this world, and by God and sunny Jesus she can take him out of it.

Also, a big thank you to Danielle Kozak. She knows why.

Nia Howard attempted to stop Jackson from making a complete fool of himself when it came to writing about the black American experience. Chances are he's still made a complete fool of himself, but that isn't Nia's fault. Thanks also to Starr Waddell at Quiet House.

Alisha Grauso usually performs a fact check for Jackson, helping make sure that his details of Los Angeles are correct.

Recently, however, she adopted two cats, Boo and Keats. It turns out they were much better at the job than she ever was, so we fired her and hired them. It was the best decision we've ever made. Thanks, Boo and Keats. The cheque is in the mail. Be nice to your human.

As always, Jackson sent early versions of this book to a few select people, because he secretly hates them. A big thank you to George Kelly and Werner Schutz for their comments, and to Jackson's wife, Nicole Simpson. I think we can all agree that she's the real hero here. She also happens to be the designer of the maps at the front of my books. That's her handwriting. Jackson's, predictably, is drunk-spider-chicken-scratch.

To every blogger, bookstagrammer, YouTuber and pod-caster who has talked about this series, and anybody who has spread the word to their friends: I love you. I really and truly love you. I'm going to name a salad after you.

Oh hey! Almost forgot. They're making this series into a TV show. By the time you read this, I might be on screen, played by Bradley Cooper. Or Idris Elba, I'm not picky. A huge round of applause to Emily Hayward-Whitlock and Fern McCauley for whacking the contract into shape, and to Heather Kadin and Alex Kurtzman at CBS/Secret Hideout for picking up the option, and for getting Idris to sign on (you guys did handle that, right?).

I think that's it. I'm gonna go stick Jackson's hand in a bowl of warm water and film the results. Adios.

extras

orbit

meet the author

JACKSON FORD has never been to Los Angeles. The closest he's come is visiting Las Vegas for a Celine Dion concert, where he also got drunk and lost his advance money for this book at the Bellagio. That's what happens when you try play roulette at the craps table. He is the creator of the Frost Files, and the character of Teagan Frost—who, by the way, absolutely did not write this bio, and anybody who says she did is a liar.

Find out more about Jackson Ford and other Orbit authors by registering for the free monthly newsletter at orbitbooks.net.

if you enjoyed
EYE OF THE SH*T STORM

look out for

THE LAST SMILE IN SUNDER CITY

Book One of the Fetch Phillips Archives

by

Luke Arnold

A former soldier turned PI tries to help the fantasy creatures whose lives he ruined in a world that's lost its magic, in a compelling debut fantasy by Black Sails *actor Luke Arnold.*

Welcome to Sunder City. The magic is gone, but the monsters remain.

I'm Fetch Phillips, just like it says on the window. There are a few things you should know before you hire me:

1. Sobriety costs extra.
2. My services are confidential.
3. I don't work for humans.

It's nothing personal—I'm human myself. But after what happened to the magic, it's not the humans who need my help.

1

"Do some good," she'd said.

Well, I'd tried, hadn't I? Every case of my career had been tiresome and ultimately pointless. Like when Mrs Habbot hired me to find her missing dog. Two weeks of work, three broken bones, then the old bat died before I could collect my pay, leaving a blind and incontinent poodle in my care for two months. Just long enough for me to fall in love with the damned mutt before he also kicked the big one.

Rest in peace, Pompo.

Then there was my short-lived stint as Aaron King's bodyguard. Paid in full, not a bruise on my body, but listening to that rich fop whine about his inheritance was four and a half days of agony. I'm still picking his complaints out of my ears with tweezers.

After a string of similarly useless jobs, I was in my office, half-asleep, three-quarters drunk and all out of coffee. That was almost enough. The coffee. Just enough reason to stop the whole stupid game for good. I stood up from my desk and opened the door.

extras

Not the first door. The first door out of my office is the one with the little glass window that reads *Fetch Phillips: Man for Hire* and leads through the waiting room into the hall.

No. I opened the second door. The one that leads to nothing but a patch of empty air five floors over Main Street. This door had been used by the previous owner but I'd never stepped out of it myself. Not yet, anyway.

The autumn wind slapped my cheeks as I dangled my toes off the edge and looked down at Sunder City. Six years since it all fell apart. Six years of stumbling around, hoping I would trip over some way to make up for all those stupid mistakes.

Why did she ever think I could make a damned bit of difference?

Ring.

The candlestick phone rattled its bells like a beggar asking for change. I watched, wondering whether it would be more trouble to answer it or eat it.

Ring.

Ring.

"Hello?"

"Am I speaking to Mr Phillips?"

"You are."

"This is Principal Simon Burbage of Ridgerock Academy. Would you be free to drop by this afternoon? I believe I am in need of your assistance."

I knew the address but he spelled it out anyway. Our meeting would be after school, once the kids had gone home, but he wanted me to arrive a little earlier.

"If possible, come over at half past two. There is a presentation you might be interested in."

I agreed to the earlier time and the line went dead.

The wind slapped my face again. This time, I allowed the cold air into my lungs and it pushed out the night. My eyelids scraped open. My blood began to thaw. I rubbed a hand across my face and it was rough and dry like a slab of salted meat.

A client. A case. One that might actually mean something.

I grabbed my wallet, lighter, brass knuckles and knife and I kicked the second door closed.

There was a gap in the clouds after a week of rain and the streets, for a change, looked clean. I was hoping I did too. It was my first job offer in over a fortnight and I needed to make it stick. I wore a patched gray suit, white shirt, black tie, my best pair of boots and the navy, fur-lined coat that was practically a part of me.

Ridgerock Academy was made up of three single-story blocks of concrete behind a wire fence. The largest building was decorated with a painfully colorful mural of smiling faces, sunbeams and stars.

A security guard waited with a pot of coffee and a paper-thin smile. She had eyes that were ready to roll and the unashamed love of a little bit of power. When she asked for my name, I gave it.

"Fetch Phillips. Here to see the Principal."

I traded my ID for an unimpressed grunt.

"Assembly hall. Straight up the path, red doors to the left."

It wasn't my school and I'd never been there before, but the grounds were smeared with a thick coat of nostalgia; the unforgettable aroma of grass-stains, snotty sleeves, fear, confusion and week-old peanut-butter sandwiches.

The red doors were streaked with the accidental graffiti of wayward finger-paint. I pulled them open, took a moment to adjust to the darkness and slipped inside as quietly as I could.

extras

The huge gymnasium doubled as an auditorium. Chairs were stacked neatly on one side, sports equipment spread out around the other. In the middle, warm light from a projector cut through the darkness and highlighted a smooth, white screen. Particles of dust swirled above a hundred hushed kids who whispered to each other from their seats on the floor. I slid up to the back, leaned against the wall and waited for whatever was to come.

A girl squealed. Some boys laughed. Then a mousy man with white hair and large spectacles moved into the light.

"Settle down, please. The presentation is about to begin."

I recognized his voice from the phone call.

"Yes, Mr Burbage," the children sang out in unison. The Principal approached the projector and the spotlight cut hard lines into his face. Students stirred with excitement as he unboxed a reel of film and loaded it on to the sprocket. The speakers crackled and an over-articulated voice rang out.

"The Opus is proud to present . . ."

I choked on my breath mid-inhalation. The Opus were my old employers and we didn't part company on the friendliest of terms. If this is what Burbage wanted me to see, then he must have known some of my story. I didn't like that at all.

". . . *My Body and Me: Growing Up After the Coda.*"

I started to fidget, pulling at a loose thread on my sleeve. The voice-over switched to a male announcer who spoke with that fake, friendly tone I associate with salesmen, con-artists and crooked cops.

"Hello, everyone! We're here to talk about your body. Now, don't get uncomfortable, your body is something truly special and it's important that you know why."

One of the kids groaned, hoping for a laugh but not finding it. I wasn't the only one feeling nervous.

"Everyone's body is different, and that's fine. Being different means being special, and we are all special in our own unique way."

Two cartoon children came up on the screen: a boy and a girl. They waved to the kids in the audience like they were old friends.

"You might have something on your body that your friends don't have. Or maybe they have something *you* don't. These differences can be confusing if you don't understand where they came from."

The little cartoon characters played along with the voice-over, shrugging in confusion as question marks appeared above their heads. Then they started to transform.

"Maybe your friend has pointy teeth."

The girl character opened her mouth to reveal sharp fangs.

"Maybe you have stumps on the top of your back."

The animated boy turned around to present two lumps, emerging from his shoulder blades.

"You could be covered in beautiful brown fur or have more eyes than your classmates. Do you have shiny skin? Great long legs? Maybe even a tail? Whatever you are, *who*ever you are, you are special. And you are like this for a reason."

The image changed to a landscape: mountains, rivers and plains, all painted in the style of an innocent picture book. Even though the movie made a great effort to hide it, I knew damn well that this story wasn't a happy one.

"Since the beginning of time, our world has gained its power from a natural energy that we call *magic*. Magic was part of almost every creature that walked the lands. Wizards could use it to perform spells. Dragons and Gryphons flew through the air. Elves stayed young and beautiful for centuries. Every creature was in tune with the spirit of the world and it made them different. Special. Magical.

"But six years ago, maybe before some of you were even born, there was an incident."

The thread came loose on my sleeve as I pulled too hard. I wrapped it tight around my finger.

"One species was not connected to the magic of the planet: the Humans. They were envious of the power they saw around them, so they tried to change things."

A familiar pain stabbed the left side of my chest, so I reached into my jacket for my medicine: a packet of Clayfield Heavies. Clayfields are a mass-produced version of a painkiller that people in these parts have used for centuries. Essentially, they're pieces of bark from a recus tree, trimmed to the size of a toothpick. I slid one thin twig between my teeth and bit down as the film rolled on.

"To remedy their natural inferiority, the Humans made machines. They invented a wide variety of weapons, tools and strange devices, but it wasn't enough. They knew their machines would never be as powerful as the magical creatures around them.

"Then, the Humans heard a legend that told of a sacred mountain where the magical river inside the planet rose up to meet the surface; a doorway that led right into the heart of the world. This ancient myth gave the Humans an idea."

The image flipped to an army of angry soldiers brandishing swords and torches and pushing a giant drill.

"Seeking to capture the natural magic of the planet for themselves, the Human Army invaded the mountain and defeated its protectors. Then, hoping that they could use the power of the river for their own desires, they plugged their machines straight into the soul of our world."

I watched the simple animation play out the events that have come to be known as the *Coda*.

The children watched in silence as the cartoon army moved their forces on to the mountain. On screen, it looked as simple as sliding a chess piece across a board. They didn't hear the screams. They didn't smell the fires. They didn't see the bloodshed. The bodies.

They didn't see me.

"The Human Army sent their machines into the mountain but when they tried to harness the power of the river, something far more terrible happened. The shimmering river of magic turned from mist to solid crystal. It froze. The heart of the world stopped beating and every magical creature felt the change."

I could taste bile in my mouth.

"Dragons plummeted from the sky. Elves aged centuries in seconds. Werewolves' bodies became unstable and left them deformed. The magic drained from the creatures of the world. From all of us. And it has stayed that way ever since."

In the darkness, I saw heads turn. Tiny little bodies examined themselves, then turned to inspect their neighbors. Their entire world was now covered in a sadness that the rest of us had been seeing for the last six years.

"You may still bear the greatness of what you once were. Wings, fangs, claws and tails are your gifts from the great river. They herald back to your ancestors and are nothing to be ashamed of."

I bit down on the Clayfield too hard and it snapped in half. Somewhere in the crowd, a kid was crying.

"Remember, you may not be magic, but you are still . . . special."

The film ripped off the projector and spun around the wheel, wildly clicking a dozen times before finally coming to a stop. Burbage flicked on the lights but the children stayed silent as stone.

extras

"Thank you for your attention. If you have any questions about your body, your species or life before the Coda, your parents and teachers will be happy to talk them through with you."

As Burbage wrapped up the presentation, I tried my best to sink into the wall behind me. A stream of sweat had settled on my brow and I dabbed at it with an old handkerchief. When I looked up, an inquisitive pair of eyes were examining me.

They were foggy green with tiny pinprick pupils: Elvish. Young. The face was old, though. Elvish skin has no elasticity. Not anymore. The bags under the boy's eyes were worthy of a decade without sleep, but he couldn't have been more than five. His hair was white and lifeless and his tiny frame was all crooked. He wore no real expression, just looked right into my soul.

And I swear,

He knew.

if you enjoyed
EYE OF THE SH*T STORM

look out for

TRACER

Book One of Outer Earth

by

Rob Boffard

Imagine The Bourne Identity *meets* Gravity *and you'll get* Tracer, *the most exciting thriller set in space you'll ever read.*

A huge space station orbits the Earth, holding the last of humanity. It's broken, rusted, falling apart. We've wrecked our planet, and now we have to live with the consequences: a new home that's dirty, overcrowded, and inescapable.

What's more, there's a madman hiding on the station. He's about to unleash chaos. And when he does, there'll be nowhere left to run.

In space, every second counts. Who said nobody could hear you scream?

Seven years ago

The ship is breaking up around them.

The hull is twisting and creaking, like it's trying to tear away from the heat of re-entry. The outer panels are snapping off, hurtling past the cockpit viewports, black blurs against a dull orange glow.

The ship's second-in-command, Singh, is tearing at her seat straps, as if getting loose will be enough to save her. She's yelling at the captain, seated beside her, but he pays her no attention. The flight deck below them is a sea of flashing red, the crew spinning in their chairs, hunting for something, *anything* they can use.

They have checklists for these situations. But there's no checklist for when a ship, plunging belly-down through Earth's atmosphere to maximise the drag, gets flipped over by an explosion deep in the guts of the engine, sending it first into a spin and then into a screaming nosedive. Now it's spearing through the atmosphere, the friction tearing it to pieces.

The captain doesn't raise his voice. "We have to eject the rear module," he says.

Singh's eyes go wide. "Captain—"

He ignores her, reaching up to touch the communicator in his ear. "Officer Yamamoto," he says, speaking as clearly as he can. "Cut the rear module loose."

492

Koji Yamamoto stares up at him. His eyes are huge, his mouth slightly open. He's the youngest crew member, barely eighteen. The captain has to say his name again before he turns and hammers on the touch-screens.

The loudest bang of all shudders through the ship as its entire rear third explodes away. Now the ship and its crew are tumbling end over end, the movement forcing them back in their seats. The captain's stomach feels like it's broken free of its moorings. He waits for the tumbling to stop, for the ship to right itself. Three seconds. Five.

He sees his wife's face, his daughter's. *No, don't think about them. Think about the ship.*

"Guidance systems are gone," McCallister shouts, her voice distorting over the comms. "The core's down. I got nothing."

"Command's heard our mayday," Dominguez says. "They—"

McCallister's straps snap. She's hurled out of her chair, thudding off the control panel, leaving a dark red spatter of blood across a screen. Yamamoto reaches for her, forgetting that he's still strapped in. Singh is screaming.

"Dominguez," says the captain. "Patch me through."

Dominguez tears his eyes away from the injured McCallister. A second later, his hands are flying across the controls. A burst of static sounds in the captain's comms unit, followed by two quick beeps.

He doesn't bother with radio protocol. "Ship is on a collision path. We're going to try to crash-land. If we—"

"John."

Foster doesn't have to identify himself. His voice is etched into the captain's memory from dozens of flight briefings and planning sessions and quiet conversations in the pilots' bar.

The captain doesn't know if the rest of flight command are listening in, and he doesn't care. "Marshall," he says. "I think I can bring the ship down. We'll activate our emergency beacon; sit tight until you can get to us."

"I'm sorry, John. There's nothing I can do."

"What are you talking about?"

There's another bang, and then a roar, as if the ship is caught in the jaws of an enormous beast. The captain turns to look at Singh, but she's gone. So is the side of the ship. There's nothing but a jagged gash, the edges a mess of torn metal and sputtering wires. The awful orange glow is coming in, its fingers reaching for him, and he can feel the heat baking on his skin.

"Marshall, listen to me," the captain says, but Marshall is gone too. The captain can see the sky beyond the ship, beyond the flames. It's blue, clearer than he could have ever imagined. It fades to black where it reaches the upper atmosphere, and the space beyond that is pin-pricked with stars.

One of those stars is Outer Earth.

Maybe I can find it, the captain thinks, if I look hard enough. He can feel the anger, the *disbelief* at Marshall's words, but he refuses to let it take hold. He tells himself that Outer Earth will send help. They have to. He tries to picture the faces of his family, tries to hold them uppermost in his mind, but the roaring and the heat are everywhere and he can't—

1

Riley

My name is Riley Hale, and when I run, the world disappears.

Feet pounding. Heart thudding. Steel plates thundering under my feet as I run, high up on Level 6, keeping a good momentum as I move through the darkened corridors. I focus on the next step, on the in-out, push-pull of my breathing. Stride, land, cushion, spring, repeat. The station is a tight warren of crawl-spaces and vents around me, every surface metal etched with ancient graffiti.

"She's over there!"

The shout comes from behind me, down the other end of the corridor. The skittering footsteps that follow it echo off the walls. I thought I'd lost these idiots back at the sector border – now I have to outrun them all over again. I got lost in the rhythm of running – always dangerous when someone's trying to jack your cargo. I refuse to waste a breath on cursing, but one of my exhales turns into a growl of frustration.

The Lieren might not be as fast as I am, but they obviously don't give up.

I go from a jog to a sprint, my pack juddering on my spine as I pump my arms even harder. A tiny bead of sweat touches my eye, sizzling and stinging. I ignore it. No tracer in my crew has ever failed to deliver their cargo, and I am not going to be the first.

I round the corner – and nearly slam into a crush of people. There are five of them, sauntering down the corridor, talking among themselves. But I'm already reacting, pushing off with my right foot, springing in the direction of the wall. I bring my other foot up to meet it, flattening it against the metal and tucking my left knee up to my chest. The momentum keeps me going forwards even as I'm pushing off, exhaling with a whoop as I squeeze through the space between the people and the wall. My right foot comes down, and I'm instantly in motion again. Full momentum. A perfect tic-tac.

The Lieren are close behind, colliding with the group, bowling them over in a mess of confused shouts. But I've got the edge now. Their cries fade into the distance.

There's not a lot you can move between sectors without paying off the gangs. Not unless you know where and how to cross. Tracers do. And that's why we exist. If you need to get something to someone, or if you've got a little package you don't want any gangs knowing about, you come find us. We'll get it there – for a price, of course – and if you come to my crew, the Devil Dancers, we'll get it there *fast*.

The corridor exit looms, and then I'm out, into the gallery. After the corridors, the giant lights illuminating the massive open area are blinding. Corridor becomes catwalk, bordered with rusted metal railings, and the sound of my footfalls fades away, whirling off into the open space.

I catch a glimpse of the diagram on the far wall, still legible a hundred years after it was painted. A scale picture of the station. The Core at the centre, a giant sphere which houses the main fusion reactor. Shooting out from it on either side, two spokes, connected to an enormous ring, the main body. And under it, faded to almost nothing after over a century: Outer Earth Orbit Preservation Module, Founded AD 2234.

Ahead of me, more people emerge from the far entrance to the catwalk. A group of teenage girls, packed tight, talking loudly among themselves. I count ten, fifteen – *no*. They haven't seen me. I'm heading full tilt towards them.

Without breaking stride, I grab the right-hand railing of the catwalk and launch myself up and over, into space.

For a second, there's no noise but the air rushing past me. The sound of the girls' conversation vanishes, like someone turned down a volume knob. I can see all the way down to the bottom of the gallery, a hundred feet below, picking out details snatched from the gaps in the web of criss-crossing catwalks.

The floor is a mess of broken benches and circular flower-beds with nothing in them. There are two young girls, skipping back and forth over a line they've drawn on the floor. One is wearing a faded smock. I can just make out the word Astro on the back as it twirls around her. A light above them is flickering off-on-off, and their shadows flit in and out on the wall behind them, dancing off metal plates. My own shadow is spread out before me, split by the catwalks; a black shape broken on rusted railings. On one of the catwalks lower down, two men are arguing, pushing each other. One man throws a punch, his target dodging back as the group around them scream dull threats.

I jumped off the catwalk without checking my landing zone. I don't even want to think what Amira would do if she found out. Explode, probably. Because if there's someone under me and I hit them from above, it's not just a broken ankle I'm looking at.

Time seems frozen. I flick my eyes towards the Level 5 catwalk rushing towards me.

It's empty. Not a person in sight, not even further along. I pull my legs up, lift my arms and brace for the landing.

Contact. The noise returns, a bang that snaps my head back even as I'm rolling forwards. On instinct, I twist sideways, so the impact can travel across, rather than up, my spine. My right hand hits the ground, the sharp edges of the steel bevelling scraping my palm, and I push upwards, arching my back so my pack can fit into the roll.

Then I'm up and running, heading for the dark catwalk exit on the far side. I can hear the Lieren reach the catwalk above. They've spotted me, but I can tell by their angry howls that it's too late. There's no way they're making that jump. To get to where I am, they'll have to fight their way through the stairwells on the far side. By then, I'll be long gone.

"Never try to outrun a Devil Dancer, boys," I mutter between breaths.

Follow us:

/orbitbooksUS

/orbitbooks

/orbitbooks

Join our mailing list
to receive alerts on our
latest releases and deals.

orbitbooks.net

Enter our monthly
giveaway for the chance
to win some epic prizes.

orbitloot.com